About the Author

Do Mostafa know what or who he is? Well, he was born and raised in Iran, the forgotten mother of civilization. And moved to the beautiful England at the grand age of thirty-five and became a bloody Englishman—He does not drink, and swears, only, if it is completely necessary. Ages ago, he read Charles Bukowski only to realize that his first novel would be good to go just a while after his fiftieth birthday, 23rd April, 2022. In all, he is a positively delusional guy who understands philosophy and loves literature and knows his way around history and psychology.

Sophie

Mostafa Ghanbari

Sophie

Olympia Publishers
London

www.olympiapublishers.com
OLYMPIA PAPERBACK EDITION

A CIP catalogue record for this title is
available from the British Library.

ISBN: 978-1-80439-232-4

This is a work of fiction.
Names, characters, places and incidents originate from the writer's imagination.
Any resemblance to actual persons, living or dead, is purely coincidental.

First Published in 2023

Olympia Publishers
Tallis House
2 Tallis Street
London
EC4Y 0AB

Printed in Great Britain

Dedication

This is definitely for you.

Acknowledgements

Hattie, grazie mille!

"Drink all your passion, and be a disgrace."

-Rumi

Chapter 1

Born in a small town in the north of England and relocated to a smaller town in the south at a very young age, Sophie had a moderate and pleasantly sweet and rather demure disposition. Her northern hometown, known as the most fitting representation of *flatness,* had occupied a larger expanse of her young mind; and her southern dwelling, the town of Town, had been laid on that large expanse with all its green and picturesque hills, mounds, dales, gorges, beaches, creeks and of course, its wealth of incongruous and obtrusively stark concrete buildings. Twenty-two years of age and tall enough not to be seen short, Sophie was, in terms of outside beauties, simply a beautiful gazelle—though not as light-footed, and somewhat rigid. Nevertheless, her otherwise *exceptional* beauty had neither been revealed to the world around her nor had it been revealed to herself, not yet.

Being an early bird, she had just woken up and sat on her bed, allowing a full chuckle to form within her and be exhaled at full force; she had entered the bed in her formal clothes and her thin muddy sneakers the night before, when she had been out celebrating her twenty-second birthday with some of her close friends. Conceding her hangover with a touch of teenage-ish pride, she changed into her two-piece light blue pyjamas and plodded out of her room and towards the small sitting room.

Pushing her light-brown sleek hair back, she looked at her birthday presents, which had been meticulously put on the dining table by her housemate, a fellow university student, a scrawny wiry girl with a very *strict* moral compass within which only the familiar things, concepts and creatures would be allowed to enter and dwell. Also of the same age, Miss Molly Wrigley was a student of Criminal Psychology. Although not yet at the top of her trade, she maintained, categorically, that man's only authentic attribute was *rascality*; and therefore, dabbling around inexplicable concepts like morality, individuality, spirituality and so on, would be a mere waste of time and also a blatant denial of the *truth*. Miss Molly Wrigley believed, very assertively, that the defusive policies and the application of mental sedatives were the only effective solutions to the ever-propagating modern ills of the modern man. Promoting herself to a premature state of intellectuality and vindication, her views were naturally not open to question! Molly Wrigley was a self-assigned mentor to Sophie!

"Good morning, my lovely Sophie!" said Molly, entering the sitting room, holding a tuft of her unwashed hair, as it was her custom.

"Good morning, Molly," said Sophie, turning towards her with one of the presents in her hand, "So you think I should return this one?"

"Yes, definitely," replied Molly emphatically.

"Don't you think—"

"Sophie, don't be so naïve," interrupted Molly, walking towards Sophie, "Throw it to his face! Tell him to fuck off! Old fucking rascal!"

"Yeah, I don't know… You might be right," said Sophie, in a most resigned tone, pulling the chair back and sitting on it. She kept gazing at the presents, laid beside each other in their colourful wraps.

She felt reluctant to unwrap them. Let them remain unwrapped and hide whatever of curiosity they contain, she thought, feeling a dismaying pain in her heart. I needed only *one* present, she thought, her eyes moistening.

"Coffee," said Molly, putting two mugs on the table, "What is it? Why are you so listless? See, it has already begun to affect you, this indecency inflicted on you! How many times have I asked you not to trust strangers? Do you want me to come with you and slag him off, this old fucking cunt? You are too susceptible, Sophie. He would have never dared to further his dirty wish had you snapped at him when he touched you for the first time and—"

"He has never touched me!" Sophie cut in, with her voice raised.

"See, this is the result of trauma," said Molly, taking a large swig of her coffee, "Human memory isn't immune to trauma. You have forgotten what you told me the other day. Haven't you? Yes, you have."

"What did I tell you?" asked Sophie, with a flutter in her voice.

"You told me that he had been touching your backside," replied Molly, biting the corner of her lower lip and staring into Sophie's eyes.

"Did I?" asked Sophie, doubt ploughing through her mind and her face revealing it.

"Sophie, you have become a danger to yourself," said Molly, hitting her forefinger on the table, "You are simply unable to see the difference between familiarity and strangeness. Those people, those strangers, have been abusing you."

Molly was right. Molly was wrong. Molly was neither right nor wrong. Molly was a brilliant absorber and glossarist of the spirit of her surroundings and well on her way to becoming its prolific propagator and its devoted advocator. Molly was the *faithful* child of her time.

"Molly," said Sophie, in a soft tone, "I think you are right. I will draw the line for them today."

"Sophie, strangers are immune to boundaries," said Molly, holding her chin, "Ward off the abuse once for good. Stay away from them."

"Yeah, I think it is a wise thing to do," said Sophie, her green eyes refusing to confirm what she said.

'Wow! There is a large mirror in here!' uttered Sophie, as if she had just noticed the mirror in the lift, *It is such a good idea to put mirrors in the lifts and all other confined places,'* she thought, looking into her own eyes… *No, I am not going to do this! I promise you. Don't frown. Believe me. I am not a danger to you. Those people aren't strangers to me. Are they? It is only Gol… Yeah, he has been confusing me! He doesn't like me. Does he? Don't frown at me. I am not going to do anything silly. I am going to grab him by the collar and tell him that I love—*

"You all right, my dear?" asked an old lady, sitting in her electric wheelchair.

"Oh, yeah, I am so sorry," said Sophie, turning around and walking out of the lift, "I was talking to myself! Wasn't I?"

"That is okay, my dear. Have a good day," said the old lady, offering her a kind smile.

Out of the building, she felt confused, her head giddy, her heart palpitating, her mind wandering off, her legs disobeying her. Inside the parking, she struggled to remember where she had parked her car last night. It is strange, she whispered with a gentle sigh.

Driving through the town, everything seemed strangely strange to her, as if she had just landed on the earth from another planet. She blinked several times. She rubbed her right temple with her thumb.

The traffic lights, red, amber, green, they meant nothing to her. Randomness offered her a green pass, amber followed, red appeared, there was no roundabout to appear, nor even a slight bend. She drove on unconsciously. Was it a neurological glitch, a heavy brain fog, alcohol aftermaths, or simply some moments of void and a preamble to a disturbing and disintegrating fear? She shook her head, rolled the window down and held the wheel firmly.

She parked her car in the small parking area behind her workplace, a large restaurant, where she held a part-time job, doing some paperwork. To her amazement, the restaurant building did not seem strange to her while the other buildings close to it did. She stood by her car, looking at the building as if it was a shrine at which she could purge her soul and move beyond her mortal existence. She turned round and looked up at the large office window behind which there was a large clean room, a corner of which had placed her during the past two years. *'Even the thought of it could rip my heart off,'* she thought, still staring at the window, the thought of not being able to step into that office for the rest of her life, that safe haven, that strangely familiar place.

"Come in," shouted Gol, turning towards the door.

"Hello, Gol," said Clement, Gol's brilliant Indian head chef and his old friend.

"Hello, Clement, my brother," said Gol, looking at his kind and smiling face, "Come here! Have a seat."

"We have two small problems," said Clement, an overdose of kindness and indulgence distorting the permanent smile on his face, "David and Franco, the Italian chef… It began with a quarrel and then got a bit too physical… a few pushes and punches…"

"Over what?"

"Apparently, David has been calling him 'a wanker'," replied Clement, his small face now a booklet of reconciliation.

"Where are they now?"

"There," replied Clement, pointing to the door.

"Call them in." asked Gol.

Seconds later, the two culprits stepped in rather languidly and stood before Gol.

"Who is going to fill me in on this issue?" asked Gol, stroking his thick salt-peppered beard.

"I asked him to stop it; I did so more than ten times," said Franco, the thin tall Italian chef, touching his aquiline nose and then his thin moustache, he added, "He has also been interfering with my job."

16

"Interfering with your job, with the same nonsense expression, 'Mate, it doesn't make sense!'?" asked Gol.

"Yes, Gol," replied Franco, folding his long arms on his chest and throwing an apologetic look at David's now blushed face.

"Yesterday, he went to the cellar and mixed up all the potatoes I had separated to be used for different purposes. And it wasn't the first time he did this."

"Clement, could you please tell me how I should deal with David?" asked Gol, a mixed hue of sadness and affection appearing on his dark face.

"He will be fine, Gol. He is just a bit hard to understand," replied Clement, raising his hand and gently placing it on David's shoulder.

"Exactly like God," said Gol, laughing, "Has anyone ever been able to define God? Will I ever be able to define David? Mate, 'It doesn't make sense!'. Even the great God didn't believe in this nonsense. If everything had to make sense to him then nothing would have happened; there would be no creation, no life, no David, no Gol… "

"Mate, I am sorry," said David, raising his rather big blond head and throwing a fleeting look at Gol's face.

"Why did you call him 'a wanker'?" asked Gol, in a low tone.

"Mate, you are taking things too seriously," replied David.

"Clement, could you please fetch me a colander and a spoon with holes?" asked Gol, fixing his gaze on David's face.

"Yes," replied Clement, a tinge of surprise appearing on his face.

Gol asked David and Franco to take a seat and as they did, he put his laptop before David and asked him to Google who was the first president of the United States of America.

"It says George Washington," said David, seconds later, in a curious and somewhat apprehensive tone.

"So, it didn't bring up the name Babrak Karmel. Did it?" asked Gol, throwing a look at Franco's excited face, "Ask Google who led two expeditions to the Antarctic region and what happened to him."

David darted a very English look at Gol's face, but it did not take him more than two seconds to curb it into a blank and baffled expression. Reluctantly, he keyed in the question and seconds later, he said, "It says it was Captain Robert Falcon Scott and… "

"Now," interrupted Gol, and stretching his hand out to take the colander and the spoon from Clement, who had just stepped in, he asked

David, "Ask Google who were the champions of *wanking* in the world! And tell us where England is on the list."

David's face blushed. He poised to sling another very English look at Gol, but he decided not to.

"What is it, Gol?" asked Clement, laughing.

"You will see," replied Gol, smiling.

"It says—" muttered David, evidently displeased with Google's answer.

"It says the English are the second most… " said Franco, cocking an eyebrow, perhaps expecting a better place for the English!

"Clement, ask Google to give us all the synonyms to the word '*wank*' in the English language," asked Gol, turning the laptop towards Clement and putting the colander before David and the spoon with holes before Franco.

"What do you want us to do with these… ?" asked Franco, pointing to the colander and the spoon.

"Count the holes in them and let me know!" replied Gol, looking at David musingly.

"Goodness!" uttered Clement with an ear-to-ear smile, "Unbelievable! There are sixty-four synonyms to the word 'wank' in the grand language of English!"

"Yes," uttered Gol, scratching his chin, "And they are mostly beautiful innocent words that have been, unnecessarily and *necessarily,* smeared and forced to mean *wank!* Humans are words and words are human."

"There are only nine holes in this spoon," said Franco, offering Gol a meaningful smile.

"And there are around three hundred in this colander," mumbled David.

"So," said Gol, lifting the colander, "If this colander accuses that spoon of having too many holes, it means this colander doesn't know that it is a colander; and a colander which doesn't know that it is a colander, well, will never understand the meaning of a 'hole'!"

"Mate, I am sorry," said David, his eyes moistening, his voice cracked.

"Franco, give David a hug, and you are off," asked Gol.

As David and Franco were leaving the room, Gol called David's name in a less admonishing tone and asked him, "You are going to Cynthia's. Aren't you?"

"I don't know… I am not sure," replied David, turning his head towards Gol and landing his now thoughtful and somewhat alarmed gaze on his face.

"I think you should, boy," said Gol in an almost pleading tone.

The relenting tinge in Gol's tone made David to form half a smile on his broad face, and merging it with Clement's full smile, he nodded affirmatively and left.

"And what is the second problem, Clement?" asked Gol.

"It is about Sophie."

"Sophie! What is up with Sophie?" asked Gol, reaching for a bundle of papers on the corner of his large desk.

"Someone," said Clement, throwing an involuntary look at Mr Gibran's desk at the very far corner of the room, "Someone has given her a birthday present—apparently two books. And she thinks—"

"Oh yes! A misunderstanding, Clement, I suppose," interrupted Gol, looking at Mr Gibran's desk with a most endearing smile forming on his face.

Minutes later, and after Sophie had been called in, Gol stood up, and crossing his long hairy arms on his chest, he looked Sophie in the eye for the second time in two years. As Sophie's face was about to reveal the signs of uneasiness, he directed his gaze down and landed it on her small hands, exactly as he had done the first time.

"Could you please unwrap those books, Sophie?" asked Gol, calling her by name for the first time.

Sophie's round white face turned rosy. With a twitch of her head, she covered half her face with a puff of her light brown hair; putting the books on Gol's desk, she gently unwrapped them.

"So, nothing of an obscene nature!" said Gol, "These two books are among the most precious works of literature, considering and examining the purest of human emotions. You are twenty-two-years-old and a university student, and well on your way to becoming a scientist. Based on what, if anything at all, have you come to this point that Mr Gibran has got bad intentions towards you? You have been with us for two years now, and you have always amazed me at how inept you are when it comes to understanding and dealing with pure human emotions. In this case, Miss Sophie Grandeur, I should say you have let your feminine psyche down."

When Gol left, Sophie marched towards Mr Gibran's desk and tossed the books on it, marched back to her desk, shoved the papers into her bag, and left the office with a touch of indignation and disquiet wobbling in her head.

She almost flew down the stairs, and when turning towards the back door, Clement called her, "What is it, Sophie? Why are you flying, girlie?"

With a quick jerk of the head, she threw a fleeting look at Clement's face and pictured half of his perpetual smile.

It was raining. She dashed to her car, holding her bag over her head. Standing by the car, she hastily reached for the car door, but a sudden inner call, completely unknown to her, urged her to stand in the rain! She laughed. She stood in the rain.

As the seconds were dying only to give birth to minutes, the rain gained rhythm, switched notes and lashed down. The lone light over the back door was overwhelmed by the now rampant rain. She took off her now drenched jacket and slung it over her head; and as it landed with a heavy and splattering thud, a seagull, which had taken refuge under a nearby car, stretched its neck out and threw a funny look at her. She held her head up, shut her eyes, and felt a soothing tingle in her veins as the raindrops were pelting her eyelids.

Minutes later, a tiny dapple dog, apparently walking ahead of an owner, appeared at the scene. Not lacking a tad in assertiveness, (which could well be denoted by his calculated and inquisitive wagging of tail), the tiny dog leered at the seagull with a tinge of warning sitting in his eyes. Turning towards Sophie and having her appraised and considered in his doggy mind, he formed half a simper on his face and after taking a few short steps forward, he stood before her with his head slightly tilted and his ears pricked.

The seagull stretched its neck out again and throwing another funny look at Sophie, waddled out from under the car and darted a creepy look at the dog. The dog's owner, (almost half of his or her stature disappeared under a very large black umbrella), appeared and immediately called the dog in a voice so hard to tell its gender—half feminine, half masculine. The dog took no heed and spurned the call with an erratic wagging of tail and a vague and gibberish yelp.

Sophie held her hands up and looked at her palms, and failing to spot anything readable, she turned them around and stared at the back of them…

Nothing.

There must be something! There must be something in my hands! Something worth looking at… something worth forming a desirous look on a face…

The tiny dapple dog took a step back, and forming a full simper on his wise-looking face, he bestowed upon Sophie a very intricate and prolonged bark enhanced by some head gestures so very akin to those of Clement's!

Sophie smiled. The simpering dog put an end to his curiosity with a long yawn and joined his mysterious owner. The seagull waddled back under the car with a low and rather pleased squawk.

Minutes later, Sophie grabbed her bag and jacket and marched back towards the back door. She banged on the door with her fisted hand, took a step back, and laughed and laughed and laughed again.

"The mother of Jesus Christ!" exclaimed Clement in his overly twisting Indian accent as soon as he opened the door, and exhibiting some very confusing head bobbles and hand gestures, he asked, "What have you *actually* been doing, girlie?"

Sophie threw a look at Clement's face, pictured the other half of his permanent smile, and ran towards the stairs; and before Clement could make an accord between his words and his confusing body language to say something else, she climbed upstairs languidly.

"I will bring you a heater!" shouted Clement, with his right hand raised, performing a lightbulb-changing gesture!

Sophie entered the office, tossed her bag and her jacket on the floor, and gently walked over to Mr Gibran's desk. Bending down, she looked at the books again, this time, perhaps, just perhaps, through a more cogent mind and a more discerning pair of eyes. She pulled back a few wisps of hair covering her right eye and read what was written on the back cover of one of the books:

'*It is only with the heart that one can see rightly;*
  What is essential is invisible to the eye.'

She looked at the back of her hands again, this time, perhaps, just perhaps, knowing that what is essential is invisible to the eye.

21

"Are you actually in your clothes or out of your clothes?" shouted Clement from behind the door with another unnecessary use of the word 'actually'.

"Come in. I am in my clothes," shouted back Sophie, still looking at the back of her hands.

"You need to get your clothes dried before you go home."

"I am not going home. I want to stay here," replied Sophie, now looking at the other book.

"Well, I have never been able to understand you," said Clement, putting the heater on the floor and plugging it into a socket by the large leather couch, "Take off your clothes and put them before the heater, and when you are back in them, send me a text."

"I think I could do with a proper meal tonight," said Sophie with one of her rare but unique smiles.

"What would you fancy?" asked Clement, now offering Sophie the fullest version of his permanent smile.

"Lamb Balti with fresh chapatti," replied Sophie, taking off her thin light sneakers.

"Okay. I will be back when you have actually sorted yourself out."

After getting undressed, she walked over to the wardrobe by Gol's desk and took out the blanket and the pillow that Gol would use for his midday naps on the couch, wrapped the blanket around her body, and walked back to the couch.

Watching the steam rising from her clothes before the heater and swirling up to the ceiling, she mulled over the past two years she had been working for Gol. To her amazement, her mind revealed to her a full archive of the apparently insignificant and transient moments, each of them impregnated with tacit hints and cues towards a destination unknown to her.

She placed her bare feet before the heater, and as the warmth began to vibe her nerves, she recalled the day, the first day, when she had come face to face with Gol: he had looked her in the eye—a falcon looking into a sparrow's eyes. Had he seen her as prey? Was she going to be hunted? What had he seen in her hands? Why had he looked at them in that manner? The days had gone by but Gol had neither looked her in the eye, nor had he looked at her hands again until a couple of hours ago.

Staring at the glowing heat, she tended to a slide show in her young mind. Each sequence, a slide show on its own, revealed to her an aspect of the nature of the connection between them. But what kept baffling her was the fact that Gol had never exhibited any explicit interest in her: he had always sat at his desk with his back to her! He had never had any verbal connection with her, except for the occasional mumblings about a piece of paperwork. He had always ordered lunch for both of them without asking her what she would like to eat! And strangely, she, the fussy eater, had always eaten, with gusto, whatever he had ordered!

She looked at the square wooden dining table where Gol and she had eaten the first lunch together. He had ordered Lamb Jalfrezi, a dish full of onion and garlic which she had never liked, but not only she had finished it off, she had also wiped up the dish with a piece of bread, exactly the way Gol had done.

She held her hands before the heater; looking at the back of them, she smiled.

How could have he said too much by just saying nothing! He has said too much! I have heard too little!

"Eat or it will get cold," said Clement, pushing the round black tray before her, "And tell me what is going on in your head."

"I think my head is empty," said Sophie, picking up the knife and fork and putting them on the table.

"It is very good *actually*," said Clement with a gentle head bobble, "Full heads are foolish."

"I can't understand what you mean," said Sophie in a flat tone.

"You don't have to. Eat your food and tell me what was that lunatic thing you did, I mean the standing in the rain."

"A call from somewhere else, it made me do it," replied Sophie with her head tilted.

"I didn't know an English girl could sound so eastern!"

"There was no geographical insinuation in that call!" said Sophie, tearing off half a chapatti.

Clement said nothing. He watched Sophie eat in silence.

"Are you looking at my hands?" asked Sophie, wrapping the last mouthful of her meal.

"No, I am looking at how you eat."

"How do I eat?"

"You eat like Gol."

Sophie looked at the mouthful in her hand and smiled musingly. And when she finished eating, she held her hands before Clement and asked, "Clement, look at my hands and tell me what feelings, if any at all, they induce in your mind."

Clement stared at Sophie's hands for some seconds, and narrowing his eyes, he said, "I think working with Gol and listening to his words has taken you to another dimension."

"Gol has never spoken with me," said Sophie with a pout, and after a long pause, she asked, "How well do you know Gol?"

"Very well, actually. We are old friends."

"Tell me about him."

"Well, when just thirteen years of age and in a very deplorable and unfortunate situation, he was fortunate enough to cross paths with a unique young man in Iran. The Soviet invasion of Afghanistan forced Gol and his family to flee to Iran. The young Iranian man, born only to love and forgive, dwells in Gol as a second soul; and this is what has made Gol a bit strange. Whenever he is quiet, his second soul is in charge."

"What does his second soul look for when it is in charge?" asked Sophie, narrowing her eyes.

"For beauty, the most sublime form of it, the beauty imbued in innocence," replied Clement, sounding like a little Buddha.

"Do you think he is interested in me?" asked Sophie, tilting her head.

"What type of *interest* do you mean?" asked Clement with a full smile.

"How many types of *interest* do we have when it comes to forming a relationship between a man and a woman?" asked Sophie in a rather sagacious tone charged with a pinch of sarcasm.

"Well, in your English mind there is only one type of *interest*," replied Clement, apparently fully connected to the little Buddha within him, "Although not too old but he is just old enough to be your dad, and so very immune to degrading pleasures."

"So, why have I been feeling this strange sensation in my heart since I have been working for him?" asked Sophie, sounding somewhat frazzled.

"I suppose, I just suppose that he has spotted a little amount of something precious within you," said Clement, now looking at Sophie's hands, "And bearing in mind that he has not shown any interest in having a verbal communication with you, I should say that he has been waiting for your heart to respond."

"I just can't understand this!" uttered Sophie, her eyes moistening.

"Sophie, you are only mind and only mind," said Clement, getting up to his feet, "Lock the door and don't forget to switch the heater off."

"Why did he not give me a birthday present?" asked Sophie, as Clement reached the door.

"Well," said Clement, pausing for some very long seconds, perhaps referring the question to the little Buddha within him, "Because you are not born yet."

Chapter 2

"She has been in this suicidal state for a considerable amount of time. Hasn't she?" said Gol, looking at a few empty bottles of cheap booze on and around the low bedside table.

"I suppose so," said David.

"You suppose so!" said Gol, "God's sake! She is your mother, Cynthia is your mother, David!"

"Gol, she just couldn't bear my presence around her," said David in a low and desperate tone.

"I think it is time to test your expertise," said Gol, pointing to the big ashtray on the table, "They look like half-smoked spliffs. Don't they?"

David kneeled, and summoning all his practical knowledge, he examined the subject meticulously, and with an assumptive air appearing on his face, he confirmed Gol's supposition.

"What is in that small bag?" asked Gol, pointing to the plastic bag among the empty bottles.

"It must be kat," said David, tearing the bag off, "Yes, it is kat."

"So, four half-smoked spliffs and some kat," mumbled Gol, scratching his chin, "Some Asian guys!"

David pretended he did not hear what Gol said. Gol walked towards the black make-up table by the window. He looked in the mirror. He was dragged in and disappeared in the breaking waves, reappeared and stood before himself, the young passionate Gol, the true lover, the selfless one. He looked at his fresh face and touching his hastily greying hair, he smiled bitterly. The mirror, the object of honesty and deception, waved, broke, shattered, and when reformed, it showed him Cynthia, standing before him with her young fresh face shining. He, the old Gol, looked the young Cynthia in the eye. She remained undisturbed. Her eyes revealed no signs of uneasiness. He directed his gaze down and landed it on her hands… Nothing.

"Is that a letter?" asked Gol, turning away from the mirror.

"Yes, mate," replied David, getting up and handing the letter to Gol.

"What century are we living in, *mate*?" asked Gol, as soon as he read the first paragraph of the letter.

"Twenty-first, mate?" replied David without looking at Gol.

"This is an appointment made in the sixteenth century!" said Gol, shaking his head, "Can you believe this, *mate!* Today is the 25th of February and this appointment has been arranged for the beginning of August! Utterly inexplicable! Even a cat could have seen the desperation and even the vibration of death within this suicidal woman! Whoever has made this appointment for this wretched woman, must be an alien from another planet! Some so-called psychiatrists who have no clue as to what the human psyche is! A bunch of so-called lovers who have no clue as to what the bloody love is! *Mate,* it just doesn't make sense!"

"Mate, I just can't understand why you should care about Cynthia to this extent," said David, turning around, and looking at Gol's face, he added, "She ruined your life. Didn't she? So she did with my father's life. She saw herself above you. Didn't she?"

"She saw herself above love, David," said Gol, crumpling the letter, "She saw herself above life and humanity! Nonetheless, if she goes down in this unbecoming manner, she will drag down with her a chunk of you and me, if you just get my drift. Therefore, she still matters to us, and we should do our best to forestall her disgraceful fall."

David sat on the bed and stared at Gol. A heavy silence fell over the damp and smelly room.

It was hard for David to digest or even imagine that even the faint dated memories of an unrequited love could yield such an unwavering sense of loyalty and responsibility. Equally hard for him to understand, was the fact that Gol had always seen him as his son; that he had always treated him that way.

Remembering the day when his father had just passed away, brought a few tears to his blue eyes. On that sodden overcast day, Gol had embraced him and appeased his unbearable pain. He had stayed with him all day, helping his young mind to grasp and accept one of life's most poignant and inevitable exigencies.

"Where is Emily now?" asked Gol, gently placing his hand on David's head.

"She is with my grandma," replied David, his voice cracked.

"She is too old to be able to tolerate a boisterous fifteen-year-old girl," said Gol, walking towards the window.

"There is no one else," said David, scratching the back of his head.

"There is, David," said Gol, opening the window.

"Who?"

"You and I," replied Gol, shoving his hands into the pockets of his trousers, "You have to wake up, David. You are now a man. Although a bit wasted, but still a man, I suppose."

Gol's sincere and rather laconic words, as always, hit David with a dual impact: they put a dent on one part of him and slightly elevated the other. So many dents and so little elevations, but the young soul had just begun to realize, unconsciously, that no elevation would come about if there were no dents; that no true love and respect would be bestowed upon unconditionally; that the lovers and the respectful are like roses—they would come with thorns!

"Do you mean—" asked David.

"Yes," interrupted Gol, "Yes, I mean you and Emily can move to my place."

"David's face brightened up. His eyes shone. Ruffling his thick hair, he said, "Mate, I just can't understand you. It is simply too much."

"*Mate,* before you understand me you need to understand yourself," said Gol, now laughing, "And for David to join and live with me, there would be only two simple conditions: first, David would never use the word, '*mate*' again. Second, he would never use the phrase, '*mate, it doesn't make sense!*' when it comes to making connections with other human beings."

"Okay, mate," said David, staring at Gol's face for some long seconds; he burst into hearty laughter.

"Now you need to go back to the hospital and make sure Cynthia is being looked after," said Gol, shutting the window, "And when she is fully recovered, I think we should just leave her alone, as she has always been."

Chapter 3

"Gol," said Sophie, sounding diffident and unsure, her heart pounding, her face blushed, "I—I—I just want to speak with you!"

Gol raised his head gently and looked into Sophie's eyes for some long moments, long enough to notice the colour of her eyes for the first time—something between green and whitish jade.

"Speak, Sophie," he said, now looking at her hands, "I am all ears."

"I—I want to—"

"Sophie!" uttered Gol, stretching his hands out and holding hers for a few seconds, "Relax. Go on. Tell me whatever you wish to."

A surge of delight and contentment washed over Sophie's white face. The colour of her eyes changing, now green, and then whitish jade.

"Tell me," asked she, putting her hands on the table and looking directly into Gol's eyes, "What have you seen in these hands that whenever you look at them my heart palpitates like a headless chicken?"

Gol, touching his greying beard, offered Sophie a kind smile and said, "Two years is a long time for a heart to respond, but I am glad that it has eventually come, the response, or at least the desire to respond. But before I tell you what I have seen in your hands, I need to know why you rejected Mr Gibran's gift, I mean those two precious books."

Sophie averted her eyes from Gol's face; dithering for a few seconds, she replied, "I thought it inappropriate to accept a gift from a man who is old enough to be my dad. It just didn't make sense."

Gol kept looking at her face for some seconds, and when she gently raised her hands and held them before him with a smile, he leaned on the chair arm and said, "What I have seen in your hands is a dormant great human attribute—It is, in fact, the essence of you. It is a shame that it is dormant, but I am so glad that it is not dead, and it could well be revived."

"Tell me! Tell me, please! What is it?" pleaded Sophie, an air of absolute innocence appearing on her face.

"If you wish to know, if it matters to you," said Gol, now his black eyes shining, "You should apologize to Mr Gibran and accept his gift. And when

29

you have read those books, I will happily let you know what I have seen in your hands."

The air of *absolute innocence* on Sophie's face vanished as if it had never appeared. Her eyes widened. Her forehead wrinkled. Her eyebrows wiggled. Her thin lips shivered. She pushed the chair back with a huff, got to her feet, and walked towards her desk. Slinging her bag over her shoulder, she turned her face towards Gol, and as she opened her mouth to say something to him, she quickly raised her hand and covered her mouth, now looking at Gol's calm face with an apologetic hue appearing in her eyes.

"I—I just wanted to say nothing!" said she, now on the verge of bursting into tears.

Gol said nothing. She knew he would say no more.

"Where was Sophie going to?" asked Clement, coming in with a small tray over his hand. "I bumped into her on the landing. She just brushed me off. She looked a bit flustered."

"She is fine, Clement," said Gol, asking him to take a seat with a gesture of his head, "There is a battle going on in her head; and her head is not the most suitable of battlefields—tough, rugged."

"How has she been pitched into this battle?" asked Clement, lifting the small China teapot and pouring tea into the two tiny glass cups, "As I told you the other day, she has been, for quite a long time, dealing with what she calls, '*An inner call!*'"

"She was pitched into this battle," replied Gol, "When her heart, inadvertently and momentarily, became responsive and detected some pulses emitted from another heart."

"*Inadvertently* and *momentarily!*" uttered Clement, the little Buddha in him taking over, "I see, that is why she is always on and off, on today, off tomorrow! A warm friend on Monday! A resentful acquaintance on Tuesday! And simply a mean enemy on Wednesday! I have never been able to understand this girl, and I don't think I will ever be. She is just like a placebo medicine! Something, yet there is something about her, something which is nothing! Something which is and is not there! And perhaps this is the reason we have been trying to find a way to love her."

"Well said, Clement," said Gol, stroking his beard, "What you mentioned is a shackled and muffled angel within her, and that is exactly

30

why we have been trying to find a way to love her."

"Oh, I think we are getting late!" said Clement, checking the time on his mobile phone, "Mrs Aziza Baygum is waiting for us."

"Cuckoo Restaurant! This is *The* name for a restaurant owned by Mrs Aziza Baygum!" said Gol, laughing.

As they entered the massive restaurant, Mrs Aziza Baygum, who was pouring two shots of whisky for two white gentlemen, greeted them with a gesture of the head and a big smile.

A middle-aged woman, Mrs Aziza Baygum was something of a woman: a broad dark face attired with a pair of black and so very bewitching eyes, rather thick and luscious lips, a shock of soft and now greying hair, a busty torso, and an equally thick and solidly swaying backside. As such, she was very much aware of what she owned and of course, so very apt at using it to her advantage.

What else would she need to promote her delightful existence to even a higher echelon? A faith, the best of them, the one that could guarantee an eventual unconditional exoneration and salvation! She did have such a faith: she was a proud and so very devout Muslim woman! So much so that she would always wear a green pair of fabric gloves whenever handling a bottle of whisky! Devout in the same light and to the same extent, she was also categorically against any sort of physical contact with the non-believers, perhaps for the fear of cross-contamination! In all, she would uphold the concept of *halal* and *haram* to its core! Mrs Aziza Baygum had raised her three children single-handedly.

Her husband, a man of her kind, had deserted her and disappeared right after their last child was born. '*For no good reason, my dear*'. It was her response to the curious and the blabbermouth who did not mind to put their noses into her business for no good reason.

"My dear Gol!" uttered Mrs Baygum, opening her arms, "May my Allah bless you. I am so glad and obliged, and thank you very much for coming to help me. And you, dear Clement, may my Allah bless you too. My dear Gol, you own five restaurants, which are five gold mines. I am sure you can spot the problem with my restaurant and tell me why I haven't been making enough money. I need to fill the bellies of my poor children. Only Allah knows how I have been suffering. Only Allah knows."

31

"Well, let's go to the kitchen to see if we can help you fill the bellies of your children!" said Clement, apparently the little Buddha in him already in charge—did Buddha ever use caustic remarks!

"We don't need to go to the kitchen," said Gol, "I know where the problem is."

"Well, if so, you dear sirs take a seat, there, by the window, and I will join you with some refreshments," said Mrs Baygum.

Minutes later, Mrs Baygum and her two sons, Usman and Islam, and her daughter, Nadira, joined Gol and Clement.

Usman, like his mother, was a very God-fearing Muslim who believed that the philosophy of Islam was inseminated in God's mind long before the Big Bang! That the word 'Muslim' was the first fruit of God's first thoughts when the Big Bang was taking place! And that the entire universe was infested by some very immoral and illegitimate creatures, and it was the duty of the dear Muslims to sort this out! And in this, the Almighty would be on their side! Twenty-five years of age, Usman was a self-proclaimed genealogist of the very 'sublime' Islamic morals, values, and *legitimacy,* and above all, he was the patriarch of his clan!

On the other hand, Islam, the younger one, was a self-proclaimed proud *phony* man who would only put on his Islamic cape whenever he needed to acquire a bit of extra credit and secure a span of sitting space among the Muslim brethren. To him, the words 'fuck' and 'money' would sound more tangible and blessing than any religious and sacred words! 'Inshallah Allah will see to it' was the only religious phrase he would use every now and then. In short, he was more like a bad Jew than a good Muslim!

"Dear Gol, you know how my Usman and my dear Islam are fond of you," said Mrs Baygum, adjusting her red headscarf on her head, "So please feel free and advise them in any manner you wish to."

Not being into sugar-coating and pleasing people for the wrong reasons, Gol's way of advising was clear: short and stark, yet so very piquant.

"Usman, dressing himself in oversized apparels," said Gol, looking at Usman's dark and rather handsome face, "Has now become overly belligerent and presumptuous, and therefore, if he stays in this business, he will only be a source of disruption and damage, irreparable damage. Aziza, your son is, needless to say, much more important than your business. With

32

Islam, this happy chap, you will never have any problem, as he is a marvellously amoral and self-interested young man! But Usman is in sharp contrast with him: he is, unfortunately, intelligent, and naturally tends towards meaning in his existence. Unarmed and unequipped, he has hurled himself into this challenging battle, thinking by wearing oversized shirts, trousers, and shoes and watching Mike Tyson's life story every other day, he can fight his society and earn his place! Quixotic, consciously, he is consciously quixotic!"

"My dear Gol, I just can't understand what you are trying to impart!" said Mrs Baygum, trying her best to abort the forceful hysterical laugh forming within her.

"If you were able to spot and understand this, you wouldn't have asked me to come here and lecture you," said Gol, looking into Aziza's large black and now moistening eyes, "There is only one place for Usman, one Kaaba, and one oracle: university. Only knowledge can help him out of his predicament."

Usman's reaction to Gol's words was a mild and reserved smile.

"Gol, we have got to go now. You are supposed to have lunch with Mr Gibran's family today," said Clement, offering Nadira one of his fullest permanent smiles.

Chapter 4

"Don't take it too seriously, Mr Gibran," said Gol, pouring a glass of wine for him, "You have just been living here for five years. You will need at least another five years to learn only ten percent of the idiosyncrasies of the English culture."

"That is exactly what I also told him," said Jamila, Mr Gibran's Lebanese wife, "Lateefa and Aisha, who know this culture better than we know, have also been trying to calm him down."

"There is a little innocent boy within my dad," said Lateefa, Mr Gibran and Jamila's eldest daughter, "It is he who is suffering."

"There is no room for an inner innocent child in here," said Aisha, getting up and walking towards Gol, "Such a child would suffer immensely. My dad will eventually understand this."

"Aisha, you sound as if you are the mother of all inner innocent children!" said Gol, beaming at her young face.

"I am, Uncle Gol," said Aisha, approaching Gol from behind and wrapping her arms around his neck, "And I would readily die for such children."

"Sit here," asked Gol, pulling back the chair beside his, "And tell me what exactly happened."

"Although I had never seen her before, I recognized her when I opened the door," said Aisha, pushing her brown curly hair back, "Dad had told us a lot about Sophie, about her unique modesty and her very gentle manners, and also about her facial similarities with me. She refused to come in. And when Dad came to the door, she said hello to him, apologized for rejecting his gift, and asked for the books back. When Dad brought the books to her, I saw something very confusing in her eyes: a mixture of pure love and pure malice. She took the books, put them in her bag, and left without saying a word. But just seconds later, she came back, handed the books back to my dad and left!"

Gol didn't seem to be disturbed by what Sophie had done. The fact that Aisha had rightly observed *pure love* and *pure malice* in Sophie's eyes, evoked in him even a more serious and curious interest towards Sophie.

"Clement, you have smashed it, boy!" said Gol, smiling at Clement, who was coming in with a platter of Lamb Biryani over his hands.

"Mr Gibran is a true Muslim," said Clement, placing the platter in the middle of the table, "He drinks wine. I like it."

"There is no vice in drinking a glass of wine," said Mr Gibran, the quiet history teacher.

"This is a perfect Indian treat!" said Aisha, looking at a variety of curry dishes on the table, "Uncle Clement is a very soulful chef."

"Uncle Gol believes there is a little Buddha within him," said Lateefa, reaching out for a dish of Lamb Dhansak.

"Well, let's eat, and we will see what a little Buddha could do in a kitchen!" said Gol, putting his arm around Mr Gibran's shoulders; he whispered to him, "You are a piece of gold, and Sophie is not a goldsmith."

As Clement was busy explaining to Jamila and Mr Gibran how he would go about cooking, and in particular, cooking curries and other Indian dishes, Aisha leaned towards Gol and asked, "Did Sophie ever ask you anything about the paintings and the objects lining the walls of your beautiful office?"

Gol's hand froze midway to his mouth. He lowered the spoon, looked at Aisha's face, and with a musing smile, he replied, "No, she never did. This is a very thoughtful question. How have *you* seen those paintings and objects?"

"There is a connection among them," said Aisha, "Something has bound them together, something so inviting. I just don't know how to explain it."

"You are right, Aisha, there is a uniting element," said Gol, "And that comes from the heart, and therefore could only be felt by the heart. I am so sad that Sophie wasn't even willing to have a keen look at them."

"Uncle Gol," said Aisha, putting her hand on his shoulder, "You pronounce her name with such care, love and respect as if she is now an important part of you."

"Sophie *is* now an important part of me," said Gol. "She has with her half of my soul. If she doesn't come back, one and a half souls will be lost."

"I will stand by you, Uncle Gol," said Aisha in a most assuring tone, "And I will give you half of my soul if Sophie doesn't come back."

A wave of absolute gratification came, lifted him, high, higher and higher, to a point of weightlessness, to a point of beatification. He could now see his own self standing before him, still smelling of the purgatory he had pitched himself into. Now he could clearly see, in the mirror of Aisha's soul, the shackled and muffled angel within Sophie.

Chapter 5

"What happened in here?" asked Sophie, looking at some shattered glasses on the floor and a few overturned tables.

"A geezer came in and asked for breakfast," replied Usman, now looking at Sophie's bloodshot eyes, "And when we told him that we didn't serve breakfast, he got angry and went a bit too far with it."

"Have you called the police yet?" asked Sophie, her voice cracked, her lips shivering.

"Sophie, you look very indisposed," said Usman.

"I am fine," said Sophie, desperately trying to pull herself together, "I just had a sleepless night. It is a severe headache."

"You are still drunk!" snapped Islam.

"I am speaking with Usman," said Sophie in a low tone without looking at Islam.

"Shut it! Just shut it, you fake little bitch!" Islam snapped again.

As Sophie turned around and scurried towards the office, Usman took a napkin, and wiping the tiny stream of blood off his brother's forehead, he said, "I just can't understand these irrational grudges you have been holding against this girl!"

"Big brother, you are an intelligent man, and I am a moron," replied Islam, "As a matter of fact, the intelligent man tends to see the bright side of things. Let me do my job. Let me see the other side for you."

"So, you think there is something between Sophie and me?" asked Usman, taking a step back and looking intently at his brother's face.

"She is trying to induce you to love her," replied Islam, examining the wound on his forehead, "You might ask what is wrong with it. I will tell you. Listen, we both know Sophie very well. We used to be schoolmates. It is your good and sound heart that she is after. What would she do with a good and sound heart? She would stab it. She would rip it off. She would make it bleed! This angelic tender little thing would draw, pathologically, an immense pleasure from watching your bleeding heart!"

Usman said nothing. Islam got to his feet and walked towards the door.

"I am going to sort that geezer out," he shouted to Usman before reaching for the door handle.

"I made a coffee for you, Usman," said Sophie, throwing a timid fleeting look at him.

Usman grabbed the mug of coffee and walked towards his desk in absolute silence. He sat in his chair, sipped his coffee, and thought about his brother's words and, in particular, about the intelligent man and his inability to see the dark side of things. He turned around on his chair and looked at Sophie, sitting at her desk as silent and motionless as a marble statue, the nape of her white neck and a few wisps of curly hair shining under the neon light. He had wished, so many times in his life, that he could live his life without the troublesome need for love, but he had always found it impossible; he had always confounded this desire with a fresh set of desires.

He got to his feet and walked towards Sophie. Crossing his arms on his chest, he stood behind her and gently landed his gaze on the top of her head, right on the top of her head, the spot he had kissed ten years ago, when they were schoolmates. He lowered his gaze and landed it on the nape of her neck, the spot he had touched ten years ago. He took a step forward with the sheer intention of kissing... No kiss. No touch. No more. No more memories. He thought, pulling his slightly shaking hand back.

"When are you going to go on your pilgrimage trip?" asked Sophie without turning around.

"Tomorrow," replied Usman, walking towards his desk, "I can't wait. It is going to be the beginning of a journey, a journey of liberation and breakaway."

"Tell me more about it?" asked Sophie, a rueful hue appearing in her tired eyes.

"It is called 'Hajj'," said Usman, "Embarking on a journey in search of liberation, true liberation, when you break away and get yourself unburdened and unshackled. Muslims go there and meet Allah face to face, at His own House, at His grand House that is the gate to eternity. People go there and ask Allah to purify their souls and set them free; they also ask Him to fulfil their worldly desires."

"What worldly desires are you going to ask Allah to fulfil for you?" asked Sophie, tilting her head.

"I am going to ask Him for a good woman," replied Usman, emotion ringing in his voice.

"What type of woman?"

"A woman for whom I would readily die," replied Usman, "And I am going to pray for you, too."

The word 'pray' hit Sophie hard. It did not take her long to feel the full impact with all the cells in her body. It was not just her body, it was more than that, it was as if she had had more than one body without knowing it. Bodies and souls, she was, she felt. Too young, too old, she was, she felt. Her eyes moistened. She wondered, she wondered at her own eyes and how quickly they would surface a vague and so very transient interpretation of what was going on within her. Not lasting enough, elusive, undefined, the moments now had become her torturous predicament. It was now apparent to this young soul that she had become the contention point between two unequal and opposing forces, one fully able to drag her around and the other so bewitchingly able to enchant her soul.

"I will be away for a while, and I want you to help my mum, and avoid bickering with Islam," said Usman, noticing Sophie's wet eyes.

"He calls me a 'loose girl'!" moaned Sophie, now shedding tears, "He calls me a 'fucking stinky bitch!'."

"Come on, Sophie!" interjected Usman, cocking an eyebrow, "You sound like a Muslim girl, as if you have never heard or used these kinds of remarks! Just yesterday you used the bloody word 'fuck' twelve times in less than ten minutes."

"I am not a loose girl!" sobbed Sophie.

"Is there anything good in not being a loose girl?" asked Usman musingly.

"A loose girl will become a bad mother," replied Sophie, wiping her eyes with the heels of her hands.

Usman stood before Sophie and looked her in the eye only to see something he had never seen before: in her eyes, in her now whitish jade eyes, he saw a holy woman with a splendid face so very akin to that of Holy Mary's. And as he was about to let out a yell of joy, he noticed an unholy presence too, sitting by the holy one: a witch, an ugly witch with a pair of piercing eyes and elongated extremities. He looked at the holy woman and then at the witch. The witch looked at the holy woman and then at him and

39

let out a laughter, a laughter tolling like a copper bell, resounding like the hammer blows on an anvil, a laughter metallic, dated and deafening. The witch rose, threw her long arms around, and now smiling at Usman, she began to dance. She turned and turned, the hems of her red and dirty robe flailing around her long legs, her long crooked fingers snaking in the air. She whirled, she twisted, whirling twisting like a tornado, a red tall rotating mass, now elongating, now shrinking, winding, unwinding, there she stood, a slim gentle angel dressed in white. The holy woman offered him a half-hearted smile; the slim gentle angel began to turn. Twisting, winding… elongating…

Meanwhile, the door opened and Cynthia appeared at the threshold.

"What! Are you waiting for a discreet invitation to come in?" said Usman, looking at Cynthia's deep-green-dyed hair curiously.

"I have got a new painting for you," said Cynthia, coming in in a swaggering gait, "I thought you might like it."

"Take a seat," asked Usman, taking the painting from her hand, "Look! This is something, so compelling, so vocal."

"I have spent hours on it," said Cynthia, throwing an indifferent look at Sophie.

"How have you done this?" asked Usman, evidently impressed with the painting.

"Same as usual. Using painting paper, pencil, colour—"

"Man, I mean the mixing of the two faces!" interrupted Usman.

"There is only one face. I have no clue what you are talking about," replied Cynthia, her pale face now a banner of self-denial and rejection.

"There are two faces, mixed craftily: eastern and western," retorted Usman, "Sometimes I doubt if God knows his job properly. Why has he endowed you with this fine talent! You, the epitome of denial and duplicity."

"Man, I think you are being unnecessarily devious with me," said Cynthia, pushing her hair back with a touch of childish huff. "Just tell me how much you are willing to pay for this."

"Let's show it to Sophie," said Usman, getting up to his feet, "If she confirms what I have seen in this, then I will pay you two hundred pounds for this."

"Sophie! This little—" said Cynthia, forcing herself to abort the harsh words that were about to tumble out of her mouth.

Sophie held the painting up, and after staring at it for two full minutes, she threw half a smile at Cynthia and said, "Two different beautiful female faces are excellently mingled."

Usman took out his wallet from the breast-pocket of his jacket and paid Cynthia two hundred pounds, and offering her a smile, he asked, "Any new tattoos?"

Cynthia threw a rather resentful look at Sophie, and rolling up her sleeve, she pointed to a curved dagger finely tattooed on the top of her right arm, and said, "I have done this in the memory of one of my boyfriends, an American bloke; he had the same tattoo on his left arm. Poor bloke, he committed suicide."

"Why did he commit suicide?" asked Usman, pushing his wallet into his pocket.

"He was not good enough for me," replied Cynthia, shoving the money into the back pocket of her jeans, "So I rejected him when he proposed, and he said he would kill himself. He did. He shot himself in the head the next day. Poor bloke."

"One Thousand and One Nights is not even a patch on that of yours and your lovers!" said Usman, laughing, "Apparently, so far only Gol has managed to survive! Why did you reject Gol?"

"I rejected Gol for a completely different reason," replied Cynthia, rolling her sleeve down, "Gol was too good for me. Too good, if you get what I mean."

"I can't. Explain it to me."

"Even at that age he was a bloody mirror," said Cynthia, an unjustified amount of indignation appearing on her face, "The first time he looked at me I thought I was completely exposed! It was impossible to hide at his presence. There was nothing you could keep for yourself because it was impossible to lie to him. Back then I used to think I didn't like it, but now I know that I just simply couldn't bear it. Standing before a mirror while you have so many things to hide, wasn't easy; nevertheless, there was a point at which I would have accepted him had he come back to me. He never did. He retreated to a life of solitude, polishing that bloody dazzling mirror."

"Why did you not go back to him?" asked Usman, throwing a look at Sophie, who was attentively listening.

"Mate, this is one of those questions," replied Cynthia, throwing another dejected look at Sophie, "When you exist and do not exist at the same time; you will become a master of self-destruction.

"There will be always something to be destroyed, something to be lost. There were and there were not two Cynthias, two selves. Oneness was missing. Oneness is missing. Cynthia was and is a historical failure, a historical victim."

Sophie was now staring at Cynthia's face. Usman picked up the painting and gazed at it. The faces smiled at him. Eastern and western, the smiles merged, separated, and merged again. A pair of large black eyes, deep brown hair, a mixture of gold and jet, the complexion, a mixture of a sunny day and a dark night, the lips, a mixture of sublime opium and honey. The pair of eyes, hued with a touch of light blue, drew Usman in and landed him in a place where there were no boundaries and barriers, where there were only gold, jet, honey, and opium.

Usman had known Cynthia since he was a teenager. She would come to see his mum every now and then, and it was, as Usman could recall now, when she had discovered (as she had put it) a piece of God within herself! She would come and listen to his mum and her overly zealous lectures on God and his undeniable presence in every and each human being. Needless to say that the *piece* of God in this and the *zeal* of Him in the other had eventually brought them to this 'profound' point that God (even a piece of him) could not dwell in Cynthia as she was an infidel! And Cynthia reminding Mrs Aziza Baygum that the words *each* and *every* predicated inclusiveness and not exclusiveness, had practically put an end to their short and mutual love escapade with God!

And now, years later, Cynthia, this disintegrated entity, was yearning for *oneness* and unity, the one thing she had always been escaping from.

Usman turned around and looked at Sophie's face, and on the screen of his mind, he drew her face, changing her eyes with a pair of large black eyes and adding a hue of whitish jade to it, mixing a generous amount of gold and jet and applying it to her hair and her eyebrows, blending a sunny day and a dark night and adding it to her complexion and honey and sublime opium for the lips.

"Why does she look at me like this, with a touch of venom?" asked Sophie when Cynthia had just left.

"Perhaps it is because of your connection with Gol, I suppose," said Usman.

"I have never had any serious connection with Gol. I don't like him at all," said Sophie.

"Sophie, you are off. You need to get some rest," said Usman, evidently displeased with what she said about Gol.

"Uh, you, my dear Sophie," said Mrs Baygum as soon as Sophie stepped out of the office, "I have a quick word with you, my dear. Just listen carefully! I pay you to come here and work. No one would pay people to come here and chat. Would they? So, work more and chat less! And remember, no romance, not in my place. My Usman is on his way to Mecca. Such a great pilgrimage! The mother of all pilgrimages—coming face to face with Allah in his grand house, Kaaba. I don't want you to stand between my son and Allah, if you just can take my meaning, my dear Sophie."

"Yes, Mrs Baygum, I can 'take your meaning'," said Sophie, desperately trying to hold back her tears, "I assure you that I am not going to stand between your son and Allah."

"I am going to believe your words and ignore what your eyes are telling me," said Mrs Baygum, putting on her green fabric gloves, "Now you can go, my dear."

Sophie left the restaurant mentally disturbed and with a heavy heart. Out and on to the fresh air, she felt utterly undecided, not even willing to inhale some fresh air and exhale with it some of the gnawing pang of pain in her heart. She wheeled her way around the restaurant and entered the parking lot. Approaching her car, her tired gritty eyes caught sight of something on the bonnet of her car. She stopped immediately, rubbed her eyes, and looked again. Her heart pounded against the walls of her chest, her brain froze, and her bloodshot eyes lost sight. Her handbag! It was her handbag, her brown leather handbag. She stared at it through her blurred and now badly dimmed vision and wished that she had never had a brown leather handbag; that she had never had any bag at all; that she had never had something called 'memory'; that she had never been pitched into the game of 'right' and 'wrong'. But it was there, the truth, as real as the burning pain in her heart and her eyes. She had left her bag at the place she had spent the night before. A glimmer of hope roused her to quicken her steps, reach the car and grab the bag. It vanished, the glimmer of hope, as if it had never appeared. Under the handbag, there was a note written in a familiar handwriting. She raised her hand and covered her mouth and read the note:

Base and worthless, you are!

You slept with that geezer last night and asked him for a favour in return! The rancorous nature of yours is even stinkier than hell! You slept with a sixty-two-year-old rotting man only to have my arse kicked! You were too drunk to remember to take your handbag with you, and the geezer wasn't clever enough to hide it somewhere just in case mad Islam barged in!

The name 'Sophie' doesn't suit you! You are just a fucking stinky cheap bitch! Never show yourself to us again!

Islam

Sophie's world came down and hit her like an avalanche, wrapping her in its white and dark layers, rolling her around like a dead weightless bird. "I did ask that geezer for a favour," she whispered, her thin lips shivering, a hysteric laugh gaining momentum within her, her round and now wan face looking like a preface to a book of utter misery and desperation. She laughed, a laugh coming from her womb, containing the entire history of insemination, birth, and the pain of growth. "I did ask that geezer for a favour," she whispered again.

Out of the parking lot and on to the street, and when the anguish in her was reaching its peak, she geared up and drove towards the city centre, and in twenty minutes and as she had done so several times since she had left Gol, she turned towards the narrow street leading to Gol's restaurant. As soon as she parked the car in the small parking area behind the restaurant, she felt a calming surge of relief and contentment in her heart. This time, she did not need to see if the back window of Gol's office was open, she was sure it was. This time, it was her heart that could feel the presence of a man who would always leave a window open, even when the weather was most inclement and bitterly cold.

Minutes later, and when a gentle and rhythmic rain had just begun to fall, she grabbed her umbrella and got off the car with the sheer intention of running towards the back door and banging on it with all her might. But, like the previous times, her heart let her down as she reached the door. She leaned against the door and sighed. The raindrops, now hastier and bigger, kept tapping on the umbrella in a strange note and rhythm, a note and rhythm insinuating to her a timeless time, full stagnation, full- motion, all meaningless, all meaningful.

She took a few steps back, and letting go of the umbrella, she raised her arms and stood in the rain. It fell, the rain, generously, soaking her frame and suffusing through her burning veins. Tears welled up in her and seconds later ran down her cheek and mingled with the large raindrops. She looked around as if looking for the tiny dapple dog that had appeared and stood before her when she had stood in the rain for the first time. There was no dog around. There was only a seagull, sitting under a windowsill and looking at her with a malicious pride sparkling in its widened eyes.

The seagull is proud of me! The bloody creepy thing is proud of me! I need a tiny dapple dog.

There is something in my hands…

I did ask that geezer for a favour! I didn't sleep with him just for nothing! I am not; no I am not a loose girl!

I need a tiny dapple dog.

I hate all the black umbrellas and the people who hide themselves under them!

"What have you done to yourself, Sophie?" asked Molly as Sophie entered the flat, "Look at you! Look at your bloodshot eyes! Come here, here, sit down and tell me what happened to you! Oh, my dear! Why are you so reckless, Sophie?"

"I was sacked," whispered Sophie, tossing her handbag on the floor.

"Where were you last night?" asked Molly, kneeling down and holding her hands.

"I don't know," murmured Sophie, staring at the floor.

"I did warn you. Didn't I?" said Molly, assuming a *motherly* tone, "I asked you not to go to Mrs Aziza Baygum and her sons."

"I am sorry, Molly. I should have listened to you," said Sophie, now looking at the back of her hands.

"Good!" said Molly, holding Sophie's shoulders, "Do you want me to get you a job at my own workplace?"

"Yeah," replied Sophie, looking at Molly apologetically.

"Brilliant!" said Molly, holding Sophie's face in her hands, "My boss is a Greek man named Garry, and he is such a kind and exceptionally well-mannered gentleman. And what can I say about his son, Draco, who loves to apologize to everyone and everything time after time? They are both most discreet and generous to young girls. And there is a very special man, a Mr Christopher Lambrakis, a middle-aged married and very chivalrous man who loves to protect young girls like you. Yeah, he has been protecting me since I got the job. And there are also some other men who know how to generously respect and appreciate beautiful girls like you. Yeah, I am sure they would love you to pieces. And I promise you they would never sit with their backs to you, like that fucking uncivilised man, what was his name again? Yeah, Gol."

"Are there any English men, too?" asked Sophie perfunctorily, her tone half-dead, her face blank, as if the question tumbled out of her mouth without her permission.

"Yeah, there are, two of them," replied Molly, now attentively twisting a stack of her unwashed hair, "A thirty-two-year-old Mr Jack something and another Mr Jack something else, also of the same sort of age. Although they look like two sedated Spring hares—, it is what a fucking Iranian man used to call them—, but they are coming from a very bad past: Mr Jack something raped his own wife five times within a week, and was given five years for it. And Mr Jack something else dared to turn the light off when his wife was reading the most climactic chapter of a crime novel, where a cheating husband and his whore were to be shot in an attic. He was forced to divorce his wife and was given three years for his careless crime. Mr Jack something has married a Polish girl, and Mr Jack something else has married a young Filipino."

"Molly," said Sophie, apparently set to cheer herself up, "Was Mr Jack something else charged also for what the cheating husband was doing in that crime novel his wife was reading?"

"Sophie," said Molly, her tone most serious, "That is why I believe you have become a danger to yourself! You should never ridicule or question our ways of living and doing things!"

"I do apologise, Molly," said Sophie, now staring at the back of her own hands.

Chapter 6

"David, change that sheet on Sophie's desk, please," asked Gol, closing the book he was reading and throwing it on the desk, "It has gathered a good amount of dust."

"So you haven't heard the news?" asked David, walking towards the cabinet by Gol's desk.

"What news?"

"Sophie has left Mrs Baygum's restaurant," said David, taking out a white sheet from the cabinet.

"Where is she now?" asked Gol, touching his well-trimmed beard thoughtfully.

"Cynthia is coming to see you. She knows it all."

Minutes later, Cynthia arrived. Entering the office, she threw a fleeting look at Sophie's desk, and forming a smirk in the corner of her lips, she took a seat beside Gol's without saying a word. The loquacious Cynthia had never found it easy to trade words with Gol as she knew that he would not pay a penny for inauthentic words. Silence had proven more beneficial to her. She put her new painting before Gol and turned her face towards David.

"Mum, Gol wants to know how Sophie is getting on," said David, throwing the white sheet on Sophie's desk.

Cynthia gently turned her head towards Gol, who was now intently looking at her painting, and kept looking at his profile for quite a while before she managed to get hold of her disdainful attitude towards Sophie and said, "Sophie was sacked by Mrs Baygum. Apparently, because of a bit of romance that was going on between Sophie and her elder son, Usman. But I think there was something more serious than this."

"Perhaps she stole something," said David, tying a corner of the sheet to the desk leg.

"Sophie is a timid little rabbit. She doesn't have enough courage to steal," said Cynthia, "I have just heard, I am not sure about it, that Sophie slept with a sixty-two-year-old rotting man only to have him kick Islam's arse! And it was Islam who sacked Sophie. I have also heard that Usman was immeasurably in love with Sophie, and that he hasn't been told yet. It will hurt him deeply."

"I just want to know if she is fine. I don't care why she was sacked," said Gol.

Cynthia dithered for some long seconds, looking at David and Sophie's desk, and then at her painting on Gol's desk; she cleared her throat and said reluctantly, "She is fine. She just got a job at Garry's restaurant. She works as a waitress."

"Garry! Garry's family!" uttered David, turning towards Gol. 'Gol, that is not the right place for Sophie."

"They are some *people!*" said Gol, shaking his head.

"Do you want me to go and bring her back?" asked David, tying the last corner of the white sheet.

"No, David," replied Gol, now looking at Cynthia's face, "I think she is destined to meet those people."

"It has been ages since she left," said Cynthia, avoiding eye contact with Gol, "If she was supposed to come back she would have come back by now."

"She will come back," said Gol; pushing the chair back, he got to his feet and walked towards Sophie's desk. He bent down and picked up something from the floor, and looking at it, he added, "David, give Cynthia five hundred pounds. Her new painting is brilliant. Frame it and put it on the wall, over Sophie's desk."

Cynthia said nothing, and when Gol disappeared behind the door, she turned towards her son and pointing to Sophie's desk, she asked, "I just can't understand this bloody thing! What is this! A historical treasure that should be wrapped in silk and kept for the posterity?"

David fully felt her mother's feelings towards Gol and Sophie: a good deal of indignation, a touch of jealousy, and self-deprecation.

"Mum, you should stop this," said David, putting his hand on his mother's shoulder, "I know you are more than sensible enough to understand that it is over; the Gol's story is over for you. He wouldn't be happy with anything less than a twenty-one-year-old innocent Cynthia. Can you get your innocence back? Never try to disturb him. He has been living with the memories of a young innocent Cynthia all these years. Does it mean anything to you, Mum?"

Cynthia let out a sigh, a very old sigh, containing old and painful

48

regrets and irreparable mistakes and failures that had smeared not even her innocence but also her soul. She looked at his face and, tilting her head, she said, "For this to mean anything to me, the entire history of a nation has to change. Understand me, David. Jealousy is the only thing that can keep me going. I am just jealous. I am not going to disturb him. I promise."

"Whom and what are you jealous of, Mum?" asked David.

"Sophie's vulnerability and innocence," replied Cynthia, "If I was as vulnerable as this bloody little girl is, I would have surrendered myself to Gol when I was just twenty-one."

"I assume you just denied it, the vulnerability in you," said David.

"I like it, boy, you are growing into a wise man," said Cynthia, touching her son's face, "I denied it when Gol spotted it in me. At that age, I wasn't percipient enough to understand why a man should fall in love with the innocence and vulnerability of a woman, and now that I am completely disabused and able to grasp it, I am simply unwilling to accept it! You know, my son, I am a historical denier, a most susceptible denier of vulnerability and innocence. That is exactly why I am jealous of Sophie and hate her."

"But Gol isn't interested in Sophie in that way," said David, ruffling his thick hair.

"Boy, it is Sophie. It is the sublime historical innocence within her," said Cynthia, a rueful air appearing on her face, "Do you know what I mean, my boy. I mean that sublime and historical innocence that can enchant even a piece of iron, or even melt it."

"Being jealous of something as precious as this," said David, "Can simply exert on you an immeasurable mental pressure."

"The bloody guilt," said Cynthia, "The exquisite bloody guilt makes punishment bearable, and somehow pleasurable! I deserve pressure. I deserve punishment."

Chapter 7

"Do you feel any better, David?" asked Gol, as he entered the sitting room.

"Much better," replied David, who was sitting on the couch with a blanket over his shoulders, "Emily made me a magic soup and then a soothing drink. They have actually sorted me out."

"Emily is the mother of all true friends!" said Gol, turning towards the kitchen, he asked, "Have you fed the dog, Emily?"

"Yes, I have," replied Emily, coming out of the kitchen and looking at his face, "Is there anything wrong, Gol?"

"If you quickly make me a pot of tea, I will tell you," replied Gol.

"I guess it is about Sophie," said Emily, pressing the kettle's switch down, "I like you most when you speak about Sophie."

"You are so very right," said Gol, pulling a chair back and sitting at the dining table. He pulled out from the pocket of his jacket what he had found under Sophie's desk: a clear plastic keyholder holding a picture of Sophie and a very gentle-looking handsome young man. He picked a napkin, dipped it in the jug of water before him, and wiped it patiently. Looking at it again, he spotted, in the eyes of the young bearded man, a genuine aristocratic air enhanced with a justified hue of pride.

"Well, now you can tell me the new story about Sophie," said Emily, putting the tea tray on the table.

"First tell me what soup and drink did you make for David, and then tell me when it began, I mean your interest in my stories about Sophie?" asked Gol, throwing a look at David, who was now watching Three Lions playing against USA.

"Gol, don't tell him," whispered Emily, "I phoned Clement and asked him how to make a soup good for cold. And he also sent me some herbs for the hot drink. As for my interest in your stories about Sophie, well, it began when I came to your office for the first time, and saw Sophie's desk," replied Emily, a cheerful smile sitting in her large blue eyes.

"Have a look at this," said Gol, putting the keyholder before Emily, "And tell me what you see in those faces."

"Oh, this is Sophie!" said Emily, holding the keyholder with both hands, "And this gentleman. They look like very close friends. Perhaps this gentleman is Sophie's boyfriend."

"What can you see in Sophie's face," asked Gol, picking up a chunk of sugar from the small ramekin before him.

"She looks happy. Doesn't she? No, wait, no she doesn't look very happy," replied Emily, now staring at the picture, "It is something mixed, perhaps it is an anxious form of happiness."

"And how about the young man?" asked Gol, offering Emily a well-deserved grown-up look.

"He is not ashamed of anything," replied Emily, a covert smile running across her round face.

"Can you just say it again!" asked Gol, knitting his thick eyebrows.

"He is not ashamed of anything."

"You have learned this from one of those books?" asked Gol.

"Yes, I have learned this from one of those books you have been forcing me to read," said Emily, laughing.

"Are you unhappy that I have been—?"

"No," interrupted Emily, "No, I am not unhappy that you have been forcing me to read those books. Now I read them eagerly. And above all, it is now a lucrative business—you pay me to read books and explain them to you."

"Brilliant! I like this business side of you. Now, can you just explain to me why you think this young man is not ashamed of anything?"

"Because the smile on his face is just a smile, like yours," replied Emily, carefully forming a smile on her face.

"Because the smile on his face is just a smile," repeated Gol, smiling at Emily and thinking of all the smiles that have been just smiles. He picked up the picture and gazed at it while Emily was silently watching him. The young man's face seemed to him like an open book, attired with very simple words that together would insinuate a rich and compelling sense of authenticity and righteousness. On Sophie's young fresh face, he spotted an old sense of reservation and uncertainty, an old and unjustified sense of wanting and not wanting at the same time, pushing away and pulling forth, loving and hating, laughing and crying, celebrating and mourning— contradiction, absolute and unjustified. The more he paid attention to the details of the two very contrasting faces, the more baffled he became, the

51

more contradicting elements he spotted on Sophie's face.

"Gol, shall I pour you another tea?" asked Emily.

"Yes, please," replied Gol, still gazing at the picture.

"Why is Sophie so important to you, Gol?" asked Emily, lifting the teapot.

"The answer to this question is too complex for you to understand," said Gol.

"But I think you need help, Gol," said Emily.

"How could you help me with this?" asked Gol, smiling.

"I have a heart and I can use my instinct. It is what you told me just the other day," replied Emily.

"Emily, I think it is time for me to feel proud of you," said Gol, smiling musingly, "Why Sophie has become a matter of profound importance to me is an intricate matter of heart and soul. And as you have just begun to show me some heart, I think I should explain this to you in the briefest possible way: my heart has spotted something precious in Sophie's heart, and as you will learn in a near future, hearts do not ask for permission when it comes to interacting. Helping Sophie to see what she has inside is the most elevating reward that my heart is after."

"David believes you want Sophie's soul to complete an incomplete image in your mind," said Emily.

"What image?" asked Gol, evidently impressed by David's suggestion.

"Cynthia's," replied Emily, offering Gol a bittersweet smile, "He believes a young Cynthia with Sophie's soul would have fulfilled your life."

"David might be right," replied Gol, gently stroking his beard, "But the problem is that Sophie's soul needs to be awakened. A soul vanished in the thick fog of a stagnated slumber, would never be a complement to anything that is supposed to bring about a sort of fulfilment."

"Gol," said Emily, "I think I can understand your views on Sophie and the way she is, but I just can't understand how a person can live most of his life only with the image of something."

"Good girl! Good question," said Gol, asking for another tea with a gesture of his head, "Emily, love is not 'something', love is THE 'thing', and therefore even the image of it can satisfy and enrich a soul. Just to put it in a simpler way for you to understand, I should say if one reaches the state of entitlement to love and feels worthy of it, then one is already in the terrain of love, and thus fulfilment is guaranteed."

"Gol," said Emily, tilting her head, "Would you please allow me to come to the office and do some work for you, so that I could spend more time with you. I think I could do the job Sophie used to do."

"Why do you wish to spend more time with me, Emily?" asked Gol, offering her a kind smile.

"I am eager to learn, Gol. I just want to learn," replied Emily, her face revealing the depth of eagerness within her.

"Emily can come to the office and do some work for Gol," said Gol, smiling, "And by the way, if you finish The Catcher in the Rye by the end of this month and come to me with a savvy review, you will get two hundred pounds to spend on whatever you wish."

"None of my friends believes that I am being paid to read books!" said Emily, laughing heartily, "'No way!' they say. Gol, it has been an amazing business! You have coaxed me into reading thirty-two precious books since David and I joined you."

"If I was in a position of power and authority," said Gol, "I would spend half of the budget of this country on coaxing the youth into reading all the worthwhile works of literature and philosophy."

Gol went to his room. Emily made another hot drink for David, and continued reading The Catcher in the Rye. Steve Gerard scored for Three Lions. David yelled, "Yes! Yes! Yes!" now running around the room and punching the air. Emily laughed at him, flipped through the book and began reading the next chapter.

David let out another yell, this time a yell of disbelief and despair. The Yankees somehow pulled off an equalizer by an unlikely and almost dead shot. Emily watched the replay: the goalkeeper missed an unmissable moment; the ball rolled under his belly, going, going, going, he tried most desperately to reach it, the ball crossed the line and announced the goalkeeper as the loneliest man in the world. Emily felt for him.

Chapter 8

Garry, sixty years of age and a self-proclaimed exceptionally successful businessman, was, in terms of appearance, a very straight and ironed man: rather tall and somewhat lanky, his stature would always look like a sandwich meticulously done in a sandwich press. So erect, so much so that he would walk so upright as if he had a long straight ladder in his stomach! Adding to this, his straight face plus his spiky hair and his long thin nose, you wouldn't dispute his state of straightness! In terms of inner attributes, he was, to an amazing degree, as *straight* and piercing as his spiky hair! By his name, you might imagine him as an alcoholic and somewhat eccentric English chav, but he was of Greek descent, the grandson of a Greek cobbler who had migrated to England when the English had just managed to set the tracks for the train of industrialisation to wriggle around and spew smoke at the world.

Why a man with Greek blood in his straight veins and vessels had been named Garry, was a question and a matter of curiosity for the ones who tended to look at human affairs from a merely sensual viewpoint and assert that Garry's mum had named him after one of her lovers. Having said that, it must be noted that no one could call Garry a 'bastard'—not in its biological terms, as he was as Greek as a Greek could be.

Obviously, born and raised in a no-go-area of the proud city of London, one might expect such a creature to have acquired the entire principles and trappings of the Englishness; but, ironically, he had only, so far, acquired the art of English chavness and the most exquisite form of the English arrogance—unjustified and a hardly tenable form of it. In this, Garry was so accomplished and adorned that he could simply be the undisputable candidate to represent England in any related competitions! Perhaps this analogy would define him comprehensively: Garry was simply a mixture of English mustard and Greek horseradish!

Anita, forty-five years old and uniquely beautiful and lyrically sensual, was Garry's wife. Rather tall and slightly busty, Anita resembled a black tulip, but there was, in the large eyes of this black tulip, a mournful air of perpetual discontent and bereavement, simply rendering her as a black tulip symbolizing martyrdom and sacrifice.

Anita, also Greek by descent, and the granddaughter of a Greek teacher of mythology, was also born and bred in England. Apart from the language, Anita had neither acquired the sophisticated sense of Englishness nor the badly distorted sense of Greekness. At the age of eighteen, when she was a most enchanting young woman, she had married Garry in a bitterly cold and confusing autumn. What Anita had seen in Garry—or what she had failed to see—was still a befuddling question for the people around them, as none of them had ever felt any sense of intimacy and affection between Anita and Garry. And it was also true about Garry and the five children she had born for him. They, the children, would rarely call him 'dad', or if they did they would sound like some reluctantly adopted children. In all, Anita was a beautiful black tulip grown over the grave of her own heart.

Garry and Anita owned three restaurants, five children, a big house, four cheap squalid hard-to-rent flats plus two cars and a spayed despairing female dog and a castrated depressed male one. How Garry had managed to succeed in business, like his marriage to Anita, was a big question for anyone who had known him long enough to notice that he lacked even the most basics of faculties, let alone the needed intelligence to create and progress.

Draco, Garry's eldest child—who would only refer to him as 'dad' whenever bragging about his achievements—would always go: "My *dad* came to this town ages ago. He worked as a dog-walker for a while, walking all sorts of dogs. And guess what? Mate, you just won't believe it! Just three years later, more or less, he managed to own his first restaurant, and shortly afterwards, he got the other two! And then, as you know, he managed to buy a good number of houses and flats!"

Although Draco was a super bombastic master of deception and duplicity, but the true side of the story would always appear in his small eyes and on his irregularly bearded face. And of course, there was always a bird around to confide the secret to the curious and the inquisitive: it was just dropped down from the sky, Garry's fortune. It was bloody and horrendous! A crowbar and a human head, red wine, skull, skin, brain, all mingled. A drunk sturdy Englishman and Garry's nephew, alcohol, lust, the lush semi-naked bodies of Lilith-like females, jealousy, the imbalanced hormones, they all converged to make the drunk sturdy Englishman shatter Garry's nephew's head. It was bloody, Garry's fortune. It was blood money, a good amount of it, enough to turn a donkey into a horse!

Garry's nephew was the only survivor of his eldest brother's family who had been killed during the Turkish invasion of Cyprus while on a vacation.

Of Garry and Anita's other children, whom this story has business with, was Calypso, a twenty-three-year-old who was a chameleon in the form of a very shy, cunning and mysterious girl. Her slim body was as straight as that of his dad, but she could be, in certain situations, as flexible as a rubber band! A rather thin long face, a pair of black eyes canopied with a pair of thick eyebrows, and a fair amount of long sleek black hair could simply render her as a female version of her dad. Like Draco and other children, she also was not very much in favour of calling Garry 'dad'. Strangely, the word 'dad' had, in Garry's children's vocabulary, a demeaning connotation to it! Similarly, Anita also was not much in favour of using the words 'my husband' whenever referring to her husband! In all, the word 'family' would simply refuse to include this couple and their children. They were just a small group of people who did not believe in the normal functions of human language, unity, and love!

Chapter 9

Although she had applied for an office job, Sophie was imposed upon the position of waitress. Demanding and imposing, leaving no room for any chance of rejection, Garry asked Sophie to work for him as a waitress, stating that she would earn more by serving the customers than sitting beside Anita and him in the office and doing *nothing!* She had not applied for an office job to sit beside two other people and do nothing! Too mindful to be able to use her mind, she gave Garry a look, a look that made him offer her a gentle and triumphant smile with a touch of pity.

"Now," said Garry, putting his right hand on Sophie's lower back for the fourth time since she had entered the office, "You will go to Mervyn, Draco and our head-waiter, Christopher, and they will teach you whatever you need to get you started. Just listen to them carefully. Pay attention. Be smart. Prove to us your mettle, and we will look after you. You are off. Oh, by the way, I like your name. I think it is a Greek name. Isn't it?"

Both unsure! The Greek man and the English girl. The origin of the word 'Sophie' remained unknown!"

"Nice to meet you, Sophie Sophia!" said Christopher Lambrakis, the head-waiter, "My name is Christopher. Nice to meet you."

"Hello, Sophie," said Draco, stretching his hand out to shake hands with her, "I am Draco. Nice to meet you."

A touch of embarrassment and a bigger touch of bafflement made Sophie speechless for some long seconds. Managing to get hold of her nerves and forming half a smile on her face, and still not sure why the two men standing before him were receiving her so intimately, she said, "I am Sophie, and I am twenty-two-years-old."

"Oh, young enough, young enough!" said Christopher Lambrakis, letting out an unnecessary and disproportionate laugh, his chickenpox-hole-ridden blotchy face resembling a crumpled brown paper bag.

"Awesome! Awesome!" said Draco, offering Sophie a very-hard-to read smile.

"Now, if you please come with me, I will show you around, and I also introduce you to the other staff."

"Yeah, good!" said Sophie, still sounding embarrassed.

"Well, let's begin with these two quiet gentlemen," said Draco, turning towards the bar, "Jack and Jack are simply the most civilized men I have ever come across, honestly. They only mind their own business. Honestly, it takes a lot to be so civilized."

"Hi, guys," said Sophie, smiling, "I am Sophie."

"Hi, Sophie," said the two Jacks at the same time, two completely bland smiles distorting their handsome faces.

"Let's move on," said Draco, turning around, "As you can see for yourself, this isn't a very large place, which is, more or less, a plus side to it, as it makes it easier for us to manage it best, which means we can look after our customers much better. Well, fair enough. Let's go."

Like his way of talking—elongating the sentences unnecessarily—Draco's extremities were also a bit more elongated and lengthier than the normal size: he was a young man of arms and legs plus a bit of belly and a good amount of chest and a barely noticeable amount of backside.

"Oh, you walk too fast!" said Sophie, now almost running behind Draco.

"I am sorry," said Draco, stopping and turning towards her, "This is an unorthodox way of walking, more or less, I believe. Fair enough. Awesome. You will get used to walking with me."

Unorthodox, perhaps this was the only word that could define Draco comprehensively. In fact Draco was a most unorthodox creature who was fully capable of playing the role of a very orthodox one—except for the fact he could not do anything to make his unorthodox extremities look orthodox! And also the fact that he would overuse the phrases 'more or less', and 'fair enough' could well be taken as a remote tendency towards orthodoxy within him.

"This is Mehmet, our head chef," said Draco, as soon as they entered the small but well set-up kitchen, "Fair enough. He is very good. More or less. Oh, yeah, fair enough."

"Me Mehmet. Nice meet you does," said the rather young plump smock-faced chef with an intricate smile splayed all over his spacious face, "I am me happy meet you it is. I am me happy work us with does. I am brother Draco my is does happy us with very."

"Where is Ghena?" asked Draco, when he had introduced Sophie to the other kitchen staff.

"I am here. I am coming," shouted Ghena from the upstairs.

Seconds later, he appeared, Ghena, the reticent and reserved young chef.

"Ghena, this is Sophie. She is our new waitress," said Draco as soon as Ghena put a tray of chicken breast on the large steel table.

"All right," said Ghena, throwing a fleeting look at Sophie's face, he added, "Good."

Evidently, Sophie felt uneasy when Ghena threw at her a second brief look. On Ghena's rather Christ-looking face, she saw an austere smack of reprehension. She quickly turned her face towards Mehmet and offered him a most pleasant smile.

"I liked the head chef very much," said Sophie, as they left the kitchen, "I absolutely loved his English."

"Sarcasm! Yeah?" asked Draco, laughing.

"No, not at all, I really mean it," said Sophie, "I have never heard anyone speak our language so correctly and so beautifully."

"Oh, okay. Fair enough. More or less, it should be so! Awesome, yeah, perhaps it is because of the fact that he has been married to an English woman for fifteen years now!" said Draco, the smile on his face drying breaking flaking shattering.

"How is his cooking?" asked Sophie, overlooking the disintegrating smile on Draco's face.

"Somehow, more or less, as good as his English is! Fair enough!" replied Draco without looking at Sophie's face.

The last of the waiters and the waitresses whom Sophie was to be introduced to was Maria, a twenty-two-year-old Greek girl with a face that simply seemed as a brief yet most inviting preamble to a story of exquisite love and affection. Maria's face, shaded by a heap of thick curly hair, was simply a mirror which was designed to reflect only the goodness.

"Maria, this is Sophie, our new waitress," said Draco, the traces of the shattered smile still visible on his face, "Garry believes she will make a unique waitress. Now I will hand her over to you. Take her upstairs and show her the bar area."

"Sophie!" uttered Maria, in a tone denoting years of acquaintance,

"Glad to meet you, Sophie!"

Something in Sophie's heart melted; perhaps a chunk of ice. She stared at Maria's rather dark face for some long lingering and heavy moments, loaded and full moments, each containing a call and a cue.

"Maria!" uttered Sophie, her round white face turning rosy.

Before Sophie could say anything else, Maria's raised arms embraced her firmly, her warm face touching hers, her heart feeling hers, her unadulterated feminine soul mingling with hers. Sophie pressed her face against Maria's and closed her eyes. A few hasty moments of self-realisation. She became all but eyes. She looked into her own mind, the anticlockwise mind, the reversed settings, the wrongly attached and the badly detached synapses.

She pressed her face harder against Maria's and whispered to herself, "Gol, Aisha, Maria and Ghena, they are the mirrors, they are the hints. I love them! I hate them! I love them, I hate, hate, hate, hate, hate them... I just hate them! I love to hate! I love to hate the calls and the hints! I love to hate the people who see innocence in me! What is Maria's heart doing in mine if I am not innocent! I am and I am not! I love and I hate! And I love that I love and hate!"

"Is there anything wrong, Sophie?" asked Maria, holding Sophie's shoulders.

"No, no, I just love you, Maria," replied Sophie, her lips shivering.

"Good!" said Maria, kissing Sophie's face most affectionately, "So let's begin. First and foremost, this place is just a bit out of its normal sense."

"What is it, Maria?" asked Sophie, a blank smile appearing on her face.

"Nothing too serious. Nothing to be worried about," replied Maria, lowering her voice, "I mean this place might not be as normal as other places you have experienced; and it is natural, Sophie. Isn't it? People and places differ from each other. Don't they?"

"As long as they pay me for what I do for them, I would be fine with whatever," said Sophie, her face still blank and somewhat baffled.

Sophie had long been fine with *whatever!* Normality and abnormality, to her, had long lost the opposing element between them; and that was why *love* and *hate* had become the same for her.

She turned towards Maria and stared at her face, perhaps in search of the traces of the sublime moments of love and affection she had just experienced with her, but she found none, not even a tiny mark or a faded hue. As a university student studying biology, she could remotely feel—just remotely and fleeting—that she was on the verge of being trapped in her biological form of existence and remain there forever.

"Calypso!" exclaimed Maria as Calypso entered the bar area, "This is Sophie."

"Hi, Sophie," said Calypso in an overly gentle tone, "You seem to have already gained a level of popularity for yourself. The guys are very fond of you, and as I can see, so is Maria."

"I am happy to hear that," said Sophie, half a smile appearing on her face.

"But you will be on a week of probation," said Calypso, offering Sophie the kindest of smiles.

"I am fine with it," said Sophie, evidently struggling to interpret Calypso's smile.

"Now, could you please come with me?" asked Calypso, looking at Sophie with a tinge of a covert sensual delight sitting in her eyes, "I want to introduce you to Mervyn, our manager. He is upstairs, in his office."

"Oh, yeah, okay," said Sophie, evidently affected by Calypso's eyes.

Minutes later, they entered Mervyn's office: a few spans of a tight and crammed space, hardly bigger than a kennel, lined with all sorts of cables and wires overhead, a desk overwhelmed with mostly unattended stacks of paperwork and festooned with a few dirty coffee cups, all sorts of wraps and even a few mouldy half-eaten sandwiches! The very low ceiling and the dirty floor plus a gurgling sewer pipe were the other aspects of Mervyn's office. So who was this rather young piece of a man? Contrary to his office, Mervyn seemed, in terms of his appearance, very tidy and neat, and even somewhat smart and posh-looking. Resting his rather broad lower jaw on his interlocked hands, he was staring at the dirty screen before him, apparently contemplating upon some very profound matters.

"Mervyn, this is Sophie, our new waitress and Molly's friend," said Calypso, "She is beautiful. Isn't she?"

"Oh, hello, Sophie Sophia," said Mervyn, turning around, "How old are you, Sophie Sophia?"

"Oh, me? yeah, I am twenty-two," replied Sophie, a silly smile distorting her face.

"Good. Good enough," said Mervyn, in a tone denoting it would be much better if she was much younger! "Yes, twenty-two is good enough. I like you. I will look after you. Just listen to Calypso and Molly, and not anyone else."

"Oh, thank you very much! I will," said Sophie, her face blushed.

"You are off. We will talk later," said Mervyn, shoving his hands into his rather curly brownish hair and turning towards Calypso, "Could you send Mehmet upstairs? I need to talk to him."

"Oh, yes, I will," replied Calypso, holding Sophie's hand and throwing a covert wink at Mervyn.

"I liked him," said Sophie, as soon as they stepped out of the office, "But his eyes, you know, they were oozing confidence and—and—I don't know how to explain it…Yeah, he is good."

"Did you notice how masculine he is?"

"Oh, yeah, I think I noticed."

Minutes later, Mehmet entered Mervyn's grand office with some speculations already formed in his large head and now delineating on his spacious face. He took off his apron, and with the air of a 'man of ladies' bulging within him, he put his palms on the edge of the desk, and after puffing himself up like cats do, he said, "Brother, what does you would want tell me to?"

"You sound as if you already know what I am going to tell you. You bloody fucker!" said Mervyn, laughing, "This new girl. I just wanted to give you a heads-up. She is mine."

"Brother," said Mehmet, his face turning blue, his eyes widening, "See what does you do would brother! You good fair man not are! I—I—I—has oooonly ttttwo! Got has you many how? You does got that blonde! You does got that other the blonde slim is very other! You does got curvy ginger that! You does got Molly… Shis new girl loves does me much very too!"

"Brother," said Mervyn, now staring at Mehmet's face, "Calm yourself down and tell me how you found out she loves you very much so quickly."

"Bbbbbrother," stuttered Mehmet, "Face shis would does me told said!"

"Oh, well, her face told you!" said Mervyn, his eyes now blank and fixed.

"Bbbbbrother, you does got wait a second!" asked Mehmet, lowering his voice, "You like does got only twenty under! Not does got you? But shis is twenty-two-old-years is."

"Yes, brother, I like only under-twenties, but she is an exception," said Mervyn, his eyes now readable only to an expert.

"What does got is it she?" asked Mehmet, narrowing his eyes, his gaze slightly shifting, up and down, left and right.

"She is too silly," replied Mervyn, his hazel eyes sparkling, his right hand creeping down his groin, "The silly ones are natural lustful bitches, all of them. They are only meant to be shagged. They are pure orgasm. What do you know about orgasm, you fucking villager? It is only the pure female orgasm that can make a man feel like a man."

"Bbbbbrother," stuttered Mehmet, sounding like a car gear being changed without the use of the clutch, "Bbbbbbrother—yyuuuuooo—ffffuckkkkkking—"

"Okay, you fucking bugger," interrupted Mervyn, laughing, "Cut it out. I will try her first and then you can have her. Happy now?"

"Okay, you fucking dickhead brother," said Mehmet, now sounding like a car coasting down a slope, "Me I give can orgasm good women to. Me I not gay half like you is! Me not like you!"

"I see!" said Mervyn, smiling, "Bugger, make me a halloumi sandwich and give it to Sophie to bring it to me."

"You bugger does is, Brother, not me I not like you," said Mehmet in a mirthful tone.

He grabbed his apron and as he turned to go, Mervyn said to him, "And by the way, you could have Molly as well. I have gone off her. Her cunt has become too loose and her boobs are shrinking."

"Brother, should you does give Garry her to," said Mehmet, letting out a loud laugh, spewing raw lust.

"I have given him the curvy ginger one and the short busty blonde one," said Mervyn, a strange mixture of innocence and extreme lewdness appearing in his eyes and on his face!

"Brother, you fucking bugger is does," said Mehmet, an ejaculation taking place in his eyes, "You told said blonde busty short give does to me!"

"Garry will soon go off her, and then you can have her. I promise," said Mervyn, getting to his feet.

Half an hour later, Sophie stepped in, put the sandwich before Mervyn, offered him a smile and as she turned around to go, Mervyn called her,

"Sophie Sophia, why don't you come here and give me a kiss?"

"Oh, me? Yeah," said Sophie, turning around.

"Come on, come here," asked Mervyn, pointing to his bearded face.

"I like you," said Sophie, bending down and kissing his face.

"When are you going to give me a proper kiss?" asked Mervyn, holding her hand.

"Oh, me? Yeah, I don't know," replied Sophie, letting out a gentle gasp—hard to tell what it was supposed to impart, "You sound like a Londoner. Don't you?"

"Oh yes, I am a fucking Londoner," replied Mervyn, gesturing her to kiss him again, "But I am originally Italian."

"Really!" uttered Sophie, kissing his face, "I have always wanted to learn the Italian language. Maybe you can teach me."

"I can't speak Italian."

"How come?"

"An English woman brought me to this country when I was little," replied Mervyn, his hand creeping between Sophie's legs, "I will tell you the full story whenever you are ready to give me a proper kiss."

"Oh, me? No, yeah, I have got to go now!" said Sophie, a distant call ringing in her head, she was not fine. She was fine. It all sounded wrong. It all sounded right. Unsteadily, she turned around to go, and as she was reaching for the door handle, Mervyn asked her, "Do you like Mehmet?"

"Oh, me, yeah, yeah," replied Sophie, her face now a tapestry of silliness, "Yeah, I do love him. He is such a decent man, and he speaks our language so beautifully."

"Oh, I see!" said Mervyn, his mouth gaping.

The days passed, and Sophie was deemed not fit for the job by Garry, Anita and Calypso. 'Too shy and a bit silly' believed Garry. 'Unable to make a decision on her own' observed Calypso. 'Not engaging enough and somewhat confused' asserted Anita. But Draco, Christopher and Mervyn believed otherwise: 'hard-working and obedient' they professed.

As one of their expertise—spotting the trait of *obedience* in young girls—Draco, Christopher and Mervyn succeeded in substantiating their views by arguing that hard working and *obedience* would definitely make up for shyness and a bit of silliness! Delving a bit deeper into this, one should add the attribute of *silliness* to *obedience* for a better understanding of Draco, Christopher and Mervyn's mind. It is to mention that Garry's opposition to taking Sophie on was tactful and not real!

"Sophie Sophia, you got the job!" said Christopher, letting out one of his trademark laughs, "Whatever the problem, no matter what, whatsoever, just let me know. No worries at all. I have your back. They believed you weren't good enough for this job, but I am here, and I will have your back."

"I thank you very much, Christopher," said Sophie, her eyes moistening.

"No worries, no worries," said Christopher, touching her arm, "I will protect you. I will protect you. My daughter, you are like my daughter. She is, like you, a bit shy, and she also needs to be protected. I will protect you. You need protection. I have been protecting Molly since she joined us."

"What are you saying to Sophie, Christopher?" asked Draco, pulling a high stool towards Sophie's.

"Nothing important. I just was telling her that she would do well here," replied Christopher drily, with his head held down.

"Oh, fair enough. She needs a bit of support, more or less, I think so," said Draco, forming an air of absolute authority and confidence on his face.

"Sophie Sophia, go and check the tables. Make sure things are where they must be," asked Christopher, throwing a look at Draco, who was staring at Sophie's face.

"Oh, me? Yeah," said Sophie, now awkwardly trying to save an aborting smile on her blushed face.

Work, an escape from something, a refuge to something else, she felt it when walking away from the two men who had just concluded, in such a short amount of time, that she needed *protection* and *support!* Not being very good at translating humans, due to a complacent reliance upon her mind, she felt an inexplicable self-deprecating indignation gaining momentum in a layer of her disturbed mind. She moved among the tables, checking that things were where they must be.

Everything needs to be moved around. They are all mismatched and misplaced.

No, they seem to be all right with the way they are. They are somewhat out of place. No, it doesn't matter. Place doesn't matter, any object could be placed anywhere, almost anywhere. No, objects ought to be placed in their designated place. Symmetric, these objects in here aren't symmetric; they are also scientifically wrong. No, the placement of such objects doesn't have to be scientifically right.

"Can I wash this cloth here?" asked Sophie, entering the kitchen.

"Oh, yes, can does wash you the here cloth," replied Mehmet, with a smile polluted with a good deal of mawkishness, "Sorry, my English enough good doesn't is."

"Don't say that. Your English is just perfect. Honestly," said Sophie, smiling.

Under Ghena's questioning look, the hearty smile on Sophie's face turned into a silly expression.

She turned her face away from him and stumbled out of the kitchen, carrying another misplaced moment with her. Since the first encounter, she had found it almost impossible to make any sort of connection with this Jesus-looking young man whose piercing gaze would penetrate into her mind and demand nothing but heartfulness and honesty.

"Chandeliers, Sophie Sophia, clean the chandeliers!" shouted Christopher, laughing raucously, as if cleaning some chandeliers was the most laughable job ever!

"Sophie, I stepladder you bring for to," shouted Mehmet from the kitchen.

"Mehmet, I will do it. You need not put yourself out for her!" shouted Draco, now marching towards the kitchen in a giraffe-like gait.

"See what doing does are you, Brother!" snapped Mehmet, jerking around like an incensed baboon.

"Not this one, Mehmet! This one is mine," said Draco with a slushy laugh, "Fair enough. More or less, you should understand this, I suppose."

"If she wants does you, it okay does is. But she me I wants, brother!" replied Mehmet with a gripping stutter, "Brother Mervyn gave does shis me to!"

"Fair enough, more or less, we will see," said Draco, lifting the stepladder, "Mervyn is a fucking manager! I am a fucking boss! More or less, you both should understand this."

"Brrrrrrother, meee I not am like you!" said Mehmet, taking off his apron with a heavy huff, "That is why shis is does like me! Me am is man the does got one only personality! All got you two personalities or three!

Understand, me not like you! Even Jacks the two does did told me am is am man only good for Sophie!"

"Oh, I see!" said Draco, narrowing his eyes, "You might be, more or less, right."

"Be careful, Sophie Sophia," shouted Christopher, as Sophie was climbing the ladder, "If you fall, you will land on the cutlery and the wine glasses!"

With each rhombic crystal cleaned a collective reflection appeared in it, some moving and some static, some reflecting the light back and some other absorbing a good portion of it, some elongating and some twisting. Among the moving ones Sophie's eyes caught sight of two unchanging faces, both bearded, both calm and serene.

This one is Ghena's. And that one… no… no! Is it Gol's!

She jumped off the ladder and meandered through the tables and chairs, reached the door and pushed it open with all her might. Out and on to the street, she saw no one, no moving thing. There were only the overwhelmed lights by the fog and the churlishly cold autumn breeze.

I wouldn't wish to see him, anyway.

"Sophie Sophia, what was that?" asked Christopher, laughing like a horse.

"Nothing—it was just nothing," replied Sophie, her eyes moistening.

"For *nothing* people wouldn't run so recklessly, see all those glasses and cutlery!" said Christopher.

Sophie said nothing because she had nothing to say. She had run towards the door for no reason. She had run towards the door for a reason. There was a reason. There was none. The two Jacks turned around and threw a merged and very coordinated and very indifferent look at her.

Meanwhile, Garry walked in in a pace so similar to that of a field marshal who had just routed the most sophisticated army on the earth! Taking off his jacket and checking the straight collar of his meticulously ironed pink shirt, he eyed around for some long seconds, and ignoring Christopher and Draco, he kept gently marching towards the kitchen, but midway on his course, he came to a slow, thoughtful and somewhat alarmed halt, as if he had just spotted a battalion of enemy's special forces. He held his head high, rolled his eyes down and focused on a spot close to the back door. Contrary to his strict habit of straightness, he was looking obliquely—he would look obliquely only at moving things!

"Draco, rat! Christopher, rat!" he shouted, dashing towards the back door, "Sophie, Rat! Sophie, shut the back door! Shut the back door! Hurry, hurry up, Draco! I want it alive!" Sophie stumbled, the fat rat made it, just a second before Sophie went down on the threshold.

"Bloody hell, I didn't know there were such fat rats around here!" said Christopher, letting out a horsey laugh enhanced with a few notes of disgust.

"Draco, I want this rat alive!" said Garry, now biting the remains of his fingernails.

"Is he a rat-catcher, Garry?" asked Christopher, letting out another laugh, this time sounding mulish and enhanced with a few notes of derision.

"I will do my best, Garry," replied Draco, darting a defused angry look at Christopher.

"I will help you, Draco," said Sophie, her face blank.

Before Sophie could manage to successfully form a silly expression on the blankness of her face, the door pushed open and three young men barged in.

"What the hell are they doing here!" uttered Garry, still biting his nearly non-existent fingernails.

"They are Mrs Baygum's sons, two of them, Usman and Islam!" said Sophie, her heart bursting, her face burning.

"Nice bottle rack," said Islam, pulling out a wine bottle from the honeycomb clay rack and turning towards Garry, "Garry, I told you. Didn't I?"

"Get out of here, mate!" shouted Garry in an overly confident tone, "Or I will let you know…" Before Garry could add anything else to his short emphatic rant, the bottle of red wine landed before his feet and shattered to pieces.

"It is a work of art, Garry," said Usman, pushing his hands into the pockets of his loose trousers, "And a very creative form of it! See, bespattered by red blobs, your stature and your face, they now look nicer! And so does your place."

Christopher and Draco disappeared. They did so as if they had never been there. Sophie took a few steps back but decided to stay in the scene. The confidence on Garry's face shattered, just like the wine bottle did. Looking at his now finely bespattered clothes, his face turned hysteric.

"What is this supposed to mean, mate?" asked Garry, his small eyes widening.

"You paid someone to come to my place and make trouble! Didn't you?" asked Usman. "You will pay for the damage caused by him or—," said Islam.

"It was me," interrupted Sophie, her eyes moistening, her voice cracked, "I asked that guy to come to your place and kick Islam's arse. It was me. Honestly, it was me!"

As Islam opened his mouth to apparently sling some harsh words at Sophie, Usman quickly raised his hand and forestalled him. He took a few steps forward and stood before Sophie, crossed his arms on his chest, and looking into her now whitish jade eyes, he said, "You are a pathetic pathological liar. You lie to justify your smeared nature. That was a demand by your nature, your devalued wayward dirt-loving nature asked you to feed it, and you did, you slept with that geezer. Sophie, this is a great achievement for you! Imagine, just imagine what it takes to devoid a soul of beauty and blessings just at the age of twenty-two! You have done it! Congratulations! You are not worth loving!"

Usman's words cut Sophie's heart but not deep enough to make it bleed; it just brought a few tears to her eyes, only to change their colour— full green to whitish jade. Her thin lips shivered, her tender shoulders dropped, she watched Usman walk away from her until he reached the door, turned around and looked at her. She felt, she heard a wrenching burning crying bleeding heart—Usman's. A part of her separated, dressed in white silk, ten years of age, Sophie, beautiful little Sophie dashed towards the door, out on to the street, she ran, faster and faster. Past a crossroad, she fell short of breath; her knees gave in, her heart pounded. She went down on her knees, her head drooping, and her light brown hair touching the wet ground. She felt, on the nape of her neck, a warm touch, an invigorating, life-giving touch. Usman, the little cute Usman, held her small hands in his.

You kissed the back of my neck!
I did.

   Shall I kiss your cute face?
   You shall.

"You all right, Sophie?" asked Draco, cautiously walking towards Garry and Sophie.

"He kissed the back of my neck!"

"Who! Mehmet?"

"No. Usman!"

"Well, fair enough, more or less, it must be so, yeah, good, I suppose," said Draco, now looking at Garry, frozen in the middle of the *creative art* created by Islam!

"Garry, your face is bleeding!" said Sophie.

"No, girl, it is red wine," said Draco without looking at Garry's face.

Garry raised his hand in a robotic manner and checked his face. One of his nail-less fingers stopped on a spot close to his right ear and seconds later, he turned towards Draco and said, "Look! It is a glass splinter. Draco even doesn't know the difference between a donkey and a horse, let alone the difference between blood and red wine."

"A donkey is actually a smaller horse!" said Christopher, who had just reappeared at the scene in a ghost-like manner.

"But a horse has got bigger balls!" said Sophie, her round face looking like a booklet of sublime sarcasm.

"Oh, I see, fair enough, more or less, you must have a point, I suppose," said Draco without looking at Sophie.

"Bloody hell, she has got a point!" boomed Christopher, braying like a horny old donkey.

"What was the matter, I mean Garry and those guys?" asked Christopher, as soon as Garry and Sophie left the scene.

"I have never interfered with his business, more or less," replied Draco, throwing a fleeting look at Sophie, who was marching towards the kitchen, "It is one's prerogative to only mind his own business, more or less, I believe."

"What is this word 'prerogative'?" asked Christopher, narrowing his small eyes.

"It means a reserved right, more or less, it must mean so," replied Draco, drawing an air of sophistication on his face.

The two Jacks remained unmoved, scrubbing the bar area and sipping their coffee. Neither the failed rat hunt nor the angry presence of Usman and Islam and the creative piece of art created by them contained enough merit and curiosity to distract the two civilized gentlemen!

"Sophie, what said did guys does?" asked Mehmet, handing Sophie a clean apron.

"He waged war on Garry, Islam," replied Sophie, lowering her voice and throwing a glance at Draco and Christopher, who were now attentively eyeing the floor in search of glass splinters, "He is a lout and a drug-dealer, I suppose. 'I have nothing to lose' he said to Garry. Now Garry has to pay him a good chunk of money."

"But did what why for does was?" asked Mehmet, elevating the English language to its highest level!

"For the damage done to their restaurant. They believe Garry was behind it," replied Sophie, proving her undisputable literacy and her unique art of discerning and understanding exquisite English!

"I know doesn't. We know doesn't. Maybe Garry something do with guy drug does," said Mehmet, looking at Sophie's face with a triumphant smile sitting in his eyes.

"Yes, we don't know," said Sophie, offering him a very sweet and almost melting smile.

"Yes, we know don't does. We say maybe. Saying not okay is does. Me am is not like others shit saying back behind over people," said Mehmet, his face now fully blushed.

As Sophie was to turn around and leave the kitchen, her eyes caught Ghena's, standing at the end of the kitchen and staring at her.

Chapter 10

"Happy birthday to you!" said Christopher, letting out a horsey laugh, "See, if it wasn't because of me these people would have sacked you. See, now you have been working here for eight months. Bloody hell! Forty-five hours a week! Cash in hand. See, this is just because you listened to me."

"Christopher, Draco isn't happy with this," said Sophie, her eyes now whitish jade, "He is going to sack Mehmet, and he might sack you too."

"Draco is still a child. He doesn't deserve you," said Christopher with a chuckle.

"He is twenty-eight years old!" said Sophie, laughing.

"It is a quiet restaurant. Isn't it?" said Christopher, evidently to change the subject, "That is why I decided to bring you for your birthday."

"Draco wanted to take me to Amsterdam for my birthday," said Sophie.

"Amsterdam!" uttered Christopher, shaking his head, "Drinking too much is a big enough problem for you—big enough without Amsterdam! And more importantly, Draco is a drug addict, and a cuckoldy man! He wouldn't mind to pimp you out in places like Amsterdam!"

"I have never been into drugs, Christopher," said Sophie with a pout, "and I am definitely not a loose girl."

"I think you should stay away from Draco all together," said Christopher, a surge of envy appearing on his sparsely bearded blotchy face.

"I like him, Christopher. We like each other," said Sophie with another pout.

"He is a user and an abuser! So is Mehmet! Why don't you want to understand this?" said Christopher, letting out a gentle hysteric laugh and revealing his large teeth; he added, "I believe you are unable to make a decision on your own."

Christopher was definitely right. Sophie was unable to make a decision on her own and discern the decency from indecency; and Christopher himself was an undeniable proof to that! So were Draco, Mehmet, Mervyn and Garry, each of them sowing the seeds of *susceptibility* in her mind and reaping it with the sickle of *protection*. If there was a scant likelihood of having an overall reassessment of her mental state, it had now been taken away from her by holding a demanding full-time job and having to study her university lessons. Moreover, her unjustifiable tendency to avoid honest and more cultivated people plus her insatiable appetite for binge drinking, had simply left no respite for this young soul.

"If, as you just said, Draco loves you," said Christopher, uncapping another bottle of red wine, "So why doesn't he ask you to join and live with him, I mean in his large flat?"

"I think Garry doesn't allow him to," replied Sophie.

"Draco doesn't give a god damn thing about what Garry says," said Christopher, with another horsey chuckle.

"Garry wants to give me one of his flats to live in, for free," said Sophie, a mixed air of lust, jealousy, indignation, regret, sorrow and pain appearing on her face, "He just told me yesterday."

"Oh, I see," said Christopher, the red wine and envy turning his face blue, "I think you should listen to me; only to me."

"I should listen to… " said Sophie, staring into the glass of wine before her, and after a long pause she added, "I should listen to all of you."

Christopher looked at Sophie's moistened eyes for some seconds, and let out a raucous laugh, as he knew Sophie's eyes would never reveal anything lasting, lasting enough to be taken seriously, understood and registered.

She was right, and perhaps it was the only thing she was certain about, by saying that she 'should listen to all of them'. Her mind, pullulated only with its own contents, was simply doing what a mind of such nature would: sequencing the events and confirming them; and thus, she would follow the faulty logic that if she refused to obey Garry and Draco, she would lose her job! And that if she did not follow Christopher and Mehmet, she would lose two *protectors*! Apparently, pleasing three married men, two of whom were even older than her dad, and securing the favour with them, was the only *logical* thing to do in order to avoid '*illogical*' consequences and the ills they might inflict on her! In all, she had become an overly attentive factotum and, of course, a doxy to this *fine* group of men.

"It would be better for you, I suppose," said Sophie in a most coquettish tone, "I mean me living in one of Garry's flats. Then you wouldn't have to take me to this or that nearby town and we wouldn't have to pay for staying at this or that hotel."

73

"Garry is a bastard!" said Christopher, touching his eagle-like nose and mawkishly laughing, "In this case, well, Garry is very watchful and inquisitive. I am sure he has already set up some hidden cameras in the flat he is to allow you to live in! We would be in trouble."

"I have been intending to ask you a very serious question for a long time," said Sophie, the flirtatious and playful look still lingering on her rosy face.

"Go on, ask me."

"How would your wife and Garry's react if they got to know this, I mean what has been going on between us?"

"Anita and my wife are women of action. Women of action are not very much into reacting.

"Oh, I see!" said Sophie.

Chapter 11

"'A source of trouble' he said, and asked me to leave. That is all I can say," said Franco, looking at Sophie's face curiously.

"I didn't know you could be a troublemaker," said Sophie, laughing.

"I am Italian, I would love a bit of trouble every now and then—it is like the cheese on our pizza!" said Franco, shrugging his bony shoulders, "Did you know what Gol said to me? He said 'Franco, you have gone over your quota of troublemaking, and that is why I think I should sack you'. And he did, the next day."

"I think you have come to the right place!" said Sophie, laughing, "You will definitely get enough *cheese* on your pizza!"

"I didn't know Sophie too could crack a joke so wittingly!" said Franco, now looking at Sophie's hands.

"What are you looking at?" asked Sophie, a thoughtful smile forming on her face.

"Nothing—just like that—I like some people's hands. Yours look very fine," replied Franco, now lowering his head and looking at her hands again.

"Did Gol really sack you?" asked Sophie, with a bittersweet smile on her face.

"I have never heard of *unreal* sacking," replied Franco, looking into Sophie's moistening eyes, "When you get the sack you get the sack."

"I never liked Gol. He was too serious and overly demanding," said Sophie, averting her eyes from Franco's.

"He is ruthlessly sincere, yet tolerant and forgiving," said Franco, unlocking his mobile phone, "Have a look at this."

"What is this?" asked Sophie, staring at a picture on the phone.

"A treasure in the museum of Gol's heart—Sophie's desk," replied Franco.

"Awh!" uttered Sophie, covering her mouth with her hand, "I can't believe this! This is so heart-breaking, so heart-warming, so demanding, so guiding, so confusing!"

"'At this desk either Sophie will sit again or no one at all' he said, the next day after you left." Two large warm teardrops rolled down Sophie's cheeks. She took a napkin to wipe them but she decided not to. There came, the tears, more and more, warm and salty, streaming down and falling on her small hands, each drop a beat, a note, a reminder, a hint towards purity and unadulteratedness, each a demand, a compelling expectation.

Short and passing moments of realisation, concurring, connecting and disconnecting, recidivating, Sophie's purgatory, she had just begun to notice, remotely, that she had been pitched into it.

She stared at the picture again. Her desk, her place, wrapped in a white spotless sheet. She zoomed the picture in and looked at the painting hung over her desk, Cynthia's work, the two mixed female faces…

"This is so *heart-breaking,* so heart-warming, so demanding, so confusing," she moaned bitterly.

Heart-breaking, these words came out of her mouth unconsciously, perhaps dropped into her heart before being fully formed in her mind. Confusing and as demanding, it was Gol's affection to her. Loving just for the sake of loving, she was unable to clearly comprehend it; and what had made this love *heart-breaking* to her, was its nature—an unconditional conditional love! It needed a pass, a pass to its domain and consequently to its unconditionality.

In her tears and in the muffled sighs inside her, she noticed, for the first time since she was old enough to differentiate her right hand from her left, the presence of so many neglected desires—some old, some older and some others unborn.

***

The arrival of Franco, the tall charming educated and pungently witty Italian chef, was in fact a preamble to ravelling and unravelling the dramas at Garry's restaurant. Of these dramas, the mind games going on among Draco, Christopher, Garry and Mehmet, were affected most by the presence of this new player.

Franco, inherently cogent and grasping in the field of mind games, was simply a too adroit rival for the four above mentioned guys. Though a veteran in this regard and old and wise enough not to be caught by surprise, Franco had a touch of fear of the young Calypso! Uncanny and fully camouflaged among her shyness and her other facile attributes and manners, Calypso could be a competent rival to any opponent. In the depth of her black and overly enchanting eyes, he had spotted the covert signs of lustfulness, treachery and rancour.

"Calypso, he nose got in put to everything, this guy Italian asshole!" said Mehmet, the nerves in his face entangling, causing a visible tremor.

"I can't understand what you mean," said Calypso, smiling angelically.

"He means Franco puts his nose into other people's business," interfered Sophie, offering Mehmet a most intimate smile.

"Good job! Translating English into English!" said Calypso, offering Mehmet a smile, a smile that initially untangled the nerves in his face but, just as quickly, it caused a crazed spasm appearing all over it.

"I think you should draw the line for him," said Sophie, offering Mehmet a fresher smile with a different taste, "Franco should only be an assistant to Mehmet and obey him."

"Can you specify what he does that you don't like, Mehmet?" asked Calypso, in a tone that turned Mehmet's face into a large round baked beetroot, oozing a juicy excitement and implying triumph!

"He talks much very too much most," said Mehmet, now the cognitive part of his brain rocking to a halt, "He knows says better more much me than! But believe I not do so."

"Okay," said Calypso affirmatively, "I got it. He thinks he is a better chef than you are but you don't believe so. Of course, he is not. I will draw the line for him."

Mehmet threw a fleeting look at Sophie, offering her a craftily hidden smile in his eyes, a lustful smile of appreciation.

It was drawn, the line, the line that would guide Mehmet towards securing a few more points in his competition with his very cunning rivals, Draco, Christopher and Garry.

"What were you telling Calypso and Sophie?" asked Draco, as Mehmet entered the kitchen in a gait so very akin to that of a victorious Ottoman Sultan—perhaps Sultan Mehmed II!

"I telling was Calypso *sister* Franco nose him about in putting business others," replied Mehmet, craftily denying Draco's demand for eye contact.

"I think you are being, more or less, irrational towards Franco," said Draco, biting his lower lip sagaciously.

77

"No brother," said Mehmet, turning his face towards Draco, "Muslim me am I. Allah know does. Me fair. Right always do I me. Me I not others like. Allah like no fair doesn't man. *Sister* Calypso better know me I am. Calypso I is sister me to brother like. Now is understand Calypso me I English."

"Oh, okay, fair enough. More or less. It is good that Calypso now can understand your English!" said Draco, now looking at Mehmet's face through his narrowed eyes, his forehead now resembling a hastily written chapter in a crime novel: ploughed, burrowed, grooved, ridged, wrinkled, each form cancelling or contradicting the other, each shape overlapping itself and distorting the others. His hair, now as spiky as his dad's, he huffed inwardly, put his thumbs on his temples and pressed them hard. Letting out the now imploded huff within him noisily, he recalled how Sophie not only had understood Mehmet's English, she had also praised it highly! And now, just minutes ago, his sister, the shy 'angelic' Calypso, had also acquired an honorary degree in understanding Mehmet's English! While trying to follow the faulty sequitur in his mind and thrash something out of his spelt-like thoughts, he recalled something else, something that turned the entire span of his mind into a field of spelt: he had overheard, while under the influence of cannabis, Anita confabulating with Mehmet over the divine taste of vanilla and the importance of knowing how to use it! And just seconds later, he shuddered at the realisation that he himself also had been understanding Mehmet's English!

Definitely, it was not a degree (honorary or real) in which he would take pride!

Mehmet, who would only surface his God and his faith whenever his libido got out of his control (which would happen four times in twenty four hours), was a very 'devout' Muslim who believed in brotherhood as the staple of human interconnection and mutuality. Though overridden and distorted, this mantra had yet enough merit in it to elicit the sense of goodness and decency even in a mind like Draco's in which the actualisation of beliefs had long been pushed in to a latent state. It did touch him initially, but due to the high number of unresponsive cords, nerves and synapses in his one-way operating mind, he concluded nothing but a multi-layered sense of pessimism and disbelief enhanced by a touch of a pathologically lustful pleasure.

78

"I thought only girls like Sophie could understand your English!" said Draco, now his face almost unreadable.

"Calypso me sister is why that she understand can English my," said Mehmet, his spacious face now resembling the longest Surah in the holy Quran—Baqara.

"Fair enough!" said Draco, his hair now turning into some metallic-looking bristles, "Is Sophie also your sister?"

"Brother, me all are girls sisters my," replied Mehmet, now the signs of a lingering stutter appearing on his face, "Mum your sister my is does too."

"Oh yeah," said Draco, slightly unhinged, "But as far as I know, other waitresses can't understand your English, which means they can't be your sister!"

"Brother, am I is Muuuuuslim, Muuuuuslim. Unddddddddeerestand? Muuuslim," stuttered Mehmet, "And am good I very man married Muslim. Understand, brother? I me am not like others."

"Fair enough, more or less, I can understand where you are coming from!" said Draco, now thoughtfully stroking his sparse thorny beard.

The only difference was the method. Both coming from the same zone, Draco was able to read Mehmet's game rules, but what he was ignorant to was the nature of Mehmet's approach regarding his claim to the essentiality of brotherhood within his philosophy. In this, what had always kept misleading Draco was the inexplicable amount of 'authenticity' in Mehmet's braggings about morality and righteousness where women were involved. Although a very unorthodox Greek Orthodox by blood and birth, due to a chronic suffering from a severe form of ignorance, he had always failed to parse the religious side of Mehmet's mind.

You just can't doubt what he says! he had said to his mum when she had praised Mehmet as a 'great' chef and a 'nice' man!

Draco was right, Mehmet's words were immune to being decoded by the mediocre minds or felt by the half-dead hearts.

'*Halal are for Muslims infidels*'. This was the backbone of Mehmet's worldview, the very catalyst that had infused an inauthentic form of authenticity in to his words! If the infidels (specially the females) are halal for Muslims, then the Muslim man would have a divine right (given to him by a divine mandate) to own and use them! And in doing so, resorting to any underhand and hypocritical strategies would completely be considered as *moral* and *legitimate!* And the infidels being all the non-Muslim creatures, would simply shed more light on Mehmet's *divine* worldview.

***

"Franco, Calypso is unhappy with you," said Anita, smiling.

"I only told her that she wasn't my cup of tea," said Franco, smiling.

"It is a harsh thing to say to a young girl. Don't you think so?" said Anita.

"I am Italian," said Franco, now picturing the lingering smile on Anita's face, "Being nice and considerate where there is no room for it, isn't my cup of tea. She asked me to stay away from Sophie. None of her business!"

"Is Sophie your cup of tea?" asked Anita, a touch of sensuality enhancing her tone of voice.

"No, she isn't," said Franco, watching the solemn, joyful, rueful smile sitting in Anita's large eyes, "But I would like to have a chat with her every now and then. She makes me think, if you get my meaning."

"In what way?"

"A large red ripe apple, a pig and a horse!" said Franco, touching his moustache.

"What is it!" asked Anita, half her face exhibiting aversion and the other half a sense of approval and merit.

"Would you rather be eaten by a pig or by a horse if you were such an apple?" asked Franco, laughing.

"I would definitely love to be eaten by a horse!" replied Anita, bursting into a loud yet gentle laugh, "But—Franco, you have a point. A very thoughtful one."

"Yes, I do have a point," said Franco, noticing a collage of sorrow, regret and apprehension appearing on Anita's face, "An apple that loves to be eaten by pigs, well, lacks the essence of applehood! Which simply means it is no longer an apple! Being Italian and naturally prone to seeing the entire life as a large red ripe apple, I believe when apples are eaten by pigs they will be turned into bad soil and regrow as crap apples. And this cycle will eventually leave the apples bereft of essence."

"Franco, you make me think!" said Anita, the core of applehood

80

appearing in the lines of her face and disappearing as quickly.

"In what way?" asked Franco, noticing what was taking place on Anita's face.

"Apples are responsible for being apples," said Anita.

"Exactly, as the pigs are," replied Franco.

Within Franco's analogy of life being a large red ripe apple and in his thick Italian accent, this accent of stretching, accentuating, squeezing and imprinting, Anita could feel and even taste the concept of *applehood.* The diluted Greek blood in which some of the red cells would always carry the sinful little immoralities to the oracle of *justification,* and the inherently bare and unstrained Italian sensuality converged in Anita's mind and streamed down to a gentle-flowing current in her heart. She thought of Sophie and all the red apples, the nectar, the ambrosia, the mortality and immortality of apples, horses and pigs. Anita did not need a deep philosophical understanding to grasp the core meaning in Franco's analogy, as it was a matter of heart, and hearts would only follow an irregular pattern within which *right* and *wrong* could well be interchangeable.

"So, you believe Sophie is an apple that loves to be eaten by pigs!" said Anita, laughing.

"No, I believe she is an apple that loves to eat pigs!" said Franco, forming a most unserious look on his face and offering it in a most serious manner.

Chapter 12

Sophie noticed that she had been staring at a host of sponges on her laptop well over an hour. Just a few months into her study of Biology, and based on her love for marine creatures, she had decided to take up a deep-sea diving course as well. She had immediately fallen in love with the sponges during her first dive to the seabed. Falling in love and making bonds with other elements in one's field of study or interest would definitely add another dimension to the process of learning, but Sophie's love for sponges—and only sponges—was, somehow, in a way excessive and in another deeply thoughtful. Falling in love with a mouth-less, heartless, brainless, muscle-less… creature was a matter that would add more twists to Sophie's worldview.

I love them because they succeed in growing and surviving while mostly insufficient.

What Sophie was unable to see was definitely invisible to the eye, and that was the ultimate *sufficiency* in sponges! The heart, the main element in growth, sponges had it. Was it Sophie's fault or that of science, they both had failed to feel it, the heartless science and Sophie's neglected heart.

"Sophie, what are you staring at?" asked Maria, turning towards her, "It must be something really interesting."

"Sponges," said Sophie, turning her face towards Maria, "I have been staring at these amazing creatures since I first bumped into them. They never cease to amaze me."

"Can they stare back at you?" asked Maria, offering Sophie one of her exquisite smiles.

"You also never cease to amaze me!" said Sophie, "I wish they could. They have no eyes because they have no heads."

"Perhaps they see with their hearts," said Maria, laughing.

"Maria, sponges don't have hearts either," replied Sophie.

"It is impossible. Everything has got a heart," said Maria.

"Maria, I can't understand what you mean."

"Why, because you are a scientist?"

"Science says sponges don't have hearts."

"Though I am not a very knowledgeable lady," said Maria, now sitting beside Sophie and looking at the sponges, "But I think all the existing things have got hearts."

"I have always hated literature and philosophy," said Sophie, "They enable people to play with words and estrange themselves from the truth and reality."

"What is the truth, Sophie?"

"Science, and only Science," replied Sophie robotically.

"And perhaps only sponges!" said Maria, laughing.

Suicide, this neighbour of truth, has always been patiently waiting for man to get himself rid of illusions, delusions, dreams and melancholia, these layers of protection against the ambiguity of the *truth*—if it exists at all. Eons, epochs and centuries have passed, bones and fleshes have formed only to rot and have rotten only to reform, but no *real* sign of the *truth* and *reality* have been felt or found in no atom and no cell.

Sophie, this continuation of forming, rotting and reforming, was unaware of her historical existence, of an existence formed in a bubble filled with some hallucinating fume. She was on the verge of slipping out of this bubble and falling into endlessness. She was on the verge of becoming *real!* She was on the threshold of falling into the mindlessness of the mind.

She lowered her head and zoomed on a purple and rather conical sponge.

It is moving! It is moving! Is it a sponge? Yes, it is. But why is it moving? Sponges don't move! They grow statically and die statically! No, it can't be real! It can't be a sponge. Sponges don't move. It doesn't make sense. No, science says sponges do not move. It can't be real!

***

"If you don't listen to me, you will lose a lot, Sophie," said Garry, leaning back on his chair while a very Al Pacino-like air appeared on his dark face.

"I have always been listening to you, Garry," said Sophie, now half her face a playground for innocence and the other half a squalid tavern for lust, guilt, remorse, humiliation and betrayal.

83

"Don't lie to me, Sophie!" said Garry, the fake air of charisma and resolution in his small eyes lasting long enough to induce a touch of apprehension in Sophie's heart, 'Christopher was here last night. Wasn't he?"

"I don't like Christopher at all!" said Sophie, the playground of innocence on her face now shrouded in a thick layer of dark swirling smog.

"Mate, I don't give a shit if you like or dislike Christopher!" said Garry, now a more Robert De Niro-like air appearing on his straight face, "Christopher was here last night. Wasn't he! Two years you have been living in this flat—my flat, for free! Just answer my question! Was Christopher here last night?"

"No, he wasn't here, Garry!" replied Sophie, her face now an illegible transcript of a bungled moral inquisition.

"You would have to pay the rent! Two years of rent! There is a contract for this!" said Garry, biting his nail-less fingers hysterically.

Sophie stared at Garry's face, long and deep, reading, unreading and assessing each written and unwritten line, delving into the depth of his eyes, she was pulled in, into the depth of those dark chasms. The pause dragged on, the stagnated moments gained weight, the pair of dark glassy eyes remained unmoved, the pair of green eyes—the would-be mirrors of rubies and gems—manifested nothing but miscellanea of horror, disgust, pathological lust, and amazingly, a touch of innocence!

"Christopher did come here last night. He did stay here until morning," said Sophie, her lips shivering, her face being ploughed by the fierce unrelenting clash of contentious forces, the pulling and the pushing between animality and humanity, elevation and degradation. It was another moment of realisation, the poignant stinging simultaneous surfacing of the slimy dirt and spotless purity, the undeniable existence of a source of discernment and its gentle but imposing presence. She was there, confined and compelled to stand a short trial.

"The dirtier the better!" said Garry, clasping Sophie's wrist and pressing it hard, "The dirtier the better! You little dirty beast! You little meretricious omnivorous swine!"

The words 'meretricious' and 'omnivorous' and the phrase 'little dirty beast' caused a fleeting havoc in Sophie's foggy mind. She remembered that Draco had also called her 'meretricious' just a few days ago. She also remembered that she had not felt the need for looking this word up in a dictionary. She remembered, an already vaporising remembrance, that she had never been interested in words and their hidden implications; that she had always hated the abrasive and scouring form of language, and loved the shallow and mechanical form of it, dictated to her by her surroundings.

Garry and Draco, these two tiny walking dictionaries of carnal and lecherous words, would lend each other their newly acquired words! And in doing so, it was Garry who was more attentive and seeking.

"You meretricious omnivorous swine! The dirtier the better!" said Garry, spluttering the words out from between his clenched teeth, "She deserves something very exciting, I thought. Your omnivorous nature needs food. I will show it to you, the food. It is here, just there, in the next room. I brought it in two hours ago, when you were arranging a holy meeting with Mehmet! Good, very good, the dirtier the better. Now, get up and come with me! You deserve it, girl."

Staring at the coffin-like black wooden box before her, she put her hands on her heaving chest and inhaled a good deal of air, and with it, a rather familiar reek—a mixture of toilet and death.

"Come here, girl!" demanded Garry, pushing back the sliding cover of the box, "You deserve it. You truly deserve it. Come here and have a look."

"No!" uttered Sophie, raising her hands and covering her mouth.

She did not wince. She did not cringe. She gazed, a gaze framed in a shapeless structure. Four fat rats, covered in a thick old layer of grime, gazed back at her, their dejected shifting eyes manifesting the entire history of foulness and disgust. She took two steps forward, perhaps the longest distance she had ever travelled, she felt, long, torturous and timeless, each pointing to an eternity. She kneeled by the blackened black box and stared at the overgrown teeth.

"I want you to take care of them," said Garry, saliva welling up in his mouth, "Anita, this tasteless mongol woman, doesn't like them. She believes they bring bad omen and fatal diseases. What an apathetic creature, this mongol woman! She forced me to bring them here! Draco and Calypso tried to convince her that rats would bring nothing with them but a sense of *reality*, but what does a mongol of a woman know about *reality*! Nothing, nothing whatsoever. I am so glad you know, the *reality*, you appreciate it, and so does Christopher, this Greek philosopher of *reality*! Look after these precious creatures, Sophie. And forget; yes forget, about the rent. You won't be paying a penny. You know the *reality*."

"Garry, the teeth of *reality* have overgrown, and they can kill it!" said Sophie, pointing to the dagger-like rats' teeth.

Garry shoved his hands into the pockets of his trousers and summoning whatever of lust and carnal lechery he had inside, he gazed at Sophie for some long lingering seconds. Now standing behind her, he lowered his head and kissed her neck. The wet kiss and the reek of Garry's breath mixed with the reek of death and toilet and turned into the *scent* of *reality!* Among the screeching chirping sound made by the rats, Sophie heard a weak and almost dying voice, a poignant lamentation, a desperate flagellation of her own innocence.

"Rats like it!" said Garry, the remains of human hue on his face fading away, "Rats like it, these creatures of appreciation. They know what is about to take place in here, and right before their eyes. Look at them, Sophie, just look at them and see how they are ogling at you, these creatures of appreciation! These epitomes of the sense of *reality*. Look at their eyes, right into them, and you will see how passionate these creatures are! But Anita, this mongol of a woman, is unable to exhibit even a very bland form of passion! You know and you are very apt at exhibiting the core of passion, you truly are. More or less, Mehmet, this little round fat brat, is also very capable of letting out a flood of passion. I like him. He is good. And you know this very well, Sophie. Don't you? He knows how lust must be cooked: let it simmer in its own juice, reabsorb the juice, turn it into slime and simmer in it again. This little round fat accomplished brute, knows his way around dirty meretricious omnivorous swine like you!"

A streak of light, heatless and languid, trickled in through the half-done dirty green curtains and flowed over the bed, spotlighting Garry's hand with bleeding fingers on the ivory of Sophie's bare back, reaching further and indolently landing on the four rats leaning against the opposite wall.

Disturbed by the light, the rats milled around until they placed themselves out of its reach. A gentle breeze swayed the curtain and a bigger column of light flooded in, revealing a stream of dark blood flowing down the chiselled ditch of Sophie's back.

"Garry spent the night with you. Didn't he?" asked Calypso.

"Oh, your dad? No, yes, he did stay with me?" replied Sophie, her tired face and her red eyes unable to convey her inner feelings.

"And you made him overly excited. Didn't you? His fingers—"

"No, it wasn't me!" Sophie cut in hastily, two wrinkles appearing on her forehead and twisting around each other like two newly hatched white snakes.

"So who was it then?"

"The rats! Those rats; they made him chew his fingers so hard! They were watching it. Yes, they were watching it all the way!" replied Sophie, raising her hand and covering her mouth, an immediate and fully unconscious reaction to her own stark assertiveness, to her own mental numbness and indifference. She stared at Calypso's jet-black eyes and the unreadable smile sitting in them and laughed, a laugh obviously fashioned in a subliminal mental workshop, where no tool was being used in accordance with the purpose it had been designed for. The wrongly burdened and unburdened nerves, the alcohol, the overwork (now fourteen days a week!) and the laborious task of *memorising* the hefty scientific lessons had left no physical respite for her, let alone the very vital mental form of it.

Watching the reflection of her own face in Calypso's eyes, she felt the criss-crossing convergence of a few nerves in her face, entangling, untangling, coiling, uncoiling and creating some pulses, the pulses that would be relayed only to remain undelivered, due to the detachment of some of the main receptive nerves in her perception system. She shed a few large tears, large and warm, larger and warmer than usual. They rolled down and dropped on her hands. The last of them, the largest of them, paused and seconds later, broke up and spread under her eyes, highlighting the small number of freckles under her eyes. Symmetric in all aspects and hued by a gentle green light, those freckles, in an unknown spot of her mind, created in her mouth a mixed taste of honey and opium.

"Stay away from Mehmet, Sophie!" demanded Calypso as Sophie turned around to go to the kitchen, "I think you have more than enough on your plate."

"Oh, me, no," said Sophie, the intention of disobedience appearing on her face and disappearing as quickly, "Oh, okay. I actually don't like him at all. Not my favourite. No, not at all, and you should have noticed this by now, Calypso."

"I know, and you know that I know," said Calypso, now staring into Sophie's eyes.

Calypso's eyes grew darker, darker than jet black. The whitish jade in Sophie's eyes kept fading until no sign of jade left to be seen. She blinked;

a roughshod of pain wriggled in her eyes and moved down to her face, irregulating the symmetric freckles. She tried to summon a touch of courage and confront Calypso, but to no avail, as there was no relevant piece of courage left within her heart.

"In an hour or so, go to Draco's flat and clean it properly," ordered Calypso, placing her handbag on the counter, "He wasn't happy with how you cleaned it last week. Don't forget to scrub the bathroom and the toilet bowl."

"Oh, me? Yeah, okay. I will go," replied Sophie, taking a short sigh of relief with a sense of being *useful* washing over her face.

"Oh, Mehmet!" uttered Sophie in a most affectionate most flirtatious tone, and now hurling herself into his arms; she added, "I have badly missed you!"

"I badly too you miss very much so," said Mehmet, a mixed hue of confidence and *justified* lust washing over his spacious face.

"Calypso," whispered Sophie, now kissing Mehmet's neck, "She just asked me to stay away from you. None of her business. Is it?"

"No worries," said Mehmet, holding her arms, "Calypso my sister is. I sure make is she will."

"Oh, you will make sure she is your sister!" said Sophie, half her face exhibiting daftness and the other a tinge of wittiness, "You mean you haven't made sure yet!"

"Enough not. Good very not," replied Mehmet, a god and a prophet appearing in his right eye and the entire of Sharia Law in the left one.

Gazing at Mehmet's face, Sophie was engulfed by a heavy multi-layered silence. The pungent smell of vaporising vinegar and fried green chilli hit her sense of smell only to remind her that it had long been brought to a halt. She moaned inside, she shed a few more tears, adding another moan to the unregistered and forgotten ones, and a few more tears to the unexamined and wasted ones. She spotted a moment of void in her mind, she watched it, it was lone, a lone and visible moment of void. She reeled back and held her head; it was a lone moment sitting among the myriads of bleached and almost invisible moments of void. There was an invisible hand moving behind Sophie and wiping up her memory with a sponge tipped in bleach.

"I Calypso sister out sort," said Mehmet, throwing at Sophie a very Ataturk-like glance over his shoulder, "Understand you said what I did?"

Sophie nodded, but not sure what she understood. The only thing she noticed, and she was sure about it, was a consistent change in Mehmet's English: now more Latinate in terms of grammar and sophistication—the verbs always landing at the end.

"Out not tonight don't we not go," said Mehmet in an alpha male tone!

"Why? Because I hassled you the other night?" said Sophie, noticing the signs of perfection in her art of understanding and translating exquisite English into simple English!

"No worries Calypso about. Shis decent good you are is," said Mehmet, his face now manifesting an exaggerated sense of virility and potency.

"Oh, she is as decent as I am! What do you mean?" asked Sophie, half her face showing a tiny touch of resentment and the other half a tinier touch of jealousy.

"You is does decent very much. I does me loves you only," said Mehmet, "Jack and Jack does believes me am I best the man for you."

"Awh, do they?" uttered Sophie, her eyes shining, "They are very nice guys. Aren't they?"

"They not nose in business people put does," said Mehmet, his spacious face now a transcript of ethics and decorums, "They bit a little like me are. They decent does are."

Decency, this stillborn child or otherwise subjected to infanticide, in Mehmet's mind had no actual place, be it a small grave or a tiny charpoy in a dark niche. Decency, this non-existent existence in Mehmet's existence was a cover under which he would nourish his own version of *decency.* *Sister* Calypso being deemed as *decent* meant he had already got access to her pants!

Apparently, Sophie was about to become the first and the most qualified *decent* apostle to this philosophical prophet of transcendence and viability!

Chapter 13

"Boy, you made me proud by this! Good catch, a triumph," said Garry, his small dark eyes brightening up, "More or less, yes, more or less, I am proud of you. For this, you will get five hundred pounds to go to Amsterdam and have some quality time. You do deserve it, boy."

"Don't mention it, man," said Draco, ruffling his spiky hair, "Sophie and Christopher helped me with it. It was actually Sophie who caught it at the last moment!

"She is bright, Sophie. She knows how to deal with rats. Doesn't she?" said Garry, ruffling his spiky hair, "And rats, those equally bright animals, also know how to deal with her. They understand each other very well. They love each other very well. Rats are great animals. Remember this, Draco."

"I will remember this," said Draco, pushing the cardboard box before him towards Garry, "I will take Sophie with me to Amsterdam."

"No, you won't," said Garry emphatically, and now pointing to the cardboard box before him, he added, "Now we have *five* rats, five fat healthy rats. This new one needs to be tamed as soon as possible. Only Sophie can do this for us."

"Fair enough," said Draco, "But I think Christopher and Mehmet also could do this for you. More or less, they also know the language of rats."

"No, boy," said Garry, now lifting the box, "Only Sophie. A rat would only become a rat if tamed by Sophie."

"You might be right, more or less," said Draco, narrowing his small eyes, "But I don't think she is very much interested in rats. She actually hates them."

"Boy, you will remain naïve for the rest of your life," said Garry, now pressing the box against his chest with a hysteric pleasure sitting in his eyes, "I bet no one has ever loved the bloody rats more than Sophie loves them. She just doesn't fully reveal it. She knows, Sophie knows how rats can guide one to the core of pleasure."

"Fair enough, more or less." said Draco, now staring at Garry with a most blank face.

They, these two little philosophers of *pleasure,* had recently noticed a change in each other, each thinking it had taken place only in the other: in their cognitive system the relevance has lost its *relevance.* Large and bold full stops had become the only familiar punctuation signs in their minds. They would take and see each sentence independently, with no link or relevance to the one before or after it. And in Draco's case, he was on the verge of taking each *word in*dependently, simply getting himself rid of the necessity of dealing with a full sentence and its implications and, of course, dodging the obligation of sequencing a number of sentences and responding to them accordingly. By having a quick peek into their most favourite sets of vocabulary, one could see the contour of a structure within which the wooden and lifeless words were being cut and carved using the tools of sophistry and distortion.

The next day, Draco travelled to Amsterdam—this Mecca of legal drugs and the gate to a sort of Nirvana!—for the forty-second time since he had found himself sensible enough to tell his right hand from his left. As devout as a Muslim, this pilgrim of psychedelia and derangement had already broken the records held by the most zealous of Muslims—both in terms of devotion and the number of visits. For his age it was already an unmatched achievement! Although intrinsically unicellular and unilateral, his trips to Amsterdam had also played an undeniable role in his fall into an irreversible singularity.

***

"Tia Maria, happy birthday to you!" said Christopher, in a tone horsier than ever.

"Happy birthday to you, Maria!" said Sophie, touching her hand.

"I thank you both for being with me today," said Maria, pressing Sophie's hand.

"We love you, Maria," said Christopher, letting out an inbred laugh, conspicuously mulish, and mawkish than ever, "But I think you haven't been able to appreciate this."

Maria smiled a smile, comprehensive and telling, wise, brave and decisive, decisive enough to evoke a tiny rusty speck of shame in Christopher.

Sophie threw a look at Christopher's face and then a more lasting one at Maria's. Was it the effect of alcohol or another fleeting moment of realisation, she felt a current of euphoria mixed with a stream of ruefulness bulging within her, an undertow not forceful enough to surge and impact.

"You are very old-fashioned," said Christopher, craftily hiding the hue of shame on his face within a sagacious air sitting in his eyes, "It is your prerogative. It is people's prerogative to be whatever they wish to be. You are old-fashioned. You know, it is hard, appreciation. Bloody hell!"

"I can't understand what you mean, Christopher," said Sophie, her face revealing a dual sense of disbelief, "The old-fashioned are called so just because of the strong sense of recognition and appreciation within them."

"Oh, I didn't know you were able to understand these kinds of things!" said Christopher, unleashing a wayward multi-layered laugh, "The world has changed, girl. You couldn't pay for a cup of coffee using a sixteenth-century coin. Could you?"

"The world has changed, but what deserves recognition and appreciation will always remain the same. This is what I believe," said Maria, the telling smile on her face now fixed in a frame of unwavering belief.

"I can't understand you young girls," said Christopher, craftily denoting pity and ridicule by the calculated shaking of his head, "I am not interested in this. Let's eat and drink. It is Maria's birthday. Celebrate, just drink and celebrate, as it is the only thing you are good at."

"This isn't a Greek restaurant. Is this?" asked Sophie, opening the menu.

"No, this is Iranian," replied Maria, pushing her puffy hair back and throwing a questioning look at Sophie.

"Iran is an African country. Isn't it?" asked Sophie, almost sure about her suggestion.

"What!" exclaimed Maria, "You don't know where Iran is located!"

"What did I say just seconds ago?" said Christopher, his face proving its capacity of containing the entire history of derision and degradation at once, "Didn't I say you young girls are only... You are only good for *one thing*... A university student doesn't know where Iran is located on the world map! And she is an English girl, the descendent of those who ransacked the world and fucked up its map!"

"Does it really matter?" asked Sophie, half her face abashed the other half indifferent.

Nothing matters if you have diminished yourself to be deemed as 'good only for *one thing*' and taught to lead a map-less existence. Location would become a matter of no importance at all, and as a consequence, time, this inherently hard-to-understand concept, would also remain untouched.

"Very good birthday! I like it!" said Christopher, his face now bearing an eerie horse-like look, "Maria is a very generous girl, I believe. But I can't understand why she is unable to appreciate some certain things; I mean the things which matter most. Look at Sophie, this fine young lady; she is so quick and appreciative when it comes to treasuring love and decency. I love her. I love Sophie. I think you should learn from her."

Maria stared at Christopher's face. Sophie watched the gently wriggling lines in his face, each carrying a stream of greed, lust and categorical entitlement.

"What! Why are you looking at me like that?" asked Christopher, the stream of sublime greed and lust now being polluted by a streak of *decency* and *chivalry,* "You ungrateful girl! I have been protecting you! Remember that black guy, that pervert of perverts, who was going to abuse you. You little naïve thing! You didn't know he was a classic pervert. Did you? No. What about that Romanian guy, that gypsy of gypsies! If it wasn't because of me now you would have been looking after a couple of chickens and a sick pig in a remote village in Romania! He wanted to take her to Romania! Would you believe it, Sophie! Draco and Mervyn aren't happy with you either. They believe you are an indecent girl."

"Maria, what have you done to Christopher? Why is he so livid?" asked Sophie, touching Christopher's hand most empathically.

"My decency is not in my underpants! You keep looking after him. You keep appreciating him," said Maria, grabbing her handbag, "He is a truly *decent* man! Treasure him, Sophie!"

"Leave her alone! Let her go!" demanded Christopher, as Sophie got to her feet to go after Maria, "Did you know what she said to me last night! This ugly girl! 'You are old enough to be my dad' she said to me! Am I old enough to be her dad?"

Sophie held the chair handles and stared at Christopher, a stare that quickly was inverted and shed a dim light on her own mind. Was Christopher old enough to be Maria's dad? Was Maria old enough to be Christopher's mother? Was fifty-five a bigger number than twenty-three?

I believe only in science and scientific methods.

"Am I old enough to be her dad?" Christopher asked again, his horsey face now as wooden as that of Troy's.

"No, not old enough to be Maria's dad. Definitely not," replied Sophie, the entire history of heart, soul, intuition, mind, science and mathematics turning into a doodle of mockery and appearing on her beautiful face. The beauty distorted, the mind—the crucible of *scientific methods*—turned into a disused wood-burner in a derelict medieval church, spewing dense dark cold smoke.

No, fifty-five was not, and had never been a bigger number than twenty-three! Or if it was, the difference was not worth mentioning!

Christopher's face underwent a difficult and spasmodic interchange, now horsey then human, a couple of lines breaking, some others stretching and perverting, now horsier then more human, now a face then a wooden span of incredulity, anguish and indifference. The look on his face changed, a touch of venomous hatred appeared in his eyes. He darted a look into Sophie's eyes. Sophie remained unmoved. The hatred was weak, a damp squib, and a projection from the void, from the depth of futility. Christopher looked like a horse. He was a horse. Christopher looked like a human. He was a human.

"Bloody hell!" exclaimed Christopher, "I just can't understand why some people behave like that! They just disappoint. They let themselves down. I am happy you know. You know, Sophie. You know very well. You are decent. I will protect you."

***

"Garry also believes that Maria isn't grateful, not enough," said Calypso, her eyeballs rolling like those of a large chameleon, "And that she interferes with other people's gratefulness!"

"None of my business, but I think you should sack her right now!" said Christopher.

"I don't want to interfere with this either, honestly," said Draco, throwing a look at Sophie's tired face, "However, I think it is our prerogative to sack her if we wish. If Christopher and Garry believe so, then, well, more or less, I should hold the same belief."

"Not shis good grateful more and not good decent," said Mehmet, glancing at Sophie over his shoulder, "Shis good out now better. Shis nose in business all bad."

"What do *you* think, Sophie?" asked Christopher, letting out a mulish broken laugh.

Sophie heard nothing, she said nothing. She noticed only one thing: a new change in Mehmet's Latinate English: he had stopped using verbs all together! Perhaps due to his confusion over their designated place!

Minutes later, Maria appeared. Consuming love and consumed by it, she quickly felt the sense of rejection towards herself, and spotted it on those faces, those mirrors of *justified* injustice and permitted nonsensicality. Nonetheless, she offered them a smile, a melting shaming reminding one. She looked round at them and landed the last note of her meaningful smile on Sophie's exhausted face. A sudden moan formed within Sophie, and before she could get hold of it, it rushed out and as quickly it fell back upon the heap of aborted and unexamined emotions in a remote part of her heart.

"Maria," moaned Sophie, as Maria was marching towards the door, "Wait! I want a word with you."

"Go! Go away, Maria!" ordered Calypso, her tone as stinging as that of her dad's.

Sophie got to her feet and ran towards the door. Out on to the fresh air, she inhaled a good deal of the cold damp early autumn air and ran after Maria.

"Please!" shouted Sophie, panting heavily, "Maria, please stop."

Maria stopped, took off her woollen hat and ruffling her thick puffy hair, she turned around and as Sophie approached her, she embraced and pressed her against her chest with all her might. The well of tears within Sophie sluiced out, ran down her wan face and through Maria's hair. She cried, blubbered, lamented and heard an inner flagellation. She took a step back and wiped her tears with the heels of her hands. She held her wet hands up and looked at them, and now looking at Maria's face through her tearful eyes, she uttered something, something coming from the depth of her unconscious mind, "My tears are old, Maria. Look! They are too old!"

Maria held Sophie's face in her hands and gazed into her eyes for some long moments. Two large warm tears gently squeezed out of her eyes and remained on her cheeks, rolled, hesitated, rolled and fell... they landed in Sophie's heart and caught fire, two clear gently burning flames.

"Go, Maria, go away," whined Sophie, evidently trying to curb the pain within her heart. Once again, she felt the loss but failed to register the true pain and meaning of it.

Minutes later, she hurried back in, escaping the piercingly cold autumn wind. It was warm inside.

Someone had made her a mug of coffee and someone else a breakfast.

There were smiles, overly zealous pampering words, tilted heads and bulged hearts, admiration, confirmation, they all generously cascading over her.

"I am glad she left," said Calypso, offering Sophie a motherly smile while a nun-like hue washed over her dark face, "She was bad company for you. Plague, Garry believes a bad company is like a contaminating source of plague. Garry is right. His life was plagued in the past. I would advise you to ignore her in case she contacts you. Yeah, this ugly girl is a harmful creature."

"Maria isn't an ugly harmful girl!" said Sophie, slightly amazed at her own quick assertion and the urge to defend beauty, Maria's beauty.

"I mean she isn't a good-natured girl. Yeah, it is what I mean," said Calypso, sounding most elderly and most sanctimonious.

"At all not she decent! Shis girl open very bad!" said Mehmet, putting two fried eggs before Sophie, "I knew first. Some girls never not decent. They mother never to nothing them good. Shis beetle very much too ugly. Shis nose Sophie business very bad."

"More or less, I think you did the right thing, Calypso," said Draco, sounding as righteous and sagacious as an undisputable master of morality, "She was really harmful to Sophie. It was your prerogative to sack her."

It was only Mehmet's ever-improving Latinate English that Sophie's mind could register. She noticed, with a flag of admiration rising in her mind, that he was now placing the adjectives at the end, after having managed to craftily get rid of the verbs all together!

"You can take the day off if you wish to, Sophie," said Draco, his face now very akin to an altar and the sound in his voice to that of Jesus Christ's, "More or less, I think you should. You know, stress and all these … I think it is your prerogative."

"Thank you, Draco," said Sophie, getting up to her feet and offering him a most appreciative smile.

Jack and Jack remained unmoved. They kept themselves busy with cleaning the two large electric fly killers over the bar area while quietly conversing over the importance of flies and the role they play in the improvement of the economy. Jack and Jack threw a fleeting disinterested look at Sophie as she was walking towards the door.

96

Chapter 14

As she entered the squalid flat, she felt a heavy weight on her heart, a weightless weight, the heaviest for a heart to endure. She walked in through the open door and stood before the rats.

Unusually quiet and resigned, the rats gazed at her, a gaze coordinated and apparently rehearsed beforehand. She tossed her handbag on the dirty couch and sat on the floor. The damp air, the smell of toilet and death, five pairs of hypnotising little eyes, the stinging cold and a lingering subdued and almost painless pain in her heart made her shudder.

'*A painless pain is most painful!*'. They were Gol's words, now ringing in her ears. This paradoxical man, this epitome of most vocal silence, had kindled a light within her, a light of a different nature—it would either turn into a flood or a smothered fire and eventually a heap of damp ash and darkness.

'*There is a level of innocence in all existing creatures, in the entire universe*'. Gol's words again, echoing, reverberating.

Even in the rats? she whispered to herself, an immediate mixed hue of silliness and wisdom washing over her blank face. *Rats are some creatures, and they are within the universe!* she mumbled, a dark laugh gaining momentum deep within her. *But they can't presage the future. Can they? No, future doesn't exist in their minds, neither does the past. No, they can't be foreboding something to me! They are just worn out. Garry adds Whisky to their food! It must be it. Alcohol has exhausted them. Yes, that look on their faces is the look of resignation and indifference caused by alcohol.*

She got up, and throwing a weary look at the rats, she turned around and plodded towards her room. She prostrated on the bed, shut her eyes and tried to arrange her thoughts and go through them. She tried and failed, tried again and failed… her brain had long become a defected magnetic field for the tampered and crazed atoms of irrationality and incongruity, where each particle had become an opposing factor to itself and to the ones around it. She tried to shut her brain down but to no avail.

Her brain, fed up with hard-to-process commands, began to phase out.

She was swept away by a fast sleep.

Is it a museum? It looks like… it is a museum and a library. Look at those marble busts! They must be the busts of some important people. Look at that statue dressed in a sky-blue shirt and a pair of black jeans! It has got a wristwatch on. I have never seen statues wearing wristwatches! No, it is not a statue. It is a man, deep in thought and staring at something. What is he staring at? Oh, I haven't come here to find out what a statue-like man is staring at! Why… ? Do I know what has directed me to this place? Apron, I am wearing an apron! I was on my way to work. Oh, you never know, this is human mind; it could sometimes take you to the places you never intended to go.

Come on! Come and hold me! I know it is you. Can't you see that I am about to collapse? Franco believes you are a lion. A strange type of lion, you are. If you don't chase, well, you can't be a lion. I will walk over to you and stand right before you… Don't push your hands into your pockets… Look, it is me. I have come here just to see you. You know that I am not interested in books and museums… What? Me in this funny apron? Oh, I see. A museum is not a kitchen! I will go and change… look, I am back in this fine long dress—white velvet with large red roses printed on it. Look at my dress, now the background is red and the large roses are white! Did you notice the change?

Pull your hands out of your pockets and hold me! Timidity is not a lion's attribute. You are timid. A lion with the heart of a fox! I put my face on your chest to find out. Yes, it beats, your heart, like that of a fox does! I will go away and never come back to you…

"Sophie, it was a dream. Wasn't it?" asked Garry, standing in the threshold, holding one of the rats in his hands, the one Sophie had caught.

"What have you done to these rats?" asked Garry, now looking at her, half his face distorted with jealousy and the other half with suspicion.

"It is not me, Garry. It is the alcohol," replied Sophie, rubbing her eyes.

"Oh, I see. You know better. You know science," said Garry, putting the rat on the bedside table, "What were you dreaming of?" asked Garry, sitting on the edge of the bed.

"Of some horny rabbits chasing each other in a green meadow," replied Sophie, now staring at the dejected rat.

"You are a salacious omnivorous swine," said Garry, caressing the back of the rat, "You were asking someone to hold you, perhaps one of those guys who hate rats. You are such a mendacious creature. There is no true pleasure in true creatures. For this, I love you *dearly*. You know your prerogatives. You know your portion and your way around the bloody pleasure—the bigger and the dirtier the better, your portion. Well, for once and only once, I want you to tell the truth; sure it won't hurt us. We won't repeat it. We hate it. Don't we? I have been told that Mehmet has promised you to get rid of his wife and marry you. Is it true, Sophie?"

"No, not at all! Whoever told you this, is a very mendacious person, and as malicious!" replied Sophie, half her face oozing innocence and the other half simply a full chapter of mendacity.

"I love it!" uttered Garry, lifting the rat and gently placing it on his lap, "I have been looking for such a bloody type of woman all through my life!"

"What type of woman?" asked Sophie, the innocence and the chapter of mendacity on her face now a scribbled demand for approval.

"Your type," replied Garry, now playing with the rat's tail, "The type that wouldn't be able to tell the truth even for once; that would faithfully remain honest to dishonesty! I have already found only two of them—the deans of their type, you and another one."

"Who is the other one?" asked Sophie, her face now resembling a gazelle being torn apart by a savage starving hyena.

"She is on her way to come here and meet you," replied Garry, saliva welling up in his mouth, "Get up! Pull yourself together. She might arrive at any moment. Behave yourself. Show her your mettle. She is a queen, a real queen of somewhere."

Minutes later, she, 'the real queen of somewhere', appeared, and was immediately introduced to Sophie as a Miss Julie Atkins. By name and manners, she seemed and sounded most English, especially with her way of speaking and pronouncing the words: allowing each word enough space and time to tumble out safely and gracefully—though somewhat smeared with a touch of pungent arrogance. She was, in this respect, very much Churchillian: plosive, glottal, plosive again, low pitch, high pitch, descending a note and ascending another meticulously, and in intervals indulging herself with a bit of syncopating. But there was a contrast, an obtrusive and off-putting contrast: Miss Julie Atkins, this dean of her type and the queen of somewhere, seemed most foreign and most masculine! Apparently, in her late fifties, she had obviously more balls than boobs! And this could be seen even by a blind pair of eyes. To cut a long story short, she was very much akin to a beaver, privileged with a wealth of jet-black moles scattered around her mouth and on her forehead. And a meagre amount of curly grey hair, a bit of height, and to be fair, a fairly feminine backside, were the other assets the apple of Garry's eye owned.

As the Persian saying goes, 'Your flaws and your good attributes will remain undisclosed until you open your mouth'. Miss Julie Atkins, (though she had already opened her mouth but not enough) opened her mouth only to reveal that she was a character to reckon with! Initially revealing that she was from academia and a smatterer around some other less important subjects, she went on to proudly announce her newly undertaken *academic* mission: a thoroughgoing research and study of the Victorian catacombs in London! And that it would be done, as she put it, along with a scouring study of Christianity and death plus a peep into witchcraft, and the effects of all of these on the zoology of man!

"What is a catacomb?" asked Sophie in a low tone.

"Oh, a catacomb," said Miss Julie Atkins, inhaling a good deal of air and going on, "It was an underground accommodation for the dead, my dear. The Romans, those delusional pioneers of the desire for immortality, would treat the dead bodies as if they would shortly reanimate and roam upon the earth again. Based on this belief, they designed a safe underground resting place for the dead, where each body would be placed in a recess and remained there, waiting for the second call to usher them back to life. Those self-lovers, the Romans, caused their own demise by going after the wrong quest, the futile quest of eternal existence, not knowing that the only eternal truth was death and rotting. Rotting to die and dying to rot, this is the only quest I have been able to grasp; that is why I am so zealously obsessed with the ethology of man!"

"I love you, Julie," said Garry, putting the rat on her lap, "I love Sophie as much. You both are of the right nature. Now tell me how have you seen Sophie so far?"

"She knows how to rot," said Miss Julie Atkins, the moles on her face wriggling, "She would rot most exquisitely. She is beautiful. The rotten beauty is the complete definition of rottenness. She is good. She is really good. Even this rat can confirm this."

Sophie stared at the rat. The rat stared back at her. Half her mind cried, the other half laughed. She tried to get to her feet. She failed. The words *rat, rot, zoology* and *man* ran after each other in her mind, crazed around and disappeared in a recess, leaving behind an eerie silence.

"Sophie, go to the restaurant and get us some food and drink," asked Garry.

"Oh, me, yeah, well, okay," said Sophie with a blank smile on her face, "I will ask Mehmet to make you some food. He knows your taste. Oh, by the way, Garry, did you know Jack and Jack believe Mehmet is the best man for me?"

"Do they?" asked Garry, musingly.

"Yeah, they do believe so!" said Sophie, her cheeks turning rosy.

"I am not sure, but they might be right," said Garry, his hand creeping between her legs.

An hour later, Sophie came back. Entering the room, she was intending to put the food and the drink on the small table that was in the left corner of the room, but she was faced with the five pairs of eyes looking at her forbiddingly. Placed on the table in the order of their title and size (Garry had recently dubbed them as bastard, pimp, courtesan, cuckold and scallywag!), the rats seemed to Sophie as only rats, relinquished the traits that had qualified them for the endowment of their lofty status! They wriggled for a short while, and now averting their eyes from Sophie's, they lapsed into their subdued mood and remained motionless.

Miss Julie Atkins moaned feebly. The blanket bulged, waved and receded. Garry hissed hysterically. The rats raised their heads, and with the already instilled unknown fear in their eyes enhancing, they looked at the bed, winced back, pressed themselves against the wall and shivered as if cornered by two old vipers.

Garry and Miss Julie Atkins hissed, twisted, rolled and moaned. Twisting, wriggling, wobbling, coiling, sinking in to the mattress, descending to culminate, culminating... they rolled off the bed... On the dirty carpet they rolled again, twisted and remained motionless, still hissing.

Sophie carried the food and the drink to the kitchen and placed them on the old dirty wooden table. She walked towards the window with the sheer intention of opening it and inhaling some fresh air but her hand froze midway towards the window. She stood there. A compelling urge formed in

101

her brain and trickled down to her heart and ran through her veins and vessels: she eagerly wanted, craved to see the world outside, as if she had never seen it before. She moved closer to the window only to notice that the windowpane was covered in an old thick layer of dust and grease. She turned around and looked at the wooden table.

A floundering mental state and the moments that were passing her by and carrying away the unnoticed and unregistered connotations and implications within them, had left a gnawing effect on her overall cognitive abilities. The dirty windowpanes and the dirtier wooden table, stained coffee cups, decaying cabinets, rusty hinges and creaking doors and… she had not noticed them. Blind and impervious, she had become.

"Sophie, where is the food?" shouted Garry.

"Here, in the kitchen. I have set the table," shouted back Sophie.

Naked, Garry and Miss Julie Atkins entered the kitchen, resembling two dead bodies who had just escaped from a mortuary with the help of a corrupt and brazen undertaker! Soulless, as the dead bodies are, they were free of obligations and considerations and therefore, modesty and shame were, to them, two completely irrelevant concepts. What was evident to Sophie was the undeniable fact that they were a complement to each other—a rotten potato cut in half. She looked at Garry with a blank face, and blinking several times, she directed her gaze towards Miss Julie Atkins and landed it on the withered remains of her breasts.

"Pour us some wine, girl!" ordered Garry, leering at her from the corner of his eyes.

"Oh, me, yes, okay," replied Sophie, her face turning red, her heart pounding.

"Fill my glass up," asked Miss Julie Atkins, stretching her long lean arm out and touching Sophie's face, "You love Garry very much. Don't you?"

"Oh, me, yes, I do love Garry. Very much. Yeah, very much," replied Sophie, lifting up the large flagon, "Mehmet also loves Garry. I do love Mehmet too."

"Oh! Who is this Mehmet?" asked Miss Julie Atkins, turning her face towards Garry and nodding thoughtfully, "He must be the best of his kind, the best ever."

"Oh, he is indeed the best of his kind," said Sophie, her face turning rosy, "He is to get rid of—no, he is just perfect."

"I love him too," said Garry, lifting up his glass of wine, "Though a bit awkward, but I genuinely believe he is simply perfect."

"I am now a bit jealous of you, Sophie," said Miss Julie Atkins, taking a swig of her glass of wine, "I wouldn't mind to be fully envious of you were not you Garry's friend. You know your essence; and I believe it is your true essence that has attracted you towards this marvellous gentleman and Mehmet. Only a few, only a small number of us, are fortunate enough to realize their true essence and be guided towards what they really deserve. We all deserve absolute freedom. You have already made it to the free zone of life, where there is nothing to restrain or warn you whenever you grab the chalice of whatever. Latitude, my dear Sophie, this is perhaps the only word which the mortal man should try to dissect and study thoroughly. Being from academia and as well as an ardent latitudinarian, I should congratulate you on your insightful takes on life at this very young age. You will definitely ascend to the summit of pleasure, this true height of human existence."

"She is omnivorous! And so fucking paraphilic!" said Garry, finger-brushing his spiky hair.

"The more the better," uttered Miss Julie Atkins, reaching for the flagon, "She knows her way around pleasure. She will soon become a great *latitudinarian* in the field of pleasure, breaking all the barriers and paddling in the pond of now and only now."

"Paddling in a pond!" exclaimed Garry, "She is a deep-sea diver. She is a scientist. She is a salacious lover of the depth!"

"Marvellous!" said Miss Julie Atkins, lifting her glass, "She would definitely become the trawler of the depth of pleasure. Moreover, there is another profoundly important point I should point out: beauty and science, if mixed, would rot thoroughly. She is privileged. She will rot thoroughly. She would set a precedent, a unique one, exhaustive and inclusive, pervasive and contagious. She is already a philosopher of pleasure, a very rancid and putrefied one."

"I am glad you are so impressed with Sophie," said Garry, touching Sophie's face with the back of his hand.

"I do take pride in getting to know such a fine young lady," said Miss Julie Atkins, touching the other side of Sophie's face with the back of her hand, "Quiet, she is quiet. The silence within her is an undisputable denotation of a free soul, free of *free will*. It would be easier for a scientist

103

to reject the existence of *free will* within an utterly conditional existence. Why do potatoes decompose? They would refuse to if they had *free will*. Is there any difference between a human being and a potato?

"No, they are of the same nature. Sameness is a bog, and what could one do other than decaying when in a bog? Decadence, if there is any form of fulfilment and satisfaction to be obtained by any existing creature; it must be sought within decadence and degeneration. It is there, instilled in her consciousness, the purport of decomposition and decadence, and for this no one would be able to divert her from the path to ultimate joy and pleasure. Sophie is a free soul; an ethologist and a seeker of the only truth available to man. To add a few more defining touches to this, I should assert that animals, in general, and some of them in particular, experience very long-lasting orgasms, which can produce even a more invigorated and lasting pleasure. And it must be, certainly, put down to the fact that animals are free of nonsensicality. In the same light, I could also imagine the enviably aroused and horny cells of a free potato (free of nonsensicality) which is maturing towards putrefaction."

"Oh, thank you, Miss Atkins," said Sophie, in an ambivalent and rather schizophrenic tone, a tone void of any emotional intelligence.

Miss Julie Atkins' hand crept on Sophie's chest. Garry's eyes turned into a mirror of ethology.

The dim light grew dimmer. Sophie, and only Sophie, could hear the muffled and ominously lamenting squeaks being emitted by the rats. Sophie's blank eyes fixed on the dirty windowpane. She blinked, she blinked again and again and with each blink the parts of a picture formed and sat beside each other: flailing, there appeared a large beating heart... A large beating heart in an iron cage and five fierce lustful rats dancing around it.   A large encaged beating heart on a background of dirt and grime.

Walking towards the bedroom, she put her hand on her chest. She felt nothing, not even a dying vibration or a single pulse. With a heartless chest, she approached the bedroom open door. Standing in the threshold, she felt, she heard the unmistakable and the ever-lasting sound of silence. Nothing, nothing born or aborted, nothing existed. She stretched her hand out to turn the light on, and as she did, her disappeared heart emitted a pulse, a one-off warning one. She turned around, and immediately dashed towards the door. She stumbled and went down headfirst. Her head, now a mass of an ever-lasting pain, grew bigger and bigger, enlarging only to contain more and more pain.

Subsided, descending, descended, the pained brain revealed a series of long-neglected contents and demanded immediate attention. Delirium and hallucination took over. Images, scenes and words mingled and flickered before her eyes: with Gol and the twelve-year-old Usman standing in the background, Mehmet, Draco, Calypso, Christopher, Mervyn and Garry were circling around her, performing an exotic form of dance and laughing at her diabolically. Christopher's horsey head elongated, his large teeth growing larger, Calypso metamorphosed back and forth, now a chameleon with large unreadable rolling eyes, hiding a mine of lust and appetite, and then a thin girl with a pair of modest and calm eyes behind which there was nothing but an endless span of darkness. She stepped closer, Calypso the chameleon, her eyes rolling, her colours changing, poising to lash out her sticky tongue. Lashed out, the tongue stuck to Sophie's right eye and was pulled back swiftly. The tongue was held before Draco. He looked at the eye stuck to it and laughed, his spiky hair now turning into dark needles dipped in poison. Garry stared at her; chuckled, laughed, snickered.

Mervyn's eyes showed her the depth of schizophrenia. Mehmet was bucking around like a stout Cypriot donkey and laughing at her. The two now disappearing shadows of Gol and Usman were walking away; they faded, turned into tiny specks of light and vanished. There was nothing in the background but a heavy emptiness, as heavy as death.

It felt eternal, the pain in her head, but it came to a halt. She rolled on her chest, crawled, moaned and toiled to get her body on her feet. Leaning against the wall, she fearfully turned her face towards the bedroom and felt a crippling horror in her heart. She hurled herself towards the door, pulled it open, and now standing on the top of the long narrow steep stairs, she noticed she was in her pyjamas and with no shoes on. The thought of going back into the flat and getting changed backlashed and propelled her forward. Almost tumbling, she reached the bottom of the stairs, and seconds later, she saw herself running at full pelt. A gentle drizzle was descending through a swirling layer of thick fog, the rays of light wriggling through the bed of fog most submissively, eager to be overwhelmed and contained.

She slipped, threw her arms around, in vain, nothing to hold onto. She fell, landed like a shot bird. No pain; it did not exist, it was not felt. Prostrate on the wet asphalt, she felt an unprecedented form of warmth within her body, a self-existent warmth, soothing, purging, cleansing, healing, liberating—perhaps a last resort for the contingent mental breakdown. She pulled herself up and sat on the asphalt and watched the blood streaming out of the sole of her right feet. A few yards away from her, there was a shard of glass covered in blood.

It was still dark and quiet. Out of reach and not yet disturbed by the light inside, the windows seemed most oblivious to the secrets they had witnessed during the night. Not a soul, asleep or awake, could be seen or heard.

She touched the gash on her sole, a large drop of blood gushed out and landed on the back of her hand, beating like a full heart, containing a complete set of pulses, some of which were unknown to her. She looked round the narrow street, ascended her gaze and looked at the blind silent deaf windows. She wondered how many people would cease to exist behind the blind silent deaf windows.

The mingling fog and light rolled, wriggled and gently descended on her. She laid her wan face on the wet but warm asphalt and shut her eyes…

"I found her lying in the street, like a dead bird!" said Clement pushing the office door open and letting Cynthia and Emily in.

Cynthia walked over to the couch where Sophie was sat. Kneeling down before her, she looked into her eyes in silence for some long whole moments. Whitish jade and blank, Sophie's eyes began to respond, growing greener and greener, now full green, observing, engaging, and communicating.

Emily stepped forward, sat beside her mum and tended to Sophie's wounded foot. Clement remained quiet.

Emily felt the true presence of her mother for the first time, a rich gentle yet compelling presence. Moments dragged on. An hour passed. Franco appeared and shortly afterwards, three police officers entered the office and arrested Sophie on the suspicion of murdering Garry and Miss Julie Atkins…

"Gol will be back shortly," said Cynthia when Sophie was being handcuffed.

106

Chapter 15

"Unfortunately, the evidence and some very hard facts are against her," said Melanie Maxwell, the officer in charge of Sophie's case, "She will definitely be convicted. A tiny whisky bottle containing morphine was found in her handbag. Based on the initial investigations, it is believed that morphine, a good deal of it, is responsible for the death of the victims."

"Can I see her now?" asked Gol, his face pensive, his eyes mirroring a rather tenable sense of eventuality.

Minutes later, Sophie saw Gol standing before her. Undecided, unsteady, shaking, she summoned some courage and rose to her feet. Her heart, untested and raw, became overwhelmed by the barging of the long-neglected, unsettled and unsorted thoughts, emotions and desires into her mind. Her eyes, contradicting each other, dithered, dodged, observed, ignored and eventually met Gol's. One eye emanating a blind and unjustified form of hatred and the other a muffled cry for love—a tiny flame deep under the ashes of denial.

"I hate you!" whispered Sophie, her whole face shivering, limping back and leaning against the wall.

"Good. Keep hating me," said Gol, now gazing into her eyes intently.

"What are you searching for in my eyes, you fake lion?" asked Sophie, a sudden unprecedented sense of amazement and disbelief towards herself washing over her face. So assertive, she had never been.

There was a pause, some moments of solemnity and weight, requiring an attention of the same nature. Officer Maxwell, though bound by duty, was also touched by what was appearing in Sophie's eyes and also by Gol's quick and potent emotional intelligence. The moments dragged on, intensified and lingered. The corners of Sophie's eyes ticked, shivered, her chest heaved, her nostrils widened, down she went, crumbled on her knees.

"In my eyes, you are searching for my *innocence!* Aren't you?" she moaned, holding her face in her small hands, "I have smeared it, the thing you loved most! I sold it, I sold my innocence! There is nothing left for you to love. I hate you! Go away! Leave me alone!"

Gol bent down and lifted her up; holding her shoulders, he said, "In your eyes, I am searching for a lost and disheartened lioness. Sophie, innocence is divine, and therefore, to wash and cleanse it you would only need a glass of water."

"Really!" uttered Sophie, a childish naiveté rang in her tone, "And you called me by name! Didn't you?"

"Sophie," said Gol, "The pit you have fallen into is too deep; and it might take us a considerable amount of time to pull you out of it. Promise me you will never give in."

"Promise you! You want me to promise you!" shouted Sophie, her face now remotely resembling that of a young lioness, "You call me by name. You ask me not to give in! You did know! You fake lion, you did know! In two years, you called me by name only once! In those two strange years!"

"I did know, and that is exactly why I am here today," said Gol, kissing her on the head, "Even a fake lion is lion enough not to be happy with anything less than a lioness. A heartless lioness would eventually get metamorphosed into a hyena—a miscreant and unprincipled creature whose saliva would unleash and drool over whatever only to define her unrefined nature. Inured to degradation, such a creature would become an adroit master of smearing what is most precious in life."

"What is the most precious thing in life, Gol?" asked Sophie; the last note in her voice lingered on his name and resounded like a tiny bell around the neck of a lost lamb in a distance.

"What one cherishes for most is the most precious thing in one's life," replied Gol, now staring at her hands, "Mind you, if one is not good enough to be cherished for, well, one would never learn what and how to cherish for."

"Gol, you kissed me on the head. Didn't you?" said Sophie, touching the spot Gol had kissed; she added, "This kiss—and—and the fact that you have come here to see me, or perhaps to help me, is just—is just baffling me. I—I—, Gol, I hate you! I really do hate you!"

"I am happy that you hate me," said Gol, crossing his arms on his broad chest.

"What!" boomed Sophie, her eyes widening, "You are the most confusing human being I have ever come across!"

"And you are the most *confused* human being I have ever met," said Gol, laughing, "You failed to understand and appreciate your own heart, and now you are putting the blame on me. And most importantly, you are about to fail to understand why I have come here today. You are going round in circles. You are chasing your own tail."

"You need a confession. Don't you?" said Sophie, her face blushed, "You want to break me down. You want to watch me shatter into pieces. You want to build the castle of your manly proud love on the ruins of mine."

Gol took off his jacket and wrapped it around her, rolled his sleeves up, took a step back and poised as if there was a message (partly semantic partly physical) for him to receive, requiring his vigorous arms, his heart and his mind. Was it a simultaneously jumping and dying sparkle, or was it a cameo presence of the real Sophie, the Sophie whom Gol had seen through her small hands? The Sophie standing before him was too bold and assertive, reckless, unshackled, full of bravado and alien to fear—just like a lioness, furious at herself and the prey.

"Can you repeat the last sentence you just said?" asked Gol, knitting his eyebrows and looking at her musingly.

"You want to build the castle of your love on the ruins of mine," repeated Sophie, her eyes now greener and more penetrating than ever.

"So, you know Sophie, and you know her very well," said Gol.

"No!" snapped Sophie, the green in her eyes fading into a barely visible whitish jade, "I don't know Sophie. She is dead. She is rotten. Gol, I hate you! Just go away! I have never loved you! Leave me alone!"

"It is not me, Sophie. It is you," said Gol, stretching his hand out to take his jacket.

"No, it is too cold in here," said Sophie, wrapping the jacket tightly around herself, "Though too large for me but it is warm. Leave your jacket for me. Go, go away."

A commotion broke out. The quiet police station yawned and welcomed it. The drunk twisted words were unleashed, pampering everyone and everything indiscriminately: 'this fucking chair is too fucking cold!' blared out a young drunk girl. 'Mate, you are a fucking bunch of fucking maggots!

You have lost your fucking bonces!' bellowed a young man, who was being firmly held by two male officers. 'I am not fucking drunk! I am just pissed off by the fucking society!' roared a middle-aged man, foaming fuming and revealing the only teeth left in his mouth—two and a half.

'I am fucking practically unable to restrain my daughter from drinking and all that! Why? Because she is fucking sixteen! Her piss isn't foaming yet!' blatted a not-so-very old mum whose sixteen-year-old daughter had smashed a bottle of beer on the head of a not-so-very-young-gentleman!

Sophie watched Gol walk away, pulled the jacket over her head and moaned plaintively. The commotion culminated, and a while later, it died down rapidly.

Chapter 16

"I thank you very much, Christopher, for arranging this meeting," said Draco, drawing on his face not even an air of mournfulness but a full book of songs of bereavement and lamentation, "The loss of my dad has devastated all of us. We have practically been out of this world. And as you can see for yourself, Calypso is about to lose her sanity under this backbreaking loss inflicted on us by a bitch!

"And only God knows if Mervyn survives the pain of this loss. Honestly, Dad was like a father to him."

"You know, your dad was a very decent man," said Christopher, throwing an empathic look at Calypso—who was crooning a rather gibberish song, apparently about the unappreciated decency of her dad— "He was a man of his word. You know, bloody hell, we just didn't know how decent and gentle he was, and I think it became his enemy, this gentleness and decency; otherwise he would have never fallen for a bitch like that girl. You know, we all know whom I am referring to. Bloody hell! How did she bring herself to put poison in a drink and offer it to Garry, this very good gentleman whose manners were second to none. Bloody hell! She didn't even show a bit of mercy to Garry's poor friend, Miss Julie Atkins. They both left the world unfulfilled. You know, man, bloody hell! Nine times, nine times I told Anita! I warned her about, about that harpy of harpies, that monster of a girl! She was hovering over Garry's head like an eagle that had eaten a good number of vipers alive! That girl is a viper! An old white viper! Bloody hell, man, bloody hell."

"Dad saw it as his prerogative, Christopher," said Draco, "And his prerogative, it was. That is why Mum decided not to interfere with it, as she had never done with any other issues since she married my dad. All of us, literally, are not into the bad habit of interfering with other people's business. Yeah, I think it was definitely his prerogative, but I do agree with you over his careless approach to this absolutely disgusting girl. In all, I honestly believe Dad left a legacy behind, a legacy of decency and defined and fully understood *prerogatives*. I should also mention that Mum should

111

not be held accountable for Dad's bitter end. You just wonder how disgusting some people really are! This disgusting girl could have spared the rats so that we could seek a bit of solace in taking care of them. They loved my dad, those marvellously intelligent creatures. They truly did love my dad.

"And what should we do now? Well, there are more important things going on in the world right now, the worst of which is the waywardly multiplying humanity and the overwhelmingly overpopulating earth and its catastrophic future consequences. Although overpopulation is the main concern, but there are countless other issues that are equally dire and forceful enough to push the world over the cliff of annihilation, issues such as animal cruelty, child poverty, caesarean, abortion, genetically modified foods, rabid dogs and Muslims, Greek Orthodoxy, meretricious nuns and paedophile priests, suicide bombers and illuminati, Nicola Tesla, Quantum Physics, parallel universes, and not to mention those bloody mother-fucker Iranians and their voracious love for weapons of mass destruction... More or less, I think there are far more important things going on in the world... Yeah, a proper man was given a proper burial... Yeah, we did it. We paid him back. Let's move on and see where the world is going to take us. Honestly, more or less, I really don't trust this world. I have never done. Backstabbing, betrayals. This is what this world is all about!"

Anita stared at her son incredulously, as if she had noticed his existence just seconds ago. His words, alien and unrecognisable, hit her hard, reverberated in a far corner of her mind and echoed back to her. Perverse, uncarved, evasive, impertinent, immune to relevance, the words stirred up within her a long and bitter sigh. Hastily, she turned around and looked at Calypso through her squinted eyes. She too seemed alien to her. She winced back at the thought of alienation permeating through her mind and her heart. Was it an unveiling or a veiling, the lifting of a thick dark cover or the falling of it over her existence? Though unspecified in terms of direction, but it was a revelation, a regurgitation of a mind fed with nonsensicality, and a heart grown accustomed to passivity and contradiction. She looked at her children again. She felt empty, alone, deserted, forgotten, and wasted. Light-headed, she got to her feet and tottered towards the door. Ignoring the calls behind her, she disappeared behind the door. She was free, she thought. Unburdened, defeated, had lost whatever could have been lost and had mourned for her losses beforehand. She had mourned for Draco the moment

112

she had felt his existence in her womb. She owed nothing to anyone, she thought. All settled. All cleared.

"I am here, I am here, don't worry," said Christopher, now watching Anita, through the glass window, crossing the narrow street, "I will help you both to manage the business. You are definitely capable of managing this even better than your dad used to. He was too rigid. You are open to the fresher ways of doing things. You know, bloody hell, life goes on. So, forget Garry and promote your business, earn more money and bloody hell, enjoy your life. We all die. No one will remain here for ever. Just listen to me. I am your friend. Bloody hell, I have been your friend through all these bloody years."

"We both appreciate your friendship and your support," said Calypso, in a tone rather self-pampering than denoting grief, "Our loss is big. Dad was a great man and the undeniable symbol of decency. And as you just mentioned, life goes on, and therefore we should get over this quickly and move on. We have always been pushed forward by your encouraging words, and we will keep appreciating your presence even more than before."

"I will support you, Calypso," said Christopher, his voice now fully horsey, that of an old drunk stallion, "You need protection. I will protect you. Yeah, bloody hell, I will protect you."

Mehmet, who had remained quiet up to that point, threw a slightly alarmed look at Draco's now distorted face, prepared himself to let out a few words, but he decided not to.

Draco looked at Christopher, pictured the word *protect* on his forehead, threw a fleeting look at Mehmet, captured a blurred reflection of the word *sister* in both his eyes and blended them in his mind. His face, this cinematic whiteboard of pathological inner desires, showed an initial projection of jealousy and indignation but, same as usual, it was turned into a picture of sheer pleasure.

Getting to his feet, Mehmet turned towards Calypso and said, "I sorry forgive me for dad your dead. Sophie bitch very very. I know from first from. I now kitchen in too much work have. Go now me."

"Wasn't it him who was to divorce his wife and marry Sophie?" asked Draco, turning towards Christopher, "Honestly, I am very suspicious of this guy. I think it was him who made that bitch kill my dad! Honestly, more or less, he is the most two-faced man I have ever met. It is, I believe, more or less, our very prerogative to be suspicious of him. Why? Because of

113

Sophie's passionate love for him. He was, and I think still is, Sophie's only favourite man in the world."

"I think we wouldn't be far wrong—" said Christopher.

"Oh, yeah!" Calypso cut in, a touch of bereaved and bitter sarcasm ringing in her tone, "Guys, just leave him alone!"

"I can't understand why you are defending this guy," said Draco, throwing a fleeting look at Jack and Jack, who were preparing themselves to leave, "Honestly, have I ever been into the bad habit of throwing shit at other people behind their backs? I wasn't intended to say this, but you made me to. So listen: one of his fellow countrymen, who knows him very well, described Mehmet to me as 'half gentleman half gay man!' which I think he actually meant to say 'a bugger', a bugger in its literal sense!"

"How about you two?" asked Calypso, holding her chin and tilting her head, "Are you full *gentlemen*? You hate him because he isn't interested in you, which is a proof to his good taste! You hate him because he is a touch cleverer than you are."

"What the fuck are you talking about!" asked Draco, pulling the sleeves of his flowery shirt up, "This guy is evidently a fucking retard!"

"I know," said Calypso in a low tone.

"Bloody hell, man!" said Christopher, elongating his neck, "I think you are being a bit too rude to us! It is definitely not your prerogative. Bloody hell, man. Bloody hell."

"Don't be so tender," said Calypso, laughing, "I will ask him to take care of you! And there is nothing wrong with being half gentleman half gay man, as we live in a free and very accommodating society. Don't we, guys?"

"I think we are going off track," said Christopher, now looking like a unicorn without a horn, "Bloody hell, man! Bloody hell."

Jack and Jack bade a quiet farewell and slipped out of the door, carrying with them a picture of Calypso's face and some snippets of what they had unwittingly overheard.

"It is such a quiet lovely night. Isn't it, mate?" said Mr Jack something, a mini Jesus-looking blonde man.

"Yes, mate, it is," replied Mr Jack something else, also a mini Jesus-looking blonde man.

"Mate, you seem to be itching to get home," said Jack something, quickening his pace, "So am I.

"Let's go, mate, let's go. I am sure your Filipino is impatiently waiting for you to arrive and knock on the door."

"She sits by the window every night, looking down on the street," said Jack something else, "And she opens the door before I knock on it. And then she holds my face in her hands and that, mate, makes me feel like a little boy; and I rejoice in every second of it. I hope it is the same with you and your Polish."

"Exactly the same, mate," said Jack something, his green eyes shining, "My Polish has been giving birth to me every day since we married."

"Mate," said Jack something else, indulging himself with a gentle hearty laugh, "We have become too wise! And it could be very dangerous."

They reached a crossing point. The light turned red for them. An oncoming car slowed down, and as it reached them, two of its young passengers flipped them off and called them 'wankers'. They both turned their heads and stared at the car's taillights while it was wheezing away. The light turned green for them.

"Mate," said Jack something, as they were crossing the road, "Do you think we would be allowed to cling only on to the first half, I mean *the half gentleman*, and leave the other half for the guys who don't wank?"

"Don't worry yourself, mate," replied Jack something else, smiling at his mate, "My Filipino believes the world will cease to exist before we grow old enough to qualify for a death certificate."

Chapter 17

"Plead guilty, and we will let you off the hook," said Calypso, touching Sophie's hand and throwing a look at Molly, "There is not any other way we can help you with this. Be wise and understand that every single piece of evidence in this case is against you. Practically, there is not even a tad of hope. Do not make things more complicated than they already are. We believe, Draco, Mervyn and I, and even your very close friend, Molly, that it was a moment of madness that forced you to take my dad's life, a man who had pure love for you. We also believe that it was your pure love for him that caused that madness within you. Madness caused by jealousy, this is what Draco believes was the main reason behind this senseless crime. You know that my dad was very interested in words and phrases due to his love for knowledge and decency. I used to learn from him a new word or phrase each and every day. 'Double whammy', this was the last I learned from him. You would face a *double whammy* in case you decided not to plead guilty: you would land behind bars for god knows how long; and most importantly, you would lose your most favourite man ever, your only soul mate, Mehmet. He was so down he couldn't come and see you today. I seriously doubt it if he would survive without you. Poor lovely Mehmet!"

"My dear lovely Sophie," said Molly, holding a tuft of her unwashed her, "Last night I was with Mervyn, and he was so unbearably pining for you. He was actually crying like a baby. And what can I say about the other guys and the pains they have been enduring since you were arrested. Oh my gosh! Poor Christopher and Draco, I would be very much surprised if they wouldn't sustain some visual damage! The poor guys have been weeping nonstop! And, yeah, I also believe Mehmet wouldn't survive without you. Based on so much love and respect they have for you, I should advise you to trust and listen to them, or you will waste the rest of your life needlessly."

Sophie stared at Molly's pale face for some long and heavy moments and remained silent. Her mind already strained, she felt exasperated. An hysterical laugh stormed within her, waved, raged and hit an undisturbed undercurrent deep within her. Seconds later, it bulged, burst and blasted out.

116

She laughed uncontrollably for a long while. Calypso and Molly watched her in silence. On the last note of her laughter, she came to an abrupt halt, remained voiceless and motionless, raised her head and looked at Calypso through a cold painful stare.

"A double whammy! My life and Mehmet!" she uttered, her voice sounding elastic, containing a volcanic energy, "Why would you let me off the hook?"

"My dad was the essence of humanity and decency," said Calypso, her large black eyes shining, "To pay a proper tribute to a proper dad we would graciously forgive you. At the end of the day, it was love, the purest form of it, that my dad paid with his life for. My dad was intended to marry you, as he had seen it as his prerogative, and it is what Draco believes. He also believes that our dad's life would have become fully fulfilled if he had married you. Just for this cause, and of course, out of sheer kindness we would forgive you. And… as for Miss Julie Atkins—well, she was a great undertaker, the best at all aspects of it, from grave digging to pulling the guts out of the dead, embalming, makeup… a loner, a fruitless tree, nothing to be claimed… we would sort this out for you as well."

Sophie was about to say that Garry was to marry Miss Julie Atkins; that it was her that would become a source of fulfilment for Garry, and consequently, for them as well. She bit her lips, raised her head and remained silent. Some long heavy minutes passed. Calypso's calculating mind crippled Sophie's.

What would be emitted from a mind religiously identified with too much physicality and morbid carnal pleasures; a mind disconnected from its source, a tantamount to hollowness, a transmuted structure within which no concept would live long enough to be noticed, defined and delivered. Calypso's large eyes rolled, right and left, up and down and were fixed on Sophie's now submissive face. Sophie's mind gave in. Her face turned into a page of scribbled nonsensicality and folly.

"I have got to go now," said Calypso, holding Sophie's hands in hers, "I have always believed in you as a very intelligent girl, and I wish you are not going to prove me wrong. Be advised that failing to make the right decision in this story, will definitely be a fatal failure."

"I will plead guilty. I promise you. I don't want to lose Mehmet," said Sophie, offering Calypso a most foolish smile.

"Good!" said Calypso, touching Sophie's face, "Mervyn and I will help

117

Mehmet to get over his traumatic mental state and make himself fit and ready for you. It is a promise."

"Awh, thank you!" said Sophie, her tears raining down, "You and Mervyn have always been so kind and caring towards me."

"No worries," said Calypso, her large eyes shining.

"I have always been proud of you, my dear lovely Sophie," said Molly, kissing her face, "You made the right decision. And I assure you the guys and Calypso will definitely help you out with this. They aren't like that primitive fucker, Gol, who would sit with his back to you! No, these guys will never turn their backs to you. And, oh by the way, even Jack and Jack believe your life without Mehmet wouldn't be a life any more."

A black and white picture of Molly's face was imprinted in Sophie's mind, perhaps a map to guide her towards the *truth*... What was the truth? She contemplated, a smile of satisfaction gradually forming on her face. '*It is the belief that will give birth to the truth*'. Draco's words, echoing in her ears, '*If you believe rhinos grow on trees, well, then rhinos will grow on trees for you*'. 'Yeah, I do believe that I murdered Garry and Miss Julie Atkins...' she thought contentedly, 'Yeah, I do believe that those guys are pining away because of me... Yeah, they love me dearly. They have always loved me. Yeah, Jack and Jack are right; Mehmet and I would die without each other.'

"Are you all right?" asked a male officer.

"Oh, me? Yeah, I am fine!"

***

Sophie pulled the chair back, wrapped the large jacket around herself and slowly and hesitantly lowered her body and sat on the chair, as if she doubted the existence of it. She wriggled on the chair, dithered for a while and turned her face towards Mr Gibran and gave him a blank and lifeless look.

Aisha's hand touched hers. She blinked, looked at Aisha's hand on hers and blinked again. Full but not imposing, Mr Gibran's presence was felt, in Sophie's mind, through Aisha's hand.

"Sophie," said Aisha, leaning towards her, "We thought it would be a good idea to come here and see you."

"I do know... " uttered Sophie, pausing for some long seconds; and turning her blank face towards Aisha, she said, "I can't understand why you people have come here to see me! I don't know you at all. Strangers, I have never associated myself with them. Yeah, strangers can cast negative spells on you, the ones that could steal one's senses and replace them with vicious distorted pulses, guiding one to this mazy alleyway or to that never-ending back road. All those directions, futile cues and soul-draining dreams…"

A heavy self-justifying silence fell over the stark cold room. The breath in Aisha and Mr Gibran's chest refused to exhale. Unconscious, dreamy, she sounded, she seemed, a projection from the unconscious zone of her strained mind or a conscious denial of acquaintance and recognition?

In no-man's-land, acting unconsciously and reacting consciously, it was apparent to Mr Gibran that Sophie's mind had become a borderless terrain within which *direction* meant a demanding trouble, a futile concept.

Mr Gibran got up and walked over to Sophie, kissed her on the head and said, "But we know you; that is why we are here. We knew who we knew and why we would want to see her."

Sophie closed her eyes, put her hand on her chest and remained silent. A flashback, a kiss on her head, in a long-forgotten past, Usman's, in those blissful days of innocence and divine passion. She raised her hand and touched the top of her head, where Mr Gibran had just kissed, turned her face towards him and stared at his silver beard.

Another while of silence. She rose to her feet, took off the large jacket, handed it to Aisha and said, "I don't know you. Go away. Give this jacket to Gol and tell him I do not wish to see him again. I shouldn't have crossed paths with him in the first place. I wouldn't. It was fate. It made me to. No, I don't think so. Fate is also nonsense, one of those misleading beliefs people like Gol sling at others for no good reason at all. Yeah, tell him— tell him I don't wish to see him again. Honestly, I—I really hate him. Tell him. Tell him I hate him. I have never liked him."

Aisha folded the jacket, held it under her arm and offered Sophie a kind smile.

Mr Gibran, the wise gnostic, the history teacher, once again spotted the zone Sophie was wondering off to: an inner zone, an inward search in a directionless direction. In the depth of her green eyes, he spotted a cut of silk and a shard of glass.

Aisha walked towards the door. Mr Gibran was still sitting, waiting for Sophie to raise her head, and when she did, he darted his wise calm fatherly

119

gaze into her eyes. Though refractory and cocooned in a mesh of irrationality, she allowed her mind to picture Mr Gibran's face, a fleeting *conscious* act. Remembering Cynthia's painting, her now wayward mind blended the green of her own eyes with the jet black of Mr Gibran's, the silver of his beard with the brown of her own hair, perhaps an unconscious attempt to test her sense of vision and its distorted connection with her other senses.

Chapter 18

"Gol, why did you ask me back?" asked Franco, "You sent me to Garry's restaurant, to that mental asylum of mental asylums, to make sure Sophie wouldn't put herself in trouble."

"I asked you back because you told me Sophie was beyond help. Didn't you?" said Gol, stirring the bowl of soup before him, "And you were right."

"You went to the police station and talked to her the other day," said Franco, "Does it mean she can now be helped?"

"No, not yet," replied Gol, gazing into the bowl of soup, "I went there only to show myself to her.

"It is me, Franco. I am Sophie's problem. I am her predicament. And it is not me."

"Interesting!" uttered Franco, a wise glow appearing in his black eyes, "*It is you and it is not you.*

"I fully understand this. This is a unique story. A bane and a boon at the same time, you are to Sophie."

"Well said, Franco," said Gol in a whispering tone, "And what would you say if I asked you to go back to that 'mental asylum' again?"

"To do what?" asked Franco, narrowing his eyes.

"To look after another Sophie, your Sophie," replied Gol, smiling.

Franco kept staring at Gol for some very long heavy meaningful moments. Gol kept himself busy with his soup, allowing him to sort the misgivings and the discrepancies in his mind. It was just a weak inner desire with no real prospect of getting materialised, or a secret short pleasant dream at its highest possibility. However, it was real. It existed and was augmenting.

"You should go back to that mental asylum and make sure nothing will happen to Anita," said Gol, looking into Franco's eyes.

"But Gol how did you—?"

"Franco, humans are words and words are human," interrupted Gol, shaking some salt into his soup, "You mention Anita's name only to savour its aftertaste."

"What could, if anything, happen to Anita within her own business, her own household? I don't understand."

"Whoever planned Garry's murder, might decide to get rid of Anita too," said Gol.

"Garry was murdered by Sophie; and she will definitely land behind bars," said Franco, "All the evidence is against her. And I am sure she will admit this senseless act to the judges. I have no doubt about it."

"All the evidence is against her, and she will admit… " said Gol, "That is exactly why I believe this murder was planned by someone else, and Sophie had no role in it."

"If I want to agree with you over this," said Franco, "Then I would definitely mention two prime suspects: Draco and Calypso, Garry and Anita's children. Calypso is a young witch with an old dark mind."

"They might have played a role…," said Gol, but I believe there is a far more mysterious and darker mind behind this murder, a fierce predator with an angelic face, I would imagine. And it must be one of the people within that business and household, or as you rightly put it, that *mental asylum!*"

"It is getting amazing! This story!" said Franco, a mixed smile distorting his face, imparting a feeling of self-reproach, perhaps because of his rather cursory initial take on the story, "Have you managed to spot any suspect yet? And by the way, I am wondering why the police questioned everybody within Garry's business, myself included, but not Mervyn."

"Based on a brief inquiry I have secretly done," replied Gol, "Now I have a list of three suspects, but Mervyn isn't in the list. No, I haven't seen him as a suspect. He is a lamb. Isn't he? Meanwhile, I want you to go back to that mental asylum and, plus taking care of Anita, gather some information about every single person within and around that mental asylum, in particular, Mehmet. I believe if there is any easy-to-open window into this story, it has to be Mehmet's head."

"Gol, you are talking about *investigation* and all these…" said Franco, "So what are the police and the law doing in this case?"

"Good question, a very good one indeed," said Gol, "They have already got what they needed: enough facts and evidence to put an end to Sophie. Truth, Franco, truth is what they hate most. For them, this case is already done and dusted. Truth is too human, expensive and demanding, requiring the right container and the highest price; that is why some societies decide

122

to get rid of it of all together and replace it with *duty.* The solely *dutiful* man would eventually lose it all together; that is certain. They are doing their duty, the police and the law, and none of them cares about the truth or the dying love in Sophie's heart."

"As I can gather now, you will definitely be able to help Sophie out of this."

"Yes, but not definitely," replied Gol, immediately, "Not because I am not sure if I can find the truth and present it to a court of law, but because of Sophie herself. It is now up to her. If she can muster enough moral courage to help herself, then I will definitely resolve this issue within a short amount of time. Trapped in an inner cage, and now encaged within an outside one, I seriously doubt it if she can break out of the first cage so soon. On the same note, I should append that no initial steps will be taken by me in freeing her… That would certainly be offering her the freedom of not being free. If she takes the first step, then I will guide her towards a form of freedom within which there is no *free* space, no pockets of uncertainty, no recesses of treachery and regression."

Would Gol's ideals remain some mere moral and philosophical projections, or would they turn into the seeds of reality and bear the expected fruits? Would his conviction—a conviction based on purification and self-realisation—be able to kindle a light in Sophie's mind and force her to see the long-neglected treasure in her heart, or would it prove only as a blind shot in the vastness of an eternalized darkness? Would Sophie allow the ever-one-off chalice of love and light be spilled on the arid and plagued part of her existence while tittering and ogling at it foolishly, or would she grab and drink it in one go?

Chapter 19

She stared at the cold silver handcuff and interlocked her fingers. They were cold, colder than the silver handcuff. Her mind, now completely out of her control, was free, free to roam around and resurface her most immediate and most *relevant* memories, one of which was Draco's words when he had visited her five days before she had been sent to the court: 'more or less, I think you have made the right decision. You know your prerogatives. I honestly do believe you do know'. He had told her when she had assured him that she would plead guilty and accept the full responsibility for the murder. He had also told her that he had never loved any other human being more than he loved her; that she had to forget all about Mehmet, deeming him as only a fucking sister-banger Muslim who had no respect for women at all; that he, Mehmet, had been calling her 'a bitch' since she was arrested. He had also expressed his unwavering love for her, stating that he would marry her as soon as she stepped out of prison.

A smile appeared and dissolved the painted painful foolish look on her face, when she attended to the last part of Draco's promises: 'I am now literally the owner of whatever Garry has left behind. Imagine, Sophie, just imagine you and me and all these assets: four flats, three restaurants, a massive and very expensive house, a beautiful six-bedroom mansion in Cyprus, a villa of the same size, more or less, in Turkey, a five-acre farm in South Africa, where Garry used to raise some Arab breed of horses... And above all and most smashing, a fat, more or less, very opulent bank account! Guess how fat? Two and a half million pounds! You would be spoiled. I would spend all of that on you, and only you. You are worthy of it. And so much more. It is our prerogative, more or less, to design our own lives in the most lavish way. Extravaganza, I think this is the word. A life of extravaganza in the heart of Amsterdam. Yeah, I have already, more or less, planned it; I mean moving to Amsterdam, you and I, and settling down there...'

She pressed her fingertips against each other. They were cold, colder than the silver handcuff. *I would rather we move to South Africa instead of*

Amsterdam. Though I know nothing about some breed of Arab horses, but I love horses. I would ask Draco to take me to South Africa. Yeah, it would be much better—peace and adventure together. I have always loved Draco so dearly. He is the prototype of authenticity. He really is.

***

"She looks more like an asexual little rabbit than a hot lustful treacherous killer!" said one of the inmates, a middle-aged middle-height woman with a wide white face and a most languishing pair of eyes.

"Half of her is hidden under the ground; I would bet on it," said another one, a scraggy well-matured woman with short hair and a freckle-bespattered face with a strange halo around it.

"Even a penny would be a big loss! I would say," said a teenage-looking petite brunette, her voice sounding old and coded.

"Mate, you are wrong," said a rather young curvy redhead, now standing before Sophie and thoughtfully assessing her, "Look at her! Of a middle-stature, two bespoke fucking boobs, as round and well-shaped as a pair of fucking grapefruits! With this innocent-looking face and those modest- looking eyes, mate, she would kill twice. You killed your victims twice. Didn't you?"

"A daft vagina is the only thing that can kill twice. She is a daft vagina!" shouted another one, in a rather testosterone-driven voice, "And I don't think she would make a good licker! Her mouth is too small."

"Her heart, like mine, is between her legs! She is definitely a daft vagina. She would kill twice," belched another one, an overdose of oestrogen easily detectable in her tone.

"Leave her alone!" demanded a voice from the end of the narrow corridor leading to the dining area.

Sophie turned around, an unconscious turn, and smiled an unjustified smile—the most justified form of it. Watching the woman, who was now approaching her, she tilted her head and completed the smile on her face. In a flash, her strained brain resurfaced a carved memory in her mind: she had offered Gol the same smile with her head tilted when she had met him first. A tilted female head, she wondered, is perhaps caused by an honest and salient desire for the purest form of goodness, or an unconscious acknowledgement of its presence. Now looking like an innocent gazelle

125

standing before a mature well-experienced lioness, she looked at the woman standing before her. Rather tall and full, full in any sense, the woman stretched her hand out and touched Sophie's face while intently looking into her eyes.

"Eileen, my name is Eileen," said the woman, in a thick authentic Scottish accent.

"Sophie, my name is Sophie. Draco calls me 'Soph'. You could also call me Soph," said Sophie, her face blushing.

"No, this name should never be torn apart," said Eileen, "And who is Draco, a sort of serpent or something?"

"Oh, no," replied Sophie, her face exhibiting a mixture of naiveté and displeasure, "A lovely handsome man who is going to marry me. He is to help me out of this, I mean this prison thing. He promised me, Yeah, he did promise me. He is now a very rich man. And he is so generous, a generous inheritor who is going to spend all of it on me."

Eileen raised her hand, and now holding her chiselled chin, she gazed into Sophie's eyes again. Deep, scouring, questioning, solemnly reproachful, Eileen's eyes made Sophie so uneasy that she winced back and immediately covered her mouth with both hands. Gol's eyes had once unhinged her in the same manner, she remembered, but they were too modest to linger and reproach.

"Come with me, you fucking undeserved little lassie!" demanded Eileen in the fullest Scottish tone and accent, and grabbing Sophie's hand, she went on, "Place, time, occasion, relevance, appropriacy are connected to each other. Eileen uses the relevant language, the language of place and time. In this location, the location of dislocated hearts, rotting oestrogens and shrinking pussies, the language should be chosen accordingly."

"Can I sit down, here, on the bed? I am feeling a pain in my back," asked Sophie.

"Feel free. Make yourself at home," replied Eileen, in the softest tone Scottish accent would allow.

"Oh, you mean you want me to be your room-mate?" asked Sophie, looking round the room, one of her eyes happy and the other slightly alarmed.

"Yes."

"Why?" asked Sophie, now noticing Eileen's round broad face and her rather large hazel eyes and her long sleek brown hair.

Eileen raised her head and paused, a long and upsetting pause. Aligning her eyes with Sophie's, she gazed into them, her pale white complexion growing brighter, her eyes widening.

"Why do you want me to be your room-mate?" asked Sophie again.

"Tell me the name of the one person whom you hate most, and I will tell you why," asked Eileen.

"Are you a fortune-teller or something?" asked Sophie, now noticing a pile of books behind Eileen's bed.

"Tell me the name of the one person whom you hate most," asked Eileen, smiling.

"Gol. I hate Gol. I do really hate Gol. He, Gol, is horrible," said Sophie, her eyes moistening, her lips shivering, "Gol is a fake man. Yeah, Gol is really fake. Gol is timid. They, the people around Gol, think of Gol as a 'lion', but Gol is just a phoney man. Have I ever hated any human being more than I hate Gol? No. Will I ever hate more...? No. His name, Gol's name, means 'flower', but I think, he, Gol, is a poisonous plant from hell..."

"Interesting!" interrupted Eileen, kneeling down on the floor and holding Sophie's hands in hers, "And you would keep happily chewing this 'poisonous plant' for the rest of your life if you got access to it! Wouldn't you? Lassie, it is not only your heart that has herniated down between your legs and metamorphosed to vagina, it is also your brain. I heard one of those lassies calling you 'a daft vagina'! If you let your brain be herniated and metamorphosed in the same manner, then you would definitely become a full drooling *daft vagina!*"

"You are looking at my hands. Aren't you? You are treating me like Gol used to," said Sophie, her head tilting, some of her unsorted suppressed feelings appearing on her face, each ploughing a corner of it, "He also would look into my eyes and then at my hands as if... as if... as if I was holding a god... a very old god in them!"

"And what did he see in your eyes?" asked Eileen, pressing Sophie's hands in hers.

"I don't know."

"Lassie, you are a fucking liar, a fucking blatant self-deceiver. He would have seen nothing had not you seen it first."

"Do you mean it was within me, I mean whatever which was seen? No, there was nothing within me. He was being... yeah; he was being a lunatic... And, Eileen! Why don't you tell me what YOU have seen in my

127

eyes and what are you searching for in my hands?"

"A vagina," whispered Eileen in a most serious tone, "I have seen a vagina in your eyes, the first vagina, the sacred one, the one from which the most important thing was tumbled out. What was the most important thing, Sophie? I will tell you. The very first product of the very first vagina was God. He, the god, jumped out of it like a—well, just like himself, and landed in a non-existent meaningless existence! He was meaninglessly meaningless. He was meaninglessly alone. He was and he was not. Was the vagina—the first one, the sacred one—as meaninglessly meaningless? No. Inside *her* (see, she had inside, outside and even a gender name), there was a pair of shut eyes. She opened those eyes. What do open eyes do? They observe. They did observe, and thus meaning gained meaning and, as a consequence, God's existence was seen. Nothing could be a source if there is a source to it. It was, Sophie, the source-less—and obviously the timeless—vagina that became the source of whatever. Because of not being an always-drooling silly vagina, she would *experience* volcanic orgasms, spewing out universes after universes, marvels after marvels, all meaningful, all meaningless. In all, the first vagina was the only place to be, the only place to come out of, and the only place to go back to. God's existence is still unknown to Him, because He has been away from home since He tumbled out of it!

"Sophie, that man, that old acquaintance of the world, has seen, in your eyes, a whit of that first vagina, that ever-existing mother of existence and meaning. A history, if you like, he has seen in your eyes; and in your hands, a guiding map towards all of that."

Now silly, then wise, now dark, then bright, Sophie's eyes seemed. Half her face promising a chuckle, the other a vague utterance. Was she awake or asleep? Was it the confinement, the thick walls and the low ceilings, or was it a sudden change to her always-imbalanced level of oestrogen? She felt most confused, most bewildered by the confounding fresh emotions crazing in her head like a barrage of hot bullets being fired by an ever-firing machine gun. This strange vagina story and its volcanic orgasms within a sacred lust, sounded, initially, to her as another travesty of the inevitable ambiguity of human existence; but as she noticed the rationally converging aspects of a moment of realisation in her mind, bespeaking a step, perhaps, towards disambiguation, she turned around and asked, "Eileen, that old acquaintance of the world, as you put it, believes that human soul can be

128

washed and cleansed with a glass of water. Is it true, Eileen?"

"That old acquaintance of the world is right," replied Eileen, now watching Sophie's face intently, "He is a gnostic, someone who has, to a certain degree, broken out of his biological shell."

"Eileen," said Sophie, her face now the perfect definition of the word 'innocence', "Do you think he has forgotten me, I mean Gol?"

"You hate him. Don't you?" asked Eileen.

"Oh, yeah, no—yes, but I don't want him to forget me," replied Sophie, slightly embarrassed.

"Unforgettable, become unforgettable," said Eileen.

"Eileen, can I read some of your books?" asked Sophie, pointing to the stacks of books behind the bed with an awkwardly sagacious hue appearing in her eyes.

"Yes, of course you can. I wouldn't mind even if you ate them!" replied Eileen, laughing.

***

When freedom is taken away, it would be replaced by uncertainty, presumption and prediction. Confined physically, fettered mentally and confused generally, Sophie soon became an interesting subject to bet on for those whose freedom had been taken away from them. All confined, all betting, all being betted on, those female prisoners would bet on almost anything and everything, even each other's age! The latest of those bettors interested in betting on Sophie, was Magdalena Martinez, a young enough Spanish dance teacher who believed, and had bet on it, that Sophie and dance were equally alien to each other. To make her bet even more contentious, she had also proposed that Sophie's soul was too inflexible to allow moves to find each other and become dance. Magdalena, in a night when all her moves had found each other very well, had killed her portly English husband: wearing a pair of Irish Dance shoes, she had danced on his unconscious body until morning, beginning with Irish dance, moving on with some stomp African ones, ascending with Samba, descending with Flamenco and ending with Tango in high-heels! Magdalena was a tall, dark and mysterious woman, a Lilith-like figure with the Eve's pretentious naiveté in one eye and an ever-tempting red apple in the other. An ardent Gothic-dresser from Granada with a dancing snake within her was definitely an instigator of a different nature, touching the good and the vice at the same time.

"Sophie will prove you wrong, Magdalena," said Eileen, handing her a chocolate bar,
"There is a very flexible dancing snake within her. It is frozen, the snake. It only needs the right heat."

"Eileen, I have always been afraid of the frozen snakes," said Magdalena, in a pristine Latinate accent, elongating the words and adding an elastic *e* to the end of each, "When warmed up, they would become voracious and viciously wise."

"Will you teach her how to dance?" asked Eileen.

"She hates dance. She is too clumsy for it," replied Magdalena, unwrapping the chocolate bar, "The other day I was dancing and she was looking at me. How was she looking at me? She was looking at me as if I wasn't dancing!"

"She hates all the things that she loves most," said Eileen, pushing back her hair.

"How come!" said Magdalena, "And based on this rationale, she should love the things that she hates most! How come, Eileen?"

"There she comes!" said Eileen, "The girl with a frozen dancing snake within her."

"Hello," said Sophie, furtively throwing a rather fearful look at Magdalena, "I am sorry for being a bit late."

"Come here, Sophie," asked Magdalena, pointing to her own lap, and when Sophie showed no interest, she added, "Come here and sit on my lap. No worries, I haven't seen you as a potential pussy-licker. Plus my long fingers, I am also privileged with a long tongue and an elastic body. I would happily lick my own pussy…"

Sophie dithered for a while but when her eyes met Magdalena's, she sat on her lap with a lingering smile.

"Why are you afraid of me, Sophie?" asked Magdalena, putting her arms around her, "I killed only one, while you killed two. I danced my victim to death. You killed them with a bottle of morphine. Mine was an incident. Yours was premeditated and evil. So, who should be afraid of whom?"

Sophie looked into Magdalena's eyes, and seeing a playful smile sitting in them, she formed one in her own and said, "You danced on your victim for five hours, pounding, kicking, stamping and eventually stabbing him in your high heels, and yet you call it an 'incident'! Who is eviller? Magdalena or Sophie? And remember, you had knocked him out by lashing a kick to his balls before 'dancing him to death'!"

"It is feeling a bit of warmth. Isn't it? The frozen dancing snake within you," said Magdalena in an evidently affable tone, "Mine was an incident, a historical *incident*. And don't forget, I was drunk, intoxicated. He used to make me drunk. '*Shagging a wise woman is a thankless fagging!*' he would go. He would take away my sobriety only to dampen my intelligence and make me 'fuckable'! And fuckable, I would become. It is so easy; it has always been, to fuck wise women up. It went that way for ten years before I underwent some severe inner challenges, which in turn led me to an inevitable self-realisation: Magdalena, being a fucking historian and driven by a black wise dancing snake within her, had allowed to be turned into a *fag hag*, a very cheap woman, cheaper than a pack of cigarette. What would such a woman get? A man minus manhood. In all, Magdalena had become *a vagina with a woman!* And thus, Magdalena began to miss the *woman-with-a-vagina* she used to be! I asked him to let me go away, but he refused. What else could I do? It was a historical anger, a mini Big Bang, accumulated, formed, imploded and immediately exploded. In all, I should say it wasn't premeditated. It was a self-calculated incident, like all historical incidents."

Sophie looked at herself and the way she was sitting on Magdalena's lap: submissive and contented, childishly present, unprecedentedly composed and engaged. She raised her head, and holding a tuft of Magdalena's long black hair, she asked, "What is the highest price of a woman?"

"See, the dancing snake within her is defrosting!" said Eileen musingly.

"The mother of *existence* is beyond *price*. She is the priceless evaluator," replied Magdalena, her dark face now a collage of beauty, intellect, passion and a knowingly diluted form of rationality.

"Will you teach me how to dance?" asked Sophie, feeling her own words resonating to each other and expressing her desire from the depth of her heart.

"I will," said Magdalena, "But I need to know why you want to learn how to dance."

131

"I am not sure why. I just want to learn…" replied Sophie.

"Good!" said Magdalena, "An unknown desire is *the* desire."

Sophie's eyes glued to Magdalena's, her mind wandered in Eileen's, and her heart flew to Gol's; and some other fractions of what she was, to the other *Unknown-knowing* strangers she had been, perhaps, destined to cross paths with. 'An unknown desire is *the* desire' she repeated to herself inadvertently. Ironically, this student of biology, this deep-sea diver, had no clear understanding of the depth, where the unknown resides. Used to remaining on the surface, where there are only foam and foliage, she had always emerged with some random pictures stored in her short-term memory, her only form of memory, as she had turned her long-term memory into a stretch of stifling peat bog. Nonetheless, now she had found an unknown and unexplained *desire* within herself, the desire to dance. Will this flame-like desire set fire to her memory, or will it be only another dead flame at the end?

Chapter 20

"Cynthia! You are back again!" said Eileen, raising her hand and covering her mouth.

"Yeah, man, I am fucking back in this cunt-wasting place," said Cynthia, laughing cheerfully and opening her arms to embrace Eileen, "Man, I have badly missed you! Honestly."

"You seem to be fucking chuffed about it!" said Eileen, embracing her firmly, "What the fuck did you do this time?"

"Not a fucking hair removal spray this time," replied Cynthia, letting out a hearty laugh and pressing her face against Eileen's. You wouldn't be able to guess in a million years, mate. A book, mate. A fucking book... no, I shouldn't use the fucking word 'fuck'! It was an old religious book. I nicked it from a Jewish synagogue."

"So, you are still dabbling around your love escapades with God," said Eileen, smiling.

"No, not really. I was just fucking curious about the... the book itself," replied Cynthia; holding Eileen's hands, she asked, "Where is fucking little bird?"

"Who?"

"Sophie."

"You know Sophie!"

"I don't know her. She knows me," said Cynthia, now looking around eagerly.

"She is with Magdalena, taking dance lessons," said Eileen, pointing to a door at the very far end of the corridor, leading to a small yard.

"Let's go there. I would love to see how a fucking little bird dances," said Cynthia.

"The little bird is growing into an eagle," said Eileen, leading the way towards...

"Sophie!" said Cynthia as soon as they entered the yard.

Sophie turned around, released her hands from Magdalena's, and after

133

going through some long moments of hesitation, she dashed towards Cynthia and hurled herself into her arms.

"You are sniffing a scent. Aren't you?" asked Cynthia.

"I am not sure, Cynthia," replied Sophie, now exhaling heavily, "I am not sure."

"Sophie has now become a dancing mass of uncertainty, Cynthia," said Magdalena, holding her chin, "What the hell are you doing here!"

"My dear Magdalena!" uttered Cynthia, turning towards her, "Glad to see you again. They should have let you off the hook by now, those bloody eccentric judges. Yeah, mate, I am back again."

"Okay, welcome back!" said Magdalena, hugging Cynthia, "I am not that bothered about being let off the hook. I have been living a life of freedom here."

"I fully understand what you mean," said Cynthia, patting her back.

"You are looking at me as if you have been missing me!" said Sophie, sitting beside Cynthia on the lone bench in the fenced yard.

"I have been missing myself, Sophie," said Cynthia, "And that is why I have come here to see you."

"I don't understand what you mean. You sound like these bloody foreigners," said Sophie with half a chuckle, "Having a life of freedom in a prison! Magdalena said this just seconds ago. They just don't make sense, these foreigners."

"I was missing an important part of myself," said Cynthia, two large drops of tears appearing in her eyes and immediately rolling down her cheeks, "I saw it within you. This is the human way of seeing this, it has always been, and will always be, the way you and I knew very well in the past.

"And let me be fully *foreign* with you: if you have become *uncertain,* then remain so, or you will become too certain and deem yourself simply as irredeemable."

"What was it that you were missing?" asked Sophie in a heavily mixed tone.

"The very *'foreign'* and pleasantly lunatic part of my existence," said Cynthia, unaffected by Sophie's tone, "The love and innocence I lost to a hollowed, degraded and impertinent existence; the one-off opportunity of seeing my own face and making it worthy of being stored in a memory for ever; and also, the pleasure that turned into a gradually-killing poison.

134

Sophie, a big chunk of life is made of dreams and therefore, the ones who stop seeing and living it as such, will eventually relegate themselves to the terrain of animality."

"You committed an offence only to get yourself imprisoned so that…?" asked Sophie.

"I did," interrupted Cynthia, holding Sophie's face in her hands, "I have come here to make sure you are safe. The ones who murdered Garry and that undertaker and. . .well, would be much safer if you were dead too."

"It was me!" said Sophie, an unmistakable conviction ringing in her voice, "I poisoned their drink. I didn't like Garry. I was going to marry Mehmet and he was standing in my way."

"Well," said Cynthia, evidently set to ignore Sophie's ardent claim, "Why was it Mehmet?"

"Because he loved me in a different way. He would make me miss him," replied Sophie.

There was a pause, long and heavy, heavy differently—self-weighing and imposing. In Cynthia's mind Sophie turned into a wounded pigeon, haplessly trying to open her wings and fly away from a ferocious crow. Pecked, pecked and pecked again… a leg was taken… a wing broken… the heart ripped out. A world ended, the world of pigeon-hood… there was only a pair of eyes left, still seeing, still searching, still innocent.

"He would never make you miss him again," said Cynthia, getting up to her feet, "He would never love anyone else differently again. He is dead."

"Dead!" exclaimed Sophie, her face revealing raw pain—unjustified, coming from the depth of her biological existence, rather vagina-breaking than heart-breaking!

"He is dead. Your most favourite man ever! During the police investigation he tried his best to convince the police that you were a 'bitch from hell'! He downed a tiny bottle of whisky during a flight to Tenerife. Poor guy! He would have had an unforgettable honeymoon with his new wife, the very snide young Calypso. She would have been loved *differently*. She would have been made to miss him. Pure whisky, it wasn't. Morphine, enough of it, was the exquisite impurity that put an end to a man who was himself a chunk of sublime impurity. What does it have to do with us? Sophie's fingerprints were found all over the fucking bottle! He died three weeks ago, while you have been in this cunt-wasting place for exactly ninety two days! Perhaps you are from Hogwarts, on a mission to torture

135

the bloody muggles! Who is next, Sophie? How many more of these tiny life-ending bottles have you prepared? Gol believes Draco is the next."

"No!" exclaimed Sophie, her face blank, denoting nothing—neither heart-breaking nor vagina-breaking!

"Oh yes! A bride and a battalion of potential grooms! Another fucking Cynthia! Another fucking smeared piece of humanity!" said Cynthia, shoving her hands into the pockets of her jeans with a mild huff, "Did he also love you differently? Made you miss him? How about Garry, that metamorphosed rat? And that fucking rotten Greek god, Mr Christopher Lambrakis! We miss what we wish for. You have been missing dirt and, girl, you have managed to get loads of it! You might wonder—and you might not because you have not been allowed to wonder for ages—how I have managed to acquire this amount of detailed personal information about you: let me explain it to you in a very *foreign* way…"

"It is Gol. Isn't it?" interrupted Sophie, her eyes moistening.

"Good! Fucking good!" said Cynthia with a muffled chuckle, "So, you can *wonder*. Can't you, Sophie? It is Gol. There is a team of people around him, all doing their best to help him to pull Sophie out of this deep pit. It sounds very *foreign,* Sophie. Doesn't it? But none of those people wishes to think of a rational reason as to why Sophie has now stood in the centre of Gol's life! They have been going around gathering a piece of information from here and another from there, as if they are looking for their own lost pieces. Emily, my own young Emily, has become so *foreign* that she believes Gol's interest in Sophie is divine. See, my Emily believes in *divine* intention, interest…

Aren't they mere metaphysical nonsense? No, they are human dreams—and not fucking *foreign*—, or I should better say harmless mediums towards the mostly unattainable qualities we wish to acquire; and those qualities are nothing but fucking mollifying dreams. And a two-legged dreamless creature is nothing but a mass of hidden pain and shame."

"I just can't understand why it is me," said Sophie, looking at Cynthia through her tearful eyes, "He can simply have any woman he wishes."

"You do understand. You just lack enough courage to believe it," said Cynthia, her tone revealing an affectionate motherly smack, "Gol is coming to see you. This is going to be your last chance. Be wise. Try to be *foreign* for a short time. Do not let it pass you by."

"When is he coming?" asked Sophie in a moaning tone.

"This weekend," replied Cynthia, "And remember, I don't want him to know I have deliberately got myself imprisoned."

"Oh, okay. I won't tell him."

***

After performing a life-affirming feminine show of affection, Sophie pulled the chair back and throwing a rather apologetic look at Gol, she gently sat down beside Eileen, and glancing at her face over her shoulder, she smiled at Aisha, Maria and then at Emily, who was offering her a kind smile.

"Hello, Sophie," said Emily in a velvet tone.

Emily's face and tone of voice unhinged Sophie, a sort of unhinging that is meant to hinge properly. She gazed at Emily's face. She had never seen a face as beautiful as this, she thought. Almost enchanted by the beauty and tenderness she was eagerly observing, she wished she could become *foreign* for a while and rejoice herself in the flood of euphoria and appreciation surging in her heart. She wished she could incorporate Emily's immaculate beauty in to all sorts of *foreign* dreams and relate it to—to whatever, to a source where all the ideals exist, or to the more popular forms of it such as 'heaven', 'God' and the 'world of transcendence'. She remembered Cynthia's painting once again—the two mixed feminine faces, a fretwork imbued in reality and dream with a mixed taste and odour of honey and opium. Emily's beauty, needless to no superlatives, was unique, but the element in it that had made Sophie euphoric was unknown to her, demanding a level of mental elevation for it to be perceived, conceded and tasted.

"You didn't know Emily?" asked Aisha with a big smile on her round white face.

"Cynthia's daughter," said Gol.

"Emily, you are very beautiful!" said Sophie, her eyes moistening, her heart palpitating, her mind crazed, almost overwhelmed.

"Frighteningly beautiful. Isn't she, Sophie?" asked Gol, looking into her eyes.

Sophie said nothing. She became a heavy full stop before an impassable moment. Unable to bear Gol's eyes, involuntarily her eyes were directed at Eileen's face and then back at Gol's again, and asked in a rather childish tone, "Gol, can I have your jacket? It is too cold in here. Isn't it?"

137

Aisha smiled. Maria confirmed the low temperature in the room by wrapping her mustard shawl around her neck. Eileen, an always fuming warm-blooded creature, folded her arms on her chest so tightly as if she had been hit by a nipping sudden chill. Gol, an always unshackled soul in his body, found it unnecessary to testify the cold. He took off his jacket and handed it to Emily.

Emily wrapped the large jacket around Sophie's body and sat beside her with a smile on her face, a smile beyond description.

"I have always wanted to have a large jacket—something exactly like this one," said Sophie, rejoicing in her own words most childishly, her eyes shining and revealing a most pristine form of contentment.

"And now you have it," said Eileen, putting her arm around her, "I just hope you remain in it. It is large and warm. In it, you will look bigger and feel warmer."

Emily leaned forward and had a proper look at Eileen's face. Maria and Aisha looked at Gol, and so did Eileen and Emily; four pairs of eyes, all conveying the same request, met Gol's. Folding his arms on his chest, as it was his habit whenever dealing with emotions, he rejected the request with a touch of pain and ample conviction sitting in his black piercing eyes.

Emily hugged Sophie. Maria and Aisha offered her two rather modified but warm smiles. Eileen and Gol shared a wise and fully understood smile.

After some long lingering minutes of dead silence, Gol got to his feet, walked over to Sophie, and stood before her. Sophie raised her head, and seconds later, she stood up. Looking at Gol, up and down, she said in a childishly excited tone, "Gol, I saw you in a dream just hours before—you know what I mean. And you were dressed in the same clothes: the very sky-blue shirt and this pair of black jeans! And more interestingly, the same wristwatch with this beautiful green dial! Dreams are strange. Aren't they, Gol?"

"Dreams are, indeed, very strange, Sophie," said Gol, now looking at Sophie's long hair.

"I knew, David told me, that you were not a fan of wristwatches. I was intended to buy you one but—but—I just didn't," said Sophie, raising her arms, apparently to throw them around in regret or... but instead, she held the back of her hands before Gol's eyes.

Gol smiled, turned around and paced the length of the room with his hands in his pockets. He paced back and stood before Sophie, crossed his arms on his chest and said, "Sophie, you are not going to miss your last chance. Are you?"

"It was strange right from the beginning. Wasn't it, Gol?" asked Sophie, half her face a full picture of innocence and the purest of desires and the other simply a picture of misery, guilt, confusion and exasperation.

"It would take you only a whit of courage," said Gol, coming to an abrupt halt and throwing an involuntary look at his own arms, perhaps a passing temptation of stretching them out and holding Sophie's shoulders, "You have already gone through the pain of it, the elevating pain of becoming a butterfly. I know you live in a time and age when butterflies are being turned into slugs! Strange time, Sophie. Isn't it? In such a bizarre age of mockery, it is a rare opportunity for us, for both of us, to share the beautiful story of saving an almost emerging butterfly. Flowery language. Isn't it? The language of human soul. The elegant language of dreams and rationally rationalised 'irrationalities'! The language of creating a shield against the inevitable eventuality of falling into the pit of amnesia and dementia headfirst. Sophie, you need to recognise and learn this language. If I ever hear you have spent another single minute of your life on studying science, you will never see me again. You have already taken gigantic steps towards turning yourself into a fully unnatural creature. Any more science and you would simply put an end to your human form of existence. The disappearance of God was a disaster because He was the biggest of dreams, though somewhat nightmarish. And thereafter, humankind plagued other dreams, and eventually saw them off in a promenade of *rationality,* and for the second time, became too wise, so much so that they did not notice their nakedness—the *shame* had also been plagued and seen off! Naked, exposed and dreamless, they were devoured by their own bodies and became resistant to dreams for good. And thereof, a self-existent dream emerged, materialised and named itself *suicide.* And thereon, another vital concept was distorted: uniqueness was forced to mean uniformity, an act that required a defusing and disturbance of the hormones. I am not talking science fiction, Sophie. I am talking about the untouchable but neglected human soul."

Some more silent but deafening moments. Sophie's face became a collage of fast-flickering images, conveying their messages from a timelessness to another, from a non-existent spot to another. She stared at Gol's wristwatch so intently as if she was waiting for it to be exploded. At

139

last, she blinked, took a step forward and asked, "Gol, can I—can I have your wristwatch as well?"

Gol walked towards Emily, took off the watch and handed it to her. Emily's large blue eyes slang a question at Gol's. Maria and Aisha's eyes revealed the same question. Gol's eyes provided no answer but a touch of a very solemn pain distorting his face.

"Too big for your wrist," said Emily, laughing.

"I like it. I like it. I like big watches! I have always been intended to buy one!" said Sophie, her face turning rosy, her eyes changing colour, now full green, then whitish jade.

"Sophie, we have got to go now," said Emily, holding her face in her hands, "Tell my mum that I am so proud of her. Gol believes we should leave her alone with how she has decided to put her pieces together, that is why we are not going to visit her today."

"Maria, stay with Gol," said Sophie, as Maria turned around to follow Gol and others.

"I will, Sophie. Take care of yourself."

"I think Emily is unhappy with you, Gol," said Maria, as soon as Gol pulled out of the parking.

"She wanted me to give Sophie a hug," said Gol, turning in to the main road.

"She was begging for it," said Aisha, looking at Gol's face in the rear-view mirror.

"Emily will one day thank me for denying Sophie a hug at this stage," said Gol, smiling at her, "A badly needed touch becomes a piece of memory, and if not received and registered properly, it would turn into an infected wound. Sophie's soul, at this stage, is too repellent to be able to deal with anything that carries a level of authenticity. Emily's soul is gaining more and more depth and insight. She thinks, and she is right to think so, that it would only take one single hug to save Sophie, but she does not know the one-off nature of all the *single* things that could save and heal. No wise soldier would use his last bullet, the only one left for him, carelessly."

"Gol, it is cold. Do you want to use my jacket?" asked Emily in an apologetic and so very motherly tone, a tone echoing out from her unconscious.

"No son has ever been privileged with having such a kind beautiful mum," said Gol, laughing from the bottom of his heart, a laugh coming from an untouched corner of his heart, "If you think I am your son, so let it be."

Emily joined Gol, and soon after, Maria and Aisha followed suit. There was an explosion of laughter and contentment.

To Maria, this sample of nature, this owner of an always-purging soul and an always-self-disabusing mind, Gol had appeared, the moment she had stood before him, as a multilateral existence within which there was a crucible where each piece of pain would be turned into a shining gem of knowledge and realisation. He had looked at her as if they had known each other for centuries, as if they had a shared but unfinished tale back in a time when affection and passion were ends and not means and excuses. And when he had opened his arms, she had flown into them like a sacred bird flying towards a sacred shrine. 'I did not know Sophie could afford to have friends like Maria!' he had said.

"Gol, would you mind to tell us the details of Sophie's case?" asked Maria, as soon as they sat at a table in a restaurant Gol had promised to take them to, "So that we would be able to help you better."

"Good suggestion," said Gol, "Well, listen carefully. You might have thought of Draco and Calypso as the prime suspects, in which case you wouldn't be that wrong. Dragging Christopher, or even Anita, into this story could also be justified in terms of the conformity of the existing aspects to this case. But I am certain that there is an evil mind behind this story, a psychopathic spiteful mind, a creation of Garry's mind."

"A creation of Garry's mind?" asked Aisha, narrowing her eyes.

"There must be a very close connection between this person and Garry," said Gol, "And I strongly believe there also must be a close connection between this mysterious person and Miss Julie Atkins. Apparently entering the world as a loner and leaving it as such, we have not been able to trace this undertaker back and find her footprints in this case. Having said that, Franco believes Anita could well be the key to unravelling this and the whole story. At the moment, Anita is grappling with a severe and draining form of depression, and therefore, we should wait and see if Franco's affection for her can turn her around."

"Oh, I am so happy for Anita," said Maria, "She deserves love and peace."

"Only a big miracle can turn such a woman around," said Aisha.

141

"It is there, the miracle, the biggest of them. Is there any miracle bigger than love?" said Emily, two blue flames burning in her large blue eyes.

"Emily!" exclaimed Maria, pressing her face against hers, "You have become too *foreign!* You actually look like a beautiful dream, a fairy tale in an ideal place. And I hope you are right with believing that love can turn Anita around."

"Gol believes I will one day become the most *foreign* woman who ever existed," said Emily, leaning on Gol's arm, "And then I would become the mother of the world, a brand-new Eve, giving birth to brand new children."

"I wish you a brand-new Adam!" said Gol, kissing her on the head.

Chapter 21

"My first day. The university is waiting for Emily to arrive," said Emily, her eyes an exhibition of gratification and pure love, "Gol, I want to thank you, and I have been thinking to find the best way of doing so. As you have always been encouraging me to stay away from clichés, I am not going to say that 'I am unable to put it into words'. Instead I am going to put it into words and say to you: Gol, I will never take you for granted."

"The best possible way! Very wise," said Gol, smiling, "That is why I believe philosophy is the best subject for you to study."

"I am off," said Emily, hoisting her backpack over her shoulder, "And by the way, I have managed the Latin course as well. And then, I will, as you put it, invade all the Romance languages. And Gol, don't forget tonight's dinner, Zereshk Polo ba Morgh (Barberry Pilaf with Chicken), and above all, the next part of the fabulous story of brother Sohrab and Afsoon."

"Sure, I won't. I wish you endless hunger for knowledge," said Gol.

Minutes later, Gol's phone rang. It was Clement, the pleasantly loquacious Clement. He set the phone on the speaker and went, "Hoy, Clement?"

"Brother Gol, how is it going?" asked Clement, in a kinder-than-usual tone.

"Is everything all right, Clement?" asked Gol, his usual response to Clement's overly kind tone.

"Oh yeah. No worries," replied Clement with a flutter in his voice, "Just wanted to let you know that Sophie's parents are here. I ushered them upstairs. They are sitting in the office, waiting for you. No worries. David is with them."

Gol tossed the mobile phone on the couch and walked towards the bathroom. Standing before the large mirror, he kept staring at his own face, as if trying to read something written on it. It was ages ago when he had done the same: when Cynthia's parents had called him 'a fucking bloody foreigner'. Back then, he had wished he could have asked Brother Sohrab's soul to leave his body so that he could have had his own soul in charge for a couple of hours. Back then, though full of youthful pride and bravado, he had failed. Back then, he had wanted to break some bones! The bones of some necks, the stands on which some haughty heads would get the chance to jut out and spew arrogance and dirt at the face of love. The child of a rough land, a land wronged by the heaven and the earth in the most blatant manner, had allowed brother Sohrab's soul to say the last word: *a neck-breaker will never become a lover.*

And now, years later, the same child from the same land, with a hastily greying head, was staring at his own face with the same urge crazing in his head. He shut his eyes and merged them with the mirror. An apparition, Sohrab and his own sister, Afsoon… and perished roses… He turned the light off, swallowed his anger, dashed out of the bathroom, grabbed his phone and his jacket and left.

Mr Barry James Grandeur, Sophie's father, a rather tall man with a long and barren face (no sign of facial hair ever grown on it could be seen), and a rather thin long and slightly crooked nose, was so very akin, in terms of appearance and facial features, to Garry and Miss Julie Atkins. The only difference was that this gentleman was white and rather ginger-ish; and moreover, his Englishness was immune to even a second thought. The moment of truth, it landed as Mr Barry James Grandeur opened his mouth only to prove himself as accomplished and meritorious as that late rat-lover and that late undertaker from the *academia!* Reposed inwardly and outwardly, Mr Barry James Grandeur was a mine of overly abraded mettle and merits, all needless to superlatives, all self-appraised, all self-tested, all self-justified, all coming from the depth! Adding to his already superfluous qualities, the art of rhetoric and the craft of articulation, one would not dare to question his lofty place in the world!

"Nice beard, young man," said Mr Barry James Grandeur, sitting cross-legged and looking at David through his small and unblinking eyes, "It is as if you have been, I should say, cut out for growing and keeping such a marvellous self-presenting beard. There is, it is believed, a bit of science in beards: when gently stroked, the beard causes some positive changes to take place in the brain—you know, hormones and all that. But mind you, I should maintain a level of aversion when it comes to those barbate Muslims and their pathological desire for keeping beards. Those bewhiskered deranged dark creatures are the products of some faulty genomes, to wit,

144

wrong instructions and wrong results. Dabbing on this subject with a touch of cautious consideration, and bearing in mind that there is a bit of science in this as well, I should assert that stroking a Muslim beard would not yield the same result as that of yours would. It is certain, as it is backed by science, that when stroked, a Muslim beard would create some badly deranged electrical waves in the brain and turn it into a diabolic circuit of an unknown nature. I should optimistically hope that your beard is not the result of an imitation of your Muslim boss."

"I am a Muslim, sir!" said David in a playful tone, stroking his beard in the manner of one of those Imams he had once bumped into in Birmingham.

Before Mr Barry James Grandeur could summon another piece of his *self*-infested opinions, the door was gently pushed open and Gol appeared at the threshold. Walking in, he threw a hello at Mr Barry James Grandeur, and putting his right hand on his chest, he offered a warm hello to the quiet-looking woman sitting beside him. Getting himself calmly seated opposite Mr Barry James Grandeur, he kept stroking his beard for some long lingering moments.

"Mr Barry James Grandeur and his wife, Elizabeth, Sophie's parents," said David.

"I am glad to have met you," said Gol, still stroking his beard.

"Sir, may I ask you to stop stroking your beard?" asked Mr Barry James Grandeur, sounding as posh and demanding as Tony Blair, "Let us get directly to the point, if you may, my dear sir."

"Well, get to the point," said Gol, in his trademark laconic tone.

David threw a fleeting look at Mr Barry James Grandeur, walked over to the table, and pulling the chair beside Gol's back, he said, "Get to the point, sir."

"Well," said Mr Barry James Grandeur, evidently intended to sound as posh, erudite and decisive as possible, "After having traded some very much considerate and profound words with this young unique piece of a man, Mr Draco Christodoulou, the son of the late dear Garry Christodoulou, we have now concluded, without a speck of reservation, that you are behind this crime, this horrendous crime that is going to consume the life of my beloved child."

A heavy exasperating silence engulfed the room. Gol's left arm stretched out involuntarily, perhaps to prevent David from reacting. He landed his heavy gaze on Elizabeth's face, an older version of Sophie's, he observed. Identical, almost identical, the same green eyes containing the same inexplicable hue of innocence; the same finely freckle-bespattered face; the same unmistakeable illusive precious desire, a most-cherished-for desire, in the depth of her eyes. Elizabeth failed to meet Gol's eyes. A roughshod of pain distorted her forehead and wriggled down to her face and made her lips shiver.

"Go on with the point, sir!" asked David, a tinge of controlled anger detectable in his tone, his blue eyes growing darker.

"The depravity of your nature could well be perceived by a fairly virtuous mind," said Mr Barry James Grandeur, his eyes now as fiery and scornful as those of a man of God, like those of a priest within the Inquisition, "You deceived and abused my beloved child and then, with an unutterable level of cruelty, you used my beloved child as a bait to get rid of Garry, that epitome of virtue and unmatched humanity. She escaped from your bestiality and took refuge to those people of superlative virtues and unprecedented geniality, not knowing that she was going to be victimized."

"What the hell are you talking—?" shouted David.

"David!" interrupted Gol, "Go on, sir."

"With those people," said Mr Barry James Grandeur, throwing a damp warning look at David, "Well, my beloved child would have been bestowed upon pure and unconditional love and ample respect; and above all, she would have been directed to the path of righteousness. It is utterly unnameable, your degenerate nature and your apathetic attitude. Human imagination would definitely fail to conceive your despicable state of mind. Thinking of what this refined piece of humanity, Mr Christopher Lambrakis, could have added to the life of my beloved child had she been left alone by you, makes me really angry and pushes me towards insanity. Nevertheless, I am immensely happy that it is not over for her, not yet. She could still be privileged by being loved and protected by this edified piece of a man, Mr Draco Christodoulou. I have already managed it with him: he is going to, as he gave me his unwavering words, drop the case against my beloved child, and have her as the apple of his eye, the love of his life. To do so, he has put forth a number of conditions one of which is related to you, dear sir. So, listen carefully: he, this finest piece of a man, wants you to leave my Sophie alone. Failing to do so, I am warning you, dear sir, would bring about dire consequences for you! And not to hold back anything in reserve, I would also like to inform you that Mr Draco, this gentleman of gentlemen, and his very wise and adorned sister, Miss Calypso Christodoulou, are set to sue you, and I am also set to support them with all the means available to me. You will definitely face the unmistakable face of justice."

Gol pushed the chair back, and getting to his feet, he touched David's shoulder, indirectly asking him to behave himself and remain silent. He shoved his hands into the pockets of his trousers and gently walked to the end of the office. There, he stood before a large tableau on the wall, showing an elephant and some men inside a dark room. He walked back and stood before Mr Barry James Grandeur, his hands still in his pockets. Looking at David, who was stroking his beard, he formed a smile on his face, pulled his hands out of his pockets, crossed them on his chest and said, "Mr Barry James Grandeur, you were ushered to this world through an untouched and unfucked vagina, while the vagina that led me to this world was a well-fucked and pampered one. Therefore, I think I have nothing to say to you."

David, still stroking his beard, looked at Gol and the look on his face, and seconds later, he burst into shattering laughter, a rising and falling one, a laughter defying rhythm and note.

"Oh, my God!" uttered David, through his now blasting laughter, "The untouched and the unfucked vagina! This is fucking great! And fucking true!"

"Hoy!" said Gol, putting his hand on David's head, perhaps asking him to laugh only at the untouched and unfucked vagina! He offered Elizabeth a smile, turned his face towards Mr Barry James Grandeur and said, "Sir, take you auspicious leave and do whatever you wish."

"Sir, I will see you in a court of law!" said Mr Barry James Grandeur, got up and marched towards the door. Elizabeth threw a heart-breaking look at Gol and followed her husband.

"Elizabeth," called Gol while she was reaching for the door.

She turned around and looked at Gol with her head tilted. Nothing was said. She nodded. The door was pulled open. The door shut.

"Gol, you should have allowed me to slag off that arrogant guy!" said David, ruffling his hair with his right hand and fisting his left.

"He did not deserve it, boy," said Gol, looking at David's thick, well-trimmed and very soft-looking beard, "Not even good enough to be slagged off. He has been watching Coronation Street and Eastenders even before

147

they were made! Nothing can penetrate his ego and remind him of the need for correction. An absolute caveman—logic-proof and barren, rotten in his own juice."

"What are we going to do next, Gol?" asked David, smoothing his hair with both hands.

"Nothing," said Gol, smiling, "Go to the kitchen and get us some food. Due to going through these really hectic days, we have not been able to have a proper chat with each other. I need to know what David has been up to recently. Oh, by the way, contact your mum and ask her to be dead vigilant. And tell her how Sophie's dad was tumbled out of an untouched and unfucked vagina!

"Perhaps she would fancy painting one, a mixed vagina, half Eastern half Western!"

"This is brilliant, mate!" said David, blasting a laugh out, "She definitely deserves a proper laugh. I will tell her."

Gol walked over to the large window at the very far end of the office, opened it, and inhaled a good deal of the fresh air. Looking round the small parking area aimlessly, he remembered the day he had been told about Sophie standing in the rain. *'The dog was looking at me as if I was the foulest person ever existed! And the seagull... as if I was the most perfect thing ever existed!'* she had told Clement. He looked at a very old Land Rover parked by the opposite stonewall. It took him a full minute to realise that it was his own, the old green simple reliable Land Rover he had bought back in his prime days. He looked at the old vehicle again, as if he had never seen it before. He thought of himself. It took him another full minute to realise that there was no *self to* think of, not a specific confined form of it, there was, he felt, unconsciously, a fully conscious presence, flowing, rippling, waving, meandering, bulging and innately existent, positively aimless.

A couple of seagulls landed on a large black bin. A dog barked in the background. The cloudy sky let it fall, heavy, hasty and out of note and rhythm.

"Gol, come on, mate. Let's eat," said David, putting a large tray on the table, "You must be starving. Eating a meal a day, I just can't understand how you have been doing this all these years."

"The quality of pleasure comes from its quantity," said Gol, pulling the chair back, "The less you ask for it the more you enjoy it. As David's mind

148

needs a bit of more time to understand these types of subjects, I think we should eat and listen to David's narration of what he has recently been up to."

"First of all, allow me to thank you for allowing me to use the word 'mate' again," said David, laughing, "Yeah, mate, David has been up to an array of some bloody amazing things."

"First tell me about your beard and the secret to its thickness and softness," asked Gol, touching his own beard and looking at David's.

"It was this Asian woman," said David, putting the basket of chapatti beside Gol's plate of grilled Chicken Tikka, "I told her I wished to grow a beard like Gol's, and she gave me a very simple recipe."

"And who was this Asian woman?" asked Gol, a playful smile appearing on his face, "I suppose you have been a bit too naughty and too busy, growing some appetite for the mature things!"

"Oh, Gol, no, honestly not," said David, his face slightly blushed, "It is not her. It is her daughter, Nadira. She is well on her way to becoming another—another—"

"David, you are allowed to use the word 'fuck'. Be at ease, boy," said Gol, laughing.

"Gol, having a conversation with you is like playing football with Lionel Messi!" said David, smiling appreciatively, "Yeah, as I was saying, she is well on her way to becoming another fucking hot sizzling juicy bumpy chunky swaying mass of—of—of just fuck! She is just amazing Gol! Just fucking stunningly amazing! Aziza the tree and Nadira the fruit! If the fucking tree can simply kill you, well, the fucking fruit can simply turn you into a handful of fucking ash!"

"Do you love her?" asked Gol, squeezing half a lime on his meal.

"I do fucking love her, Gol," replied David, the depth and the nature of his desire being revealed in the depth of his blue eyes.

"I have never imposed my own takes on life on you. Have I, David?"

"No, never."

"But now I wish to give you a precious piece of advice on your love for Nadira," said Gol, tearing a chapatti in half, "No sane man would bite an unpeeled orange. Learn to peel your orange. Seeing the heat and the juice and the bumps in a woman before seeing the mine of the divine charm, love and affection within her, is like biting an unpeeled orange. Learn how to peel your orange, boy. I appreciate this viable level of sensuality within you,

149

which is of course a sign of a fully functioning mind and body, but putting the physicality of a woman before what she is inside, is a gross travesty of goodness and an irreparable betrayal of the one and only miracle."

"Gol, what is the one and only miracle?" asked David, looking into Gol's eyes.

"Women are the one and the only miracle," replied Gol, reaching for the basket of mixed fresh herbs, one of the staples of his diet, "We are living in a modern age of the cavemen. I do not expect you, the young caveman, to understand what I mean, but as I have always seen every single human being as a universe, I should say that we all can afford some rebellious moments and regain our long-lost individualities. Only a rebellious man would eventually learn how to peel an orange."

"Gol, I promise you I will one day master the art of orange-peeling," said David, the ever-pristine appeal of youthfulness and the priceless innocence converging on his face and turning him into a mini Jesus Christ! "I would also like to promise you that I will definitely see Nadira's mine of charm, love and affection first."

"Good caveman!" said Gol delightfully, "Now tell me the other stories."

"Let's begin with Mr Barry James Grandeur," said David, a good deal of sarcasm washing over his ruddy face, "The man who was tumbled out of an untouched and unfucked vagina! And who also has been watching Coronation Street and Eastenders even before they were made! He and Elizabeth have four children, three girls and one boy. Our Sophie, the centre piece of our now amazing story, is the eldest one in this family. They live in a tiny northern town where everything is flat, flat in all its aspects, the earth, the beers, the tyres, the rocks.   Except   noses!   The   other interesting thing in this habitat of flatness—I didn't see this with my own eyes—is a bovine farm whose inhabitants–the cows and oxen–speak, and they speak a German-sounding language! Some believe it is a hotchpotch of all the Nordic languages. But the funniest part of this was formed when Mr Barry James Grandeur, 'this fine piece of a man' and the manager of this farm, proposed that the language was actually Turkish, trying to substantiate his claim by referring to cows and oxen's tendency to cross their legs when speaking! He even set up a gallery exhibiting photos of Ottoman Sultans and prominent diplomats sitting cross-legged when speaking!"

"What a fabulous fabrication! What a fabulous bogus fable of

150

imagination!" said Gol, a gentle smile sitting in his eyes, "Have I ever enjoyed any other short story as much as I enjoyed this? Give me the conclusion to this before you move on to the next story."

"Well, based on our extensive detective efforts," said David, evidently itching to dig into his plate of Lamb Biryani, "Maria and I concluded that Mr Barry James Grandeur is a confidence-shattering, soul-infesting creature—even those speaking cows and oxen were not happy with him— and definitely responsible for Sophie's overall confusion and lack of courage."

"Good conclusion!" said Gol, "Eat your food and listen to me."

"But just to let you know that the gallery thing was not bogus," said David, laughing, "He actually set up the photo gallery to glorify the cross-legged sitting Turkish things! Perhaps his love for cross-legged things goes back to the way he was tumbled out of that untouched and unfucked vagina—cross-legged, I imagine, he jumped out!"

"Another good touch, David!" said Gol, "I want you to pull all your senses together, connect all synapses and focus on what we are going to do during the next week. We live in a society within which everyone carries a mask, and behind it they become whatever they wish to and do whatever they wish to do; and they all get away with whatever they do. Within such society the ones who fail to wear masks would seem as odd and deemed as potential dangers to the society! Not to waste any time, we must search for the *nicest* and the most *decent person* around Garry's business and household, a person with a golden mask on."

"Calypso is the only member of Garry's family who is worthy of wearing a Golden mask," said David, picking up a red radish from the basket of fresh herbs, "Draco was born with a golden mask, but when he grew up he sold and spent it on psychedelic drugs and gambling only to turn his brain into a chunk of dung. He is now wearing a second-hand silver mask, stolen from a charity shop by Calypso."

"David you describe things like those American writers do!" said Gol, smiling.

"What else would you expect when you coax or force people to read books," said David, laughing, "Emily is now well on her way to becoming an incarnated version of Emily Bronte!"

"Happy to hear that," said Gol, "There is a close connection, I suppose, between Calypso and the mysterious person behind this story. And I also…"

"Gol, surely the key to unravelling this story is in Anita's head!"

151

interrupted David, now stroking his beard sagaciously.

"Spot-on, David! Just like a good detective," said Gol, "But the problem is that Anita is now a hollow human being with a lost soul. It will take a good deal of time before even she manages to find some tiny traces of her almost vanished individuality. I believe in Anita's inherent decency, but her conscience, like her other faculties, needs time to regain a level of functionality. I just hope it isn't too late for her. Even a tree would have suffered the same had it been exposed to creatures like Garry and Draco for so long."

"If I am not mistaken, you are going to ask me to focus on Calypso," said David.

"You are not mistaken," said Gol, "We need to find out what she has been up to since the death of her dad. If I haven't been mistaken, and she is the one who finalised the murder plan, then she might have been busy trying to find a way to get rid of Draco too."

"I see," said David, nodding affirmatively, "Why did they get rid of Mehmet? He was only one of their staff."

"Judging him by the information Franco has acquired about him," said Gol, dipping a piece of bread into the bowl of yoghurt before him, "Mehmet used to be a scorpion, a type that could afford a good number of lethal stings within a short period. This type of scorpion can replenish their venom in a matter of minutes, making them capable of delivering stings after stings to whatever or whoever dares to stand in their way. Failing to see the dire consequences of stinging creatures like Draco and Christopher, time after time, he also became too oblivious to the already honed blade of revenge flailing around him, divorced his wife and married Calypso. What I have learned from his unfortunate end is that the mysterious person we are looking for could well be a rather young man. By marrying Mehmet, Calypso might have intended to hurt our mysterious man in one way or another. If this story isn't derailed, Calypso could be the last victim of it."

"So, how have the police approached Mehmet's murder so far?" asked David, lifting the glass of lemon water before him.

"They believe it was Sophie and Draco," said Gol, shaking his head, "But they haven't been able to find enough evidence to arrest Draco. They are now looking for a possible accomplice to Sophie, as they strongly believe Sophie had enough motives to murder Garry, that undertaker and Mehmet. I think we have said enough about this. Tell me the other stories."

"Based on the last overall accounting Mr Gibran has done," said David, picking up the last of the red radishes in the basket, "Your business has improved drastically."

"You mean our business, David?" asked Gol, brushing some breadcrumbs off his shirt.

"Gol, mate," said David, paused, dithered and paused again, evidently struggling to sort out his emotions and his thoughts "Mate, I—I just can't understand this."

"You don't need to understand it," said Gol, the most authentic fatherly tone ringing in his voice, 'Feel it, David. Understand what has to be understood, and feel what has to be felt. This is the modern disease—the confusion between the heart and the mind. A person suffering from such a degrading disease would always face the world with a rictal and silly smile. Becoming too mindful is the beginning of forsaking the heart and that, well, would definitely lead one to a station of no return: dementia, where one would lose it all. I do not expect you to fully understand me, but I expect you to try. You would lose nothing, boy."

There were some minutes of heavy silence. Gol got up and walked towards the large window. The rain had slowed down and gained a sort of rhythm and steady momentum. The seagulls were still patiently waiting for the bins to be overflowed. The old reliable Land Rover had contentedly given itself up to the rain. In a distance, some dogs were barking muffled, indifferent and dismayed barks; incorporated in each tone there was a sense of futility and dryness.

"Gol," said David, walking towards the window, "Would you please help me with this Nadira story?"

"Is it her family?" asked Gol, turning towards him.

"It is," replied David, his face now so very akin to that of John The Baptist, implying a deep desire to baptise and initiate himself into the sea of peace and love.

"Nothing, even God, cannot stand in the way of a true lover," said Gol, smiling, "Prove yourself as a true lover and leave the rest to me."

"Gol, mate!" exclaimed David, his face not able to handle the miscellaneous inner thoughts and desires rushing to it, "It is incredible that even God can't stop a true lover; and it simply means that a lover is even greater than God!"

"Bravo, David!" said Gol in an admiring tone, "And it is even more incredible that you have managed to learn the alphabets of the language that you have been deprived of: the language of heart and dreams. David, this

153

language doesn't have to make sense. If you tell your mind that a lover is even greater than God, it will definitely mock you; but your heart will fully understand it. Learn to use your heart as a kitchen and your mind as a workshop."

"Gol, can you tell me a bit more about the language that I have been deprived of?" asked David musingly.

"See, boy, you have just begun to throw questions at yourself and at your world," said Gol, stroking his beard, "All through the history, disheartened and indifferent masses have been turned into concrete slabs and used in the foundation of the empires. Concrete slabs don't ask questions, and therefore, they don't move or change, and this makes them most solid, the ideal base for the creation of what is called *greatness!* You are the inheritor of an empire and a good deal of *greatness.* Find a little alcove for yourself, kindle a light in your heart, make a cosy place in it for your Nadira, and live a viable life. Out there, nothing is going to change. The womb of the empire, the only part left of it, is still giving birth to concrete slabs! David, we live in a society that lies and believes its own lies, but thankfully we are both self-sufficient enough to stay away from it and live our own lives."

A heavy silence devoured David. The desire appearing in his eyes, reminded Gol of that he had spotted in Sophie's when he had visited her at the police station: the ardent desire for liberation, the unequivocal desire for being irresponsibly human.

In his neglected and rather subliminal intuition something sparkled, jumped and flared before his eyes, illuminating the world within him. He raised his right hand and placed it on his heart. It was beating, as it has been since it has been; he could not recall since when and how.   He pressed his palm against his chest, as if trying to scan and register his heart and the notes to which it was beating. He raised his head and looked at Gol and, for the first time, he felt no restraint, no reservation, now he could, he thought, gaze him in the eye as long as he wished. As he was turning around, he heard a gentle voice calling his name: *David, from now on I will not beat unless you ask me to.* It was his heart, he thought.

"David, ask Clement to make some Barberry Pilaf with Chicken for Emily," asked Gol, while David was walking towards the door.

154

Chapter 22

Mrs Aziza Baygum reposed herself on the chair somewhat ceremoniously, and with an air of casual forgetfulness, she took off her mustard headscarf, let her newly dyed thick hair down, smoothed the sleeves of her blotted pink Kashmiri long dress, and raised her head and looked at Gol. Engulfed by a deep calm feeling of full presence, Gol allowed Mrs Aziza Baygum to read his face through her inquisitive mind.

"My dear Gol," said Aziza, her large black eyes revealing a taste of some unsuccessfully suppressed or curbed connotations of what she was about to say, "May Allah bless you. Would you mind if I said, well, you look like a married man? Your eyes, they are reflecting a woman to me, a very charming but sad-looking woman. Your eyes, together, look like a clean lake in which a naked woman is leisurely swimming. And I wish, I pray to Allah, that it is true."

"What does she look like, this charming but sad-looking woman?" asked Gol, smiling.

"She looks like no other," replied Aziza, pushing her hair back, "Otherwise she wouldn't have been allowed to swim where she is swimming now."

It was not fortune-telling. It was Aziza-telling! It was the ultimate femininity and a blazing soul and a thirst-seeking body connected to a hidden mine of passion and sensuality, invigorated by justifiable guilt and a dual and always-warping worldview. Aziza was a daughter of God, but not the god she claimed to believe in, not Allah. She was, and she was secretly aware of that, the mortal daughter of one of those pleasantly corrupt mythological gods! Allowing herself a certain level of impertinence, craftily wrapped in a cut of Allah's shirt, Aziza was a clairvoyant in the terrain of love and fermented sensuality, and therefore she would never fail to detect it—even in the eyes of a man like Gol.

"Do I really look like a married man?" asked Gol, laughing.

"You have been looking like a married man for years now, my dear," said Aziza, her innate flirtatious and casually quizzical rhetoric coming on,

"Busy, bracing your faithfulness and patiently waiting for her to arrive. Old wine, you have become old wine. And someone has seen you as such. Limited with her tastes and wont to cheapness, she is still dithering, unsure if she should grab a cup and throw it to you. She is afraid of real drunkenness. A married-looking bachelor who has proudly been fathering two lovely children. How are they doing?"

"Well, very well. They are doing very well," replied Gol contentedly, "Aziza, I have come here to ask you for a favour."

"Gol asking Aziza for a favour! Go on then!" said Aziza, holding a tuft of her hair and giving a gentle slow-rippling twist to her upper body.

"It is about David and Nadira," said Gol, crossing his arms on his chest.

Aziza kept gently twisting and untwisting the tuft of hair around her forefinger. The slow-rippling twist in her torso got a touch intensified and seconds later, it wobbled down to her rather thick legs. Some sort of movement, unknown to Gol, appeared around her mouth, deepening the two lines at its corners. She was, it seemed to Gol, masticating, ritualistically, two small cuts of two different things, one being ground in the left of her mouth and the other in the right.

"Allah," uttered Aziza, letting the word out from the left corner of her mouth, "See, my dear Gol, I am—I am befuddled—I—I just don't know what to say. You know, my dear, after all the good you have done to me and my children... After Usman squandered the business and left us totally broke... You know, his unfortunate love for that English girl and all this... and falling into gambling... and losing faith in himself and humanity... You saved us. We are back on our feet again."

"Aziza, this is not a business. I am not asking for anything in return," said Gol, smiling.

"Oh, my dear Allah! My dear Gol," said Aziza, a pang of pain appearing in her eyes, "I know it is love. I know love is not, and should not, be approached as business. But as you are very well aware of it, I have always been following what Allah has said in the Holy Quran. You know, my dear, my Nadira being a very devout Muslim girl and your David being... well, a non-believer, Allah is against it. He has clearly said it in the Quran. Non-believers are unable to appreciate love and goodness. Because they are non-believers. They believe only in pleasure—cheap and easy-to-access pleasure. Sins, and the scourge Allah would verily impose on them. I took my sons back home and found two decent girls for them, two girls of

156

their own kind. And now they are happily living a life of faith and love. I want the same for my Nadira—a young man of her own kind.

"A messed-up woman is like a car without engine—worthless, useless. To a car as such, the road makes no sense. My life was messed up. Aziza, the woman, was messed up. I don't want this to happen to my Nadira. What would she get in the end? Dementia. Allah sheds tears when a woman falls into dementia. My husband was a good man, but he was not enough, or perhaps it was wrong of me to think so. When I married him, I was a very skinny anorexic almost skeletal dark girl who was more than happy, or even lucky, to have a husband of that calibre. But things, as they always do, changed: shortly after I gave birth to Usman, my body began to open up, and soon after I was transformed, as the society proudly let me know, into a *sexy* woman—the *hottest,* as they said! *Recognition,* the society gave it to me, and with it, came the demands. Society would not glorify a woman's backside for nothing! Aziza, the woman, was messed up. And now with a lost Allah and a de-glorified backside, she is preparing herself to say hello to dementia! You are listening to me with the same old patience. Aren't you, old boy?"

"I am," said Gol quietly.

Nothing was said for a while. They looked at each other as if they had just come across a few interesting and interestingly written lines in each other's mind. Aziza's began with Allah, Eve, Adam, Satan and a mischievous serpent, and continued with Adam thoughtfully and suspiciously counting his own ribs—did he know how to count? There were also hell and paradise: red hot thick rods for the ones who had failed, and milk, honey, round boobs and solidly swaying backsides for the ones who had spent half of their lives sitting on prayer rugs and counting their gains and rewards with strung turquoise beads. Eve remained in the background, holding her hands between her legs and wondering how her nameless and impersonal existence became so *private!*

Gol's was simple: Adam, sitting in the shade of an unknown tree and flipping through an unwritten book, was patiently waiting for God, Eve and the serpent to have the self-created discord among themselves concorded. He was patiently impatient to have a word with Eve over the newly coined concept of *privacy.*

"Gol," said Aziza, now looking into Gol's eyes while an epiphany, ascendant and transgressive, beginning to loom in her large eyes—Allah

157

was taking his heavy leave, and some gods and goddesses were descending, some mortal and some others immortal. Accompanying them, there were Jesus Christ and the very lush Marry Magdalena

"Gol, were you ever tempted to seduce me?"

Gol crossed his arms on his chest and stared at Aziza's face with a most genial smile sitting in his eyes. Aziza smiled. Gol smiled back at her, and seconds later, they shared a long and hearty laugh.

"Secretly, I think, you did, at least once," said Aziza, still laughing, "He said he wanted to keep a beard as thick and soft as yours, David. And I gave him the recipe. He is so fond of you. Secretly, he loves to imitate you; and to do so, he courageously swallows some of his unexamined English pride. I think I should stop being so cynical. Yes, I should give consent. I do, my dear Gol. Even Allah might be happy with it. He will be. He will also give consent."

"Thank you, Aziza," said Gol, stretching his hand out and touching hers, "David has begun to appreciate himself, and consequently, he will certainly not fail to appreciate the ones who are dear to him."

"Old boy, old wine," said Aziza, propping her chin on her fisted hand, "You know your words. Appreciation. This society has forgotten what and how to appreciate."

Chapter 23

"A small audience. Isn't it?" asked Gol, stirring his coffee.

"As you have already told us, this story is going to be a story of heart and pure love," said Emily, looking at Aisha, "Aisha and I have enough heart to listen to it. And if David bothers himself and shows us some, then we will be a big enough audience."

David's response was a smile and a ruffling of his hair and a gentle caressing of his beard.

"So, the Story of Brother Sohrab. Let's begin from the beginning," said Gol, "It was a time when the world had fought most of its seminal wars and had reckoned with a series of necessary or unnecessary revolts against itself. One of these wars, which had been launched a few centuries ago, was the war between God and traditions at one side and the rapidly flourishing but greed-infested human intellect at the other. As the new battle over dominance and the fierce competition over who could gain more and eat more had just begun, it came to pass that it was in Afghanistan's lot to host the bloodiest part of it. Afghanistan, Allah's last and only hard-to-penetrate stronghold, was not going to turn its back on Him.

"When the Russians invaded Afghanistan, the other big guys saw it as a serious threat to their interests and got involved with it in one way or another. And when Allah The Almighty also decided to get involved, many people were forced to flee their homeland and take refuge to their neighbours, carrying their pristine but rigid souls and their rich but neglected hearts with them. Some believed there was something underhand between Allah and the other side, believing Allah's fight was all but fake. But the faithful believed Allah was the only truth left in the world. It was an atrocious confrontation, an orgy of bloodshed; and it was all scripted by man."

"Why did the Russians invade Afghanistan?" asked Emily.

"Because if they had not, well, the others would have done it," replied Gol, taking a sip of his coffee, "A foothold, they were all looking for a foothold. Well, let's get back to our story. It was on a windy churlishly cold day when we set off for Iran. Due to the size of our family and the fact that we were not the poorest of the poor, the family's move to Iran was done relatively smoothly. As soon as we reached the border, we were let in. Right on the other side of the border, and just a few short steps into the soil of Iran, I felt a telling contrast: the air contained more oxygen, the wind gentler, the sky kinder, the earth softer, even the pebbles and the rocks, everything contained a tangible sense of change in it, everything was open to time and change. Having my sister's hand in mine, I felt that she was also amazed by the drastic differences between the two sides of the very narrow line separating the two countries.

"Walking into Iran with unknown fears of the unknown, we all knew that life would never be the same again for us. Before the war we were some people, and it was certain to us, some ordinary people with a streak of primitiveness still lingering within and without us. My dad was sort of a farmer and my mother, well, was only the wife of a farmer. Our small village and our small piece of land, as you may imagine, was our own planet, calmly orbiting around itself and rather impervious and oblivious to the other existing objects around it. Pervious, it was only to Allah, the smell of damp earth and the life-giving smell of bread. It was my sister, Afsoon, and I, the only children of this family. Soon after my mother let me into the world, she became infertile—a blessing in disguise, otherwise they would have definitely added to the number of future sufferers. We had a space shuttle—an old dilapidated cart, driven by a small old donkey! He would submissively carry Afsoon and me to a nearby village where there were a small old mullah and a small Maktab, and where we would be taught Quran, Sharia Law and a bit of poetry."

"Gol, how old were you and Afsoon at the time?" asked David

"Afsoon was fifteen and I was thirteen,'" replied Gol, taking another sip of his coffee.

"Is there any meaning to the name 'Afsoon'?" asked Emily.

"It means 'charm', 'spell', 'magic'," replied Gol, "Back to the story. We entered the land of abundance with an unknown compelling feeling squirming in the back of our mind. Deja vu, it was not. Imagine you have been separated from your mother for ages, and now you are back, so close to her, almost in a touching distance. You stand before her, put your hand on your heart and look into her eyes only to realise that she might not remember you; that you might not be remembered. It would give you ample

160

pain, and the pain would become ampler when you have no home to return to and cry your heart out within its walls. It was us and Iran: the wandered children and a mother affected by amnesia.

"After a long journey, we arrived in the beautiful city of Shiraz, the city of exquisite wine, rarefied poetry, lush gardens and ever-in-love nightingales. The whole city was like a lover, privileged with prosperity and abundance and all adorning aspects of a fulfilling existence. But an already full-blown war was going on. Iraq had been pitted against Iran. As a teenager who had been fed Quranic teachings by the parents who had also been fed the same stuff, I was overtly proud that God had descended on the soil of Iran after the revolution of 1979; that Allah and Iran were well on their way of routing out the heathens and restoring the ever-exalting fidelity in the world. We all were proud of this, except Afsoon."

"She had also been fed the same stuff. Had not she?" asked Emily, throwing an apologetic look at Aisha, as if she had stolen this question from Aisha's mind.

"A very wise question, Emily," said Gol, throwing a smile at Aisha, "Because Afsoon was a lover. Because she was too human. Lovers would not get it wrong. It is within them, the truth. Afsoon was a lover and destined to meet her match, Brother Sohrab.

"We moved to the nearby countryside in search of agricultural or other menial jobs. When we entered this small village, it was early morning. The village had woken up, done its yawns and stretches and prepared to embrace the very close-looking sun. It was, the gently rising sun, much bigger and warmer than that of ours back in Afghanistan. Ours was too far and not warm enough, always late and always in a rush to set.

"There came flocks after flocks of sheep and goats, flooding the flat sweep leading to the green low hills, dales and valleys. A couple of dogs and a couple of shepherds appeared from a flank of the village and from another, an old man, leisurely straddled on the back of his white mare-like donkey, whistling a very merry tune. They all approached us simultaneously and came to an abrupt halt.

"Ridiculously curious and somewhat shocked, the two young shepherds blinked several times, looked at each other with widened eyes, and when became certain they were not dreaming, they burst into laughter. The dogs followed suit by throwing at us some rather defused and playful barks. The old man and his well-fed and stout donkey took an immediate

161

and different liking in us: they both looked at our loose clothes, our very old-fashioned loafers—almost primitive—and our turbans, mine and my dad's. Of my mother and Afsoon there was nothing exposed to be beheld—they were two burqa-clad human beings. Pushing up the large brimmed straw hat on his head with the tip of his finger, he threw a musing look at my dad and said, 'You must be from the past! Far back in time, perhaps from the days of catapults and flint and steel'! He was right and wrong at the same time: we were from the past with regard to some aspects of what we were, but we had seen Kalashnikovs, rockets, helicopters, thunderous jet fighters…

"The rest of the villagers did not dare to approach us at first. A gaggle of them took a few very cautious steps towards us and stood at a stone-throw away from us, whispering to each other in low muffled voices. A few gigantic dogs appeared and menacingly growled at us. My father stood before us, stretching his long arms around to defend his family. A few young boys threw pebbles and some others fresh cow dung at us. As we were anxiously looking on and as the now incensed dogs were now snarling at us, a young boy entered the scene. He directly walked over to me and gently holding my hand in his, he asked my parents and Afsoon to follow him with a gesture of his head. He was as calm and assuring as an old sage. He walked us across the village, and when we entered a narrow alleyway, my father's already hesitant feet refused to go further.

"'Father, we are safe' said Afsoon, grabbing his hand.

"'Grandma!' called the young boy as we entered the front yard of a rather large muddy house with freshly thatched walls with a fine mixture of clay and straw.

"'Is that you, Sohrab?' asked Sohrab's grandma, a rather tall old woman, coming out of a room which looked like a pantry.

"'Grandma, remember what you were telling me the other day?' asked Sohrab with an old pristine ring in his tone.

"'Yes, my son' replied Grandma, now staring at the four strange-looking strangers standing before her with a tinge of fear of forgetfulness appearing in her eyes, she added, "I said. . . What did I say? Oh yes, I said the point in being alive and living is to be seen; and therefore if there is no one around to watch you live, so there will be no point in existing. Yes, I think I said this"

"'Would you allow these people to stay here with us, live and watch you live?' asked Sohrab, a well-conceived and substantiated ray of altruism glowing in his eyes.

"Grandma's response was priceless: she walked over to us with her long arms open. My father's face was a face to watch when Grandma tapped him on the back and called him 'brother': he took the longest sigh of relief ever, as if his one and only wish had been fulfilled.

"Half an hour later, we were sat on a red Persian carpet, drinking tea with fine sugar chunks while our now slackened bodies and somewhat appeased souls were absorbing the mild morning sunshine.

"It took us only an hour to learn that Grandma was a mine of humour, and pleasantly witty. 'Brother Hassan' said Grandma, looking at my father, 'Would you mind if those two female things pulled themselves out of those sacks?'

"With my father's immediate permission, Afsoon and my mother took their burkas off, and with a deep sense of appreciation appearing on their faces, they looked at Grandma's beautiful face and offered her two big smiles.

"'I would not blame you, brother Hassan' said Grandma, now nostalgically mesmerised by the wild beauty of the two 'female things', 'You have two moons. You need those sacks. Moons must be hidden in sacks. Moons are dangerous, and that is exactly why they are moons'.

"Grandma, with a touch of intuitive gnostic comprehension and ample empathic abilities, would, inadvertently, philosophise almost everything in her own simple way of collocation.

"'We all are wont to work, Fatima. Aren't we?' said Grandma, smiling at my mother, 'So, I will show you around the house first while Sohrab is making two of the rooms ready for you, and then give you some work to do. Well, let us begin from the front yard where we are now. Until a while ago, you would see five hundred karakul sheep in this yard. See, all those folds round the yard; they would become packed with sheep. Just imagine how many lambs we would have during the spring. They left, my three sons and their wives. They moved to the big city. I don't know why. Perhaps to eat ice cream and drink, I don't know what they call it, Pepsi, Pepsis, something like this. Then my husband fell ill. Opium, they said, would rejuvenate him! The government had put all the elderly on opium for the purpose of rejuvenation! They all got pickled in their graves, and then turned into dust. Mine died while inhaling big gulps of the opium smoke to

163

get his youth back quickly! He busted his lungs. Come here, see this large room, look at those barrels and casks, those big and small kilner jars… look at that. You know what it is… that large leather bag… I would process my dairy in it… A calf's hide; myself did the tanning and the curing. There was a life here back then.

"'And the bakery, that small room. A large tandoor and all other tools. The smell of bread, the closest to God's. And there, as you can see, within those low walls, I would grow vegetables. See, how large it is, this fertile swathe of land. See, my dears, when there are no eyes around to watch you and either enjoy or hate whatever you do, you will become idle, and it is when life begins to trickle out of you. The world, mark my words, will suffer a premature death. Oh, I just don't know these deforming palates and changing appetites. Ice cream, Pepsi, opium, rejuvenation, Allah, infidels. I think I am almost there where one would lose it all. But I know how to lose it all: I would lose it hilariously!'.

"'I promise I will watch you and rejoice in whatever you do, Grandma' said my mother, turning around and embracing Grandma.

"'And I will envy your hilarious way of looking at the world' said my father, laughing.

"'You people are some wild apple trees' said Grandma, her black and still sighted eyes taking an air of ruefulness, 'You have shades and fruits within you. Well, let's deal with our emotions in a better time, when we have sorted out our heads. Now, right now, at the very passing moment it sprang to my mind… Perhaps we could… No, we can begin doing it right now: you two, father and son, this swathe of very fertile land needs a proper aeration. Dig and prepare it for a large variety of vegetable seeds. There, see that door, behind it you will find shovels and some other tools you might need. And you will be rewarded with the lunch of your life. I will make it, with the help of these two female things!'.

"And that was the beginning of the dream-like and most important and the richest part of our lives, lived with a rare grandma and her rarest grandson.

"Just a mile out of the village and skirting some low green hills, Grandma owned a rather large piece of agricultural land which had been abandoned since the death of her husband. My father and I, with Sohrab's help, brought it back to life, growing wheat and some other summer crops. My mother and Afsoon were busy looking after a hundred sheep that

Grandma had bought just three weeks into our stay with them.

"With the immediate worries over the bread and butter and shelter gone, Afsoon and I began to grow on Sohrab, and it was then that our story began to write itself, with Sohrab in the centre of it. So, who was Sohrab? Twenty years of age, he was the youngest child of Grandma's only daughter who had married a townsman at a very young age, meaning that Sohrab was actually a town boy. Being as natural as the nature itself, and understandably, not very much in favour of the fuss and the buzz and the unnatural colourfulness of the big city and, of course, the loneliness of his grandma, he had moved to the village at the age of seventeen. By the time we bumped into each other, he had managed to earn two diplomas, one in Economy and the other in Literature. In all, he was like a river: flowing and meandering was his amusement and reaching the ocean his goal. Shortly after we settled and got to know our duties and directions, Sohrab took the lofty task of educating Afsoon and I upon himself. Immaculately principled, he would manage our time in a way that no seconds of it would pass us by without being used."

"Why did you and Afsoon not go to school?" asked Emily.

"As I mentioned," said Gol, "Allah had just descended on the soil of Iran, and it was chaos, *as it was in the beginning*. Allah and the ones who had invited him to descend were too busy to consider these sorts of *unimportant* matters. We were not allowed to go to school at that time! Why? Only Allah and his friends knew! It was only after the mayhem created by Allah and his cronies had died down that *Iran* saw that it was wrong. Iran, due to its primordial culture, has always been good at putting the wrong things right."

"What did Sohrab look like?" asked Aisha.

"Handsome," replied Gol, asking Emily for another coffee with a gesture of his head, "Muscular and very manly. And above all, half soul half mind."

"Was he a fan of beard?" asked David, smiling.

"Oh yes, it was the fashion of the time," replied Gol, "I was itching to grow up and keep a beard like his."

"Tell us about Afsoon, Gol. What did she look like?" asked Emily, gently pushing the cup of coffee towards Gol.

"Dad Pashtun and Mum Hazara, imagine what you would get," replied Gol, turning his face towards Aisha, "I think Aisha, this ardent student of

165

mythology, should do the justice to this infusion of wildness, charm and beauty."

"You would definitely get a goddess!" said Aisha admiringly, "I have some Afghan friends some of whom are Hazara and some other Pashtun. I can easily envisage Afsoon's face and stature."

An inner gaze glazed Gol's eyes. The initiating piece of a bittersweet tale, perhaps. After a long quiet pause, he continued, "They, Sohrab and Afsoon, were the universal mediums of love and affection.

"Their presence would guarantee leniency and kind compromises among people. Intrinsically composed and consequently wise and soulful, they knew how to receive people's impulses, modify and convey them back to them. As some 'strange-looking' strangers, we had some distressing issues to deal with. People used to laugh at us for the way we were and looked like: our clothes and the hue in our eyes that would make us look as some untamed creatures. Sohrab's solution to this was simply unique, coming from an encompassing mind imbued in a divine heart: he became like us. He became one of us. He wore our clothes: very loose trousers, long shirt with a slit at each side at the waist, painstakingly embroidered cap and a large shawl wrapped around his upper body. It changed people's perception of us. They opened up and allowed us to do so, and gradually we became part of the village's worthwhile memories.

"By the time it had become apparent that the Soviet Afghan and Iran Iraq war was not going to end soon, we had lived three absolutely blissful years of our lives with Grandma and Sohrab. With each sunrise we would rise to live a day fresher than the day before, and with each sunset we would relish the realisation that we were far ahead of ourselves: we had been loved and allowed to love. We had been given the unique chance of having a deep and overall look into our own psyches. We had seen ourselves. We had learnt how to appreciate what we were, and it was, ironically, one of our main worries: we had got wise to the purest form of love and humanity. Eventuality, life means eventuality, and we were unconsciously afraid of it. Separation had become our nemesis, and what had added a very pungent poignancy to it was the eternal bond between Sohrab and Afsoon, who were patiently and wisely in love, having their own misgivings and reservations about the flailing events of the world around them and their own fate."

"Gol, give us an insight into the nature of the love between Afsoon and Sohrab," asked David, his face beaming, his eyes brightening up.

166

"Listening is the greatest of arts and questioning is the fruit of it," said Gol, smiling at David, "Boy, I am so happy that you are acquiring the art of listening. Well, they were there, right in the heart of love, guiding and touring each other through its vastness. And this mutual understanding of it had elevated them to a level beyond their physicality. They would sit beside each other in absolute silence without saying a word because they were listening to the cascading sound of their merging hearts. Words are not for the lovers. Love is a one-word language, and the word is itself. No carnal pleasure would ever surmise the yearning for love when one is truly submersed in it. Despite being very young and, like other human beings, creatures of full sense perceptions, they had not touched each other up to that point, not even a brief holding of hands or a stealthy stolen kiss in the dark of a breezeway. Their love should not be materialised prematurely; I think it was what they had in their unique young minds.

"A year later, it came, like an avalanche, the eventuality of separation, and landed on us with all its stifling and freezing force…

Chapter 24

It was a dreary sultry high noon when Cynthia woke up from her short nap. She had been unwell for a week or so, her pains and aches sourcing mainly from her mental state. She sighed. She inhaled and with it, a good deal of the mixed reek of tampons and stale female body sweat was sucked into her lungs and made her cringe with an inner moan. She was dealing with a culminating bitter feeling of disconsolation and discontent, to wit, though not quite out of her zone yet, she was feeling like a cat in a strange garret…

It all had begun a while ago when she had asked Sophie why she had gone off dance lessons, and also why she had fallen out with Eileen and Magdalena, to which Sophie had initially reacted with a cold indifferent shrug of shoulders. But when Cynthia had urged her to provide her with an answer, she had snapped an unseemly and rhapsodising reply at her: *this is my fucking life! I am amazed at you fucking people and the attitudes you take on! More or less, I think you people are disgusting!*

You are, you lunatic self-serving degenerate fucking people! Did I call you 'people'? I take it back! You are far beneath it! Fair enough! Degeneracy has got, like other things, its own boundaries! You perverts have crossed all those boundaries! Fair enough, you could barge into other boundaries and embrace the entire depravity and fuck yourself! Unnameable, the level of immorality you are privileged with! More or less, I believe so! Disgusting, more or less, I should say, you are! Never ever again interfere with my life! Fair enough, you will definitely face the unmistakable face of justice. As for the fucking dancing, what is the point in shaking my ass around! Only lunatics like Eileen and Magdalena believe that dance comes from the soul! There isn't even a fucking damn whit of logic in this! What the fuck is soul anyway! Has anyone ever seen a soul? I hate, yes, I hate these fucking life-wasters! Fair enough, I think, more or less, they are all some delusional melancholic fuckers!

Initially shocked by the sheer insolence in Sophie's tone and the inconceivable irrelevance in her words, Cynthia had recognised Draco's vocabulary in Sophie's spitting rant, as she had previously recognised traces of Mehmet's Latinate English, too. She had also noticed some rather educated new words Sophie had used, words and phrases such as, 'depravity', 'degeneracy', 'immorality and its boundaries', 'inconceivable rascality', 'inexorable criminality of mind'.

With Eileen's help, she had found out that Sophie had been secretly visited by Draco, Christopher and her own parents.

Promising herself that it would be the last breach of instructions and restrictions, she lit up a cigarette and dragged on it deeply. Puffing the smoke out she watched it swirling up to the ceiling, and inhaling another puff with a good deal of indignation and resignation, she reckoned, with a bleeding heart, that Sophie was far beyond the tendency of attracting light and goodness; that she was simply a container designed only to contain glorified trash! That she and goodness had long divorced each other; that she had become addicted to depreciation and hollowness; that she would eventually dehumanise herself.

"Cynthia, what is it? You look so down," asked Eileen, coming into the room.

"I am all right, mate," replied Cynthia, taking another deep drag of her cigarette, "I am positively fucked up! You know what it means, you wise woman. Lost it all. Nothing left to lose. Nothing to be worried about. Nothing to stab and poison my heart again because there is no heart in my fucking chest. Just a dead chunk of something. By saving Sophie I could have salvaged a chunk of myself."

"A vengeance against herself!" said Eileen, sitting beside Cynthia on the bed, "She is going to avenge herself against herself! What for? For allowing herself to fall in love and wish for decency! She is going to spit on the face of love, not knowing that it would fall on her own face. Instead of this disgraceful fickleness and backsliding, she should understand that her heart is cluttered up with baubles and gewgaws, and therefore, it has no room even for a speck of love and decency. What has caused this to happen to her? Well, a very expensive form of grandiosity and—even more lethal than the morphine and more resolving than acid. In all, I think she is *too great* to think of love, and if she does, she will definitely see it as a toilet roll! The coalescence of negations, she has become."

"Oh, yes, exactly like the fucking young Cynthia!" said Cynthia, reaching for another cigarette, "The fucking young Cynthia, *the Goddess of Goddesses,* also would see herself greater than bloody life! Too great to ask for love! Too great to be humble and recipient! Fucked over by her own folly and impertinence. She had even a short affair with God, when her superiority—not even to God but also to the entire universe—was proven to her! Eventually, she turned herself into a toilet roll! By saving Sophie, I would have salvaged a big chunk of myself. But Eileen, I am not that fucking wasted. Am I?"

"You are now unshackled. Freed of demeaning notions," said Eileen, putting her arm around Cynthia's shoulders, "And above all, the fruits of your life, your children, are now in safe hands. They will definitely yield the seeds of propriety and appreciation. You are enlightened, and this is the result of your yearnings for goodness. You would have sacrificed yourself to save Sophie."

"Awh, Eileen! I would have. No doubt about it," replied Cynthia, two large tears rolling down her cheeks.

"Pack up, girl," said Eileen, wiping up Cynthia's tears with the heel of her hand, "The world outside is eagerly awaiting a new Cynthia. You will be released tomorrow."

"She would have become a competent dancer. Sophie," sobbed Cynthia, another two large tears rolling down her cheeks, "She is now associating herself with the most accomplished shoplifter in the country, that sociopath woman who calls her 'daft vagina'. People get what they deserve. She loves the wiseacre and the miscreant and the impotent, an impeccable colligation and a recipe for becoming infertile and failing to become."

***

"People of the same fucking nature can easily spot each other," said Lucy, the thirty-year-old plump Liverpudlian blonde and the most accomplished shoplifter in the country, "Daft vagina, I spotted you as a daft vagina right away, using my own cant mind and vigilant cunt. We both are daft cant cunts! I mean cant and cunt in a diplomatic way. And I am so happy we have now joined. A fabulous duo who hate to be exploited or abused. Don't we, Sophie? We are daft not because we are lacking in intelligence or other faculties people are bragging about, no, contrary to this fucking belief, we are daft in a wise and diplomatic way: we deter them, we fuck them over, those who dare to distort *our beliefs* and stand in our unique and fruitful

170

way of looking at life and seeking pleasure. With all these fucking deft thieves of beliefs around, women like you and me are always exposed to being stripped of what we are made of. Some morons, out there, in this fucking society, fucked me up. I was at uni, studying Politics, aiming at becoming another Maggie Thatcher and causing another itching feat in the arse of this society! They said I was a fucking sociopath! I wasn't. I have never been. I was just living my life the way I wished. I had only a few steps left to get my degree, but they kept locking me up time after time. I believed, and still believe, in absolute freedom. What is the meaning of fucking life if you aren't free to take what you wish! No worries, my dear Sophie, I teach you how to deter the ones who are going to bungle your life up by stealing your beliefs. In all, I believe you have made the right choice: to stand by Draco and his friends and fuck that lunatic daydreamer over! What was his name? Oh, yes, Gol. He has to be fucked over! He has to be taught a lesson he will never forget. You are truly a daft vagina with an ardent inclination towards *decent* people. I am so gutted that the unimaginable cruelty of this fucking man has inflicted on you such great pains and losses. Mehmet, as you described him to me, was a big loss to you, a treasure, I should say. He would have definitely filled your heart with love and ever-lasting joy. He was, without a shadow of doubt, your first and your last true love. Dirty fucking man! Well, what can I say about Christopher, or even late Garry, these unique men who know all the isles, crevices and interstices of a woman's existence?"

"Thank you very much, Lucy," said Sophie, sounding most animated, "My dear dad, who is a very knowledgeable man and also a brilliant orator, believes that immorality is the mother of all other infestations and smearing ills of human relationships. Yeah, he told me this just the other day, when he and Draco had come here to encourage me to speak up and demand for justice. And as you already know, my dad, with the full support of Draco and Christopher, had prepared a lawsuit, which will be launched in a near future. And then we will fuck them over."

"Waste no fucking time, Sophie!" said Lucy, her green eyes overwhelmed by a wave of 'justice-seeking' desire bulging within her, "Move your arse. Put your pieces together, and before they could come up with a plan to evade the fuck, get them fucked over! The shameless fucking abuser is a rich man. Isn't he? You should hook him up, and he is done. To be let off the fucking hook, well, he would have to fork out, well, all of it.

171

And that would be the price of abusing and stealing the dignity and the soul of an innocent girl. So many thievish fucking men are around these days! The fuckers are obsessed with stealing fresh pussies! Poor innocent skirts of this country, they are utterly defenceless! You would have become an angelic mum had you not been scarred and marred in this manner. My late dad would always go: 'if skirts get deflowered disrespectfully, they will never flower'. And my mother would go: 'the days of flowering skirts have long gone'. Now, just for the purpose of appeasing your own unbearable pain—oh, my poor Sophie—would you mind telling me more about it… how did it all begin?"

"Oh, yeah, it was horrible! Traumatising! Yeah, it was," replied Sophie, the green in her eyes disappearing, "I was still a virgin when I bumped into this man… I don't want to mention his name…

"It frightens me. I hadn't been even touched before. A full virgin. Not even a kiss or something."

"Oh, blimey! An actual rose, you may say," said Lucy, propping her pudgy face on her fisted hand and biting her thick lower lip.

"Yeah, I was like a red rose," replied Sophie, her eyes now almost whitish, " He looked into my eyes, right at the first day. Oh, what horrible eyes! Like those of—those of—"

"Of a monster. I think you mean of a monster!" interrupted Lucy, covering her mouth with her fleshy hand.

"Oh yeah," said Sophie, her eyes moistening, "Did you know what he asked me for, right at the first day? He was, he is a fucking muff-diver! He is. But I gave him a… first… you know what I mean. He made me do it. And then he… you know what I mean… that muff thingy. And just in a matter of minutes, and even before I could see it coming, he humped me like a wild animal."

"Sophie, stop being such a naive fucking ninny!" said Lucy, holding her chin in her hand in utter amazement, she added zealously, "He *raped* you! That fucking muff-diver *raped* you! Never ever use any other terms. Naïve! It is good you didn't say he made love to you! Be diplomatically daft and use your only fucking ace wisely. *Rape,* Sophie, you were raped! And don't forget, the only means of defence left for us skirts, is this fucking term, RAPE! You are a so-called fucking daft vagina! Wake up. And remember, you are not going to stand before a fucking judge and say that he gave you a good wet licking and you returned the fucking favour by giving him a good fucking blow job; that you got your fucking panties off, spread the pussy before him and… Sophie, your rose was perished! It was raped. If you can't remember how you were raped—that would be quite understandable—you can watch some of those fucking numerous rape-related documentaries on the fucking internet. I don't really know, but I can imagine how he did it: bearing in mind that he is a very strong man, and by nature, very coarse, I wouldn't believe that he was tasteful enough to fancy a bit of cunnilingual play—Muslim men wouldn't fancy it. Believe me. So, he just grabbed you from behind, lifted you up, and lowered you on your knees, pulled up your skirt and, easy… Oh my dear Sophie, I can imagine how painful it was!"

"Lucy," said Sophie, crossing her legs and holding her chin, "Why can't I remember how I was raped? It is funny. Isn't it? It is so ridiculously strange that I need someone to help me recall how I was raped!"

"Oh, my lovely Sophie!" said Lucy, wriggling closer to her and holding her hand, "Trauma, my lovely Sophie. Trauma is a severe psychological wound that can wreck the entire nervous system and disrupt the normal functioning of the brain. You are lucky. In some cases, trauma can fuck people up for good. I am glad you brought this up—this fucking *trauma* thing. You were *raped* and, as a direct consequence of it, were badly *traumatised*—the most ideal case for a judge to quickly put an end to an evil-minded cruel fucking man! Brilliant! You have a fucking spiffing case! Think of, at least, a million pounds in compensation, Sophie. You are well on your way of getting him badly screwed, the fucking man who plonked down on you and deflowered you so brutally. Rape and trauma are like fucking hand grenades to us defenceless lassies. Shove them up his fucking arse, get the money and amend your perished rose and your wounded soul. Conviction, summon some conviction to your mind and go for it. And tell me about the murders, and how he managed to fool you into committing them."

"Yeah, well," said Sophie, the preambles of a 'conviction-summoning' urge appearing in her eyes, "One day, and after he had just finished brutally raping me, I cried my heart out and pleaded with him to let me go. He looked at me and said that I could buy my freedom by doing him a favour. 'You would be paid handsomely for it' he said. He looked into my eyes again, and when saw the eager desire for freedom in them, he asked me to help him murder Garry. He said he would pay me half a million pounds plus

173

a flat in the best place of the town. But I can't remember why he wanted to get rid of Garry."

"You have got to recall this," said Lucy, "Fucking trauma! See, how it has bungled your memory! When attending a court of law, this would definitely be the most decisive part of this horrendous case. But I can imagine, now knowing this fucker to a certain extent, that perhaps he had a crush on Garry's wife. You get what I mean? You know, I mean envy, lust, treachery, backstabbing, these are the games this kind of men are into. Killing two birds with one stone, I assume—owning the pussy and the wealth!"

"Lucy," said Sophie in an elongating tone, "It is really amazing that you know how to help me remember the fucking aspects of this horrible story! Yeah, I think I am about to remember the other aspects to it. Perhaps it is this sluggishness of my brain, due to a transient brain fog or something like that. Yeah, anyway, I think you could well be spot-on with your assumption. Once, while raping me brutally inside his car, he told me something about Garry's wife's arse! Oh my gosh! What a horrible indecent man! This is exactly what he said: 'If your arse was as great as that of Garry's wife, you would be the sexiest fucking chick in town. But don't worry, yours is only one size smaller. It will soon grow thicker'. Yeah, Lucy, I think he actually told me that he badly wanted Garry's wife."

"Good! Fucking smashing!" said Lucy, kissing Sophie's face, "Now I can easily imagine the rest of it: he sent you to Garry's restaurant to seduce and guide him towards a trap he had devised. Now I can see why it took you three years to bring yourself to poison Garry: you were too modest and too decent to allow yourself to even seduce a very righteous married man, let alone shag him. Any way, he kept harassing you, he amplified the mental pressure on your young mind and, understandably, you eventually gave in and became a murderer. You murdered two very dear human beings. I was very much impressed by your brief descriptive of Miss Julie Atkins. Such a spiffing enlightened soul, a beacon of truth and guidance. I really loved her takes on the nonsensicality of *free will* and her spot-on touch on the *absolute freedom.* I am deeply sad that life—very much needlessly—was snuffed out of such an amazing essence of liberty. I can't help expressing the same amount of sorrow and regret for the loss of Garry, that *father of fathers,* and the unique example of conscientiousness and piety."

"I have been severely agonising myself over this," said Sophie, taking

174

a deep sigh, "I am not sure if the remorse of this senseless crime will ever leave me alone. But Lucy, I am only twenty-six-years-old, and when those murders took place, I was only twenty-five."

"See, Sophie, right company," said Lucy, smiling, "You came to me, to your true mate, to your own nature, and this is the result: with me help you are recalling what you have forgotten, smoothly wriggling through your mind and uniting your ties. Spot-on again, Sophie, this age thing! You are still a teenager. And I am sure the fucking judges would love this. The entire judicial system would see you as a teenager. All females under the age of *forty* are actually teenagers. We poor defenceless skirts of this country should always be grateful to our very considerate judicial system within which we always remain non-aged and noncommittal. And this is actually very much in line with the late Miss Julie Atkins' views on absolute freedom. Age, Rape, Trauma, it couldn't be any fucking better! We have all the three fucking concepts in one fucking place! Underage, raped and traumatised, you would definitely be let off the hook and, as a well-deserved compensation, you would pocket a large sum of fucking boodle. And, Sophie, I just remembered another spiffing judge-convincing factor within your case!"

"What?" asked Sophie, grabbing Lucy's hand.

"Alcohol, mate, the fucking alcohol!" replied Lucy, sounding like a wise hen, "Thanks to our judicial system again! Women have never been required to drink responsibly!"

"Oh Lucy!" uttered Sophie admiringly, "Yeah, I was drunk when I committed those murders! Brilliant! Thank you, Lucy!"

"You are most welcome, mate," said Lucy, smiling sagaciously, "And the more we go through this fucking story the more I get to comprehend Miss Julie Atkins and her precious philosophy. I am, somewhat, jealous of you. I wish it was me who had bumped into that true mine of true takes on human fucking life. I reckon she, this fabulous woman from academia, must have written some spiffing stuff. I would love to read them. That would be a priceless privilege."

"Yes, she did write a good number of books and essays," said Sophie," now sounding like a woman of *conviction*, "And she actually gave me a copy of her last book just an hour before her unfortunate death."

"Wow!" uttered Lucy, "What was it about?"

"It was a tiny book with a great title," replied Sophie, pausing for some long moments, apparently trying to recall the book title, "Oh, yeah, it was 'How to Rot Without Getting Decomposed'."

"The most mind-boggling fucking book title ever!" said Lucy, her small eyes widening, "Positively mind-fucking! Obviously, you didn't get the chance to read it. Have you got any idea what might have happened to it?"

"I will ask Draco to find it for us," replied Sophie with an assuring smile.

"I would treasure the taste of such an insightful mind," said Lucy in a most desirous tone with her eyes shut, "I hope Draco has found the book and kept it safe. Well, let's get back to our own task. We need to summarise what we have so far observed and move on towards a most cohesive conclusion—a painstaking highlighting, if you like. But before jumping into this, I need to know some more details of this devastating case of rape and trauma. I mean details such as how often and how he would rape you and—"

"Oh yeah, I get what you mean," interrupted Sophie, assuming a most innocent tone and forming a most angelic look on her face, "Five six times a day, every day, and very rough, violent, I should say."

"Goodness gracious!" exclaimed Lucy, covering her mouth with both hands, "A fucking horny deranged stallion! Go on, go on, my poor Sophie."

"Yeah, he is a mad man," said Sophie, her eyes welling up, "Twice as big as I am, he would plump down on me as if I was a fucking mattress. Sometimes he would push my head under a desk or chair and hump on my back, as if I was a fucking rutting little jenny. He would actually call me this."

"Bestiality and total perversion," said Lucy, musingly, "Plus a touch of paedophilia, would definitely convince a court of law to render this man as an imminent threat to the poor defenceless skirts and the entire society. Bearing in mind that when he raped you for the first time, you were very young—obviously still a *child*—I am certain the dear judges would take this into a very subtle consideration. Needless to say that a stallion-like man who humps a very young girl and calls her 'a fucking rutting little jenny' is definitely a voracious fucking predator!"

Sifting through fairness, justice and rationality—though in a diplomatic and necessarily cunning manner—the two mates of the same nature thrashed

176

out the justice-bearing grains of Sophie's trespassed and plundered field of dignity and innocence! In doing so, they affectionately mingled their gentle feminine souls to make sure that nothing except justice would be sought after; that any other enticing aspect in the way of their quest for justice would be vehemently avoided; that, in all, nothing unblemished would be blemished! Having their own dictionary, and accordingly, their own definitions, enhanced by a self-appropriated right to footnote and sophisticate, the two 'fine ladies' had no reason to doubt their views and think again, and did not.

Lucy, the more experienced and the more assertive one, guided the less experienced and awkwardly revolutionary Sophie to the podium of litigation and demand for compensation. How far would Sophie go with her newly acquired word view and her rapidly metamorphosing soul?

Chapter 25

London had never been her favourite place, she thought, searching her pockets. Holding her gilded atomic lighter in her hand, she looked around aimlessly. She was aimless, out of prison and free, free to be aimless. "It is good. It has never been better," she whispered to herself, walking across a stretch of finely manicured turf and towards a large black poplar with its branches splayed around and low to the ground. Tossing her colourful handmade shoulder bag—a gift from Mrs Aziza Baygum—on the turf, she sprawled herself in the generous shade of the tree and lit a cigarette and immediately dragged on it. She felt an unprecedented peace within her, in all of what she was, a tellurian being experiencing the full presence of herself. She gazed around, at the prison gate and its cold admonishing gaze at her, at the tall fortified walls and the ever-entangling barb wires planted atop of them. She directed her gaze to a row of saplings planted opposite a row of very old trees. Suddenly she missed her children, a wistful potent desire, a long-neglected affection, one of the numerous lost moments of her life. Her tears came, rained, facile and unstrained, nothing to deter them, nothing to unnecessarily examine them. They were heart-washing, soul-freshening eye-clearing tears. She wept silently, looking intently at the fresh shimmering leaves of the saplings in the sun. A gentle cool breeze rustled the leafy tree branches, got cooler and wafted through her damp hair, perhaps to empathise with her broken heart. She wiped her tears and formed a smile on her face, a smile gradually formed, like a photo developing in a darkroom. She remembered what Gol had told her years ago: '*the nature realises when a woman is sad*' her smile shattered. Her smile reformed and she laughed, the saplings dancing in her glistening blue eyes.

She flung the cigarette butt on the turf, got to her feet, grabbed her bag and walked towards the narrow footpath to her left. Coming to an abrupt halt, she marched back, picked up the cigarette butt and… She put her hand on her heart… she felt… she was certain… some eyes, some familiar eyes, some much-missed eyes had been watching her since she had stepped out of the prison gate. She looked around, her heart now bursting with joy. She darted an eager look towards the open parking.

There she spotted a brand-new silver Land Rover. She shaded her eyes with her hand and looked… Seconds later, the Land Rover's engine roared… it was coming towards her… "Emily! David!" she shouted, her arms open like the wings of a martin landing before her hatchlings at the end of a long perilous flight. A random barrage of kisses, neglected in years of emotional drought, was released, and non-randomly each landed on the right spot. The eyes were the main target, the unused windows to the soul.

"It is as if we had not seen each other for ages! Isn't it?" said Cynthia, pressing her children's faces against hers.

David and Emily said nothing. Nothing was needed to be said. The long-awaited love had in itself the entire system of communication.

"Mum, look who is behind you!" said Emily, the happiest of smiles sitting in her tearful eyes.

"Gol!" said Cynthia, tilting her head, not sure what to say or what to do.

"Come on, Cynthia! Let's have a hug," said Gol, opening his arms.

Cynthia walked towards Gol with her head held down, opened her arms and embraced him. Another salvaged and most-cherished-for moment of affection, another little triumph for a big but now rather disabused and humbled loser.

"Gol, you were so loyal to your old Land Rover," said Cynthia, as soon as they got into the brand new car.

"David turned it into a bunch of scrap metal," said Gol, laughing, "He crashed it into a tractor while driving over the speed limits. Just imagine if it was one of these flimsy cars."

"Goodness!" said Cynthia, quickly turning her head around and looking at David anxiously, "You all right, my son?"

"Yes, Mum, I am completely fine." Replied David, touching her shoulder.

"We are lucky, the three of us," said Cynthia, her eyes moistening, "I think God likes us. He loves the three of us. I don't know what God is, but I sincerely believe something likes us. Something is looking out for us. And by the way, you don't seem to be interested in knowing what Sophie has been up to."

"We have already been filled in about what she has done," said Gol, "Sophie is a little cavewoman with so many cavemen around her. A seagull

179

would only listen to another seagull. I hope it is not the case. I hope Sophie isn't, by nature, a seagull. I still believe there is a white dove within this now seagull-looking girl."

"They are going to sue Gol," said David.

"Who?" asked Cynthia in an overly calm tone.

"Garry's children and Sophie's dad, the son of a virgin, the cowherd," replied David, ruffling his hair in an overly calm manner, "Apparently, Mehmet, before his death, had told them that Franco and Sophie were Gol's spies, sent to them to prepare a plan for Garry's murder. He, Mehmet, had also made up a completely bogus and lengthy story about Gol and his connection with those deranged Islamists and what they have been doing. And now they are using Mehmet's diabolic stories to get away with their own crimes."

"Did Mehmet know Gol at all?" asked Cynthia, her face revealing a deep sense of disbelief and disgust.

"No, not at all," replied David.

"And Sophie had fallen in love with such a miscreant creature!" uttered Cynthia, the two parallel lines between her eyebrows deepening. "He was a king seagull. A seagull would fall in love only with another seagull. I think Gol should leave these rascals to me. I know how to deal with them. At the end of the day, well, I have nothing to lose."

"Gol, I think Mum is right. Mum and I will sort them out," said David, smoothing his hair.

"As long as Brother Sohrab's soul is with me, I won't allow any violence," said Gol, throwing a fleeting look at Cynthia, who now looked like a resolute lioness, "That would be a storm in a teacup. Anita has just begun to open up—thanks to Franco. Therefore, I believe Cynthia is more than capable of palavering her into revealing some of the hidden aspects of this story to us."

"I will try my best, Gol," said Cynthia, "But I strongly believe iron must be cut by iron."

"You are right, Cynthia," said Gol; stroking his beard, he appended, "But remember, unlike rascality, tolerance has limits."

"I understand," said Cynthia apologetically.

Cynthia remained silent, listening to the smooth and tuned sound of the car engine, and while feeling a quivering transmission of composure within her long-stressed and strained body and mind, she caught sight of her

180

daughter's face in the rear-view mirror. Leaning her head against the window, she was looking out on the fast flickering world outside, the gold of her hair shimmering in the sun, her large blue eyes gazing at an unknown spot in the world. Not to disturb her, she leaned back against the seat and looked at her aslant. She wondered at what was happening in her own heart, a surge of life-affirming feelings, all elevating, all forgiving, all exonerating, all beatifying, all liberating. Cynthia, the master of slipshod and love-wasting attitudes and tendencies, had just noticed the unique beauty of her own daughter, the child she had neglected all through her turbulent life. She threw a look at Gol's profile. He was aware. He was present. She put her hand on her heart; it was full to the brim, full of love and goodness. She shut her eyes and drew: Emily offering an overflowing chalice of love and beauty to the rising sun.

"Have you ever watched a worried lioness?" asked Gol, without looking at her.

"Me, yes, no... Gol, honestly... I am—I am fine," said Cynthia, slightly embarrassed, "I—I will stand by you and my children. I will defend our peace and happiness. I will defend our achievements."

Gol's appreciative mind and heart was touched by Cynthia's words. Not that it was her words that he could judge, it was also her inner world that he could clearly see and feel. This woman had wounded his heart with the dagger of folly and self-punishment. Stippled on the scars of that wound, her face was still with him. As an edified soul, he was certain that she was in a fierce battle with herself, dealing with a smorgasbord of entangled emotions and beliefs. He also was certain that she had begun to appreciate goodness and beauty within their authentic forms.

The next day Cynthia woke up with a bursting desire in her heart and her mind, the desire to tear off and out her world, the world within and the world without. The desire to set alight whatever deserved to be burned. She looked round her bedroom. It was damp, dirty, littered with all sorts of objects: empty booze bottles and tobacco pouches, cigarette butts, crumpled papers and a few mismatched socks, a red pair of pants, a pair of once-pink brassieres... She sprang to her feet, pulled off the beddings... Washing, brushing, hoovering, dusting off, scrubbing, scouring... Her wardrobe, she did not need it any more... Nothing old, nothing damp, nothing unnecessary. Bin bagged and piled up by the door, there were all the discordant items which had occupied his small living space. She bleached the bathroom… Took a shower… Inside her now emptied and cleaned wardrobe, there were only a pair of faded blue jeans and an unused light green T-shirt and a pair of black thick-based leather shoes. When she got dressed, she noticed it was a bit nippy outside. She walked towards the bin bags by the door to take one of her thin jackets, but she changed her mind. She was warm inside, she thought. She checked the time on her phone, paused, dithered, check the time and the date, pulled the door open and stepped out.

It was a sunny day with a bit of chill in the air, nipping at her bare arms every now and then. She walked smoothly in her comfortable shoes. She came to a halt and looked at her shoes, like a six-year-old little girl. Comfort, she had never felt it this way, she thought. She walked on, a frivolous, carefree, childish walk, a walk of undefined and uncalculated steps. She was happy and in utter peace with herself, and she did not wish to know why; and perhaps the desire to remain ignorant to the cause of her gratification, was an undeniable proof that she had already entered the zone of her heart and her intuition. She felt hungry, hungrier than ever. She had been asked over by Gol to have lunch with him and her children.

"You are not late, Cynthia!" said David, walking towards her.
"I will never be late again," said Cynthia, embracing her son.
"Cynthia," said Gol, smiling, "Have you been meditating?"

"Oh, Gol! The same old Gol," said Cynthia, walking towards him, "Sort of. Ransacking, sorting out, discarding, cleaning, cleansing. I think it was badly needed."

"Take a seat," asked Gol, getting up to his feet, "And you will need a fire."

"Amazing! Now I can easily understand you," said Cynthia, settling herself on the chair opposite Gol's, "I will borrow your fire, the blue-flamed burning fire that burns the unnecessary desires and sets one free. The shadow and the weight, I don't need them any more."

"She sounds like a foreigner. Doesn't she, David?" asked Gol, laughing.

"She does," replied David, ruffling his hair and laughing.

"My Emily!" said Cynthia, as Emily pushed the door open and stepped in, "I love my foreign Emily to pieces!"

182

"I love you too, Mum," said Emily, embracing her.

"Is the food coming, Emily?" asked Gol.

"Yes, it won't be long," replied Emily, sitting on the chair beside her mum's.

"Cynthia, how would you manage an art gallery if you had one?" asked Gol.

"Well," said Cynthia, noticing she was looking into Gol's eyes, "An art gallery to me would be like a sea to a fish. I would swim down to the depth in search of pearls. I would resurrect all the dead fishes of art within me. I would make friends with clams and oysters."

Cynthia's answer touched Gol's heart. Emily kissed her face. David raised his hand to ruffle his hair but remembering he had done so just seconds ago, he smoothed them with a distorted but funny smile.

The idea of Cynthia having an art gallery, had occurred to Gol when he had decided to take David and Emily into his own care; and the reason it had taken so long, was Gol's unwavering belief in the *right* moment. And the right moment had arrived, when Cynthia had begun to appreciate herself as a woman, and above all, as a mother. It was mainly her regained and polished motherly attitude and love that gradually convinced Gol to see her as a dear friend.

"Shall we do it now or after lunch?" asked Gol, looking at David and Emily.

"Let's do it now. I can't wait to see Mum's reaction!" said David, ruffling his hair.

"Well, let's go then," said Emily, holding her mum's hand.

Cynthia, not knowing what they were talking about, followed them, as she was asked to. Out of the office door, they turned left and towards the stairs leading to the large flat upstairs. Before reaching the landing and the door to the flat, Cynthia's eyes caught a shining sign on the wall. She stopped, put her hand on her heart, tilted her head to one side, and with utter disbelief and with her heart pounding, she read: *Cynthia's Scintillating Art Gallery*.

The flat was empty, and looked larger than before. Stripped of all household furniture and furnishings, the flat was now breathing like a living entity, with its newly painted walls and its fine wooden flooring, and above all, with its large windows letting in a generous amount of light.

She kept walking around the flat in silence, turning, looking up and looking down, like a devout pilgrim in a shrine. She looked at Gol, who was rolling out a large fine Persian carpet, she was about to walk over to him and say 'Gol, I just can't believe this!' but meanwhile her still roving eyes caught sight of two potted plants, placed at each side of one of the windows. She, the pilgrim, sat on the floor cross-legged and glued her eyes to the two wisteria plants, gracefully sitting in black glazed clay pots.

"Mate, I can and I believe this," said Cynthia, now standing before Gol with her arms crossed on her chest, "Back then, in our prime days, in the days of Cynthia's folly and haughtiness, you sent me two potted wisterias, and I, so very disdainfully, sent them back to you. Well, it was an unconscious rejection of goodness and affection, because I lacked what goodness would take. I wish, I only wish, I could find a modicum of need in you, and based on it, I could offer you a lengthy apology and redeem myself; or at least, I could say 'I am so sorry'. But I will do what I can do: I promise you I will never be sorry again in my life."

"Now you can believe yourself," said Gol, "And this is your redemption. Look at them, your children, how attentively they are moving those objects around. They are preparing a place for their mum in their lives."

"Gol!" said Cynthia, now on the brink of bursting into tears, "I—I—"

"Say no more, Cynthia. Let's go and have our lunch," interrupted Gol, touching her shoulder.

"What a day!" said Cynthia, looking eagerly at the dishes of food on the table, "I woke up with an urging desire storming through me. On my way walking to you my beloved people, every single thing kept pampering me: the sun, the nipping chill, the passers-by, the street, the pavement, the traffic lights, the playful dogs and their owners, the pigeons… Even the seagulls!"

"Oneness, Cynthia. Isn't it?" said Gol, uncorking a wine bottle.

"Absolutely," replied Cynthia, "The moment one decides to join in, the other elements rush to welcome one. This beautiful game of thinking, questioning and comprehending, is the only essential and valid game for man."

"Gol, just to let you know Mum has been reading Rumi," said Emily, putting a plate of finely seasoned, roasted or fried starters before Cynthia.

"Really?" asked Gol, pouring some wine for Cynthia.

"Rumi is the question and the answer!" said Cynthia, lifting her glass

184

of wine, "It was a birthday present from Emily. What a sensible girl has my Emily become!"

"How about your David, Mum?" asked David, cleaning his hands with a napkin, apparently to ruffle his hair.

"A naïve-looking but wise and recipient boy who wouldn't mind to take the very bashing risks every now and then!" replied Cynthia, laughing from the bottom of her heart.

"I actually love this description!" said David contentedly, "Let's see how Gol would describe me."

"The loveliest asshole ever!" said Gol immediately.

There was a moment of silence, the calm before a joyful little storm of laughter, which followed right away. They laughed full and comprehensive laughs, each containing a simultaneous rich feeling of gratification and appreciation. Rejoicing in their laughter with all their bodies and souls, each of them were fully aware of the underlying reasons for this momentary but elaborate celebration. To Emily and David, these now unmoulded young seekers of unadulterated love and affection, it was some rewarding and soul-searching moments of recognition.

To Cynthia, well, this once-a-nymph, who had decided to represent and reflect nothing but her own demeaned image on the world, it was a precious moment of coming face to face with her real self. To Gol, it was simply another look at his own soul, reflected on the three faces before him.

Chapter 26

"Mate, I think you are being very very unjust to me," said Christopher , his face now looking horsier than before, "You know, if it wasn't for my calculated advice and encouragement, you wouldn't have succeeded in… You know what I mean… I mean what happened to Garry."

"Be a bit clearer, more or less, if you may," asked Draco, narrowing his eyes in the manner of a man of utter authority and confidence.

"Mate, I am very very clear," said Christopher, his nostrils widening, "You know that now I have lost a lot; my wife left me, and my children don't wish to see me any more. And above all, I am now penniless. You know, it isn't fair that you want everything for yourself."

"Christopher, Sophie is my red line," said Draco, exactly in Garry's tone, a tone capable of belittling and shattering a soul at the same time, "Watch out what you wish for. More or less, I am reiterating this: Sophie is the love of my life. So, know your limits and be happy with what you are promised to get. More or less, you will be paid a good chunk of money for your support… you know what I mean."

"Come on, mate!" said Christopher , the Narcissus within him badly wounded, "You all know—even Garry knew this very well—that Sophie was and is mad about me. And I am not sure if she is interested in you at all. So, be wise and leave Sophie for me. And, mind you, I want the money you promised me as soon as possible."

"Well, fair enough, more or less," said Draco, now Garry's soul almost visible in him! "In relation to your demand for Sophie, I think you are going round in circles. I will not have it! I warn you! Fair enough, more or less, as for the money you were promised, I should let you know that you have to wait until we have sorted this inheritance story among the family. Having said that, I would have happily paid you the promised money right the next day after Garry's death if it wasn't because of my very devious sister, Calypso. She believes you have already got more than what you were promised!"

"What have I got!" boomed Christopher, his neck elongating, his eyes bulging.

"Clever crafty girl! Isn't she?" said Draco triumphantly, "A 'different currency'! Fucking brilliant! More or less, fair enough. I reckon she believes you have been paid in a different fucking currency! Far more intelligent than I am. She is, more or less, a very capable player."

"Mate, I can't understand what you and Calypso mean!" said Christopher, the signs of belief and disbelief wriggling in the deep lines of his face.

"Mate, you know very well," said Draco, lowering his head and looking into Christopher's now cockeyed eyes, "Can you reckon the price of a fresh pussy? Oh yeah, you might reckon a price of, let's say, ten to twenty pounds plus a pint of beer, more or less. Well, you wouldn't be that wrong, but don't forget we are talking about a fresh pussy with Greek pride tingling in its fine layers. Mate, you have been shagging Calypso for three years now—since we got to know Garry was going to marry Miss Julie Atkins. Yes, more or less, I might agree with you that Sophie was and still is mad about you, but Calypso offered her fresh pussy to you not because, like Sophie, she was infatuated with you, but because she intended to get you involved in our plan for getting rid of Garry and that undertaker. You don't seem to understand the situation you are stuck in, my dear friend. Mate, based on what Calypso has worked out, we don't owe you a penny."

"I had nothing to do with Garry's murder. I wasn't even here the night he was murdered," said Christopher, his lopsided eyebrows wriggling, he eyes fixed, his face frozen.

"Fair enough, more or less, you played no direct role," said Draco, "But you got tempted when Calypso told you about Garry and that undertaker: you, cunning man, thought you could get your hands on a good amount of money. Calypso knew you were the only person who could convince me to join her and get rid of Garry and that undertaker. She promised you a good amount of cabbage and, well, you did your job very well."

"Bloody hell, mate! You shouldn't treat me like this," said Christopher , almost on the brink of a humiliating breakdown.

"Oh, I am sorry, Christopher," said Draco, holding his shoulders, "I am so sorry. I really didn't mean to hurt you. Go and take a seat. There, over there, by the fireplace. I will make you a coffee. It will soothe your nerves. Fair enough. No worries. More or less, I appreciate your prerogatives."

Christopher, still having problems with understanding the definition of

187

the word 'prerogative', plonked himself in the armchair by the fireplace and held his head in his hands. He had always reputed himself as a man of integrity and unswerving principles. Though illiterate, but esteeming himself as a well-deserved inheritor of the Greek blood and pride, it had dawned on him a sense of uniqueness; and to manifest this epiphany, this exalted and *recognised* state of being, he had named his grey Pitbull dog 'Zeus'! And thus, he had formally offered his divine and very much justified presence to a thirsty society of divine-seekers! Having a scant meme and lore-based knowledge of the Greek mythology, this 'fine piece of a man' had found no doubt in the authenticity of his divine state when a generous amount of choice sacrifices had kept flooding towards him. Sophie, Calypso and a good number of other even younger, fresher, and finer nymphs, were the latest of these offers to this modern but horse-like Zeus! And now this well-stablished full god, was furious with another of the same kind—though semi and yet to be promoted to his deserved strata! He was flabbergasted not because he had been insulted and badly humiliated, but because his state of Godhood and his morals had been questioned!

"Mate, sip your coffee and get hold of your nerves," said Draco, "As I was saying, more or less, it is your prerogative to assert yourself and insist on your rights to be obtained. Fair enough. Don't forget, Christopher, we are still friends, of the same blood and the same pride. As that fucking Iranian man used to say, we might eat each other's flesh but we won't throw away each other's bones. A savvy saying. Isn't it. Fair enough. To this end, I believe there is still a good chance for us to settle this like two men of essence and defined prerogatives. So, listen carefully and use your last chance wisely. If I drop the case against Sophie and let her walk away, the people around us would laugh at our very proud family. They would say 'a great proud authentic Greek man was murdered by a meretricious English girl, and his death was approached as that of a rat'. To avoid such an unbearable disgrace, I am going to ask for some blood money—a chunky chunk. Sophie's dad has to pay if he wishes his beloved child to be freed. Fair enough. And this way, more or less, I would be able to pay you the exact amount you are asking for."

"Firstly, Sophie's dad is only a cowherd," said Christopher in a resigned tone, "I don't think he could afford this. If he was a well-to-do man, his daughter wouldn't have to work fifty hours a week while going to university. Secondly, if Sophie is the love of your life, as you said this just

188

minutes ago, why do you want to screw her dad?"

"Firstly, I have done my homework," said Draco with another triumphant smile, "He is more than capable of paying for this. Secondly, his daughter working fifty hours a week wasn't down to his father's inability in supporting her, and you know this very well. Let's say no more about this. Thirdly, you didn't listen to me carefully. It isn't about screwing her father, it is about settling this case justly and gracefully. And… Listen, Christopher, I think, more or less, I actually might be willing to have a second thought on Sophie… Do you know what I mean? It is very much up to you. If you help me with this, then, well, more or less, I might leave Sophie for you."

"What do you want me to do?" asked Christopher perfunctorily.

"Reason with Sophie's dad, and convince him to pay the blood money," said Draco, preparing himself to have the last laugh, he added, "As you are such a facetious fucking talker, I am sure you would succeed in coaxing him into paying the money in no time."

"Sophie loves me, and only me," said Christopher, touching the thick gold chain around his neck, "So be honest with yourself, and don't mix things up. Bloody hell! I will do my best, of course, only if you cut off all your ties with Sophie from the very same moment. And I seriously advise you not to play with me, mate. Bloody hell, man!"

"Fair enough. More or less, I get your drift," said Draco, biting his lower lip musingly, "I am not going to argue with you over whom Sophie really loves, but you should be a bit more rational and understand that if I cut off all my ties with her, she might turn against us. Be wise, my friend, and don't allow your emotions to get in our way."

"When are Sophie's parents supposed to come?" asked Christopher, his face now a tapestry of a tragically lost battle.

"Tomorrow," replied Draco, still biting his lower lip.

***

"Well, my very dear friends," said Mr Barry James Grandeur, holding his head high; and assuming an air of unerring discernment, he went on, "May I thank you, dear sirs, for bestowing upon me the elevating privilege of being associated with you. Needless to say that man's soul needs as much nourishment as his body does, to wit, body and soul should always maintain

189

a level of equilibrium. To elaborate on this, I should also maintain the undisputable view on the importance of refined virtues, the defining qualities within which one would master the art of being human, and consequently, surpass one's otherwise subliminal existence. You are, my dear friends, as I have mentioned this before, two very precious men. I am so far very much obliged to you. Now, my dear sirs, I am at your disposal. I am certain the love between you and my Sophie will help us all out of this devastating predicament imposed on us by a base and barbaric man."

"Sir, you seem to know your prerogatives," said Draco, reaching for a bottle of wine in the ice bucket, "It is, more or less, a great joy to deal with the ones who are well aware of their rights and obligations. Christopher and I also treasure you as a man of quality virtues. Fair enough. As you might have already noticed, Christopher is like a father to me. He has always been there for me during the hard times, defending me against the treachery and the backstabbing of the world.

"Therefore, in order to show him my respect, and also benefit myself from his experience and wisdom, I leave this task to him. Fair enough. Yeah, he knows his prerogatives very well. He will be fair and rational."

"My dear Mr Barry James Grandeur," said Christopher, evidently trying to sound as Godly as possible, "You know, I am very very happy for having the honour to get to know you. And we are now eating lunch together. Very good. I am happy for this. As you know very well, Sophie is like my own daughter, who is only a year younger than her, and I will do whatever it takes to pull her out of prison. It is heart-breaking to see such an angelic creature behind bars, where every single thing is harmful to her. What can we do? This is the world we are living in. Some people are here only to exploit and abuse others. Look at this young gentleman, our own Draco, he has been betrayed as many times as the number of his hairs! And bearing in mind that he is a very hairy man, well, you could imagine how many times he has been betrayed by the world so far! And what should I say about his heart that is full of scars made by bastard stabbers. But he is fine; I have been teaching him how to come to terms with his wounds. I took him under my wings since he was a teenager. But the loss of his very fine father—one of the finest of his time—has badly affected him in a number of ways. The late Garry wasn't just a unique dad, he was also an asset to his family and his society. He was a clever money-making machine, a fine businessman who would see far ahead of himself. Only God knows how much more wealth he could have generated for his children. You know, he was an expensive loss. You know, fair people consider all aspects of what is going on among them. You are a fair man, and who is to doubt Draco's fairness? Adding to all this, the blabbermouth around Draco, I should expect you, dear sir, to see all the aspects of this issue. To get Sophie out of prison without causing any damage to Draco's social status, you and Draco need to make two deals between yourselves, one of which is going to be only for the formality of this case."

"Dear Christopher," said Mr Barry James Grandeur, adjusting the stiff collar of his pink shirt, "As your trustworthiness has already been proven to me, I entrust the fashioning of any deal to you, two gentlemen. Except for a few low-lives, who are all ungrateful and unfulfilled foreigners, the rest of your community have rendered you to me as the very righteous and empathic members who would take immense pride in defending the dignity of their community. Righteous and chivalrous, this is how your community have described you to me. Therefore, my dear sirs, hold nothing in reserve, and let me know how I shall shoulder my share of this heavy burden."

"Well, what else could I expect of a man of this calibre?" said Christopher, pouring himself a glass of wine, " As we all know, Sophie is still the prime suspect in relation to Mehmet's murder, but we know that Gol was behind this as well. The good news is that Draco and the solicitors working on the case have managed to gather some very good facts, which is a big step towards getting him hooked. And the other good thing is that Mehmet's family are also convinced that Gol was behind his murder, and they are doing whatever they can to get justice for him. Therefore, I think the late precious Miss Julie Atkins' blood money is the only serious obstacle in the way of Sophie's freedom. To spare yourself and Sophie from the hassles and time-consuming this part of the case, I think you should pay the money to Draco, as I believe he is very apt when it comes to challenging these types of issues. And the second deal: you should write a cheque to Draco for the blood-money of his late great father. Of course, as I said, this cheque will never be cashed, as it is only to gag the blabbermouth and all this. Now I think things are clear for you and Draco. You can now take your time and think about this solution. And most importantly, don't forget that Gol will soon be arrested and put on trial. And as he is a very rich man, he would certainly prefer to pay rather than to serve a life sentence. And it means you wouldn't lose a penny, and you might even pocket a remarkable amount of money."

"I prize you and your sincere and comprehensive clarifications on this issue," said Mr Barry James Grandeur, "To avoid any inordinate hesitation and delay in this crucial issue, I will return to you as soon as I have it discussed with my wife. I am very much convinced that we will prevail, despite the intricate nature of this case."

"Sir, I assure you this case is not that complicated," said Christopher, in a tone as if he was receiving a divine revelation, "Gol, this animal, abused your beloved child, and forced her to commit murder, as simple as this. And remember, there are two important things in Draco's mind: the murder of his decent dad and his honest love for Sophie. He won't allow this evil man to get away with his wicked crimes... Oh, I was about to forget a very important thing: you shouldn't allow your wife to get in touch with Gol. You know, with all due respect, I believe she is naïve and could be deceived and exploited by him. In that case, things might go wrong for us."

"I fully apprehend your purport, my dear wise sir," said Mr Barry James Grandeur, "I assure you this will never happen."

"Mate, you did a brilliant job!" said Draco, minutes after Mr Barry James Grandeur had left, "Honestly, I will do my best to make sure you will have Sophie in your life. You deserve this, my dear friend. Prerogatives are very important, more or less; it is what I have always believed all through my life. You know yours, and that is exactly why you are being guided towards your wishes. Your very unfaithful wife left you, but think how life is going to offer you a replacement! Just imagine the fresh charming intelligent Sophie by your side. Sophie, the sweetest woman I have ever had the privilege to cross paths with, more or less, it is what I believe. Well, how I could not regret this sacrifice, I mean forsaking Sophie and offering her to you. Perhaps it is, more or less, a test of what I am made of. I have always been a man of great sacrifices, despite being stabbed in the back and fingered by the world time after time."

"Mate, we have both been stabbed in the back by the world," said Christopher, a feeble echoing sound detectable in his voice, perhaps coming from the Mount Olympus! "We can't change this treacherous world, but we can stick together and defend ourselves against it. Let's have a firm handshake and stand for what we are made of."

"Mate, I perfectly understand your point," said Draco, now standing as stiff and straight as his dad used to, "We will get over this, like so many other hardships we overcame in the past."

"I like it," said Christopher, "This is the way we should look at what we have done and what we can do together. And just if you don't mind, I wish to say a few words about Calypso… You know, I mean…"

"Feel free, my friend. Be at ease and say whatever you wish to," interrupted Draco.

"Well, I don't think it was wrong," said Christopher; assuming a Zeus-like air on his face, he added, "You know, prerogatives would tell, and by this, I was sure that me having sex with Calypso was completely fine. Bloody hell, she liked it. More or less, I think she was right to follow her prerogatives, and she did, as she has been doing since a very young age. Bloody hell, more or less, I should say she wasn't fresh at all, not even three years ago! I think even ten pounds would be a bad bargain!"

"Fair enough," said Draco, forming a Godly smirk in the corner of his mouth, "We should all be thankful to my dad. It is because of his very open-minded and all-inclusive views on morality and how it must be approached that now we know how to go about our lives and get the most out of it.

"He believed once one masters the art of spotting and interpreting one's prerogatives, one would be allowed to do whatever one wishes. What happened between you and Calypso, well, was based on prerogatives, and based on her prerogatives, she was right to put such a high price on her pussy, regardless of whether it was fresh or not. Don't forget, my friend, it is the personal prerogatives that can define an action as wrong or right."

And thus, one and a half modern Greek Gods, with the help of a metamorphosed English man, and within a process of extrapolation and interpolation and applying their self-created rhetoric and circumlocutions, redefined the book of morals and reached a conclusion so incisive that no mortal creature could question its authenticity. Having this edition adorned with the stamp and confirmation of the mortal community, it was collectively agreed upon that it had to be kept out of the reach of the sophist and the cynic!

Chapter 27

"Mum, I think you should leave this Italian guy," said Calypso, sounding like Mother Theresa, "If you refrain doing so, you and all of us will soon be in trouble. He is such a sly creepy guy, and not your type—far beneath you. Do not forget you used to be Garry Christodoulou's wife. Draco also believes he is morally corrupt to his core, very licentious, a pervert. He will smear the family's reputation."

"Thank you for this wise and motherly piece of advice," said Anita, looking at her daughter in the mirror, "And thank you for giving birth to me!"

"What do you mean, Mum?" asked Calypso, offering her mum an overly kind smile.

"Garry Christodoulou's daughter," said Anita, resuming brushing her long hair, "Why do you think I am not able to tell what is good or bad for me?"

"Mum, I am sorry. I didn't mean that," said Calypso, taking the brush off Anita's hand, "Let me brush your hair. What I am worried about is your mental situation, which could easily be exploited by men like Franco. Considering the age gap between you and Franco, Draco and I believe he is after something else. Draco also believes that this relationship is a disgrace for the family as it isn't based on the right prerogatives—neither side has shown any. He also believes that it shouldn't go any further."

"Is there anything else you two might be worried about," asked Anita, watching her daughter's face intently.

"Oh, yes," replied Calypso, avoiding Anita's eyes, "Draco... You know, it is not me. It is him. He believes there has been something untoward going on between you and Gol, the man who murdered our dad. He believes you should stay away from him and this Italian guy if you expect us to forgive you for betraying Dad."

"Very interesting!" said Anita, turning around, and gently taking the brush off Calypso's hand, "I didn't know Gol murdered your dad! Let me think if he had a good enough motive to murder your dad. Oh, you know

194

my brain; I have never been good at supposing and imagining. Yes, I can feel it now, something is signalling in my head. Yes, it must be it. It was a long time ago, long before your dad's unfortunate death, that I met Gol in a party. He came over to me and said 'Anita, I am dying for your arse'! What a bloody scallywag! No proper man would die for a woman's arse! Do you know how I responded to his rude remark? I slapped him and told him that my arse had a proper owner, a very proud gentleman with Greek blood running in his veins. 'Anita, I will get your arse and your husband'! He said this to me and left, with his ego badly wounded."

"Mum!" said Calypso, a tornado of hysteria engulfing her face, "Mum, I have got to go now! Yes, Draco is on his own, and it is going to be a busy day."

"Go, my child," said Anita, her eyes moistening, "And remember, you and Draco should hurry up and sort this out before it is too late. Trap your dad's murderer before he manages to conquer your mum's arse!"

"That was hilarious, Anita!" said Franco, entering the bedroom, "I was about to blast out a laugh."

"Where were you hiding?" asked Anita, smiling.

"There, behind the door."

"So you heard what we said?"

"Yes, and loved this 'arse conquering' part of it!" said Franco, now blasting out a hearty laughter, "I didn't know Gol was a fan of your arse!"

"Oh, Gol," said Anita, aborting the winding laughter in her and replacing it with a rather sad smile, "I wouldn't have slapped him. I would have only told him 'boy, you are always late'."

"Very kind and gentle," said Franco, "Are you still fasting on thinking and making decisions?" asked Franco, laughing.

"Oh, yes, please. Just for another while!" replied Anita with her head tilted, "Tell me what should I do next."

"Pack up, right now. We are going to Italia. We will be driving to Milan," said Franco, "Now they know that you know what they have been up to; that whatever of these bogus stories they have dictated to Sophie, have been related to you. Calypso is right now running down to the restaurant to inform Draco about this 'arse conquering' thing you mentioned. Therefore, I think it isn't safe for you to remain here."

"I see," said Anita, picking up her hairclips, "I hope they quickly sort this out before it is too late."

"I hope so, as it is the only slight chance left for them," said Franco, throwing a very empathic look at Anita.

"So you know what I mean?" asked Anita, turning towards the mirror.

"I know," replied Franco, "You hope they run away before the truth of this case is revealed, in which case it would be the end of them. To take their last chance, they need money. Draco sold the house a while ago. Where is the money? As far as I know, he has already gambled away half of it, and the other half has mysteriously disappeared. Add to this all, his addiction to cocaine; I don't think they will ever have a chunk of money in their pocket. The other day one of the staff told me that Draco has been stealing from the staff's tips box since ages ago; that he also has been fiddling with their wages; that he is now paying his staff off-the-books to evade taxes. Despite all these misunderstandings they have towards me, I have been trying my best to find a way you could best help your children out of their self-created plight, but I am not sure if there is anything you could do."

"There is something I can do for them," said Anita, holding her face in her hands, "I can pray and shed tears for them. It is so painful for a mother who has never been allowed to help her children. I am not trying to justify my failures, but it is the way it was. Garry never allowed me to feel myself, and as a result, I failed to feel and understand my children. They only followed him, and eventually became him. Draco is an enhanced version of his dad: a very justified façade underneath which there is a very harmful form of rodent mischief with a streak of evil attraction in it. Strangely, there isn't even a speck of what I am in my children! I wish I had a little scientific knowledge so that I could look at it and learn if human genes can override and overwhelm each other. I think they can, otherwise, my other three children, who were brought up by my mum, wouldn't have developed the same abnormal rodent characteristics! You keep telling me that I am worthy of so much; that life will reward me with peace for the pain I have endured. I wish I had neither endured any pain nor deserved any peace. I wish I had come to this world as a tree, as trees are the only winners among the living things. They live so long that death becomes meaningless to them. They have an ever-returning spring of rejuvenation. They never mourn for the leaves they lose. I have lost all my leaves, and been cued towards a cold and unrelenting winter."

Franco said nothing. He helped her with packing up. It was the

196

unfulfilled part of what Anita was that had initially attracted him towards her, the dormant and immaculate passions, and her keen desire to surface and live them. As an inherently passionate man, he had seen, delineated on her face, the earnest will of recovering and depositing her young soul in a well-deserved and trustworthy heart. Still physically fit, she had—without the disheartening fear of disgracing herself—allowed Franco's curious interest in her to be drafted and outlined. With the wisely applied confidence of a buyer of vintage hearts, this connoisseur of his own trade had eventually won her trust. She had noticed, with a youthful grain of joy germinating in her heart, that it was not the same old story of the younger man searching for the oracle of carnal pleasures within an older woman. With a suppressed wealth of alacrity and a still-forceful-enough feminine sensuality and charm within her, she had soon let herself in to the passionate game designed by Franco.

"Franco," said Anita, folding a long light green skirt, "I think I can learn the Italian language in a year or so. In the past, I never had the chance to have a look into my heart and see to my numerous passions. I have recently noticed that I am now overly interested in word and expression, as if they had no place in my life in the past. Now I can almost feel the words and tell what they have to convey and how they do it."

"I have noticed that you have noticed this," said Franco, laughing, "How have you felt the Italian language so far?"

"Emphatic," replied Anita, a multiplying sweet and solemn smile appearing on her face, "Ruthlessly honest, for the most parts pronounced as it is written, generous with applying the stress to make sure nothing is held back in reserve or exposed to doubt, black is black and white is white. And in terms of soul, beauty, lyricality and felicity within this language, I should say speaking Italian is like having a passionate foreplay before—before—"

"Before entering the purgatory!" said Franco, in a serious tone, as if speaking Italian was actually a substitute for foreplay and, well, a pass to the purgatory and the eventual expiation!

"Franco, you are unseriously serious!" said Anita, laughing, "Sometimes you make me confused!"

"I am so glad to hear this," said Franco, in a tone hard to tell its direction, "Women fall in love only when they lose their bearings. To make a woman confused, a man must be a serious clown; but the problem with this attitude is that the serious clown would eventually promote himself to

197

a philosopher, and as women can't stand philosophy, they would look for another clown, not knowing that a clown incapable of promoting himself to a philosopher, well, is not worth loving."

"Franco, I am now really confused," said Anita, laughing, "Please, remain a clown!"

"Please, remain confused. And I promise you will never notice my philosophical promotion," said Franco, letting out a frivolous clownish laughter.

Franco gazed at Anita, a lingering and heavy gaze, one of those that sallies out of a niche in one's mind like a bird in a dark room, leaving behind a wake of silence and doubt. He had experienced this a while ago, and now a question had begun to form in his mind: was Anita's eager tendency towards romanticism and sensibility an early sign of a quick recovery from her traumatic past, or was it, or could it be a habitual try at denying her miserable past altogether?

Chapter 28

It was raining outside, generously and unhurriedly, exactly in the manner David had wished. After checking his appearance in the mirror for the last time, he walked downstairs, and as he had expected, he found Gol standing by the window and watching the rain. Walking across the large dining room, his eyes caught a new painting on the wall. He was to ignore it, but when the pair of little anxious green eyes in the painting stared at him, he walked over to have a look at it. It was a little girl in tattered clothes, with unwashed face and hair, holding an intact loaf of bread in her small hands while her anxious eyes wondered off to a distance. He walked over to Gol with the pair of little eyes lingering in his mind, and stood beside him without saying a word, and watched the rain. Unsaid hellos, unuttered things, unexpressed affections and appreciations, nothing needed to be vocalised or shown between them. He had noticed this a while ago, when he had gone through the time since he had entered Gol's life. To do so, he had taken a few steps back, to the day his dad had passed away, and to the day his mum had attempted suicide. As a young neglected teenager with his head filled up with some mechanical instructions—he had observed—he would have never reached a point at which he could take and give without the need for words and guttural expressions.

'David, feel whatever has to be felt, and understand whatever has to be understood. Do not mix them up.'

He whispered to himself the advice Gol had given him. He also remembered one of the conditions he had put forward the day he had decided to take him and Emily into his custody: *'you will never use the phrase 'mate it doesn't make sense' when it comes to making connections with other humans'*.

"It is a romantic day, mate. Isn't it?" said David, looking at Gol's profile. "It is overcast and wet, beautiful in its own way," said Gol, smiling.

"Imagine Nadira and me with a couple of children walking in the rain in a near future!" said David, exulting in his own words.

"The entire universe is somewhat melancholic," said Gol, "And that is exactly why the nature has engrained in our minds the ability to imagine. The ones who stop imagining and dreaming, will become too serious, and eventually fall into the trap of absurdity. David, you are now outside of the box; do not allow society to put you back inside it."

"I get what you mean, Gol," said David.

"Good!" said Gol, "Now, go to the restaurant, manage the food with Clement, and make sure you are back here before noon. Mrs Baygum and her children are supposed to turn up at half past ten."

"Okay," said David, "Gol, do you think you would be able to tell us the second part of the Sohrab and Afsoon's story? I think Nadira would love it. I told her about the first part a while ago."

"It has already been arranged by the brand new Eve, Emily," replied Gol, laughing.

With Emily and Nadira in charge, patiently receiving some unsolicited advice from Cynthia and Mrs Aziza Baygum, the large table in the dining room was beautifully set for a small banquet at which the date and other requirements for Nadira and David's wedding were to be discussed and determined. After all the invited guests had arrived, Gol welcomed them in a brief manner, and left the lectern to Aziza, which soon proved to be a small mistake, as she ploughed through the entire history of marriage and the importance of it. Needless to say that she conferred with Holy Quran and Allah, and using her own unique illative reasoning system, she considered marriage as the only gate to the heaven and eternal salvation. To enhance her points and nail her own colours to the mast, she used all sorts of struts and stays—some directly borrowed from Allah, and some others inferred from Sharia Law and Hadiths. But Aziza being Aziza, she knew she had to somehow dilute her views to serve the occasion and sound less extraneous: very cinematically, she pulled out from her handbag a pair of green fabric gloves, and with some gesticulation, she put them on and took the task of serving the forbidden juice to her guests upon herself!

"Well, my dears," said Aziza, lifting up a bottle of red wine, "Just for the purpose of offering you a piece of general knowledge, which I am sure you would all appreciate it, I am going to give you a brief history of alcohol while I am pouring you wine or whatever else that you may wish. Well, let me begin from here, where Mr Gibran is sat. Bearing in mind that this very fine Egyptian gentleman is a devout Muslim who believes there is no harm in downing a glass of wine, I should particularly ask him to pay attention to

200

the story of alcohol. Mr Gibran, have half a glass now, and I will come round again. Alcohol, my dears, was discovered by Allah himself—"

"Created and not discovered, Aziza," said Mr Gibran, laughing.

"Oh yes, Allah is a creator and not a discoverer. Thank you, wise man," said Aziza, "So what did he need alcohol for? For testing humans and gauging their mental strength against the corrupting temptations thrown at them by Satan. Allah, you may not know, is always testing and strengthening us. He needed a name for the stuff he had created: alcohol, he named it alcohol, which means 'a giant demon or an evil spirit'! And it was supposed, Allah had decided so, to be used as a vaccine, like our modern day vaccines, but Satan added something to it to make it overly strong, too strong for the delicate human brain to bear. Of course Allah got wise to it, but he decided to leave it as it was! You may ask why. Well, my dears, Allah is the greatest of politicians—you could ask the English establishment if you don't believe me—so He used the tampered-with-*giant demon* as a means of spotting the potential wavers and troublemakers within His kingdom. Therefore, my dears, whoever allows, knowingly or unknowingly, a giant demon into their heads, they go on Allah's rosters and rotors, which would definitely be used against them in the day of judgement."

It was a great shame that Aziza was not educated enough to open up her intuitive takes on the world around her. Suggesting that the English establishment could confirm and define Allah's political mind was not a mere humorous gesture in her fabricated story of alcohol. As a very political woman by nature—just like Allah and the English establishment—Aziza had learnt, by heart, that the art of fabrication, duplicity and acting, if mastered wisely, would yield desirable results without exposing one to judgement and admonishment. As a pragmatic woman with a thoroughly pragmatic take on Allah, Quran and the intricacies and idiosyncrasies of the English society, she had acquired a very covert Machiavellian philosophy with the word '*means*' at its very core. Though she had failed to enter the academic world, but she had successfully positioned herself at a viewpoint where she could practically learn the psychology and mores of the society. To do so, Aziza had used the first practical *means* available to her: her unique bumps and her enchanting charms, learning with all her parts— physically and mentally! Like all accomplished Machiavellians, she had also attired herself with the art of creating justifiable pretexts and spotting

201

the loopholes within whatever she had to deal with.

Aziza's humour was the humour of a successful women who had been, very wily and very aptly, playing the role of a broke one! Aziza was, curiously and understandably, very much grateful to Allah, Quran and, of course, the English establishment and society—though the latter would always be favoured secretly.

"I don't believe Allah would punish people for drinking alcohol," said Lateefa, Mr Gibran's eldest daughter.

"My dear, you have married an English man," said Aziza, putting the corkscrew on the table and standing akimbo, "The Englishman is even more religious than the Muslim man! And his religion is a mixture of alcohol and jealousy! So, don't worry. Keep drinking because Allah would only punish him. Why only him? Because if you refuse to drink he will be offended, and he might divorce you.

"Allah hates divorce more than he hates drinkers."

"Aziza, you are spot-on!" said Jamila, laughing, "All people, more or less, believe in a sort of religion; and religions are too many, alcohol included."

"You are right, dear lady," said Usman with a very educated smile, "Whatever is based on some strict principles and rituals is definitely a religion. Alcohol is the religion of this country, and it has its unbreachable rituals! The followers of this religion have to imbibe a minimum of forty-two litres of alcoholic drinks per week in order to qualify for a minimum of reward; and failing to take in the minimum required amount, needless to say, would bring about an unspeakably torturous punishment: a healthy existence! A man, who loses half his teeth and damages all his inner organs before reaching the grand age of thirty, does so because he sees it as a sacrifice towards attaining a better place in hereafter!"

"What are its rituals?" asked Mr Gibran, musingly.

"Not very complicated," replied Usman, "The higher the intake the higher the reward! And like most of the other religions, the main parts of prayers take place during the weekends: it begins with the guzzling of ten pints of beer at home; and it has to be done between six and seven o'clock; and it is only a warmup for the real bender, which begins at half past eight and goes on until the next morning. And during the mentioned time, the worshipers must trip to the loo at least seventy-two times! Throwing up is not compulsory, but it will be a bonus! Urinating in the street while tottering back home in the morning is considered obligatory! Stumbling and hitting the ground like a basketball is another highly rewarding practice within this unique religion! And the hangover is approached as a very honest yearning for the divine blessings! The main point within the philosophy of this religion is to dampen the mental existence and wear out the physical form of it in order to have an early reunion with its essence in the heaven! Mind you, their 'heaven' is actually an ocean filled up with pure alcohol, and there is no woman in there, but there are fish and chips! See, completely different from the other heavens we know! People have always been overtaking each other when it comes to being peculiar, but I don't think the English will ever be overtaken with their unique and very simple religion!"

"You are right, Usman!" said Lateefa, "My husband is dead ritualistic when it comes to drinking alcohol, especially at the weekends. He believes the weekend's drinks ought to be taken in within specific timeframes. For example, he downs the first of the ten pints, which must be taken in at home, at exactly six o'clock, and the last one at the last minute of seven! And then he guzzles at least twenty shots of spirits and six shots of mouthwash between half past eight to half past nine at a tavern (shrine), before going on a tour of other shrines in the town like a devout pilgrim! He also makes sure he drinks eight shots at each shrine he visits."

"You said there were no women in the heaven promised by this religion," said Mr Gibran, laughing, "So where would the female followers of this religion go?"

"Good question, Mr Gibran," said Usman, "The female followers of this religion will end here on earth! They are considered as ephemeral; that is why they called them 'English roses'!"

"Guys, the food is here," said Aziza, smiling at Mr Gibran, who was about to ask another question, "Let's eat first, and I think we will have enough time to go through all the religions in the world."

Now with Clement and Islam in charge, the food, mostly Indian and Middle Eastern, was served.

Aziza kept going round and asking the guests to help themselves to this or that dish, explaining the ingredients and the best way to prepare and cook them. In doing so, she refused to confirm Clement's mostly modifying comments, stating that cooking was a job for women, to which Clement responded with a smile and some head bobbles.

After lunch, Aziza, Cynthia and Gol, very much to David's delight, announced that the wedding would take place in a fortnight. And after seeing off some of their guests, they sat, drinking coffee and chatting about a variety of different subjects among which was the confabulation about the English *religion* and its unwavering rituals, with Usman revealing a new form of himself—now an educated rationalist rather than a religious man he used to be. Under Aziza's constant compulsive gestures, he, directly and indirectly, forswore some of his hard-core beliefs in Allah and Islam, and in religion in general, which plus giving up wearing oversize clothes and watching Mike Tyson's life story every other day, was a drastic change for a man who used to hold beliefs such as 'Islam was the first word uttered by Allah'! Nonetheless, and as it could be felt within his sardonic story of the English *religion*, and also his study of law, he was still very much prone to hold a level of irascibility against the English worldview. Though now evidently more composed and in peace with himself, and less likely to slur over his views, but his particular emphasis on the power of law could well be taken as an advert towards a fresh contentious strife over his identity and his place in the society.

"Gol, how happy are you with my Islam so far?" asked Aziza, kissing her Islam, now the proud father to a little girl.

"He has done a brilliant job for us," replied Gol, offering Islam an affirming smile, "Teaming up with David, he managed to turn around one of our losing restaurants, and now he is managing it like a qualified businessman. I am very happy with him."

"My dear Gol," said Aziza, "Islam is the result of my business mind. Unlike Usman, who is somewhat melancholic by nature, my Islam has always been paying full attention to my way of doing business and managing things. And above all, he is also a better Muslim than Usman, who is now changing rapidly."

"Mum, Allah knows better," said Islam, smiling placidly, "Brother Usman will get his Master's in a few months' time. An educated man would see his God differently; it is natural. Inshallah we will all be good servants to Allah."

"See, how marriage has changed my Islam," said Aziza, kissing his Islam again, "Marriage is the tradition of prophet Mohammed, Allah's peace be upon him, and all believers must uphold this holy manner of reunion. My Islam used to be like a loose cannon, ready to wage war and go for it with full force. Thanks to Allah, he is now full of peace and far

204

away from rage."

"Mum, I used to be a loose cannon against the rascals," said Islam, "And not being melancholic like my brother, I soon realised, using my instinct, that rascality was a norm. Rascality is a norm; and acting like a loose cannon against it is most abnormal! And I think this question of identity my brother is dealing with is just like a bad joke."

"How melancholic is Nadira?" asked Gol, musingly looking at Islam's face.

"As melancholic as Usman is," replied Islam, "She also keeps banging on about the importance of personhood and all these educated things."

"Gol, we are ready," said Emily from the other side of the large table.

"She has already told us about the first part of the story you are to tell us," said Aziza, beaming at Emily's shining face.

"Mate, Nadira and I just can't wait to hear the rest of the story," said David, holding Nadira's hand, "She has already fallen in love with Afsoon."

"Well, first of all allow me to thank all of you," said Gol, "We are truly honoured to have people like you as our guests on such a happy and blessed day. Before beginning to narrate the story, I would like to say a few words about the importance of the stories like this. As 'rational animals', we are credited, and our credit is *rationality,* meaning minus it we are only animals! Within an honest comparison, a dog would be deemed superior to a man minus rationality, for a dog is privileged with a natural wealth of appreciation and loyalty. An agoraphobic man, who walks backwards away from the edge of the roof without looking behind him, will definitely fall off from the other side. In the same light, too much *rationality* would become the plague of *rationality*! The story you are about to hear is the story of some irrationally rational people! The entire universe is a paradox; and the ones who try to make sense of it properly, will only cause more ambiguity. *'Drink all your passion, and be a disgrace'*."

"Uncle Gol, what does it mean 'be a disgrace'?" asked Nadira, the youngest among the audience.

"Melancholic Nadira!" said Gol, smiling, "The world owes too much to the melancholic people. Well, it simply means, listen to your heart, and avoid unnecessary mindfulness.

"So, we left the story when separation, this inevitable poignant part of life, was lurking around in a mist of uncertainty, and how it eventually loomed over and devoured us. It was a cool morning, and when we were preparing ourselves to say the morning prayers, that my dad announced that we would be going back to Afghanistan in a few days. He said that he had a dream the night before, in which prophet Mohammed had appeared and asked him to go back to Afghanistan and defend Islam; that Islam was in danger; that without Islam human life would be degraded to the lowest degree of animality. The Prophet Mohammed had also scornfully reminded him of the Iranian teenagers as young as twelve, walking on the minefields and throwing themselves under the enemy's tanks only to defend Islam! The prophet had also chided him for living a life of comfort and gluttony, eating freshly baked bread with freshly laid fried eggs and cream and buttermilk… He had also mentioned lamb chops and mutton Korma on a mound of finely cooked fluffy rice! And at the end he had reminded him that life without Islam would not be worth living; that if Islam was removed from the face of the earth Allah would turn all Muslims into *man* Korma and feed them to the giant beasts guarding the hell! It was actually a strange time for Muslims and Islam, as the 'all-knowing' Muslim leaders were trying to put the prayer rug and the worshiper above the worshiped!

"And thus, we had to go back home to defend Islam! Grandma, Sohrab and Afsoon, these creatures of heart and intuition, tried to dissuade my dad by the means of reasoning, which of course was a futile waste of breath, as he had been ordered and mandated by the Prophet Mohammed! He was adamantly set to sacrifice himself for Islam, and there was no force deterrent enough to make him even think again, let alone forgo his divine-sealed mandate."

"Gol, where did you stand on the issue?" asked Emily, musingly.

"A very clever question," replied Gol, "Being associated with Brother Sohrab had somewhat softened the steel of my metaphysical beliefs and opened my eyes. Nevertheless, I have to confess that, bearing in mind that I was only a teenager, I was undecided: half my mind was with Islam and Prophet Mohammed and the other half with Brother Sohrab. To avoid any unnecessary frictions with my dad, I kept quiet and gave myself up to the hands of fate.

"Sohrab tried to guide my dad to a point at which he might see the bigger picture. He told him that there would be a future for Afghanistan when the futile war was over; that if all the refugees like him failed to comprehend this, Afghanistan's post war future would soon become a painful past.

"Brother Sohrab was right. When the war against Russians ended years later, Afghanistan lumbered into the future like a night-blind wounded black horse and immediately rolled into a long-lasting civil war, stumbling and landing on its own limbs. Imagine shattered bones within flesh and a mental tendency accustomed to nycotophilia... Afghanistan suffered, and still is suffering because after the war there was not enough light, I mean bright educated and meritorious forces to guide the country to the right path. The little boys, who had fled the country with their families when the war broke out, became teenagers and were thrown back into the war fronts to be either perished or survive and grow into the mature voracious warmongers!

"'Brother Hassan, if you think you have to go back' said Sohrab, already knowing the nature of my dad's response, 'Then I think you should allow me to marry Afsoon and leave your family here'.

"'An Afghan man will never leave his family unattended'! boomed my dad, his eyes now two burning mirrors, reflecting pure primitiveness, 'Allah will pour boiling tar down my throat if I leave my wife and my daughter unattended! We will leave, right now, all of us! And if you love Afsoon, well, you can only marry her in Afghanistan'.

"We left. It took us two days to reach the border. It was a dark night, and we had to wait behind the gates of the border immigration office until the next morning. I threw my shawl on the asphalt and lay down with my shoes under my head. I was craving for a fast sleep, I was wishing crying begging for unconsciousness, for a moment at which my existence would be deemed as a mistake and immediately undone. I wished my existence was like those scribbles on the old blackboards so that I could grab a sponge and wipe it off. An unavailing last try before you get engulfed by a relentless surge of grief. I was fully aware of what was going on in my surroundings: at each side of the border a full-blown war had gained momentum, and only God knew when it was going to end. People had been pitched into a game of bloodshed and unspeakable pain and anguish. Was it right for me to tend to my emotions and be irrelevantly affected by them while people were being pummelled incessantly by the earth and the heaven? The answer to this question was equally easy and difficult. It was easy because I was a teenager and the heart in my chest was not a big one. And it was difficult because the consequences of emotional decisions made by me could inflict pain on my family. Even the thought that I might not be able to see Sohrab again could make me cry, it did and I cried my heart out in silence. The dark sad night and I were growing older, one slowly and leisurely and the other hastily and painfully."

"You were missing Sohrab. Weren't you?" asked Cynthia, tilting her head.

"I was missing myself," replied Gol, smiling, "I learned this years later. I was aspiring to goodness, and it was within Sohrab; and strangely, it was calling me. As the dawn was looming, I walked over to Afsoon, who was leaning against the gate with a blanket wrapped around her. As soon as I sat beside her, she whispered to me 'Kaka (brother), go back to Sohrab'. I could not believe my ears. 'Write a note and put it into Dad's pocket. Tell him you will come back. And tell Sohrab I do not want him to come after me. It is safer in Iran for both of you'.

"In a matter of minutes, I scribbled a few words on a piece of paper, slipped it into my dad's pocket and left, carrying the pang of pain of not being able to say goodbye to them with me.

"Sohrab and Grandma received me very warmly, though they were somewhat unhappy with the way I had left my family. A few days later, Sohrab and I went to the city and found an Afghan family and brought them to the village to stay with Grandma and help her with the sheep and the farm. A while later, we received a letter from Afsoon, addressed to both of us, urging us not to allow our emotions to affect our decisions. She had expressed and highlighted her worries that we might fail to see the consequences of moving to Afghanistan. In this letter, her first one, she had addressed Sohrab as *brother* which was a deterrent gesture to prevent him from going to Afghanistan and risking his life because of her.

"We were relatively happy, Sohrab had found a place for me at a college in the city, I was corresponding with Afsoon and was aware of the family's situation… And in all, our lives had taken the right turn and were well leading us towards even better days. But as all the moments of life have a designated time and place to arrive at, we were badly hit by the arrival of one of these moments: it was a Friday morning, and Sohrab and I had just woken up and were moving around in the yard, overseeing what the Afghan family were doing and checking what had to be done in the day. There was a moment when we came face to face, and there was this unuttered and alarming question in the minds of both of us: where is

208

Grandma? She should have been up and around by now! We both dashed into the house and seconds later, stood behind the door of Grandma's room, dreading the inevitable, and what had intensified this dread for me was the mental connection between Sohrab and Grandma. The moment he looked at me in the yard, I realized something had been revealed to him. I knocked on the door several times, and eventually pushed the door open. By the way Grandma was lying in bed, we realised something was wrong. Sohrab kneeled down beside her and seconds later, he painfully forced out a few words 'stroke, Grandma has suffered a stroke'! I sprinkled some water on to her face while Sohrab was holding her in his arms. The lines of her face wriggled and she toiled to open her eyes for a fleeting second. As her heavy eyelids dropped, a very faint smile appeared on her face.

If there is no one around to watch you and rejoice in whatever you do, or even show a bit of jealousy, there is no point in being alive and living. Grandma's words, ringing in Sohrab's ears. 'Call everyone into the room' Sohrab asked me, still holding Grandma in his arms. I immediately called the Afghan family into the room. Grandma toiled again to open her eyes but she failed.

"Another fleeting smile appeared on her face. The moment had arrived. Grandma was now like the sun on the summit of a high mountain at the sunset. Unconsciously, we all followed Sohrab's solemn attitude—we did not cry. We did not lament. And years later, I fully comprehended what was going on in Sohrab's mind during those bitter moments: Grandma's existence was an existence of celebration and so was her death. She gently slipped away. We watched her die, as we had watched her live.

"We both knew the days ahead of us after the death of Grandma would be completely different.

"There was an emotional void to be dealt with, especially for Sohrab, as it was Grandma's unadulterated humanity that had bestowed upon him the strength to overcome some of his material needs and live like a sage at that very young age. It took us a while to come to terms with Grandma's absence in our lives. We moved on, and were doing very well until I noticed some profound changes taking place in Sohrab's mind and heart. Once and when we both were irrigating a field of clover, he told me about a dream he had had a while after Grandma's death.

"'It was about Afsoon' he said, taking off his round straw hat, 'I was walking on the bank of a fast-flowing river when I noticed someone was swimming in the river. A while later, and when I was walking down some stone steps leading to the river, I noticed the person swimming was in trouble. I almost flew down the steps and immediately ran towards the river, with the sheer intention of diving in and helping that person. Just moments before reaching the river edge, I noticed the person in the river was a woman and almost naked. I hesitated for a few seconds, dealing with the silly question of whether it was right for me to touch a naked woman! It was a woman about to lose her life. A touched but alive woman would be a million times better than an untouched but dead one, I said to myself when frantically swimming towards her. I shouted to her before approaching her, and she turned around. When I saw her face, my whole share of adrenalin in life was pumped into my blood at once and rushed up to my brain. Gol, it was Afsoon! It took me a few long minutes to pull her out of the river, and it was then that I realized she was unconscious and in urgent need of help.

'Meanwhile and when I was taking my breath back and thinking what I should do, a tall western-looking woman appeared from nowhere and immediately kneeled beside Afsoon and asked me to leave her to her. I walked away from them, and minutes later, I found myself walking through an unknown woodland. Why did I leave Afsoon with a woman I did not know? This question banged in my head and made me turn around and run back towards the river at full pelt. They had disappeared! There was an eerie silence and a stagnated river'.

"I knew he would, sooner or later, fly towards Afsoon. Have you ever seen a butterfly fly around a candle? The love between Sohrab and Afsoon was the love of a butterfly for a candle. It is in the burning light that a butterfly seeks the end to its life. The end to Sohrab's life was Afsoon, and therefore, he would not mind going to a war-torn Afghanistan and even be perished.

"And the day came. He handed over the house and the farm to his uncles, and we moved to the city to prepare ourselves for our long perilous journey to Afghanistan. I was a million percent wrong by being a million percent sure that we both would be going to Afghanistan. As if the hand of fate was not going to allow me to be with Sohrab.

"'You will be going to Europe' he said with a bitter smile. 'Remember what Afsoon had asked us in her first letter: 'do not allow your emotions affect your decisions'. Here there is a question and based on it, there is a decision to be made: how much of our lives can we save? It is said the war in Afghanistan has turned out to be one of the most atrocious wars ever, with Russian soldiers ignoring the wartime rules and even the very rudiments of moral obligations. Your father in war fronts, your mother, and Afsoon left in God's trust in a remote village. They all could perish at any moment. I am under no illusion that your father would ask me to join him in war fronts and fight against the 'infidels', the ones who are set to 'remove' Islam from the face of the earth! And it all means chances are that we might not survive. You are a bright boy, and I think you are the part of our lives we can save. Who would be remembering and narrating our story if we all perished?'.

"Apparently, I was destined to be turned away from the cool and clear well of affection and happiness while always just inches away from it. I had to make a decision, and I had been advised not to be emotional with it. A teenager being all but emotions, I made it, I made an impossible decision. Apart from my mum, this ever-unconditional friend, this ever-loyal lover, Afsoon and Sohrab were the only human beings who loved me from the bottom of their hearts and wanted nothing for me but health and a future. Within the time we had lived together, we had become one; and adding to this, Sohrab's gnostic way of looking at human relationship, I was convinced that our story was well worth having a narrator. 'Gol, learn how to turn your pains into happiness' he told me at the moment we got separated from each other.

"With the help of Sohrab's dad I was sneaked into Turkey, and a few days later, I moved to Greece where I stayed for a while until my move to England was planned and finalised by Sohrab's dad…"

Chapter 29

"Elizabeth!" uttered David, walking towards the door, "Why are you standing there? Come in, please."

"I have come here to—to—" said Elizabeth, stepping in.

"You have come here to speak with Gol," interrupted David, ruffling his hair, "You have come here to speak with Gol about Sophie. Am I right, Elizabeth?"

"You are right," replied Elizabeth, her voice cracked, a gentle tremor running in the lines of her white face.

"Good!" said David, "We have been waiting for you. We knew you would, sooner or later, come here. You should have come much earlier, Elizabeth."

"My husband didn't allow me," said Elizabeth, a streak of pain appearing on her face, "He believes Gol is an evil man."

"Oh yes, *'fair is foul and foul is fair'*, said David, laughing, "Take a seat, over there, at the table. He is upstairs. I will go and call him."

Elizabeth, slightly unsteady and confused, exactly like her Sophie, walked towards the table while turning around and looking at the fine artefacts, paintings and pictures lining the office walls. She stretched her hand out to pull the chair back. Hesitant; she dithered, changed her mind, turned around and walked over to the rather large bookshelf in the far corner of the office. As an academic person, teaching geography for the most of her life, she was not much interested in the subjects that would fall short of being categorised as scientific and factual. In fact being excessively and unnecessarily *academic* was responsible for the lack of interest and alacrity towards anything open to doubt and in need of modification within her mind. Nevertheless, as a result of being pitched into the predicament created by Sophie and, consequently, facing the necessity of discerning the right and setting it apart from the wrong, she had begun to doubt her mentality and her worldview. She looked at the books and read the titles of some of them. They were all closely connected, those apparently muted books, each offering a piece of advice along with permissive preferences; each a

212

precious anthology of its own kind. They were books of literature, language, history, philosophy, psychology, sociology… They were all directly related to the wherefores of human life, and none of them was to advocate the necessity of a thoroughly factual way of living it.

"Elizabeth!" said Gol, standing in the threshold with Cynthia and David behind him, "I was expecting you long ago. Anyway, I welcome you, and hope we can find a solution to this problem."

"Oh, hello then," said Elizabeth, throwing a fleeting look at the books over her shoulder, and turning towards Gol, "I am very sorry for all this."

"No need to be sorry," said Gol, pulling a chair back for her to sit, "It is not going to change anything."

"Elizabeth, I am so happy that you have come here to see Gol," said David, ruffling his hair, "I seriously believe this is going to be the first serious step in pulling Sophie out of her cage! And this is my mum, Cynthia."

"I very much hope so," said Elizabeth, pushing the chair back and getting up to shake hands with Cynthia.

"Elizabeth, we will eagerly listen to you whenever you are ready," said Gol, pulling the chair beside his back for Cynthia.

"Well, let me go back and begin from the beginning," said Elizabeth, offering Cynthia a very innocent smile, "It was around six years ago when she came back home for Christmas. She wasn't the same Sophie she used to be. She was happy and unprecedently calm and composed, but what was behind her joyous state was apparently too rich to be contained within her. It was at lunch that she mentioned a name for the first time, and kept repeating it since, as if it was a most rewarding mantra. 'Who is Gol?' asked my husband. 'Oh, yes, he is the man who gave me the job I told you about' replied Sophie, and now overly animated, she continued, 'He has been so kind to me. But he is a bit strange, yes, he is. I think he doesn't like me at all. I can't understand why he is so kind to me if he doesn't like me. He doesn't speak to me at all. But the strange thing is that when he is around I am the happiest girl in the world. Every day he comes in, checks what is going on with his business, and then keeps himself busy by reading books. We eat lunch together in absolute silence. Sometimes I feel like I want to grab him by the collar, shout at him and ask him to speak with me'.

"'How old is he?' asked her dad.

"'A bit younger than you are' replied Sophie.

"'Stay away from him. He is an abuser' said his dad emphatically.

213

"As a woman, I knew what my Sophie was dealing with was pure love, but I didn't have the permission or the courage, or even the will to interfere and express my own views on what was going on within my daughter. Within our household we all had agreed that truth was an arbitrary concept, a chunk of dough, something that could be formed into any desirable shape, re-formed and even deformed, if necessary. I had also learnt that the wisest and the safest way to approach a matter was to avoid it all together by pretending that the present form of it was impeccable and ultimate! I had never been allowed to ask questions and wish to examine things and ask for evidence. Perhaps my Sophie needed only a few encouraging words from her mum, telling her to go back to Gol, grab him by the collar and shout to him that you love him. She left with an-ever-growing confusion on her face, and I *proudly* buried the desire I left unexpressed beside so many other innocent desires."

"Fair is foul and foul is fair!" said David, ruffling his hair, "When I was at school, I used to hate Shakespeare, but now that, with Gol's help, I am able to understand him, I believe that our confusion over what is wrong and what is right is rather a historical one. Who is an abuser? Is it the person who does not abuse, or is it the person who does abuse? Is *abuse* a negative term or a positive one? Or perhaps it is a bisexual term!"

Gol stretched his hand out, ruffled David's hair and let out a hearty laugh. Cynthia and Elizabeth followed suit. Minutes later, and before going upstairs to Cynthia's gallery, David told Elizabeth about the desk wrapped in white sheet, Sophie's, and that it would only be used again if Sophie was the one to use it. It deeply affected Elizabeth. She stared at the desk and shed a few tears.

Entering the gallery, Elizabeth marvelled at how she was marvelled at Cynthia's art gallery. Had she ever been so impressed by some works of art? Could she remember the last time she had been moved or wondered or even cheered up by the incorporated aesthetics within any form of art? No, Elizabeth had stopped feeling amazed at the world around her years ago, and when she had gradually become a mirror to herself, reflecting a 'perfect' self to her! She walked towards a large painting on the wall, stood before it, and raising her hand and covering her mouth, she stared at it while her green eyes exhibiting a form of delight she had never experienced up to that point.

"Emily, my daughter," said Cynthia, standing beside Elizabeth, "She is

214

beautiful. Isn't she?"

"This is a breath-taking painting!" said Elizabeth, her eyes shining, "And your Emily's beauty is simply astonishing and strangely imposing!"

"I love that, this imposing element in her beauty," said Cynthia, "You have an eye for subtleties, Elizabeth."

"Oh, no, yes, I think you are right," said Elizabeth with a very mixed smile, "And that is… let me see… that is my Sophie!"

"I did it when I was in prison," said Cynthia, "And that woman is Magdalena, who was keen to turn Sophie into a competent dancer."

"My Sophie is beautiful," said Elizabeth, now standing face to face with her Sophie, "And you have made her look even more beautiful. I was told you imprisoned yourself only to be with my Sophie and protect her. Why did you do that, Cynthia?"

"That is a lengthy and complicated story," said Cynthia, holding Elizabeth's hand, "I will tell you in a better time. Now let's go and sit. I think Gol is going to give us a delicious lunch."

"Gol," said Elizabeth, as soon as they sat at the table that was placed by the one of the large windows at the end of the gallery, "My Sophie told me about all the lunches you had together in full details. She told me that eating with you helped her to turn her hatred of garlic and onion into love; that when sitting beside you she would become a creature well beyond all her likes and dislikes. I am amazed at how you failed to understand that she had fallen in love with you. Gol, you denied my Sophie even a few words. Why Gol? Why?"

Gol crossed his arms on his chest and looked at Elizabeth's face for some seconds, and remained silent. David busied himself with uncorking a bottle of wine. Cynthia looked at her own hands, gently raised her head and smiled at Gol. The door was pushed open and Clement appeared with a rather large round brimmed steel tray over his hands. Lowering the tray and putting it on the table, he offered his trademark universal smile and got himself seated beside Elizabeth. Inside the tray, there was a large crab, two sizeable lobsters, a good number of finely seasoned and cooked red king prawns, a good deal of slightly fried asparagus, some wedged lemon and a lidded container of butter sauce. Throwing the remains of his universal smile at David, he picked up his tools and began to crack open the crab and the lobsters, masterly using the mallet, the crab cracker and forks.

"This is for you, the best part of it," said Clement, putting a mixed plate of crab and lobster flesh, king prawn and asparagus before Elizabeth.

"This is the best starter to drink wine with," said David, getting up to pour the wine.

"Once I cooked a crab for Sophie," said Clement, laughing, "She made a mess of it, cutting her hands in several places, "How is she doing in prison anyway?"

"She is doing very well," said Elizabeth; lifting her glass of wine and offering Clement a smile, she added, "Yes, now she is doing very well."

"Have you recently visited her?" asked Cynthia.

"Yes, I visited her three weeks ago," replied Elizabeth, throwing a look at Gol's pensive face.

"Does she know about what Draco and Christopher had done to her dad?" asked David.

"Yes, she does. I told her everything," replied Elizabeth, throwing another fleeting look at Gol's face, "At first, she didn't want to believe it, but when she saw my tears she relented and eventually brought herself to accept the truth. It was so hard for her to believe that her so-called friends, those scoundrels, had swindled her dad out of all his money!"

"Did she mention anything about her being innocent?" asked David, now intently gazing at Elizabeth's face.

"Oh, no, she didn't," replied Elizabeth, half her face alarmed and the other half embarrassed.

"And it simply means that she still believes in her *friends*," said David, raising his hand and holding his chin, "That she still believes Draco and Christopher are her saviours, and whatever they are doing is based on decency, love and altruism! That she believes that the one who used and abused her was Gol and not her friends! Elizabeth, you know that they have launched a lawsuit against Gol and made your daughter accuse Gol of a crime he had never even thought of! And that would be a tragedy if your daughter has believed that what she believes in this case is true!"

A short spell of heavy silence fell over the place before Cynthia deliberately changed the subject by recounting some of her prison memories, among which there was the story of 'the first vagina' Eileen had told Sophie, a messy story within which there was a precious lesson to be learned: the limitless worth and value of a woman and the importance of recognizing, highlighting and acknowledging them. Adding her interpretation and spicing it with her personal bitter experiences she supplied that if a woman fails to understand and appreciate the core meaning of her beauties—inside and outside—she will become ugly and degraded; and as such, she will become the direct and the indirect promoter of crudity and ugliness.

"Cynthia, you are as good at managing a conversation as you are at painting," said Clement with a full smile.

"She is," said Gol, gesturing David for some more wine, "Cynthia is truly good at managing things because she used to be a master of messing them up!"

"I take that as a wise complement," said Cynthia, laughing, "I think Elizabeth is now ready to go on with whatever she wishes to say about the main subject."

"Well," said Gol, looking at Elizabeth, "Let me say a few words about what Elizabeth said and make the story clear for her, and then we will listen to her. First of all, allow me to make my curiosity towards Sophie clear for you: Elizabeth, it was during those first days that I noticed Sophie had reached *the* crossroad of her life, a crossroad that not too many are fortunate or unfortunate enough to arrive at. I could hear Sophie's heart, guiding her towards me, urging her to try and lay her desire bare, a desire so pure and innocent that I would not hesitate a second in responding to it.

Although I do not expect you to fully understand my points, but I would like to say the love in Sophie's heart was too big and too heavy to be easily delivered. It was this ardent, innocent and honest desire within Sophie's heart that made me curious, and then she became important for me, and also part of me…"

"Gol," interrupted Cynthia, smiling at him, "Shall I explain the rest of it?"

"You shall, Cynthia," replied Gol, taking a covert sigh of relief.

"It is hard for Gol to speak about himself," said Cynthia, smiling at Elizabeth, "But I know how to talk about him. Well, we all fall truly in love only once in our lives, and Sophie's heart had reminded her of this; but as we all know she failed to use her one-off opportunity. Later on, Gol will tell us why she failed. Now, why did Gol become so curious that he decided to give her a place in his heart; that he decided not to leave her to her own devices. He became curious because of what he had within him and he was sure about it. He knew Sophie had fallen in love with his polished an elevated soul. How Sophie's young heart had guided her towards Gol's

217

inner world became the basis of this curiosity I am referring to. In other words, to see what she saw within Gol she had to be a dear and innocent soul; and she was. Dear Elizabeth, I would like to let you know that the same story happened to Gol years ago, and the other side was Cynthia, the very same woman sitting before you right now. She too spotted a different world within Gol and fell in love with it, but the reality was that I simply lacked what it would take: commitment, engagement, and wholeheartedness, the desire to be read and understood like a good book. Moreover, the wrong worldview made me believe that all these great attributes were shackles and fetters, not knowing that they were the very fruits of liberation, as only a liberated soul can understand concepts such as commitment and wholeheartedness and… The other thing I would like to mention here was the delusion that I was unique and always right; that I belonged to a different class, the class of inherent superiority, coming from a source only known to me! Was I really superior to anything? No, it was only a balloon, and it popped up by the fang of reality. Would a *superior thing* ever ask for love and affection? No, being *needy* is the plague of such a *thing*! Years ago Cynthia spat on the face of love because she saw herself above it. And years later, Sophie repeated it, and what makes this thoughtful is the undeniable fact that the other side could categorically be the best choice for any woman. Elizabeth, Gol decided not to forsake and forget Sophie exactly for the same reason he decided not to completely ignore Cynthia. Where would I be right now? A demented middle-aged woman, sectioned in an asylum.

"Where am I right now? I am an artist, reflecting the goodness that reflected my neglected values to me, and very much immune to dementia because I am no longer a master of denial and dressing up my delusions and illusions and foolishly offering them to the world as immaculate truths!"

"Thank you very much, Cynthia," said Gol, "I think now I can put forth my conditions for Elizabeth, and if she understands me clearly, then we will definitely do our best to free Sophie as soon as possible. I should remind Elizabeth that her daughter would have been freed long ago had not her husband hampered what we were doing—a wrong and foolish interference, I should say. And to leave no reservations whatsoever, hereby and for the first time, I let Elizabeth and all of you know that I have found out who planned Garry's murder and how it was carried out."

"Gol, are you being serious!" asked David, his eyes bulging.

218

"I am," replied Gol, now adjusting his gaze on Elizabeth's face, "The day we visited Sophie in prison, someone slipped a piece of paper into my pocket. It was a list of Sophie's favourite men! It was a rather long list. One of the names, the first one, had been crossed off and before one of them there was a cross in red ink. It was indeed a very wise and thoughtful hint by a wise person that the prime suspect could be among Sophie's most favourite men! Does it mean that Sophie would only favour the men who are capable of using abusing smearing and even of committing murder! And if it is true, then who is responsible for this tendency inculcated into her young mind and soul! Who is to justify this pathological aversion towards goodness! These are bitter questions. Aren't they, Elizabeth? Is our Sophie addicted to abuse and degradation? Once Franco described Sophie to me as a red ripe apple that loves to be eaten by pigs! If it is the case, well, why should we bother her? If a red ripe apple can draw satisfaction and pleasure from being eaten by a pig, then there is nothing wrong with it; and you and your husband should also be happy with what you have incorporated into her psyche."

"Gol, please don't say that," moaned Elizabeth, "Sophie needs your help!"

"She is still firmly holding on to the belief that she was the one who murdered Garry and Miss Julie Atkins!" said Gol, crossing his arms on his chest, "Tell me how, and I will help her. You visited her just a while ago, and she did not mention anything about her innocence, and you also were reluctant to ask her. To avoid going round in circles, I am going to put an end to this by saying the last word: Elizabeth, *fair is fair and foul is foul*, and this is the only way I can differentiate right from wrong. If you understand this term the way I do, then we will all team up and free Sophie. And if not, then I will have to wish all of you a good life. Now I will leave you alone with Cynthia. Perhaps she can help you make a wise decision."

After lunch, Gol, David and Clement left. Cynthia and Elizabeth remained silent for a long while, looking at each other while their minds wandered off to two different directions—one to a terrain where the creeks and the streams would join up to become rivers and reach the ocean, and the other to a terrain where division and stagnation were far easier concepts to deal with than the quest of flowing and reaching an ocean.

"Elizabeth," said Cynthia, pushing her hair back, "I have heard that you and your dear husband believe that Draco is the 'finest piece of a man' you

219

have ever been privileged to meet! Is the foul really that fair, Elizabeth! You are defending indecency only to help it grow and bear more fruits! You put all your savings on a plate and offered it to him, believing he would spend it on freeing your daughter; and you still believe so! Based on Gol's prediction, this story would have had another two or even three victims. The person behind this crime needed and still needs the would-be-victims to help him with swindling you and your husband out of whatever you have. No worries, Elizabeth, I can understand you because once I used to see the world through the same window you are standing at. Perhaps you have come here to ask Gol to go to a court of law, stand before some judges and confess that he deceived, abused and then forced your daughter to murder Garry and that accomplished undertaker! Wouldn't it be another spit on the face of goodness! Do you know what, dear Elizabeth, you people would have never had any problem with Gol had he abused Sophie! Foul is fair and Gol is foul!"

"Cynthia, you are being too unfair and harsh to me," said Elizabeth in a low tone, "It isn't me. It is my husband."

"What do you mean, 'it is my husband'!" asked Cynthia, "So, what and who are you? Aren't you a woman and a mother? You and your husband have been staying with Draco and Christopher during the last two weeks, helping them add more drama to their foul story! Elizabeth, there is a big difference between a thing and its shadow—they are definitely not the same, as plain as this. One would never understand goodness if half one's mind is in love with the other way. Elizabeth, the ones who are always right have never been right, and as such, they will never be right because they have never been wrong! We are all brought up in a padded box and fed with the *same* identical sets of beliefs; the beliefs that have made us believe that we have reached a unique state of oneness and harmony; that we all can taste an ice cream and see the bad and the good in the *same* way. Sameness and oneness are not the results of themselves; they are the result of difference, diversity and friction. A mirage is a mirage, but the ones who are inflated and kept in a padded box are so prone to see it as a splendid apparition of the truth. Now it is entirely up to you, stick to your own way of seeing the world—which I don't see anything wrong with it if it works for you—or turn around and see what has to be seen. Just not to leave anything necessary unsaid, I would like to say a few words about the people whom you, your husband and your Sophie have seen as the epitomes of righteousness and decency. As you were not privileged enough to meet Mehmet and be blessed by his 'transcendent' 'divine' existence, and as well as he was your daughter's most favourite man ever, I should let you know who he really was: even suffering from twenty five percent mental impairment, aggravated by a long-term use of psychedelic drugs, had not dampened the wrong nature of this harmful parasite.

"Your daughter used to work around fifty hours a week for which she would be paid off-the-books! What would she do with her money? She would spend most of it on Mehmet! And to Mehmet, well, your daughter was just a bitch! Perhaps to earn this grand title she was so generously at his disposal! What can I say about Draco: a plague, he is simply a plague; perhaps the most unprincipled man ever existed! He used to pimp for his dad! And Christopher, well, this rotten modern Greek god, married four times, divorced four times, like his ancestors, he sees himself responsible for taking care of the young girls and protecting them against the predators! Based on a divine appropriation, sealed and given to him by his ancestors, using these young girls is his undisputable and exclusive entitlement! Of course he would see them as his own daughter before using them—it is divine custom! So Zeus-like! I will leave the dead Garry alone and instead tell you about her mysterious daughter, Calypso: as a modern Greek goddess, she, at a very young age, learned how to use her vagina as the *apple of discord* and pave the way to her eternal existence!"

Elizabeth left, carrying the *thing* and its *shadow* with her, obviously still none the wiser that a *thing* and its *shadow* were not the same. Cynthia chided herself for her rather anger-driven and excessively pungent remarks about the members of the opposite front. She wished she had shown due self-control and allowed some room for moderation. She walked towards the window, opened it and wandered her gaze out and up towards the dense and rather dark clouds among which some shapes were forming. Mostly human-like, bearded broad faces, large eyes, thick brows and long hair, tall slender females with an inexplicable form of beauty, dressed in long white garments, the shapes swirled and twisted out of shape and seconds later, reshaped on another floating patch. Attuned to her aptitude mind and as a result, well disposed to see beyond and above, she marvelled at her mind and how agile and productive it had become, twisting and crazing around in search of congruity and uniting aspects. On the mirror of her now-polished imagination she set the background for her next painting: on an utterly incongruent background, where the opposing elements had gone head to head, she painted Elizabeth and herself, ambling around in a green meadow and thinking, unconsciously, of their attained or unattained shares of the beauties of the world. She painted a basket full of fresh bread and offered it to Elizabeth…

When Elizabeth returned to Garry's restaurant, she was feeling giddy and slightly unhinged.

Lounging in a cosy corner of the restaurant, her husband was busy chatting with the two 'fine pieces of men', Draco and Christopher. Gently and somewhat unsteadily, she approached them, and offering them a quick and brief smile, she placed herself on the leather couch and beside her husband. Quiet and apparently calm, she kept listening to the three 'fine pieces of men' while waiting for the cup of coffee she had ordered when she had entered the restaurant.

"Yes, my dear sirs," said Mr Barry James Grandeur, gently lifting the glass of whisky before him, "As I was saying, once one of these foreign plebs, whose so-and-so country I cannot recollect, called me 'a bionic man'! You know, these neglectful mediocre-minded pieces of abnormality and degradation have never heard of the word 'duty', which is undoubtedly the essence of man.

"'Why do you think I am a bionic man?' I asked the pleb, of course in our trademark overly remissive English tone. 'Sir, you cannot differentiate an ox from a tractor!' replied the pleb. Do these epitomes of dereliction and unbecomingness know that the entire universe is a mechanical marvel? Duty and mechanics define humans, and in the same light, I am very much reluctant to seek the non-existent differences between an ox and a tractor! It would be just a waste of time and breath arguing with these half-witted mongrel things whose beliefs are as impertinent as their whole existence. My dear sirs, I should remind you that I am very much aware of the bizarre time we live in; I mean all the baseless fuss and claims about racism and discrimination. Therefore, I only pamper the truth when I am honoured to have the company of some worthy people like you. Blood, my dear sirs, tells the difference. You are privileged with having the Greek blood running in your veins, the blood that is the honour and the dignity of the Western world and civilisation. The Greeks and the Turks, well, they have always been my most favourite parts of humanity, as they are the well-deserved owners of exquisite pride and dignity, and as such, they are inherently people of duty and solidity. And I would also like to mention a few words about Mehmet, that generous vessel of Turkish blood and pride, who was unjustly perished by a worthless pleb! As I have been told by Sophie, he was a highly righteous and dutiful man. May his soul rest in peace. He and Garry will definitely be greatly missed by this country."

Involuntarily and voluntarily, a mixture of some smirks and some other less-known-to-mankind facial expressions began to wriggle around Draco's mouth, and seconds later, they were fully formed. Christopher thought it was a disdainful reaction to what was said about Mehmet, as he also quickly formed a few of the same smirks and threw them in with a very mulish laugh. But he was wrong. Those wriggling shivering melting trickling smirks and their weird trappings were to gently pamper Elizabeth!

"Elizabeth, you were not supposed to…" said Draco.

"Oh, yes," interrupted Elizabeth, "Yes, I know who told you. Calypso. We bumped into each other when I… you know, you would all be grateful that I did go there and spoke with him. I promise you will all thank me for this. Before anything, let me assure you that I didn't believe a single word of what he said."

"Oh, very interesting!" uttered Christopher, his mulish laughter now sounding hysterical, "Okay, tell us what he said."

"Well, he mentioned something from Shakespeare," said Elizabeth, half her face shivering westward and the other eastward, "Yeah, 'foul is fair and fair is foul'…"

"How do these people dare to mention Shakespeare!" interjected Mr Barry James Grandeur, letting out a very old damp huff, "Do they know anything about poetry, these plebs!"

"Yes, as I was saying," said Elizabeth, her face revealing her share of surprise at the plebs who dare to mention Shakespeare, "Yes, he, like all wrong men, tried to deny that he did all those horrible things to our Sophie. Obviously in vain, as we all know it was him. And then he went on saying that Draco and Christopher would swindle all of your money out of you, and some more nonsense, until he mentioned something which made me think for some seconds but I did not believe what he said. Do you know what he said? He said he knew who was behind Garry's murder. 'I have already found this out' he said. And it was then that I realized how dark and evil this man was. I suppose he knows he is bound to be caught by the

223

unmistakable hand of justice, and that is why he is trying to find a scapegoat and evade punishment. And I was also amazed at Cynthia and her children who are so blindly supporting this very wrong man. By looking into Cynthia's eyes you would see that she would readily sacrifice herself for this evil man! I have never heard an English person defend indecency! And I found it so condescending of him when he said he would have to wish us a good life if we failed to change our stance on this issue…"

"This country has gone insane," interjected Mr Barry James Grandeur, staring into the glass of whisky in his hand, "That is why she has been wasting her love and energy on the despicably crooked beings only to gain more of depravity and humiliation! A very hare-brained, self-belittling attitude, I should say!"

Draco and Christopher exchanged some 'divine' looks and rejoiced in the sweet taste of vindication melting in their mouths. The last look Draco threw at Christopher seemed very much Zeus-like, as it made Christopher assume a very much Prometheus-like air on his face—alarmed but defiant. They both turned their heads towards Elizabeth, and when their divine gazes landed on her face, she offered them a very much Medusa-like smile—unaware of the hidden dangers in divine games!

"Just forget what he said," said Draco, smiling at Elizabeth, "We have known this guy for ages. He is definitely a pervert and a danger to this careless and innocent society. The poor Mehmet knew him very well. It is a pity that he is not with us today; otherwise he would happily expose this disgusting man to you. Once the late Mehmet told me that Gol once tried to rape him! Would you believe it! How morally, and even biologically, should a man be wrong to bring himself to rape an immaculately innocent man like Mehmet! Just imagine what an unbearable pain the world would have to suffer had Mehmet been raped by this evil beast!"

"Yes, we have known this horrible man for years now," said Christopher , now sounding fully divine, "Do you know what Mehmet told me about Gol just a few weeks before his unfortunate death? Bloody hell, man! He said he saw Gol, with his very own eyes, shag a donkey in a farm belonged to a very innocent British-Albanian guy! Bloody hell, man! Would you believe this? What on earth has an innocent donkey done to deserve this! Bloody hell, man! Yes, Mehmet and Draco knew him better than I knew him. You know, our Draco's prestige wouldn't allow him to open his mouth and talk about such horrible creatures; otherwise you would be appalled by the depth of corruption in that evil man!"

"Yeah, honestly I don't want to talk much about a pervert," said Draco, now inflated with a Zeus- like conviction, "The only thing I would like to mention about him is his bombastic personality. Do you know what I mean? I mean he is a man of bluffs, and bluffs only to divert attentions from his rancid nature. That is why he told you that Draco and Christopher were to screw your money out of you, and also that he had already found out who was behind Garry's murder. Yeah, honestly, there are far more important things going on in the world right now. Honestly, we should not allow our time be consumed by the nonsensical men like him. Yeah, let's move on and free our Sophie and enjoy our priceless friendship. The solicitors have already managed it. There is only one more step left, which I think will be taken by the end of the coming week. Yeah, there are far more important things going on in the world right now."

Mr Barry James Grandeur downed some more whisky, leaned against the couch, crossed his legs, and now entranced by alcohol and his bulging ego, he indulged himself some quiet moments, riding on the waves of his polished thoughts and alchemically mixing some Greek panacea and some Turkish pickles!

Elizabeth, still none the wiser, sipped her coffee and reflected upon what she had said and what she had not during the hectic day she had gone through. What she had not said could only be worked out by knowing what she had said, and that was, strangely, an impossible possibility, as what she had said was based on a baseless base! She had used some empty words when speaking with Gol, the words which she had never been allowed to examine and see what they could contain. She had mentioned that how her Sophie had fallen in love with Gol, and how this love had placed her above and beyond her likes and dislikes while at the same time imagining her Sophie in the arms of Draco! Elizabeth's mind had long been turned into a one-way road leading to a destination only known to her. She had never asked questions for the purpose of obtaining the truth, but for the purpose of learning how to smear and avoid it!

In this show of 'decency' and aversion for the other side, the *Greek blood* remained unexamined! Perhaps it was considered too assertive and even extraneous to ask for authenticity and ratification when two Greek Gods, in full flesh, were present!

Chapter 30

"I am very much impressed by Cynthia's Gallery," said Melanie, crossing her bear arms on her chest and looking at Cynthia's latest painting, "It is like an entity. There is a sort of integrity and cohesion… You know, I don't know how to explain it."

"Emanated from the soul," said Gol, "It doesn't have to be explained. It has to be felt. And you have felt it."

"Oh, I like that," said Melanie, pushing her black sleek hair back, "When I was younger I couldn't understand the language and the importance of art and literature properly; and I think it was due to the manner these concepts were conveyed to us."

"Gol, I think Melanie has got good news for us," said David, coming in with an ice bucket under his arm.

"How did you know, David?" asked Melanie, smiling positively.

"I have felt it," replied David, laughing,

"You have felt it, then you are dead right."

"Well," said Melanie, as soon as they sat, "Gol, congratulations! The court has acquitted you."

"Nothing could have made me happier!" said Cynthia, her eyes moistening.

"Thank you so much, Melanie!" said David, letting out a hearty laughter, "It was a bizarre game of mockery! Could you please tell us the details?"

"Yes, of course," replied Melanie, obviously impressed by the youthful innocent and zeal waving in David's eyes, "The case was rife with discrepancies, bizarre ones, mostly from Sophie. When she was summoned to the court for the first time, she accused Gol of deceiving abusing and using her, and when she was asked to provide the court with the details, she began with sexual harassment and rape. The judge listened to her lengthy accounts of what had happened to her since she had bumped into Gol, and assured her that justice would be done, and this emboldened Sophie to an extent that she added some really kinky aspects to her narratives of the story."

"Wine food and such a fabulously bogus story!" said David, pointing to the two waitresses coming in with two trays over their hands, "I can guess what will happen next!"

"Oh, look at this! I absolutely love it," said Melanie, looking at one of the trays which was full of some succulent mixed kebabs.

"To make a special food for a special guest, Clement needs to know only one thing," said David, putting a glass of wine before Melanie, "'Are they happy or miserable?' he would ask. And this is for you, Melanie—a very happy food."

"Thank you, David," said Melanie, laughing, "I love the food and also your unique sense of humour. And about being happy, yes, I think I am one of the five top happiest policewomen in the world."

"Not mixing up is the secret," said David, "Gol taught me how to avoid it: feel whatever has to be felt and understand whatever has to be understood."

"It is very much true," said Melanie, smiling.

"Melanie, those two chunks of pork are for you," said Cynthia, pushing the tray towards Melanie, "And when you are ready, we will eagerly listen to the rest of what you were saying."

"Yes, as I was saying," said Melanie, lifting the fork and the knife, "Sophie goes back to the prison with the hope that Gol would soon be arrested and put on trial and, well, that would be the end of the story. But contrary to her wishful dreams, the court was provided with a very decisive piece of evidence. When she was called to the court for the second time, the judge told her that he needed her to carefully look at the acquired evidence and identify Gol. So, what was this piece of decisive evidence, and to whose benefit it was going to be decisive?"

"Goodness! I can imagine where this story is going to be diverted to," said Cynthia, holding her chin in surprise.

"Yes, you are right, Cynthia," said Melanie, asking Gol to pass her the basket of fresh herbs with a gesture of hand, "In that unfortunate hour, when we carried away the bodies of the two victims, we also carried away a good number of other objects. During our search and forensic examinations of the flat and also based on what Garry's wife told us, we noticed that the CCTV cameras had neatly been taken off the walls and carried away."

"Interesting!" said David, gesturing Melanie to pass him her empty glass.

"Yes, it is. Obviously we went through this case in accordance with our procedures and full and numerous forensic examinations but we could not find out who, and how, had removed the cameras from the flat. And as Sophie was found guilty due to the existence of enough evidence and undeniable facts and, of course, her own confession, the court decided to close the case, and as a result, any further investigations were deemed unnecessary. As there are some crucial aspects of this story yet to be fully unravelled and for some other parts to be discovered, I am going to leave this here and tell you a bit about Sophie and the Judge who acquitted Gol: let me begin from the end, when the judge addressed Sophie with a few very thoughtful words before closing the case: '*Girl, you have never been abused and you will never be!*' Will Sophie ever be able to comprehend the meaning of this? I hope she will. The judge asked Sophie to repeat the details of how she was abused by Gol, and when she did, he played some of the contents of the CCTV cameras and asked her to carefully watch and identify Gol for him. Sophie had no clue that what she was about to watch was a rather fetish play whose scenario had been written by herself! She had told the judge that Gol would force her to get naked and then he would place some dirty rats on her body; that he would love to do it while rats were hysterically watching… And some other really kinky accounts of her so-called predicament, so deviant that even a policewomen would not be comfortable with mentioning them! I am so happy that it fell to my lot to deal with this exceptional case. I have dealt with a good number of cases and learned incredible lessons about human behaviour, but this case has raised some very hard-to-answer questions in my mind. How indurate and impervious can a human being become to goodness and truth that he or she could blatantly deny even the existence of the shining sun in the sky! There is another big lesson in this case that I am eager to learn, and that is Gol's conviction that Sophie might turn around and get herself disabused! I wish I could have a peek into Gol's mind."

"Take a break, Melanie. Your food is getting cold," said Gol, smiling, "If she is human, well, then there is always a chance for her. And as I strongly believe that all people are inherently innocent, and bearing in mind that Sophie has already tasted the real love and felt the true connection in a short spell, I still allow a bit of space for optimism, though she has been trying her best only to prove to me that she is only a physical existence and

228

physicality is doomed anyway."

"And this space of optimism you mentioned, must be based on something," said Melanie.

"It is," replied Gol, "It is based on my heart and intuition rather than a discursive and mindful approach. Even right now that I am sitting here I can feel the presence of Sophie's heart around me. If this desire, which means pure love and goodness, has not yet been able to enlighten her mind, and if it completely fails to do so, then we might refer to what you mentioned about the *indurate* and *impervious* minds and souls, in which case I would render Sophie as irredeemable; but as I said I still can hear the clamour of a fierce battle going on in her mind. And above all, the day she left me, she left behind a tiny piece of her heart, and she has since been fighting to take it back. The problem with goodness is that it is too expensive and too demanding—if one fails to live up to its compelling presence, well, then there will be a game of smearing and hatred. Now you can go on, Melanie."

"Well," said Melanie, filliping against the glass before her, perhaps to gather her thoughts, "After the appearance of those footages at the court and what they revealed, the judge also deemed the accusation of Gol being behind Garry and Miss Julie Atkins' murder baseless, and it all means that Sophie will spend the rest of her life behind bars unless Gol has an ace hidden up his sleeve."

"I have, Melanie," said Gol musingly, "But I will only reveal it if Sophie turns around and stops spitting on to her own face."

"I am thinking about what the judge told her," said Cynthia, taking a gentle sigh, 'That she had never been abused and she would never be! I have lived all this, this bitter irony of banging on the wrong door and asking for the wrong saint."

"But you eventually found the right door and the right saint," said David, laughing.

"Yes, I did," said Cynthia, touching her son's face, "But nothing can compensate for my losses. I lost half of myself. You might think if I could see myself at a point in my life and have the courage to listen to the supplications of my heart and face the reality, so can Sophie. But it would not be easily possible in her case, as she is not genuinely interested in any form of art and any other activities that can instigate her soul and her mind; that can enable her to hear her own voice. Sophie has become xenophobic

229

towards herself, and for such a person being *perfect* in being bad is much better than being good and *imperfect!* I still see her as a chunk of myself, and like Gol, I am very much optimistic and hope that she will recognise and appreciate herself before it is too late."

Melanie gazed at Cynthia's face, her hazel eyes merging with hers and her heart hearing hers. She directed her gaze towards Gol and gently landed it on his face and immediately remembered the day when he had come to the police station to visit Sophie. She had watched Sophie's face when she had lashed out at Gol like a lioness and a while later had turned into a kitten and asked Gol for his jacket. Perhaps it was the simultaneous presence of the lioness and the kitten—these two symbolisers of the nature of love in a female heart—that had kept Gol and Cynthia still rather hopeful about the eventual result of Sophie's confused game of hopscotch. Melanie, this experienced policewoman who in spite of having to deal with the less congruent section of the society, was a gentle and soulful creature, could effortlessly feel the pure and somewhat painful emotions emitting from Cynthia's heart and gently being received by Gol's big and generous heart. To her, Cynthia seemed and sounded like a pilgrim whose own selflessness was on the verge of turning into the most rewarding of divine prayers. It was apparent to her that Cynthia's yearnings for goodness and love were a courageous and voluntary jump into a blazing fire.

Chapter 31

"My dear sirs, I welcome you to my cattle farm," said Mr Barry James Grandeur, "As you can see for yourself, even my cattle are already impressed and deeply elated by your presence. Look at that kine, that so very united young group of calves, they are definitely most interested in you two fine sirs—you could tell that by looking at how they are gently waving their tails."

"Bloody hell! I didn't know that even cows could appreciate us!" said Christopher, letting a mixed laugh out—half equine half bovine.

"Honestly, they can, the animals can see through people," said Draco, assuming a very wise and somewhat gnostic air on his face, "My late dad used to communicate with a good number of animals, but as we all know he was religiously in love with rats. Yeah, he could see through the rats and the rats could see through him. In fact, it was his spiritual presence that would elevate the rats' minds to a higher echelon and enable them to see through him. The peak of mutuality, if you can get my drift, they were there, my dad and the rats."

"Dear sirs, this is a subject of exhaustive capacity and importance," said Mr Barry James Grandeur, looking admiringly at Draco's face, "Let's have it debated over lunch. I have prepared a lovely piglet for you two gentlemen, and I have particularly done so in a very old Greek style—cut in reasonable chunks, seasoned with the most relevant spices and ready to be skewered and barbequed over a glowing fire."

"Bloody hell, let's go. I can't wait," said Christopher, letting out a laugh with a low-tone squeak ringing in it.

"Please do follow me," asked Mr Barry James Grandeur, poised to march towards a hut to the left of the rather large enclosure, "You dear sirs should have known Elizabeth by now. She is a brilliant organiser with a mild tendency towards perfection and demand for things to be done thus and so. She has already prepared everything."

"Hello, Elizabeth. How are you?" said Draco, in a tone that made Christopher form one of his trademark Godly smirks in the right corner of his mouth.

"Hello, my dears! I am fine. Yeah, absolutely fine. And overly happy to see you!" replied Elizabeth, standing before the hut in a red shirt and a long flowery skirt, "We are very much delighted to have you with us on this gorgeous day."

"I thank you very much, Elizabeth. It is a great pleasure for us to be with lovely people like you," said Draco, looking at Elizabeth's long hair flowing down on her breasts, while biting the corner of his lower lip.

"My dear sirs, let's take a seat," said Mr Barry James Grandeur, pointing to an old wooden table to his right, "And I will attentively listen to Draco's further elaboration on the connection between his late great father and the rats he used to love so dearly."

"Yeah, honestly, they really loved each other," said Draco, reposing himself on the high-backed bench, "As I mentioned earlier, it was all about mutuality; they were actually studying each other, if you will. Yeah, honestly, I have always believed in paranormal connections among living creatures, and there was some sort of paranormal streak in what was going on between my dad and the rats, and it became apparent to me when Sophie joined them."

"Oh, interesting! I didn't know this," said Mr Barry James Grandeur.

"Yeah, honestly, Sophie and I used to catch wild rats for him," said Draco, finger brushing his hair with a tinge of paranormality sitting in his eyes, "And then Sophie would tame them for him; and this led to the realisation of another mutuality: the mutuality between my dad and Sophie, which was deeply spiritual, the sort you would witness between a good father and his daughter. Yeah, honestly, my late dad was a father to the world."

Minutes later, Elizabeth brought the food and some wine. The taste of the finely prepared and barbequed piglet was considered, by the hosts and the guests alike, as Godly! The wine, which was not that much of a Godly stuff, was sipped with a more worldly sense of presence. They ate and dug and delved into the depth of some profound issues and matters about and around the moral basis of the world and its pestering plagues, with Mr Barry James Grandeur articulating a very bold assertion that the world would need an immediate bloodletting, a thorough phlebotomy or it would become cankerous and rot in its own juice! Of course, Draco took full advantage of his first and foremost worry: the world and the important things going on in it! He, as adroit and crafty as an old Greek sophist, manoeuvred around his views as if he was located at a lookout out and above the planet earth! He would describe his observations from top to bottom. He also praised Elizabeth's new hairdo and the natural rejuvenation of her face and the unique beauty of her eyes. Christopher, now absorbing the true taste of the piglet with all his cells, got involved in praising Elizabeth's physical qualities. Using his wayward but yet curiously effective way of putting forth the contents of his mind, he first humorously imparted to Draco that a man should not praise another man's wife at his presence, and then, very periphrastically, apparently for the purpose of clarification, he put forth some hypothetical instances: 'For example', he said, 'It would be wrong of me to say that Elizabeth's lips are very sensual; that her hair flowing on her breasts would make her look even sexier; that her eyes could make a man suicidal; that her legs and backside could make a battalion of soldiers point their guns at each other and happily blow each other's head away... Yeah man, bloody hell! This is wrong'."

It was all wrong. It was all right. It was all a matter of discretion. It was neither right nor wrong. It was all Greek sophistry and the English art of deliberate justification, soaked in passivity and indifference.

Leaving the language and its paradoxes and jargons behind and moving on, one might be able to assert that Draco and Christopher could not be that wrong; and that, in the same light, Mr Barry James Grandeur and his wife also could relish their satisfaction. For Draco and Christopher, it was a matter of following the rationale of the game they were playing and also a matter of using the means available to them, and for the other side, well, it was simply a matter of trade, giving something (whatever) and taking what they eagerly needed.

"Well, bloody hell, we are having it all," said Christopher, touching Elizabeth's bare arm, "You know, I am speechless. Yeah, honestly."

"My dear sir, you have only yourself to thank for," said Mr Barry James Grandeur, wiping his mouth with a thick white napkin ceremoniously, "Whatever a man gains is the result of himself. Well deserved, you are, both of you."

"Honestly, you are very much right," said Draco, the contour of an aborted divine smirk feebly visible in the corner of his mouth, "I also believe people get what they deserve. My great late dad also used to hold the same belief. Yeah, honestly, he was, like Miss Julie Atkins, a sort of essentialist."

Philosophy has always been more beneficial to the moron than to the wise, as misusing and abusing the terms have always been much easier, or perhaps the moron is the wise and the wise is the moron!

A newly weaned and slaughtered suckling piglet, some fiery wine, a beautiful girl who used to tame wild rats for an *essentialist* whose chewed off fingernails were perhaps the denotation of an ever-orgasmic *essence* within him, and of course, a proudly self-metamorphosed cow-whisperer, they were all there to define *essentialism* and *merit*!

After lunch, Mr Barry James Grandeur asked to be excused as he was to visit a vet in the town and discuss with him the mental wellbeing of his only pair of Anatolian black cattle. "They have recently been down and depressed," he said.

A limping seagull sidled near the low wall behind the now abandoned table and moments later, another two landed, and immediately assuming an air of absolute entitlement, they threw a quick look at the limping seagull and cocked up their heads and remained motionless with their eyes wide open and rolled up, as if they were listening with their eyes. Seconds later, the two confident seagulls exchanged a wise look, and apparently having the existence of a slight possible danger overlooked, they flapped and hurled themselves on the table, sending a few dishes and cutlery flying. After letting out a few loud squawks, the other seagull limped towards the table and joined the feast. In a matter of minutes, a brazen lot of the same kind appeared over the farm, and wasted no time in swooping down on the table. The would-be-danger that the two first seagulls had detected and wisely overlooked appeared at the scene: a young-looking old Golden Retriever bitch. She seemed to be dejected, empty, out of her zone, the zone of loyalty and disloyalty, the zone of partiality and appreciation. She seemed positively disinterested in the world around her. She took a few heavy steps towards the looting birds that were voraciously gobbling the remains of the piglet, changed her direction and walked over to the two mature cows standing behind the mesh metal fence. The two cows neither ignored her nor acknowledged her presence. She raised her heavy head and stared at them. Though out of her zone, but she was still a dog, an intrinsic connoisseur of spotting and reading the natural curiosities—even if they were hidden nether the thick skin of a cow. She turned towards the birds, bobbed her head several times, as if trying to measure an angle. There was a line and an angle, travelling over the heads of the birds and reaching the door to the hut. The cows were innocently intrigued to know what was going on inside the hut. The positively disinterested dog threw half a simper at the cows and languidly walked towards the wide green meadow before her. On her way, she caught sight of a lone pigeon, innocently pecking the wet ground, unaware of the fierce crows and omnivorous seagulls around her. She changed her direction and gave the pigeon a gentle chase and made her fly away.

The air smelled of divine semen mixed with the bodily sweat of a mortal female. The rain lashed down. The two cows were still lingering around with their large eyes still dilating. The seagulls entertained themselves with putting on a short show of rascality and vandalism. The dog, now standing in the middle of the gently sloped meadow, gave herself up to the lashing rain with the rending desire for regaining her state of doghood crazing in her head. She forced herself to bark but nothing came out of her. To bark, she remembered, there had to be a good cause. No dog of genuine breed and blood would bark for the wrong causes.

She had stopped barking since long ago.

"Good morning, my dear sirs," said Mr Barry James Grandeur, "My car broke down, that is why I did not return last night. I hope you did not feel offended."

"No, not at all," said Christopher, his face looking pale, "We kept chatting with Elizabeth until late, you know, about Sophie and the young girls like her who are unable to make decisions on their own. Yeah, Elizabeth is a very knowledgeable woman, and that is why we really enjoy chatting with her."

"Happy to hear that," said Mr Barry James Grandeur, pushing a chair back for Draco to sit, "She has just informed me about the new obstacle in our way of freeing Sophie."

"Honestly, more or less, we think this is the shortcut to what we all wish for," said Draco, his Godly smirk splaying all over his wan-looking face, "As you know we have already managed Miss Julie Atkins' blood money—it will soon be paid. Not to waste any more time, Christopher and I thought we could pay a small amount of money to Mehmet's family and ask them to drop the case against Sophie until we succeed in finding some new evidence and get Gol convicted."

"What did Elizabeth say about this?" asked Mr Barry James Grandeur, landing his gaze on the thick gold chain around Christopher's neck.

"Honestly, more or less," replied Draco, finger brushing his hair, "She is happy with it. After all, she is a mother and her child would be her most immediate priority."

"Barry, we should hurry," said Elizabeth, putting three fried sausages on Christopher's plate, "It is not a big amount. I have already transferred all of my savings to Draco's bank account; and if you could quickly manage the rest, I am sure we could have our beloved Sophie with us before Christmas."

"Dear sirs, please do not take it amiss," said Mr Barry James Grandeur, taking a sip of the mug of coffee before him, "Of course my trust in you dear gentlemen will never waver; but just for the purpose of disambiguation, could one of you tell me what exactly went wrong with that pleb's case, I mean Gol, and why he was acquitted? The judge told me somethings about some CCTV footage, and he even wanted me to watch it but I decided not to, because I was sure it could never be authentic."

"Such a wise gentleman!" said Christopher, letting out one of his horsiest laughs, "Bloody hell! The solicitors are on this, doing their best to prove that those footages are completely fabricated. You know, Photoshopped and bogus. Bloody hell, man, bloody hell! There were no CCTV cameras in late Garry's flat at all. Bloody hell, these dirty games behind a dead man, late decent Garry."

"Yeah, honestly, more or less," said Draco, taking a long screechy sniffle, "We all know the nature of this type of people and how they would add a touch of their evil minds to whatever they do.

"Honestly, I am glad you refused to watch those disgusting footages. Yeah, honestly, nowadays technology has made it so easy, I mean the fabrication and tampering with materials. Honestly, Christopher and I also refused to watch it, but for the tactful purpose of knowing what we should do next, we asked solicitors for a briefing. Yeah, honestly, disgusting, the solicitors believe they have used one of those adult videos and… You know what I mean."

"It is exactly what I also assumed," said Elizabeth, putting three strips of pinkish ham on Christopher's plate, "That lunatic officer, that Melanie something, told me that the footages were authentic, and that one of them shows Sophie using cocaine with Draco sitting beside her, but I didn't

236

believe a word of it. Who would believe a fine and very athletic man like Draco be into drugs and all this. And she also gave me an amalgamation of some other evidently incohesive accounts of some really 'untoward' behaviours that had been taking place in the flat... All nonsense, I believe."

The Golden Retriever bitch took a long yawn and prostrated herself on the cool damp soil by the low wall. The limping seagull appeared. The two innocently curious cows approached the fence, stood side by side, bulged their eyes and stared at the four humans who were contentedly and so very attentively reflecting the morals of the world to each other while enjoying their large breakfast. The dog pulled herself up and walked towards the seagull, who was now leering at something out on the meadow. There was a lone friend, innocently pecking the wet soil, unaware of the dangers around her. She was made to fly away.

Chapter 32

"Eileen, why are dreams so important?" asked Sophie, sounding down and flustered, an onerous urge sitting in her eyes.

"Are they?" asked Eileen from behind the book she was reading.

"Yea, I think they are. I have read a good number of books about dreams."

"Good! I thought you were wasting your time reading those nonsense magazines in the library," said Eileen, closing the book and putting it on her chest.

"No, I have been reading loads of good books," said Sophie, tilting her head.

"Happy to hear that. Now tell me your dream," said Eileen.

"It was strange! Very strange," said Sophie, her eyes moistening, "It was a woman carrying a dead body. 'Whose body is that? Have you killed her with morphine?' I asked. 'This is my own dead body! I have been carrying it around for ages' she said, looking at me the way she was looking at her own dead body. And then she told me that when she died there was no one around to bury her body. 'If not buried quickly, the dead bodies, the earth would refuse to accept them, and they would become a burden' she said."

"Why do you think dreams are important?" asked Eileen, gazing at the ceiling.

"Because I think they remind us of our wrong thoughts and actions," replied Sophie, a long deep hard-to-release sigh gaining momentum within her.

"Have you been thinking of Gol lately?" asked Eileen, now rising and sitting on the bed.

"No, I haven't," replied Sophie, narrowing her eyes.

"I am amazed!" said Eileen, involuntarily twitching her head and covering half her face with a puff of hair, perhaps to avoid a full eye contact with Sophie, "Thinking about Gol, based on your own system of reasoning, could be the only wrong…"

"Eileen!" interrupted Sophie, now on the verge of bursting into tears, "You allowed me to come back to you. You didn't do so to tease me. Did you?"

"I am not teasing you. I am talking to you using your own logic," replied Eileen, crossing her arms on her chest. "The ones who associate themselves with roses, well, needless to say, they will dream and smell of roses and the ones who associate themselves with thorns will dream of thorns. What are roses? What are thorns? Satisfaction defines all the existing elements: if one is happy with being pricked then one's rose is a thorn, and if one feels delighted and elated by the beauty and the divine scent, then one's rose is definitely a rose. Is your rose a rose or a thorn, Sophie? If you have come back to me only to make sure your rose is a thorn, then please don't waste my time, go back to Lucy and earn your PhD in the grand field of daft vaginas!"

"Eileen!" moaned Sophie, an old dead pain scraping out of her mouth, "I am beyond roses and thorns! I am nothing! I have become nothing! Can you understand this, Eileen?"

A heavy silence took over; Eileen held her chin and stared at the floor. A commotion broke out in the corridor and its noise pierced into Sophie's nerves and made them vibrate like the strings of a harp. She sobbed and with each sob, she let out a chunk of an old and unexamined pain. Eileen raised her head and landed her gaze on Sophie's hands and thought of her dream. 'Death is the beginning of birth,' she thought, a sagacious smile sitting in her shining eyes, "And nothingness is the beginning of becoming," she whispered to herself. Was it the foamy wake behind a ship that comes into existence only to become non-existent? Was it a weakened and falling wave or a bulging body of water connected to an ever-flowing undertow? Sophie, since she had first told her right hand from her left, had made promises only to break them! She had, wittingly or unwittingly, sown the seeds of passion only to kill them as soon as they germinated! Eileen raised her head and looked her in the eye, those green mirrors, those reflectors of ambiguity and tainted images.

"Let's talk about your dreams," said Eileen, kneeling on the floor and holding her hands, "Your first one, do you remember. The one in which you had visited Gol in a place of meaning and thought—a grand hall, a masterpiece of architecture, remember, half museum half library. You had forgotten to take off your apron! You had gone back there again, wearing a unique dress… The changing background and the roses. He had stood there like a statue with his hands in his pockets. Do you know he is still standing there and watching that glass door? He has been standing there all through the history; and that is why he seemed to you like a statue. And the second one you told me about around the same time: you being a guest to an apparently most civilised woman, the owner of the most splendid human attributes, a woman attired with brilliance and ample generosity. You were both in the kitchen, with her making a very especial meal for you and bragging about her respect and affection for you and also praising you as a brilliant human being. What happened when the meal was ready? She spat on it and put it before you! Disgusting. And your recent dream, and you didn't mention what sort of age was the woman, carrying her own dead body."

"Oh, yeah, she was a thin middle-aged woman," said Sophie, now looking at Eileen's face in a most childish manner, "And she was of a middle-height stature with her back slightly stooped. Eileen, please tell me what they mean, all my dreams."

"I will," said Eileen, now looking at Sophie's face like a frustrated but most tolerant mother, "There is a balancing element within every existing thing in this world. Though still walking on a pair of wooden legs, the science of human psyche believes dreams equilibrate the overall mental state of man."

"Do you mean dreams remind us that we are wrong or right?" asked Sophie.

"You could say that," replied Eileen, getting up and sitting beside Sophie, "Where were you when you had the dream of entering that grand building and visiting Gol? You were lying on a dirty bed in a squalid flat with some rats moving around, and of course, with your mind strained and badly convoluted. That dream, Sophie, was to remind you of your most-cherished-for desires: true love, honesty, loyalty and engagement and above all, knowledge and the hard-to-attain enlightenment and self-realisation and of course, your place."

"I think I can understand what you mean," said Sophie, now sounding like a teenage girl who had just noticed her mother was going to forgive and trust her, "But why was Gol so disinterested and indifferent towards me? Why did he not open his arms and embrace me instead of standing there with his hands in his pockets?"

"Goodness is a quest and not a notion," replied Eileen, smiling, "And Gol, this old friend of the world, was unsure if you could ever see it that way. He could have opened his arms and owned you a short while after he offered you a job, but he did not. Why? It is so simple: because he wanted all of you, all of what you were, he wanted the entire young girl who had fallen in love with him. Sophie, lust was the last thing in his list, but he knew it was the first in yours."

"So, I could say Gol was a possessive man if he wanted all of what I was," said Sophie, indulging herself a touch of sagaciousness with a full smirk.

"Using the language to abuse yourself is a hidden crime," said Eileen, overlooking the smirk in the corner of Sophie's mouth, "And it has been, believe me, the main cause behind the fall of great empires. Playing with language is a dangerous and misleading game and as degrading, because this game would only be played in one way: chewing and eating the words and then regurgitating them. A possessive man is a user and an abuser, and as such, he would begin with the possessing and using the softest and the easiest-to-access parts—exactly the way a hyena does. Who did possess, use and abuse you? Gol, this so-called possessive man, or those rotten Greek gods? Eight hundred days, girl, you have been here in this place of rotting oestrogens as a prisoner, waiting for those rotten gods to help you out, the very guys who created this predicament for you! It isn't your fault. It is society's fault. It would take this society three decades to notice that someone has been abusing some vulnerable innocent creatures! Melanie Maxwell is an old friend of mine. She told me all about those CCTV footages and some other details of your mind-bogglingly strange story. Perhaps it is going to take you three decades to realise that getting shagged by an old married man while some dirty rats watching you was the unmistakable sign of a severe pathological derangement; that being pimped out by the same man and his son to men even dirtier than themselves was the unmistakable sign of degeneration and regression! The senses of beauty and youthfulness had died within you otherwise you wouldn't have given yourself up to the pigs and to the rodents! Oh yes, you will abuse the bloody language and justify this. You gave yourself up to them because they were gods! You might say. Immortal woman, you are now, impregnated mentally with a mighty Hercules wriggling within you! Imagine a rodent Hercules! I hope it isn't Garry's seed. How much is the price of your vagina? If less

241

than an arm and a leg, well, it isn't a vagina, it is only a mouse hole, a cunt to dehumanisation! You have already paid more than half a million pounds to have your vagina pampered by the least worthy of creatures ever! And it isn't the end of it, Sophie. Draco asked your dad to pay three years of rent for the flat Garry allowed you to live in for free! Thirty thousand pounds for a squalid flat that not even the rats liked! And it isn't the end of it, Sophie. Your mum has convinced your dad to sell his farm and pay the money to Draco and Christopher so that they can pay Mehmet's blood money and get you out of prison! I didn't know dehumanisation was such an expensive process! Do you remember what I told you about…"

"Stop it! Stop it!" exploded Sophie, screaming, slapping her own face, "Stop it! I did tell you that I am beyond roses and thorns! I did tell you that I have become nothing! Can't you understand this, Eileen! I am a craven little bitch! I am fucked up! I hate myself and you and all the race of the fucking mankind!"

Two prison officers rushed into the room and immediately grasped her arms from both sides. She was tearing her hair out while letting out some strange-sounding screams.

Minutes later, and when the officers were leaving the room, Magdalena appeared. Kneeling down beside Eileen, who was holding Sophie in her arms, she threw an inquisitive look at Eileen, and when she nodded positively, she lowered her head and whispered under Sophie's ear, "A dancing fucking snake will never die!"

It was the moment Eileen had long been waiting for to arrive. It did arrive and she made the most out of it: she squeezed the old rotten painful pustule within Sophie, and it burst open, letting out an old patinated fluid, smelling of rancid words and long-suffocated thoughts and slimy dead roses.

"She has fallen asleep on your shoulder," whispered Magdalena, rejoicing in her own words.

From among all the shoulders in the world there were only those of Gol, Eileen and Magdalena that Sophie could rest her head and fall asleep immediately, and that had become apparent to her.

Would she allow those shoulders to offer her comfort and peace of mind and guide her out of her predicament, or would she stick to the thorns she had mistaken for roses and draw satisfaction from being pricked for the rest of her already calamitous life? Or—that would be behind human

242

psychology—her return to Eileen would be proved only as an act of assurance that she would never forsake her wrong beliefs? Apart from these speculations, what was evident was the undeniable fact that she was unconsciously aware that holding on to her beliefs might cost her life, in which case she would definitely be recognised as a most faithful martyr by Garry and Miss Julie Atkins's ghost!

"You have been having some happy days since you returned to us. Haven't you?" asked Magdalena, without looking at Sophie, "Did you decide to return to us because Lucy was released or because—?"

"I was badly missing you and Eileen," interrupted Sophie, her voice cracked.

"Where is Lucy now?" asked Magdalena.

"She is in Turkey now," replied Sophie with a playful and covert smile, "Yeah, she moved to Turkey a few weeks after she was released. Her mother is also with her. She has married a tall Turkish guy who is one of the most notorious roughnecks of the city of Istanbul. And Lucy's mum is also busy with the younger brother of the same guy. Yeah, they are very happy. She said this in her letter to me. Yeah, she believes Turkish men are the most amazing men in the world."

"Really! I didn't know that," said Magdalena, now looking at Sophie's face thoughtfully, "So what is it about them that makes them the best in the world?"

"Oh, yeah," said Sophie in a tone hard to decode, "Like Lucy and her mum, my mum also believes that the Turkish men appreciate every single inch of a woman—like dogs appreciating bones! I think my mum also is going to move to Turkey. Yeah, she is a very passionate woman who believes all women deserve proper appreciation. My mum believes Greek men used to be also as good in the past, but not now, as an old tendency towards homosexuality has been awakened within them. Yeah, my mum is a geography teacher, and she is also very much interested in Greek mythology and the history of the Turkish Empire. She is particularly very much in favour of Zeus."

"Why is your mum particularly interested in Zeus?" asked Magdalena, gently twisting her upper body.

"Oh, yeah, because she believes Zeus was the only perfect god," replied Sophie, a strangely sardonic godly hue appearing in her eyes, "Yeah, my mum believes Zeus was perfect because he was capable of raping mortal women. And she believes other gods are imperfect because they are impotent. I think she is right. A god must be omnipotent."

"What are you talking about, you two?" asked Eileen, entering the yard.

"About the potent and the impotent gods," replied Magdalena, laughing raucously, "And Turkish men who can appreciate a woman the way a dog appreciates a bone! And also about the recurrence of the old homosexuality in the very gentle Greek men!"

"Interesting!" said Eileen, sitting on the bench and beside Sophie, "May I join in?"

"Come on, join in!" replied Magdalena, still laughing, "Eileen, this is a bloody blazing story, this story of us and Sophie! Eileen, don't be shocked. I have a strange question for you: is your God capable of raping mortal women?"

"What the hell are we talking about!" said Eileen, laughing heartily, "Well, this is one of those questions, and it is a pity that it was thrown at me while sitting in the backyard of a prison. I would have absolutely loved to be standing at a podium at a place of knowledge and thought when responding to this question. Well, is it even possible for a knife to cut its own handle? Is it even possible for god to rape his own image? My dears, a woman is an image of the god I believe in. My god isn't into self-raping!"

"Is your god perfect?" asked Magdalena.

"He or she or it or whatever, is neither perfect nor imperfect," replied Eileen, gently stretching her hand out and holding Sophie's, "He is the ultimate definer and therefore, absolutely undefinable. And could you tell me why we are cooking philosophy and theology?"

"Because we need to cook Sophie!" replied Magdalena, now holding Sophie's face in her hands, "She is such a tough meat! If you think some allegories, maxims or advice could soften her fibres, you are wrong. If you asked me I would say even the great Socrates wouldn't be able to reason with Sophie and make her understand how erroneous her beliefs are, because Sophie believes in Zeus!

"She believes he is perfect because he can rape mortal women! And what makes the whole thing a lot more difficult is her ardent love for Turkish men. And her mum also is about to move to Turkey and get herself appreciated there! And her dad, if Draco and Christopher leave any money

244

for him, will go to Thailand to get his thingy appreciated there!"

"Magdalena, stop joking," said Eileen, turning her face towards Sophie and asking her, "Can you remember what I told you when you had just entered the prison?"

"Oh, yeah, you called me 'undeserved lassie'," replied Sophie, offering Eileen one of her long-forgotten unique smiles.

"I called you so because," said Eileen, now looking into Sophie's eyes, "I could clearly see the signs of a great but smeared love in your green eyes. I could also feel the weight of that love in your freezing heart. If we are interested in your story it is because we can still hear the muffled voice of that true love within your heart. If Gol hasn't given up hope on you it is because his heart is still receiving some feeble pulses from yours. It is only the goodness that Gol, Magdalena and I care about, and that is the main and perhaps the only reason we have been trying to help you see the light of the truth before it is too late. Well, before going any further, I should make a very crucial point clear for you, and I do ask you to listen attentively—use your ears and your heart and avoid making any judgement until I have finished. Obviously, every single human being is the direct result of his or her own society, meaning that all through the history of human existence only a small number of humans have managed to materialise their full potentials and be a result of their own existence; and it is because of them that we are where we are now. Society's influence is inevitable, and there are some societies that deliberately sedate their members. The designers of such societies sterilise the growth of individuality only to hinder the multiplication of ideas, these demanding fruits of a healthy gaggle of people. And what would be the result of such degrading approach to humanity? The sense of right and wrong, Sophie, the discerning faculty, would be turned off, and that would well be the beginning of a disaster for such a society. I doubt if you have ever had a proper look at your society, the society that has wrongly and negatively been *unified* and *uniformed*. Would it be even possible to get such society disabused? Made impervious to logic and reasoning in this sinister manner, such society would categorically avoid questions and questioning only to pave the way to its eventual mental demise. Question, Sophie, has now become a comprehensive synonym to the most belittling swear words in this society. You could rip someone's heart off by throwing a serious question at them! Well, of course we are not going to correct society; I am just trying my best to save our own Sophie and the speck of the still breathing love within her heart. Just to make everything clear for you, I would like to let you know that I know more than enough about you, your family and the guys whom you believed, and still believe, were the epitomes of all blessings! Allow me to be a bit inconsiderate and say that if now more than a thousand days of confinement haven't been enough for you to realise that you have badly been wrong, I am afraid Sophie, I should say there is only another place that can definitely do this, and that will be a nice grave! If solitude hasn't enabled you to see what you are, it simply means you are dead. Now, Magdalena and I will eagerly listen to you, hoping you will stick to what you told me yesterday. That 'I am beyond roses and thorns' and that 'I have become nothing'. And I very much hope that you are not going to be distracted by the prospect of moving to Turkey with your mum and having yourselves appreciated by the guys who have canine qualities in them!"

"What if Gol has gone off me?" asked Sophie, a torturous spasm rushing to her face.

"Good!" said Magdalena, now staring at Sophie's distorted face, "So, you can feel the pain of loss. It is good! Very good! Pain is the remedy."

"You have never been a good listener, Sophie," said Eileen, 'What did I tell you yesterday? Oh yes, I said it a bit metaphorically. Gol will never go off you even if you disappoint him. He would solemnly mourn your demise."

"Well, as I said yesterday," said Sophie, forcing herself to manage the overwhelming feeling of embarrassment gaining momentum within her, "I have become nothing, therefore, I am ready to listen and learn how I can become something."

"If you wish to listen, you must ask questions," said Eileen.

"Yes, I know," said Sophie, sounding positively apologetic to herself, "I am going to begin asking questions. I question myself. I sling the harshest of questions at my much forgotten self. You, Eileen, believe there is a frozen wise dancing snake within me. You are so very right. Why and when did the dancing snake within me freeze? Magdalena might be surprised by how I will be explaining myself, but I am sure you will believe me, because you have been watching me for ages. I am definitely worthy of having a nice grave but only when I have lived a life of grace and gratitude. Confinement, I have been using it, right from the moment I was handcuffed, or even long before that, from the moment I left Gol. Let me take you back to when I fell in love with someone who had gracefully fallen in love with me. It was when I was itching to turn eighteen, get my permission, go out in to the society and sell my virginity—though I had already sold it long before that, cheaply, very cheaply, it was not one of those vaginas which could give birth to God. Eileen knows what I am referring to. I bumped into a gentleman, a rare one with real blue blood in his veins. He was only five years older than me, and perhaps one of the most handsome men in the world—handsome outside and handsome inside. We got together and broke up as quickly. It was me, he was expensive in any sense and I was not sure if I could live up to what he was. He was too good, too decent. I had sold my virginity for a tenner, a bacon sandwich and a bottle of beer. I was from a time when vaginas were the cheapest of commodities! And he was from a time when vaginas were the captivating opening chapters to greatness and meaning. See, Eileen, I can use the language figuratively and richly. Yes, I know, it is surprising to see Sophie, the naïve-sounding girl, talk rationally and seriously."

"It would be even confusing for a storyteller to deal with such character!" said Eileen, holding Sophie's hand in hers, "The frozen wise dancing snake, it must be it, Sophie."

"Definitely," said Sophie, offering Magdalena one of her unique smiles, "Gol never spoke with me during the time I was with him. It wasn't him. It was me. I never could summon enough courage and look at his face and let him know that I would cherish his voice and his precious words. Once he was having a savvy conversation with an Englishman in the office, and I was stealthy and eagerly listening to him. He was talking about the women who had given birth to the great empire-makers.

"And it was here, in this vagina-wasting place, as Eileen calls it, that I thought of my great great great great grandmother as one of those women. I thought of her vagina and its price, and it was around the time you had told me the story of the first vagina, the one from which God was tumbled out.

"Priceless, her vagina must have been priceless. An empire and all its trappings could have only been tumbled out of the priceless vaginas!"

"Eileen, should we believe our ears!" said Magdalena, gesturing Sophie to sit on her lap with her arms open, "No reader would believe this character!"

"Oh, Magdalena," said Sophie, sitting on her lap, "Sitting on your lap

247

gives me this divine feeling of childhood and innocence! Yes, you should believe your ears, because I have paid a hefty price to learn that a sedated woman is a plague to herself and to the world; that a cheap vagina is a gate to regression and dehumanisation. I am not chewing and eating the words and regurgitating them. I am feeling them. I am living them. Yes, I admit that there is still a wrong nerve within my head that can tempt me to think of moving to Turkey with my mum, find a father and son and get ourselves appreciated by their canine qualities—the father pampering mine and the son my mum's—but I promise you it will remain only as a harmless fantasy until I get the manliest of men to manly appreciate me."

"So, no more Greek men in your list?" asked Eileen with a craftily mixed smile—half feminine half masculine.

"Delusional vagina-wasters!" replied Sophie, laughing from the deepest part of her heart, "Believe me, they are. There is a feminine electric wave circulating in their backsides, holding them in between male ejaculation and female orgasm! Eileen, look at the fucking story of my life! Look at the fucking story of a sedated woman's life! If one day someone wants to write my life story, I would definitely ask them to entitle it 'A Sophomore Vagina! I mean sophomore in its literal meaning.

Okay, where were we? Oh, yes, it all began long before this vagina-polluted story, I mean when I noticed I had one for the first time and shortly afterwards, I also noticed that my mum also had one, a much bigger and older one. I didn't have to wait long to realise that the world around me was eagerly waiting for mine to ripen, of course not very patiently. And when it did ripen, I realised it was practically my ID card, a pass to the world, a most authentic piece of document to define and confirm my auspicious existence in the world! And as I mentioned, it cost the society only a tenner, a bacon sandwich and a bottle of beer to have it stamped for the first time! And just past twenty, I realised that the society had begun to see my vagina as *not fresh* and therefore not worth a penny! That I had to pay the society to have it screwed! This is an absolute degradation! An unforgiveable crime against the soul of humanity and the undisputable creator and the owner of God and the entire existence! You two are amazed! Aren't you? There is yet more to come. Brace yourself. It all began—this process of disambiguation and wising up to a false and base existence—at the moment when Gol, this old friend of the world, looked into my eyes. At that moment something exploded within me, but I was unable to see what it was, because I was a

248

sedated woman, an artificial female thing, hollowed out of its essence. It took me a long time to realise what it was, and it happened to me in the unlikeliest, or perhaps the likeliest of places: at the court and when I stood before the judge for the first time to accuse Gol of raping me. Eileen, it smelled of a rusty historical secret, it smelled of the true essence of womanhood, perhaps deposited in me from the time of the women who gave birth to the great empire-makers, from the time when the vaginas were priceless. And that moment reminded me of another moment: an inner call that had urged me to stand in the rain when I had rejected Mr Gibran's present with a blind prejudice. I began to feel my full exposure to all these perhaps unnatural mental hints since I met Gol, and when I left him they remained with me and kept constantly reminding me of my dearest aspirations. When I left Gol I cried my heart out and for the first time in my life, I felt the excruciating pain of loss; and that was a big loss, and what would make it almost unbearable was the fact that it was entirely self-imposed. What would you do when you have just let goodness pass you by while goggling at it like a clown? It is here or there, there is nothing in the middle. You wise women understand what I mean. Imagine you have a price tag on you which evaluates you as worthy as a tenner, a bacon sandwich and a bottle of beer; and with this in your mind you would say a silly farewell to goodness and offer a warm salute to the other way and would embrace the degradation, as the only thing you are worthy of. I joined Garry's people. What a thoughtful coincidence! You have just divorced the ultimate goodness and set to marry the best kind of the other side, and you get it in no time! They were, all of them, the unmatched masters of abuse and degradation. Right from the first moment I could hear the boiling of their poisonous saliva in their mouths. They had, perhaps rightly, spotted me as an easy and hassle-free prey, eager to be torn into pieces. Right at the beginning they decided that I needed protection. Imagine, between your legs there is a vagina that has been suffering from a severe form of inferiority complex, and all of a sudden a gaggle of very '*chivalrous*' men offer you and your poor vagina some divine boon of protection! I wish Clement was here to see that an English girl can sound like an eastern one; that she also can let herself into the depth of sentimentality and see through her dreams the wefts and the warps of her silky and worthy existence; that she is not 'only mind and only mind'."

"Sophie, my dear Sophie!" uttered Eileen, now holding her head with both hands, "You are the simplest and at the same time the most complicated woman I have ever met! Bearing in mind that the bloody enlightenment does not happen to people overnight, I suppose you have been going through it since long ago. And if this is the case, which apparently is, why have you been allowing those rascals to play with your life, your family's and the dignity and the reputation of the dearest person to you, I mean Gol?"

"A very good question," said Sophie, taking a long sigh, "When I was handcuffed and taken to the police station, I noticed that I was suffering from two devastating addictions: addiction to cocaine (thanks to Draco), and addiction to being humiliated and abused. Getting rid of the addiction to cocaine was easy but it was too difficult with getting rid of ignorance and overcoming the life-destroying biases and prejudices. And it is a miracle that I have managed to go through it and I hope I will soon see the face of liberation. A big chunk of me was craving for sublime indecency, and who were the most qualified to quench my pathological thirst? Of course Mehmet, Mervyn, Garry, Draco, Christopher and Calypso. It was a pity that Garry and Mehmet left the scene so soon! With them, I could have been completely satiated, particularly with Mehmet, that most accomplished parasite who had a sealed mandate from his Allah to abuse and exploit non-Muslim female things. Now I understand why Jack and Jack believed Mehmet was the most suitable man for me! Would the world believe that a twenty-three-year-old beautiful silky English girl would spend all her money on the most harmful parasites like Mehmet and Christopher only to have her degraded pussy appreciated by their canine qualities? You said it all, Eileen, you wise woman, you expensive woman, you are right, the senses of beauty and youthfulness had died within me otherwise my soul would have never allowed me to offer my historical soul and my silky body to rodents like Garry and his son!

"Christopher and Garry told me they would see me as their own daughter! And they did, only some Greek Gods can shag their own daughters and pimp them out to other fellow gods! 'The dirtier the better!' they would say. 'Meretricious omnivorous swine!' they would call me. What can make a piece of silk believe it is not worthy of a price? What can make a rose believe it is the symbol of ugliness and the source of foul odours?"

"Who is to blame, Sophie?" asked Magdalena, now gently playing with

250

a tuft of Sophie's silky hair.

"A very hard-to-answer question," replied Sophie, "Once I heard Gol say that fire is the only answer to some specific types of questions. This is a badly infected question, inflated with pus but utterly painless. Who dares to cut it open? A painless question is full of shame and misery. If there is any answer to this question, it must be sought in its ashes."

"This is a miracle!" said Eileen, two large tears rolling down her cheeks, "Although not quite sure but I felt it the day you came back to us. How can I prove this miracle!"

"If it is proven then it won't be a miracle," said Sophie, stretching out her hand and wiping up Eileen's tears.

"I believe in incarnation!" said Magdalena, laughing cheerfully, "Emily Bronte, I suppose has incarnated herself within our beautiful and well-deserved Sophie. She is back to fulfil her worthy aspirations."

"I love this, Magdalena!" exclaimed Sophie, her face now exhibiting the new Sophie, "She was, without a shadow of doubt, like all worthy women, the owner of a very expensive vagina. She would crack up at seeing so many daft and cheap vaginas around today! But I would make her happy. We would both marry Gol. Yeah, we would both marry Gol! Eileen, Magdalena, I am becoming positively uncomfortable with this amazing story! Did you know I have been receiving some very life-affirming letters from a certain Emily?"

"Cynthia's daughter?" said Eileen in an admiring tone.

"Yes, but I would love to call her Gol's daughter," replied Sophie, her eyes brightening up, "Only men like Gol could offer this world another Emily Bronte. Would you believe she is well on her way to becoming so? She is a university student, studying what Gol asked her to: Philosophy and Latin language. I will show you her letters. She is one of the brightest and most soulful girls I have ever met. In her latest letter to me I found a picture. Could you guess what that picture was?"

"Something related to Gol?" asked Eileen.

"Oh, yes," said Sophie, her now wise and talking eyes picking up the unique beauty of her face,

"A picture of my desk, the desk I used to sit at when I used to work for Gol. Eileen, he has wrapped the desk in a white sheet as if it is the rarest and most sacred object ever existed! It made me feel most innocent. It took me beyond right and wrong, where there is no question and no obligation, where there are only eternally blissful moments, and where nothing has to make sense."

"Goodness will give birth to goodness," said Magdalena, "A lion will give birth to a lion and a rat to a rat. Man has always been making a silly and most degrading mistake: inventing a language for what which is a language itself! The entire of human existence is a language, a very clear and unequivocal language, and within it a lion always means a lion and a rat means a rat. A society plagued by an invented language will eventually be plagued by the rats it breeds! This is a lesson I have learnt from history."

"I love this analogy," said Sophie, offering Magdalena the fullest version of her unique smile, "You are absolutely right. It was the invented and very much mechanical language that misled and eventually guided me towards the foulest of people. I left Gol because the fake language failed me. Imagine a beautiful young girl—and as Eileen beautifully put it, the image of that super power and perhaps the image of the entire universe—happily catching and taming wild rats for a rat-breeder and drawing immense satisfaction from it!"

"Girls, it is getting dark. I have to shut this door," shouted an officer, standing in the threshold.

Chapter 33

"Dance is rather for the soul than the body," said Magdalena, "It was your body, in the past, that is why you failed. It is your soul now and that is why your body moves like a flame. Lower, lower, your hands… Remain a flame and you will be dancing for the rest of your life… Good, now you know where the next steps must land, and you know it by heart… The bending of your back… in a second, it must be formed in a gradually formed second… No room for hasty seconds in dancing. Good!

Bravo, Bravo! The turning was impeccable! Your hands… Your hands are finding each other… They are receiving a message… both of them… so coordinated! Your breath… it is not heavy… no it is not… even your breath is dancing!"

"Join me, Magdalena! Come on!" said Sophie, coming to an abrupt halt and looking at the overcast sky overhead, "It is going to pour down. Come on! Let's dance in the rain. I have become all but melancholia. I have always wanted to dance in the rain."

"Take my hand. It is your dance. Guide me through it," said Magdalena, beaming at Sophie's rosy face.

The rain began to fall down, gently, rhythmically, as if even the nature had felt the vibrations of Sophie's heart and her ardent desire for harmony and unity. Barefooted, they danced on the now wet closely-cropped turf with Eileen and a few other spectators watching them curiously. It was Sophie's dance, disorderly ordered and choreographed sets of moves formed in a defiant mind. It was Sophie's dance, a small flailing flame to herald a looming little sun within her now bigger heart. It was Sophie's dance, a covert rebellion against her own self, an inflexible self that had pushed her towards a severe mental aphoria and stagnation…

"Sophie, you have a visitor!" shouted Eileen, now standing beside the officer who had come to inform Sophie.

"Messages, Eileen, messages!" shouted back Sophie, holding Magdalena's hands and going for the final move.

"Yes, they are coming from each and every direction!" shouted Sophie,

253

"Any idea who might be my dear visitor?" asked Sophie, now guiding Magdalena towards where Eileen stood.

"What would be the difference, Sophie?" shouted Eileen, "What matters are the messages, and they are coming."

"And they are coming!" said Sophie, now standing before Eileen. "I think I look like a wet sparrow. Don't I?"

"You look like a wet white dove," replied Eileen, touching Sophie's face.

"Once a hawk looked me in the eye and made me feel like a sparrow," said Sophie, laughing childishly, "Eileen, I can't wait to be hunted. I have been missing that divine and most sensual moment. Hawks don't hunt miserable sparrows. Do they?"

"You are being soaked in metaphors. You are living the language. You are rehearsing your freedom," said Eileen, wiping Sophie's face with the sleeve of her shirt.

"Am I, Eileen? Am I?" asked Sophie, with the excitement of a child who had just been promised her ever most favourite toy.

"You are, without a shadow of doubt," replied Eileen with a most assuring smile.

"I want you and Magdalena to be with me," said Sophie, now dashing towards the door, "I am going to have a quick shower. I won't be long."

"It is Gol's jacket!" said Magdalena.

"And his wristwatch!" said Sophie, pulling the jacket's sleeve up and holding her wrist before Magdalena.

"How does it feel to be in this jacket?" asked Eileen.

"It helps you feel the essence of womanhood," replied Sophie with such care and devotion as if trying to impart that the essence of womanhood was the main element of the entire universe.

"Oh, my God!" exclaimed Sophie, as they entered the visiting area, "This can't be real! Look, who has come here to visit me, Usman!"

Sophie stared at Usman, who was standing a few yards away from her and looking manlier than ever in his expensive grey suit. There was only one part of Sophie's existence that could contentedly fly towards Usman and cherish his ever honest and loving presence. It broke away, the ten-year-old beautiful innocent Sophie and dashed towards him with her arms wide open.

"Usman! Is it really you? Have you come here to see me?" asked Sophie, her body demanding a firm and long embrace.

"It is me, Sophie. I have come here to see you," replied Usman, holding her in his arms, "We are old friends. Aren't we?"

"We are. We are! We have always been!" said Sophie, tears running down her cheeks.

"Let's sit down," said Usman, now noticing Eileen and Magdalena's presence.

"They are my friends. They are very wise women, both of them. They are my dearest friends."

"Glad to have met you, wise women," said Usman, pulling the chair beside his back, "A miracle is only the fruit of wisdom."

"Amazing! Eileen also believes so," said Sophie, her face rosier than ever.

"And Magdalena believes it is only the last move of a soulful dance," said Eileen, offering Usman a full smile.

"How would you define it?" asked Magdalena, delightfully looking at Usman's wise-looking and kind face.

"Well," said Usman, already impressed by the two women sitting before him, "A miracle is like a lost child who is eventually found after years of separation and pain."

"I love this, Usman!" uttered Sophie, "I love these kinds of analogies. I am about to find my lost child."

"I can't recognise you! You are a completely different Sophie," said Usman, putting his arm around her shoulders.

"I am so glad to hear this," said Sophie, looking into Usman's eyes, "Now tell me about your little children and your wife."

"They are fine. They are my life. I love them to pieces," said Usman, his dark face beaming with joy and pride, "And who told you that I have married and—?"

"Gol's daughter," interrupted Sophie, "Yeah, let's call her Gol's daughter. The beautiful Emily, she told me, in one of her letters. She loves me. Yeah, I am so happy that Emily loves me. Yes, she is also very happy for you and what you have achieved. You are now a competent lawyer, she told me. She also told me about David and Nadira… What? You are looking at my jacket? I prised it off Gol when he came here to visit me! And this

255

watch. Yeah, I did prise them off him! They are the best things I have ever had."

"I hope they will remain as such for the rest of your life," said Usman, now holding Sophie's hand and examining the expensive watch.

"You guys should trust me," said Sophie with a pout.

"We do trust you," said Usman, "These two curiously wise women and I are sitting here with you, we are here for you, and it simply means you have made us to believe in you. Emily showed me some of your letters and I read them carefully. Within each single word you had used there was a smack of heart and intuition, a good deal of fervent desire for goodness; and above all, a loud and clear cry for liberation. Language, Sophie, is the only reliable mirror in which we humans can watch the true images of each other. And most importantly, I felt a sense of rebellion in your words, which means your desire for liberation is well received and soaked in your heart. Only a potent force can remove the shackles."

"Usman, you are the same honest ten-year-old boy who loved me so dearly," said Sophie, kissing his face, "But I broke your heart and ripped it out your chest. But you have come all the way here only to make sure my heart isn't going to be broken and ripped off my chest. If I could only understand this divine sense of loyalty within men like Gol and you I would…"

"You are almost there, Sophie," interrupted Usman, "You are ready to sacrifice yourself, and there is no proof more assuring than this."

"Usman," said Sophie, now really sounding ten-years-old, "I might join you and we both revolt against the society! Are you still intended to find your place in the society? Are you still in search of your identity? Are you still demanding recognition and all this?"

"No, Sophie," said Usman, "That would be a futile act, an upward spit. We would be devoured and dissolved in the stomach of this society. Out there, Sophie, there is no room even for a simple and sound debate, let alone revolt. This jacket, Sophie, is the safest place for you when you are released to go back to the society. Remember, a society whose most chivalrous men are creatures like Garry, Draco, Christopher and Mehmet—those womb envy-sufferers—will never tolerate an awakened and belligerent Sophie. A society that so generously bestows ample adulations upon the ugliest of souls, will never stand a liberated beautiful Sophie. Hold onto this jacket firmly."

256

"I know what you mean, Usman," said Sophie, clasping the collar of the jacket with both hands.

"Wise women," said Usman, smiling at Eileen and Magdalena, "Can one of you tell me how it happened, I mean this unexpected change within Sophie's mind?"

"Well," said Eileen, evidently impressed by Usman's unadulterated affection and attention towards Sophie, "I personally believe it didn't happen that unexpectedly. Sophie should be grateful to the hand of fate that made her cross paths with Mehmet, the purest and the most lethal form of poison. Although Sophie had given herself up to those guys only to be abused and humiliated, but there was a moment when she realised that even the humiliation and abuse could have some boundaries and limits—though far-reaching and wayward. The taste of degradation and depravation that Mehmet imposed on Sophie was too dehumanising even for these concepts to contain and absorb them. Allow me to use a bit of bad language to make this immaculately clear: imagine a toilet refusing to accept a load of shit because it is too shit! It was Mehmet. What Gol had spotted within Sophie, that speck of light, goodness or whatever else of the same nature, began to vibe Sophie's nerves and prevented her from falling into a deeper form of numbness and slumber. And bearing in mind that around the same time Draco had deliberately pulled Sophie into drug addiction, I don't think if it wasn't because of Mehmet's unspeakable and unprecedented depravity, our Sophie would have ever noticed her eventual painful demise. Let's see what our Magdalena has got to say."

"Don't forget Garry and the rats!" said Magdalena, laughing light-heartedly, "And that horsey Greek God, Christopher, the bearer of the baby Jesus! The protector of young and innocent girls! The buyer of cheap virginity and pickled twats! Forgive my language. Talking about a story created in this manner would only be possible by using its own language. In all, I think Sophie should be grateful to all of these human-looking creatures and of course, that speck of whatever within her that is still alive and able to remind her of what she had been in a far past, what have become of her in the present and what she can be. As a historian who happens to be a dance teacher as well and also familiar with philosophy and the art of rhetoric, I believe if the blood running in Sophie's veins is the same blood that in the past became a river and ran in the veins of the world and provided it with ample oxygen and made it take an ever-soaring leap, then she will

257

definitely become a beacon to her own existence."

"Did you carefully listen to what Magdalena said," asked Usman, smiling at Sophie.

"Oh, yes," replied Sophie, sounding more serious than ever, "She means I am a historical being, a discontinued continuation of merit and morality."

They stared at Sophie's rosy face incredulously, each of them thinking of some aspects of her personality that had been exposed to them in different ways. Was she the same female thing who had slept with an old rotting toothless man only to quench her pathological thirst for dirt and degradation while knowing that Usman was ready to offer her his kind heart? Was she the same female thing who had happily offered her historical silky body and her most elating soul to the rodents like Garry and Draco? Was she the same female thing who had helped Draco and Christopher to loot her family's wealth and dignity? Was she the same female thing who had sold her virginity for a tenner, a bacon sandwich and a bottle of beer? Was she the same female thing that had shamelessly spat on the face of love and goodness by standing before a judge and accusing Gol of the crimes that had actually been inflicted on her by others? Was she the same female thing that… Was she the same female thing that… This, if dragged on, would definitely turn Sophie into the biggest question mark ever—even bigger than the ones related to the origins of life and the entire universe with all its big and small bangs! But there was a piece of truth—with its limpidity immune to taint and sophistry—and that was the fact that the tendency towards degradation within Sophie was not historical. History cannot recall any great past founded on degradation and cheapness.

"Sophie," said Usman, holding her hand in his, "I am going to go to Mecca again, next week."

"Oh, that pilgrimage trip you told me about… that liberation, breaking away… and all good wishes…?" said Sophie, now her face acting as her memory, "And you said you would pray for me! Do you remember, Usman? Did you pray for me?"

"I did," replied Usman, "I asked Allah to grant you grace so that you could become a good mother. Remember when Islam had called you 'a loose girl'? And you were crying your heart out and moaning that a loose girl would become a bad mother."

Sophie's heart burst. She buried her face in Usman's chest and let the

258

flood of her tears come and wash away the clutters around her forgotten heart. Her body remembered that day, when it had accommodated a child, a teenager and a woman at the same time, a woman half of whom was craving for motherhood and the other half, well, for utmost pleasure. Her body remembered its divided parts: the part containing the child became dormant and soon forgotten. The part containing the teenager suffered a severe immaturity and was lost in a drunk alleyway. The part containing the women became a no-go-area for motherhood and womanhood. The ten-year-old Sophie pressed her face against Usman's chest and listened to his heart, and for the first time in her life, she felt the presence of friendship in her own heart; and in the same light, she also realised that she had never been accustomed to love and friendship; that she had always been trapped in a body that had been chained and abused by... No, she was too confused... She had used her body to abuse her soul. She had used her soul to abuse her body. What was she? What was her body? What was her soul? How had it been even possible to create such a disconcerting and confounding division of whatever she was?

She raised her head with a painful demand sitting in her wet eyes. She opened her mouth but nothing came out of it. It was lost; it was erased. It was a need. It was no more a need. It was a need already fulfilled. She was going to ask Usman if Gol still wanted her. She found the answer within herself, uttered by her soul, her body and all of what she was. Just an hour ago she had told Eileen that she could not wait to be hunted. 'I have already been hunted', she whispered to herself. The world within Sophie had now become like a puzzle—almost done, with a few small but strangely similar pieces left to be clicked in. Would she be able to discern the slight differing edges and see the game soundly through and throw her arms around triumphantly and celebrate her rebirth with a flame-like dance of growth and joy? Or would her body, this unaccustomed-to-mental-growth mass of sensuality stand in her way?

"Sophie," said Usman, putting his hand under her chin and raising her head, "Although I am now fully convinced that you have had a clear and guiding insight into all the aspects of what you have gone through so far; but there is a very important point that I would like to remind you anyway.

"Listen carefully. The moment you step out of this prison, the society will receive you with open arms. So far so good. So kind and caring of this society! But it will receive you warmly only to make sure you will hand yourself over to men like Mehmet, Garry and so-and-so! This society, like all other societies, has its own ways of living its life, and it is not to be blamed. Would this society allow one of its still very much *useable* members go the wrong way and join an 'evil man' like Gol and become *useless!* This Society is, particularly about its female members, as *divine,* watchful and jealous as Zeus! Out of this prison, an unmasked and enlightened Sophie would be considered as odd and a potential threat to the morals and values of the society! An enlightened and disabused Sophie would eventually give birth to some children, some immune to sedation little pesky creatures, the seeds of 'trouble' and 'disgrace'! This society, by no means, is lenient when it comes to safeguarding its values; otherwise it would have been plagued by men like Gol long ago! Did you know the street leading to Garry's restaurant has been named after him? Did you know the government granted half a million pounds to Garry's family after his death? Did you know Mehmet was granted citizenship after his death and was hailed as a fine and most scrupulous man? Did you know your parents have promised Christopher that they would convince their Sophie to marry him? And this deal is apparently about to be finalised because your mum has been the main negotiator! What would one offer to one's gods? Of course, the sweetest and the most beautiful sedated females! Sophie, gods and masks are the only things that this society can care about!"

Sophie wrapped the large jacket tightly around her body, turned towards Usman and gazed at him for some long seconds while engulfed by a heavy silence. She remembered, with a touch of shame sitting in her eyes, that a *call* had always prevented her from reciprocating Usman's genuine love for her. It had, the still unknown *call* to her, deemed Usman as untrustworthy, *alien* and evil! She remembered, with a bigger touch of shame sitting in her heart that the same call had approved of her pathological love escapades and the wriggling of her silky body in the beds of abuse and dehumanisation. She remembered, with a wrenching pain in her heart, the tiny dapple dog and the seagull on that rainy day with the dog's innocent-looking face engraved into her conscience. She wondered at how nature had kindly been chasing her only to show her the right path, and at how inexplicably she had eagerly been walking the wrong one. She thought of all the alien, evil, untrustworthy people she had bumped into during her not-so-long presence in the world: who could be more qualified and deserved to proudly sit at the top of the list than Gol! Who would have

260

the honour to be entitled as the second best! Perhaps her Maths teacher, or the bus driver who would offer her fatherly smiles on her way to school, or her first boyfriend, or Mr Gibran, Aisha, Emily, Maria, David, Nadira and a small number of others! Unfortunately, she did not remember a big number of *alien, evil, untrustworthy* people!"

"Usman, can I ever be a free woman?" asked Sophie, a bleak hue appearing in her eyes.

"Yes, if you can afford the price," replied Usman.

"What is the price?" asked Sophie, her face thoughtful than ever.

"Give up your freedom!" replied Usman, now looking into Eileen's eyes, "Give up the freedom of feeding on crap and getting yourself bloated. Give up the freedom of getting yourself filled with the hot air of grandiosity and uniqueness. Give up the freedom of undoing yourself. Be your own bird, sing your own song. Be a nightingale and not a grackle."

"How can I get rid of the indelible abashing past mistakes?" asked Sophie, her thin lips shivering, a surge of a different pain surfacing an unprecedented hue of exoneration and forgiveness on her face.

"Keep yearning," replied Usman, Eileen and Magdalena listening to him attentively, "And write a shining future of pride and grace on the indelible scars of the past. What matters is the eventuality of our beautiful Sophie. Get your first trophy as soon as you can."

"You are not a religious man, Usman. Are you?" asked Eileen, smiling musingly.

"I used to be relatively religious," replied Usman, his face now fully confirming his witty nature, "But now I am most religious, because I believe in no religion at all! I used to be a good Muslim.

"Now I am a devout Muslim! I am not making sense. Am I? Well, whatever makes people believe they are entitled to some rights, or are allowed to justify their otherwise rationally untenable actions is simply a means of demeaning and metamorphosis. The only true religion available to man is growth and the pain of it. Humanity is a responsibility. That is what I believe."

Usman left, leaving behind a wealth of warmth and a good deal of pain and responsibility for Sophie to deal with. Would she have visited an imprisoned Usman had he broken her heart or deemed her as alien, evil and untrustworthy? Would she have rejoiced in his return to the path of

261

goodness and enlightenment? Would she have been able to even think of forgiving him? These were the heart-wrenching hefty questions that Sophie's awakening conscience had to answer. She tried.

She struggled. She hesitated and tried again. There was an impelling desire gaining momentum within her mind, so rendering that it made dodging and whitewashing impossible for her. *I would have definitely cursed him for ever* she thought, her face turning into a twisting question mark. She mulled. She remembered. She whispered:

A painless growth is responsible for a painful life, And a painful life is a cheap life.

Had I ever felt the pain of a painful life?

No! No! This is a crime! They gave me the pain but not the pain of it! Pain is a force. Isn't it?

This is a crime! They have even faked the pain!

Pain is a boon. Pain is a call. Pain is an opportunity to cure.

Would I have still sold my virginity for a tenner, a bacon sandwich and a bottle of beer had I learnt the meaning of cheapness? Hollowed out, empty, dry, dead, all the human-defining concepts, nothing is real!

Fake the death too! Fake the death too! Put an end to a painfully painless existence of non- existents!

This will turn into vertigo, this painfully painless process of castrating, sterilising and pasteurizing humanity. An everlasting painful vertigo. An ever-rising blood pressure.

"Sophie, what is the matter with you?" asked Eileen, turning the light on, "Why are you wriggling in your bed like a wounded gazelle?"

"I am full of pain," replied Sophie, her face looking wan and lifeless, "Come here. Let me hold your hands."

Eileen walked over to Sophie's bed and lay down beside her. Sophie put her head on Eileen's arm and remained silent. The light was left on. The dark within Sophie grew darker. Her pain amplified. She clasped onto Eileen's bosom, inhaled her intact scent of motherhood and exhaled it with a long and relieving sigh.

"Eileen," whispered Sophie, "I have recently been experiencing a strange feeling.

"Tell me." whispered back Eileen.

"I have been feeling as if I am pregnant!" said Sophie, letting out a

262

short gentle giggle.

"You are," said Eileen, putting her hand on the top of Sophie's head, "Just like a fertile piece of land, eager to embrace the seeds and feel the pain of growth and yield the best of crops."

"I love the way you people use the language," whispered Sophie, "I wouldn't mind being jealous of you."

"It is a good jealousy," murmured Eileen.

"Eileen, why do I feel most authentic whenever I speak with you?" asked Sophie.

"It is a question for you to answer," replied Eileen.

Chapter 34

"Mate, I have to admit that you were dead right," said Christopher, letting out a laugh with a new sound easily detectable in it, "This rat business has actually helped me to land on my feet again. Bloody hell, yesterday we sold a hundred and eighty-five rats with a profit of ninety-eight percent! Would you even believe this! Bloody hell, it was even impossible for me to think of this lucrative business. We are now practically earning more from this than the three restaurants put together! Yeah, bloody hell, man."

"It is always there, more or less, the business thing," said Draco, giving his nose a proper quick massage, a habit he had recently acquired, "It is inside people's heads. You just need to use your head and see it in theirs. And don't forget, we have this from my dad. It was actually his idea, a much bigger and utterly ambitious idea. If death had not claimed him so unfairly and so untimely, this country would have boastfully owned the first rat-breeding factory. Yeah, he was going to sell all his properties and invest all of it in his first factory."

"Bloody hell, man!" said Christopher, "Do you mean he had spotted it in society's head? What a genius! That is why they named a street after him."

"Yeah, and he had spotted so many other things as well," replied Draco, swallowing his saliva and now looking as boastful and cocky as a French rooster, "He was going to shed light on this society in a variety of ways."

"I think we should fulfil his wishes, beginning with this rat-breeding factory thing," said Christopher.

"I have been seriously contemplating about this," said Draco, sniffling noisily, "Now that we are almost sure that Dad's murder case is over, and I think we can turn one of our restaurants into a small rat-breeding factory."

"Bloody hell, that would be a cracking business, mate!" said Christopher, the new sound in his voice now almost identifiable, "And, mate, I have been intended to have a word with you about my overall state. You know, bloody hell, this loneliness thing. Now that we all know who is going to spend the rest of her life in prison and why, I think you should help me get over this loneliness thing. Bloody hell, do you know what I mean? I mean if you allow Calypso to get involved in this rat business, then I can somehow coax her into marrying me; or, I don't know, maybe I just can have her as my woman."

"Mate, you know me very well," said Draco, offering Christopher a pair of dead eyes and a wriggling smirk, "I have never interfered with people's business. As you know very well we live in a society in which nobody's business is nobody's business, and therefore I don't think I would be able to bring myself to interfere with this. Having said that, I can assure you that I will have no problem with Calypso joining our rat business, provided that you promise me to have her under control by relaying to me whatever she thinks or says. Do you know what I mean?"

"Mate, I guarantee this," said Christopher, assuming a most righteous air on his face, "I have always admired you for being so bound by your philosophy and morals. Bloody hell, some people are really crap. They put their bloody noses into whatever they come in contact with. Good, very good. You know, man, bloody hell, it is all about taste, Calypso knows my taste very well, and I am also happy with her taste. Bloody hell, man, you know, Sophie deceived all of us. She is going to rot in prison. She deserves it."

"Mate, I think we should never mention her name again," said Draco, "She was only a cheap bitch, the cheapest ever. We all learned our lessons with whatshername evil presence in our lives. Honestly, more or less, I was almost sure, right from the beginning, that this so-and-so would spoil our blissful lives."

"What was the word?" asked Christopher, narrowing his eyes in a very rat-like manner.

"Whatshername or so-and-so," replied Draco, squeezing his nose.

"Yeah, bloody hell," said Christopher, "This whatshername and her mum are useless bitches who are even unable to taste a man properly. I don't think they have ever enjoyed sex. Bloody hell, man. I think it is their thingy, yeah their thingy is numb."

"I understand what you mean," said Draco, "Once I heard my dad say whatshername was unbelievably cold and vapid."

"Yeah, man, bloody hell," said Christopher, scratching his face, 'Only the girls who are fathered by men like us can offer the world some charm and real pleasure. Bloody hell, Calypso is like a furnace. She is good, really good. She knows how to properly taste a man."

"It seems you have already spoken with her," said Draco with a half-dead smile.

"Yeah, man. No worries, no worries," replied Christopher, "I will treasure her. Yeah, bloody hell, I will look after her. She likes it. She has always liked it with me. She knows her portion. She is decent, that is why she wants me. And she also can spot it in society's head, I mean this business thing and rats."

"Fair enough," said Draco, the signs of jealousy and a dark rendering pleasure appearing in his eyes, "As it appears, things have taken the right turn for us. It is a big shame that we lost Mehmet. I think we failed to understand and appreciate him. I think he was only second to my dad, I mean in terms of philosophy and mentality. Imagine what a great help he would be to us with this rat-breeding business."

"I do agree with you," said Christopher , now scratching his neck, "We all failed to see what he had and what he was in his core; and I suppose it was because of his somewhat wild and unpolished nature. Bloody hell, I don't know, perhaps he could have become another Garry. But I am happy that this society appreciated him by offering him citizenship after his death. He was a Muslim. Wasn't he? Yeah, bloody hell, he is now in paradise, roaming around with an English passport in his pocket and being slobbered over by English girls."

"Mate, English girls are not allowed in Muslims' paradise!" said Draco, letting out a laugh with a very squeaky screechy sound in it.

"If we believe he could have become another Garry," said Christopher, now scratching his nose with the rapid movements of his thumb, "I am sure he has already smuggled some English girls into his paradise! Remember, Mehmet was a teacher of ratness."

"Fair enough," said Draco, scratching the back of his neck; and now musingly gazing at Christopher's face, he added, "Wittingly or unwittingly, you have just proposed a great idea…"

"Bloody hell, man. Have I?" interrupted Christopher, now scratching his forehead very wittingly!

"Yeah, man," said Draco, throwing a touch of admiration (wrapped in a smirk) at Christopher, "I am quite impressed by Mehmet being a teacher of ratness! Honestly, imagine a logo for our rat-breeding business! Man, this is awesome! I am fucking loving it! Imagine a large glossy sign with

Mehmet and Garry teaching a gaggle of plump healthy rats! Give me a piece of your fucking imagination, mate!"

"Aha! I am getting what you mean, mate," said Christopher, now scratching his right ear, "Well, we could imagine a good number of locations and situations: how about a classroom, perhaps one of those old traditional ones with blackboards and chalks, with Garry and Mehmet in rat costumes teaching the rats how to be rats?"

"Mate, this is fucking awesome! Honestly. It is," said Draco, hysterically excited, "I absolutely love the last part of what you said: *teaching the rats how to be rats!* Mate, it would smash it, it would insinuate to society this craftily mixed sense of humanity and ratness!"

"What does insinuate mean?" asked Christopher, now scratching his left ear.

"Don't worry, mate. Go on with your fucking awesome imagination…" said Draco, biting his lower lip.

"Bloody hell, well," said Christopher, thoughtfully stroking his now non-existent beard, "Let me add some other things to the first one and then I will tell you the second one. Bloody hell, man, yeah I am thinking of a background where you and Calypso, in your very colourful clothes, are shepherding a gaggle of rats in a farm of peanuts. Seriously, just imagine two young cute human beings shepherding a big number of cute rats. Bloody hell, it is what I think; it moves some things inside people. Do you get what I mean? I mean, bloody hell man, yeah, I mean it touches some parts of society's brain."

"Mate, you know the entire biology and psychology of bloody rodents!" said Draco, an eerie air appearing in his small eyes, "Honestly, you are fucking awesome! It couldn't be any better, this idea of Calypso and I in the background!"

"Mate, I am not finished with it yet!" said Christopher, evidently enjoying the rodent animation wriggling in the lines of Draco's face, "Mate, imagine Mervyn and me too in the scene! Imagine us partially hidden among the branches of a chestnut tree to the left of the peanut farm, overseeing the grazing rats! Imagine Mervyn's face and what it could do to the heads of observers!"

"Man, this is pure fucking genius!" said Draco, laughing cheerfully, "Such a brilliant logo will definitely serve the main purpose behind this business best. For me, it is all about my Dad's legacy and his ardent desire

267

to offer something to this society, the society that offered him numerous opportunities and ample support. He spotted this in the head of society; I mean this craving for moving on and leaving the dogs behind. As a man of thought and meaning, he was always trying to offer this society a meaningful service. Meaningful, he would always say a meaningful and cultivating service is worth millions of pounds. He was well aware of society's tendency towards a big and badly needed shift: the shift from dogs to rats."

"What a genius! What a genius!" exclaimed Christopher, now bending down and scratching his right lower leg, "He was spot-on with this! Bloody hell, man. Yeah, he was right. People are actually going off dogs!"

"Honestly, they have already gone off dogs," said Draco, squeezing his nose, "And the reason that my dad spotted behind this was beyond the realms of sociology and all this. He believed the concepts have changed and therefore the society also has to change accordingly. What does loyalty mean, if anything at all? Concepts like this are fetters and chains. Dogs keep signifying and reflecting outdated restrictions—wrongly defined as morals and values—to this society. My dad and the great late Miss Julie Atkins had some lengthy and profoundly savvy debates on the issue. They both believed the quintessence of this society could only be reflected back to it by the initially wild and the partially tamed rats."

"Oh, I see!" said Christopher, now scratching his palms one after another, "So how are we going to go about this, I mean having them wild at first and then...?"

"A very good question, mate," replied Draco, now posing as an undisputed intellectual, "We would only follow Dad's simple method: whisky and a whit of human sex hormone."

"Human sex hormone!" exclaimed Christopher, scratching the top of his head.

"Yeah, mate," replied Draco, hitting his forefinger against his temple, "Miss Julie Atkins used to be sort of a scientist. It was her idea, and Dad being an intellectual, was more than capable enough to see the point in it. Whisky would enhance a rat's brain and human sex hormone, well, would make it horny, simply enabling it to fully grasp the fully flourished concept of wildness. So we will apply Dad's method at the farm stage, when we will be shepherding them in a peanut farm. And then during the next stage we will stop giving them the dose of whisky and double the human sex hormone; and this will eventually enable them to identify themselves with human beings. Amazing! I actually learned some philosophy and logic from my dad. Based on his belief on this particular subject, now I can assert that if a being identifies itself with another being, it means those two beings have inherently been connected to each other. Yeah, I think we are well on our way of guiding and helping this society to get rid of the overly inquisitive, irrelevant and pleasure-spoiling dogs and embrace the rats, these creatures of briefed and concentrated values."

His father an *intellectual*, himself also privileged with a good deal of the same stuff, Draco, though draped in a cloak of folly and impertinence, was the child of his surroundings, and therefore he was very much right to be wrong with his arguments! Where the fine line of discernment has faded and, as a result, *foul* can be painted and sold to the defused and sedated souls as *fair*, Draco was the most appropriate and qualified intellectual to appraise the ills and the defects of his society and issue healing and corrective prescriptions! Appropriated to him what society had sealed and appropriated to his father, Draco was devotedly set to appreciate his society that had appreciated his father and him so devotedly! Thinking of that now 'expired' soft cheese (Sophie), and her mum, that lover of rough Turkish men and a zealous former admirer of the-now-half-potent Greek ones, had always made Draco feel overly *humbled* and indebted to the society! Despite having a defected memory system—the short-term part was too short and the long-term part clogged—he was still able to recall the numerous faded female faces that had readily and unconditionally bestowed upon him all their charms and offered him their silver bodies for free; he could also recall that he had never recalled—or even felt the necessity of doing so—any male faces of the society! He had already begun to recall that he had never recalled Mr Barry James Grandeur's name or face! To him, his dad and their cronies, this society had always been only a lush female thing!

In all, Draco and Christopher had already proven themselves as two adept and very persuasive pied pipers to the society that loved them dearly! Was it down to their own merits or was it all down to an out-of-tune gaggle of people who would knowingly favour any awry melodious noise only to avoid the tuned and demanding reality? Had they really believed that Sophie would have spent the rest of her life in prison, or was it another unexpected piece of strategy devised in their divine heads? Would the warmth of pure love, loyalty and friendship be able to melt the ice within Sophie and make her immune to these pied pipers, or would she fall for another *mesmerising* melody and follow them to her demise? Would the historical black dancing snake within her goad her to action with a tiny touch of venom, or would they both become a forgotten history for good?

***

"How on earth could you bring yourselves to do this to me?" asked Anita in a hapless tone, "You have sold my flat! You have sold the roof over my head! You, ungrateful apathetic creatures!"

"Mum, please calm down," said Calypso, sounding like the mother of Jesus Christ, "We will buy you another one, a much bigger and better one, by the end of this year. Please understand us. We had no other solution. This business can be the most lucrative business in this country, and remember, it was formed in Dad's great mind, meaning that we can register it and ask for a monopoly over it. We must hurry and set up this rat-breeding farm or factory or it could easily be stolen from us. Draco has sold two of the restaurants and we are hoping to sell the other one and all of our flats so that we can put up the money for this massive business. Mum, we, all of us, are moving towards a great and colourful future. Do you understand what future is, Mum? No, you don't, otherwise you wouldn't have been wasting your life with that lunatic Italian who doesn't even know the difference between a dog and a rat!"

"What is the difference between a dog and a rat?" asked Anita, in a most resigned tone and with a most indifferent look washing over her dark face.

"A dog is yesterday and a rat is the future," replied Calypso, her large eyes fixed in a frame of insatiable greed and lust, "This society is going to have it all, Mum. Can you understand this? A dog is a matter of the past. This society is itching for full satisfaction. Imagine rats as big as pillows! This society wants rats, bigger and fuller rats. This society wants orgasm, a much bigger and lasting one."

"Interesting!" said Anita, sounding like a prisoner who had just been told she would be executed before the dawn, "So why has this society chosen you and your brother to provide it with a much bigger and lasting

270

orgasm?"

"See, Mum, you have now learnt how to ask good questions," said Calypso, her eyes rolling, "Just yesterday we threw this question at ourselves, Draco and I, and when we failed to come up with a good enough answer, Christopher, as always, provided us with the right answer: 'It is because society has seen it within you'. He said, and needless to say that he meant the rat, yes society has spotted the rats within us and therefore it has decided to eagerly allow us to be the guiding shepherds to it.

"Christopher believes this society has always been ambushing this opportunity, and now that it has arisen, society isn't going to let it pass it by. Yes, Mum, you also should be proud of us. Christopher believes Draco could well be recognised as one of the greatest intellectuals of the 21st century. I can remember Mr Barry James Grandeur also saying the same thing: 'this young man is in connection with another world, the world of supernatural' he said. And I am sure you would be amazed if you knew what Elizabeth said about Draco! Do you wish to know? So, listen carefully: 'Any woman who sleeps with Draco will become immortal'! Do you think she and her husband paid Draco half a million pounds just for nothing! She has now become immortal, and knowing that Sophie also had become immortal long ago, they are absolutely happy with what they have paid for it."

"Has Mr Barry James Grandeur also become immortal?" asked Anita, a dark pungent humour ringing in her tone.

"Mum, I didn't know you could be so witty!" said Calypso, "I am not sure, but he looks like an immortal man! Once Christopher told me a story about Zeus and how he would grant a form of semi-immortality to the men whose wives he would bed. Fair bargain. Mr Barry James Grandeur is a businessman after all."

"Do you really think you are right with what you have been doing?" asked Anita, gazing at her daughter through her now glazed eyes.

"Mum, we are well beyond right and wrong," replied Calypso, now Garry's voice coming out of her, "This is what Draco and Christopher believe, and I also think they are dead right. Dad and Mehmet also used to hold the same very exact belief. Draco believes if you think of England as an African country, then England is an African country."

"Interesting," said Anita, her face now completely blank, "You are beyond redemption, my poor children. You are lost."

"Nonsense!" snapped Calypso, "Let's suppose it was the case, then who would be most responsible for us being beyond redemption? We have nothing to be ashamed of. We are proud of ourselves, and our pride comes from the society that has always been supporting us. It is so simple to understand: if the society is happy with what we are and also with what we have done and achieved, then it means that we have been walking the right path."

Anita said nothing. She had nothing to say. She was responsible. She remembered how Franco had observed and described Sophie long ago: *'Sophie is an apple who loves to be eaten by pigs. An apple is responsible for being an apple'*.

She sighed and vanished into her past, those blissful days of youth and jovial moments, those innocent moments of applehood that she had failed to imprint in her mind. She had soon allowed her soul to get accustomed to being bitten by the wrong teeth. She had, knowingly, received the seeds of wrongness and carried them to the stage of fruition one after another. She was responsible for failing to be responsible, and it was a multiplier of her pains and sorrows. She remembered the day she had dared to stand up to Garry and what he had told her: *'Talk to me only when you need food and sex!'*. He had said, injecting a touch of venom into her heart, it had crept up to her brain and reduced her down to a mass of confusion and deprecation. That was the first and the last time she had felt the need for responsibility, and since then she had only received food and sex! She was responsible and her responsibility was backbreaking. She had turned herself into a broody hen only to lay and hatch the eggs of indecency. She was more than responsible. She would be, in the court of her conscience, deemed as criminal. She sighed. She remembered: *'I have never trusted women! They are not worthy of a man's trust'*! Garry had shouted at her when she had demanded for trust and respect. She sighed. She remembered that she had always mistaken wrong for right; that she had always wasted her love, affection and time on the wrong people. She bitterly laughed at how she had deemed Mehmet as a 'great and nice man' while knowing that he was a most harmful human-like creature. She sighed and remembered how she had, knowingly and unknowingly, played a devastating role in the demise of her children by passively confirming and allowing Garry's teachings determine their future. *'I have no trust in humanity! I do not believe in deceptive concepts like 'love' 'affection' 'empathy' 'forgiveness'*...

Humanity is a dirty joke! Love is a plague!' Garry had spewed these words out when she had dared to remind him that he could be wrong with his takes and views and the bringing up of their children. She sighed and remembered that Sophie was not the first and the last young girl Garry and her son had used to satisfy their ever-aggravating rodent souls. She kept remembering, regurgitating the wrong stuff she had swallowed unchewed, the stuff she could and she should have never downed regardless. She sighed and remembered how passively she had turned a blind eye on so many untoward happenings in her life, happenings such as the realisation of Mervyn, and later on Christopher, abusing her Calypso since a very young age and… She sighed… But she failed to remember more… There were, in a niche of her mind, some stories that her memory had classified as 'not-to-be-disclosed'. She got up to her feet, threw a *last* look at her Calypso and pictured her face in her mind… She shuddered and failed to remember… Her memory had already classified the last picture of Calypso's face as 'not-to-be-disclosed'. With a heavy heart and a giddy head, she walked away, leaving behind the passivity that had led her into a world of darkness and unspeakable degradation.

Chapter 36

"The little things, Mum, all the little things," said Emily, gently sitting on the chair beside her mum's and looking at the painting she had crouched over with all her attention concentrated on the tip of the tiny brush in her hand.

"What is it, Emily? Are you going to teach me another piece of philosophy?" asked Cynthia, turning towards Emily with a smile on her beaming face.

"Am I being a pain?" asked Emily, looking at the brush in Cynthia's hand.

"You have always been a pain," replied Cynthia, putting the brush in a small ceramic bowl to her left, "The sweetest and the most nourishing pain. Has any mother ever been privileged with having the most elevating pain in the form of a beautiful daughter? I doubt it. Now tell me whatever you wish to. What is it about, 'all the small things'?

"The other day," said Emily, now staring into the pair of eyes in her mum's painting, "Gol was telling me that Cynthia shouldn't crouch over her painting desk for so long. 'It can hurt her neck and her back and affect her overall posture' he said."

"What are you trying to impart to me, Emily?" asked Cynthia, the answer already revealed in her own eyes.

"Someone is set to prove the English storytellers wrong," said Emily, still looking at the painting, "That they should stop using the name 'Cynthia' to implicate all the ills of the world; that this name contains some hidden treasures within it."

"Emily," said Cynthia, holding Emily's hand, "We have become too foreign. Haven't we? Since we got closer to Gol, we have unconsciously been using a very flowery language, romanticising and adding a touch of melancholia to whatever we think and say. I love this very much. So, he thinks I should avoid hurting my neck and back and… and my overall posture. Interesting! Has he been mentioning my name differently?"

"Mum, you have become so percipient," said Emily, "He wants you to move to his place and live with us. He believes you don't deserve a life of loneliness. You would reside in one of the large rooms upstairs."

"All the little things!" uttered Cynthia, "Too much rationality is the plague of all the little things, as it yields an invalid form of selfhood, and a self-created this way, will become most irrational and of course a source of confusion. Do you know what I mean? Oh, what a silly and irrational question! Of course you know. You are a brilliant student of philosophy. I mean a very *rational* mind would see breastfeeding in public as an act of smearing society's dignity while drooling over the picture of a twenty-year-old naked girl on the front page of the Sun!"

"I fully understand what you mean, Mum," said Emily, "You mean what has been happening between you and Gol has been based on two open hearts with the partial interference of two flexible and compromising minds."

"You said it, my dear child. You said it," said Cynthia, her heart overwhelming her mind, "Emily! Have you noticed? Yes, of course you have… That this story is going to take us all by surprise. We all know that Gol is not going to forget Sophie (neither are we), and it means—that would be—see what would happen when you allow your heart to lead you through your life! It wouldn't cease to surprise you time after time. It would keep pumping large amounts of euphoria into your veins. All the little things. Someone feels the pain in your back and your neck. Someone wishes to see you standing upright and proud. Someone wishes to have you closer to them. These are not the little things, Emily. Are they? Or perhaps they are the bigger little things."

"What is the difference?" asked Emily, evidently delighting herself in watching her mum's euphoric face, "When all the differences have been seen, no difference will be seen."

"Emily," said Cynthia, "I have it in my guts that you will soon become the first most prominent female philosopher, the one who could sit and have a dinner with the greatest of the other side."

"Mum," said Emily, putting her hand on Cynthia's shoulder, "A female mind is too delicate, and this delicacy makes it too considerate, and a mind considerate to this extent, won't be willing to reveal the entirety of what it observes. A female mind is overly aware of the unpredictability of the details and the perils they might contain."

"Emily, shall we have lunch together?" asked Cynthia, "I am so

275

fascinated with this subject. I would like to have it fully examined with you."

When Cynthia went downstairs to order lunch, Emily got herself amused with walking round the gallery and looking at her mum's old and new paintings, which had lined the walls like the pages of a history book. There she spotted, in each painting, a modifying and correcting element intuitively incorporated into her works. Right opposite the entrance door, her eyes caught a new painting on the wall: the portraits of all of them in one place with that of Gol in the middle. There she observed the craftily hidden piercing hue in Gol's eyes and the unuttered questions without question marks on his wide forehead. There she noticed the regained innocence in her mother's blue eyes. There she spotted on David's charming face a full book of sincerity devotion and love. There she spotted an ocean in her own eyes… There she also noticed that some details had deliberately been left out.

***

"The light of my eyes!" said Aziza, lifting the round China teapot to pour tea for Cynthia and Emily, "Have I ever seen anyone as the light of my eyes. Emily is the light of my eyes. Seeing Emily enables me to see the unseen."

"I love this, I absolutely love this, Aziza," said Cynthia, looking at the tiny glass cup of tea before her, "Can you explain it to me?"

"Some people question Allah's existence—or whatever else it might be called; a super power or the source," replied Aziza, assuming a very religious tone, "Blind, they are, as Allah himself said. If you wash your eyes and then have a proper look at Emily and also know how to use your other eyes, you will clearly see the reflection of that beautiful creator in her eyes. And my very dear Cynthia, we are all eyes, every single part of us is an eye, and it is because the creator wants us to see him. What is the purpose of this wish by the creator, we don't know for sure, but it doesn't make any difference because it is good."

"Is Emily the most beautiful girl you have ever seen?" asked Cynthia musingly.

"Definitely," replied Aziza, the religious air on her face now gaining, unconsciously, a gnostic hue, "And this beauty comes from inside, my dear. It is the awareness of the beauty inside that has doubled Emily's outside

276

beauty. I mean her soul and the way it has been nourished. And that is why whenever I look at her, I think of the source of her unique beauty. I think there is a source to all the existing things in this world. I also think it is very important how we get exposed to the world. My dear, Emily's heart is a highly educated heart and therefore she could be the light of the eyes of the wise and the lover."

Knowingly or unknowingly, Aziza was philosophising her views in a jargon-free manner.

Although not quite happy with the way she herself had been 'exposed to the world', but she was evidently elated at the intuitive realisation of how Emily had been exposed to the world and its blissful results. By saying that 'seeing Emily enables me to see the unseen' perhaps she meant to highlight the importance of holding on to the tendency towards the search for the source (meaning) in human life. Both Aziza and Cynthia, had experienced this game of heart and love and light, getting infatuated with heaven and its creator whom they both once had called 'Allah' and had fallen in love with Him, a love that Cynthia had quickly fallen out of. They both had kept falling in and out of love, with Aziza turning her emotions into a lenient politicised philosophy and Cynthia giving herself up to silence and art. And they both had begun to see the light with Emily being a guide towards it.

"My dears, I welcome all of you from the bottom of my heart," said Aziza, cheerfully looking at her guests, "I take ample pleasure in having you with me again. I would like to thank Gol, this old boy, who brought you dear people into my life. Well, just before your arrival, Cynthia and I were talking about our children when we both remembered that we had another child who had been kept away from us for so long, I am talking about our beloved Sophie. As you all know, Sophie is now an inseparable part of us; and in fact it was because of her that we got closer to each other and became friends for life. A few days ago Gol gave me some very good news, and I decided to ask you my dears over and share them with you: we will soon manage to free our beloved Sophie from prison!"

Maria and Aisha dashed towards Aziza with their arms wide open. Mr Gibran's eyes revealed the most unadulterated and universal fatherly joy and relief. Jamila and Lateefa shared a hearty smile with Gol and Emily. David and Cynthia shared their happiness with Nadira and Usman. Islam kept nodding to all this affirmatively.

After the emotions had been dealt with and the unuttered reservations had been left to be dealt with in a better time, Aziza put on her green fabric glove and poured wine for her guest, beginning from Mr Gibran and repeating her old worn-out story of alcohol and how Allah used it as a political means… And that the English establishment was as political as Allah was… But this time she poured a full glass of red wine for herself, and after giving her guests some rather short explanations on why she decided to have a glass of wine with them, she sipped her wine with a tinge of guilt covertly wriggling under her dark complexion. "My dears," said Aziza, pouring herself some more wine, "I have recently learnt that Allah is a drinker himself! Why did he discover the alcohol—no, 'discover' isn't the right word—he created it. Why? Because he wanted to brew a whit of His own knowledge in it. He did so, tested it Himself and offered it to man. Even our great prophet didn't mind it. He would sit with his Jewish friends and down a few cups every now and then. Some believe a big chunk of those world-changing revelations occurred to him right after visiting his Jewish friends. And we all know that our beloved Jesus also wouldn't mind it. We all know that how he would turn water into wine."

"Aziza has rebelliously been ploughing through the history of God, religions and philosophy!" said Gol, laughing.

"'Ploughing' is the best term, Gol," said Mr Gibran, returning Usman's confirming smile with a nod of head, "She knows how to philosophically not to be philosophical at all! And how to irrationally be rational!"

"See, my dears, true knowledge is always within the quiet heads," said Aziza, putting a few chunks of lamb on Mr Gibran's plate, "This peaceful quiet man knows how to read people's minds and kindly understand them. All great-looking societies are built on the shoulders of the rationally irrational people. I heard Gol saying this."

"Aziza, this lamb is so delicious!" said Mr Gibran with his eyes closed.

"It is braised, my dear, my special and exclusive way of cooking lamb," said Aziza.

"What is 'braised'?" asked Maria, narrowing her eyes, apparently trying to guess the meaning of the word.

"It means cooking slowly in little moisture," replied Aziza, assuming a donnish tone, "See, my dears, that is why I believe the English establishment is as political as Allah is: to create a great country you would need a language so massive that the ordinary people would never get past mastering its alphabets—just like Allah's Quran!"

"Mum, leave Allah and the English alone," said Nadira, laughing, "Tell us more about Sophie and when she will be released."

"Oh, my dear lovely Sophie," said Aziza, putting her right hand on her chest, "My heart has been crying for Sophie. Well, my dears, some women know how to fall in love and some others don't know, and they are the ones who land in a mess. The ones who know how to fall are the ones who have already learnt how to land. Our sweet beloved Sophie didn't know how to land and that is why when she fell anyway, she landed in a mess, in a very sticky mess. As you all know, since my dear Usman, this very competent solicitor, took Sophie's case on, and also considering the fact that we all have been doing whatever we could, we have now reached a point at which we can clearly see a free and overly happy Sophie in our lives. The details of how we have succeeded in doing so should, understandably, be kept safe until we knock on the prison's door and call our beloved Sophie out. It won't be long, my dears. It is what I can categorically confirm. My dears, you know that if you allow me I will be speaking for days nonstop. So, to avoid this, I will leave the rest of this to Gol. He may wish to say a few more words."

"Aziza, you are a sweet and savvy speaker," said Gol, smiling, "I think what you said will suffice.

"First of all, allow me to thank all of you for your sincere support all through this really challenging struggle we have been involved in. What began to amaze me right from the beginning of this struggle was the manner you all got involved in this: you all have been trying your best to help Sophie without even asking yourselves why. And today I can see it on your faces and in your eyes that how you have been growing on her. Before I tell you the next part of the story of Sohrab and Afsoon, I would like to hear a few words from Mr Gibran and Aisha who have visited Sophie eight times since she was imprisoned."

"Well," said Mr Gibran, smiling, "For me it began when I noticed she had fallen in love, a love that had turned her into *love*. Being modest and intelligent by nature, that love had turned her into a butterfly that could readily fly into the flames of a burning candle. What I found most confusing about her was her hesitation, which was obviously due to alienation. Love, that form of it, Sophie was alien to it. In other words, she had never been allowed to have a look at love through a window other than the window of

279

carnal pleasures; she had never been allowed to understand her own heart and let it guide her through her life; she had never been allowed to be *silly,* and that I think turned her into a wise fool who eventually followed her own way of following. There was nothing more pleasing and elevating for me than imagining beauty, charm and purity entrusting themselves to wisdom and appreciation. It was around the same time that I decided to offer her a present with the sheer intention of exposing her to the light and the taste of heart and the importance of listening to it while under the impartial observation of mind. Of course, I did not expect a twenty-two-year-old girl to undergo a drastic change by reading a couple of books. It was only a shot in the dark. And now I am overly pleased that things are going to take the right turn for her, and I hope our Sophie will soon learn the meaning of her own name and let it shed light on her future path. Our Sophie deserves our love and affection, and we will happily receive her with our hearts."

"Very pithy and heart-warming," said Gol, looking at Aisha.

"Well," said Aisha, her now mature face looking wiser, the signs of a well-acquired and fully absorbed level of knowledge clearly visible in her eyes, "For me, it all began the day she came to our home to apologise to my dad and ask for the books back. The moment I looked her in the eye, I spotted a mixture of love, hatred and indignation in them. She was not upset with my dad. She was indignant at herself. She used those books only as a pretext to vent the maddening indignation within her. At whom her anger should have been directed? During one of our latest visits she told me that an hour before coming to our place, she had decided to lash out at Gol and let him know that he should have shown her some heart and loved her back when she had fallen in love with him. I wish she had done so. The past is past, but what matters now is the courage she has gained by standing up to herself and getting rid of the wrong form of the sobriety that had made her excessively self-conscious and consequently self-centred. She is now standing in the middle, in the middle of her own existence and the world. And this is the blessing result of carrying a heavy pain with her for so long, the pain of true love. I am impatiently looking forward to having her among us as soon as possible."

"My dear Aisha speaks so beautifully," said Aziza, offering Aisha a big smile, "That is why I was telling Cynthia that the way people get exposed to the world would determine their quality. My dear Aisha has been exposed to the world in the best possible manner. I wish the same to happen to our still young and understanding Sophie. I will pray for her and ask Allah to grant her peace and grace. Yes, my dears, we will all be fine when our Sophie is back with us. Please keep praying for our Sophie. May Allah bless all of you."

From which viewpoint had these people looked at Sophie that had enabled them to see her as part of their own lives? What had they seen within her and how? What had convinced Mr Gibran and his bright daughter, Aisha, not to give up hope on Sophie and keep trying regardless of Sophie's repellent attitude towards them? What could have healed Usman's wounded heart and cued him back to Sophie as a friend? What could have changed Sophie's unacceptable image in Aziza's mind and turned it into a most-cherished-for image? What could have been valuable enough to convince Cynthia to imprison herself only to protect Sophie? And above all, what could have encouraged the young Emily to keep secretly corresponding with her, and even sending her money and birthday gifts?

These were the questions to which none of them could or wished to provide an answer, as they all had followed an inner call, convincing and reassuring enough to enable them to see the contour of the final image and what it would represent. These were not the questions to be answered. They were to be lived, and how beautifully these *daydreamers*, mostly foreign, had lived their questions within a self-existing and self-defining intention to provoke an undertow within Sophie and help her to resurface her real self.

Were they all mere coincidences, all these encounters in Sophie's life since she had been imprisoned? Was it a coincidental encounter when she had found herself standing before Eileen and looking into her eyes as if searching for the key to eternal freedom and happiness? Was it a coincidence when she had encountered Magdalena, historian and dance teacher? Was it a coincidence that the young Emily had been spending a good deal of her time on writing lengthy letters to her and expressing nothing but her unconditional love and support for her? These and so many others were the questions for Sophie to deal with: would she wisely choose to live them or would she carelessly choose to answer them? Or would she take the last remaining step wrongly and get herself rid of the obligation of answering or living these questions altogether?

"Gol, we are ready," said Emily, putting a cup of coffee before him, "Tell us the next part of the heart-warming story of Sohrab and Afsoon.

281

Although I have already braced my heart, but I hope the end of this fabulous story is not going to be bitterly heart-breaking."

"Well," said Gol, looking at Emily's face with a tinge of pain sitting in his eyes, "Pride has always overcome and surpassed bitterness. This story is the narrative of pride and loyalty, and the ones who played its roles faced their fate with their heads held high. They will be living in my heart as long as I am alive."

"And they will definitely be living in the hearts of your children!" said Maria, in an infectious and animated tone.

"Of course they will be," said Aziza, "Allah will see to this, my dears. Allah knows how to write stories with good endings and make them live for ever."

"Well, where did we leave off the story?" asked Gol, smiling at Aziza.

"You entered Greece, waiting for your move to England to be managed by Sohrab's dad," replied David.

"Thank you, David," said Gol, "My stay in Greece lasted more than it had been planned, which soon turned out to be a blessing in disguise for me, as years later I found it to be one of the curiously important parts of my life. Sohrab had made me literate enough to be able to think and see beyond my age. He had also taught me a good deal of history, and therefore I knew where I was. As it had been managed by Sohrab's father, I stayed with a very kind Greek family, an educated middle-aged couple and their three lovely children: Marta, Alex and Costas. Well, this story was not meant to be much about me, but as I was an indispensable part of it and now the narrator of it, in this part I might highlight some snippets of my part. So bear with me. As I mentioned in the first part, I was born and lived the bigger part of my childhood in a remote and hardly frequented village innocently hidden among some high mountains. Perhaps 'pristine' would be the right word to describe that spot of the earth, where all the existing elements were blissfully satisfied with the way they were, which was the way of nature—a fully conscious presence. And I was the child of my time and my surroundings, pristine and natural. Then came the war and the tolling bells of a new world and a new presence. I moved to Iran almost as a primitive boy, and there faced with two pristine lovers who taught me the grand art of falling in love."

"Gol, did you fall in love with Marta?" asked David, ruffling his hair with an air on his face expecting nothing but an emphatic yes.

"David, I am now fully proud of you," said Gol, smiling at him, "You are now able to detect and smell love naturally. I did fall in love with Marta but it did not take me long to realise that I had to quickly fall back out of it! Imagine how hard it was for a sixteen-year-old boy to shoulder a massive and heavy responsibility that himself had happily accepted to take on. I was fully committed to Sohrab and Afsoon's pure love and aspirations for me. Although they had not imposed any confining demands on me, but my unwavering love for them would not allow me to get diverted from the path they had put before me: they had asked me to move to Europe and to a country where I could become something. Even a teenager as I was, could tell that Greece was not the place they meant. I turned the love for Marta into a unique form of friendship, and it was my first practical try at dealing with the alchemy of love and other human emotions. By the family's generous love and patience, I managed to quickly learn some Greek, and when I had become relatively able to work out what they were saying, Marta's dad began to mention some things about Greek philosophy and history—as all the Greeks would proudly do—which became a prefatory to my future love for philosophy and thought. It was during the last months of my stay in Greece that I received the news that Sohrab had moved to Afghanistan, and as I had predicted, my dad had put forth some conditions in order to allow Sohrab to marry Afsoon, one of which had been that Sohrab would join the Mujahedin and fight against Russians for five years, or 'infidels' as he used to call them. That Sohrab had accepted all of my father's conditions without any objection. My father asking Sohrab to fight for 'five years' raised a big question in my mind even at that age. How did he and so many others know that the war was going to drag on? It was a war and not a wedding, this was the way my teenage mind could see it. In a way and unconsciously I was happy that I was only a teenager and should not have thought about the manner in which grown-ups would write scenarios for each other and make the innocent and the most vulnerable to play the bloodiest part of their stories. But it did not last long; this short existence of frivolous indulgence, as I had to grow up, it was nature's order. I had to think; I had to endure the pain of thinking; I had to learn how to love the world the way it was. No one was able to help me understand why people like Sohrab, Afsoon and my mother had been pitched into a game of bloodshed by the people whose main worries have always been their bellies and a span below it. Let me wrap this part up by saying a few words about

Marta: she was highly intelligent and very humane, and as I had predicted that she would sooner or later leave Greece in search of a bigger and more accommodating place, she moved to America a few years later, and has since been living there. She is a prominent NASA scientist.

"I moved to Italy with an Iranian man, who shortly afterwards managed my move to England.

"Though my stay in Italy was short but it reminded me of an interest that had been formed in my heart and my mind. And it was related to Sohrab and football. Before moving to Iran, I had not even heard the word 'football'. Although Sohrab was an unconditional lover of all positive human activities, but he was more interested—I realised this years later—in the activities that could surface and reflect the soul and the essence of those involved in them. He was an ardent fan of football, and in particular Italian football. He had a small black and white television, on which we would watch a football match together every now and then. And when I had relatively familiarised myself with football, I also began to like Italian football, an interest that was initially induced in my mind by those musical-sounding Italian names and the blue colour of their jersey, which I had seen on the front page of a magazine. 'They play it from the heart' Sohrab would say, 'They give it whatever they have at their disposal. They fight for every second of it even when they see no prospects of victory'. In all, Sohrab would always look for the traces of heart in whatever he was interested in, and his hearty search for hearts became an enlightening philosophy in my future life. When I grew older I realised that Sohrab was impeccably right with his observation of the Italian football and the amount of soul and heart they put in to it, and play it exactly the way they cook and eat—patient preparation, even more patient cooking and, well, eating with gusto and full attention. Well, allow me to leave Italia and move on to England before I, very much unwittingly, take you back as far as the Divine Comedy!

"I arrived in England in the morning of a windy and churlishly cold day, and was safely handed over to an Iranian family—some distant relatives of Sohrab's father. I was immediately fascinated by the beauty of England, and a few days later, I felt this unknown and very mesmerising feeling sitting in my heart and creeping up to my mind: it definitely was not the immediate result of infatuation; it was a true and existing feeling, and it was arriving, and it meant that it was coming from somewhere. How was it possible for a teenager to feel and picture the entire stature of a historically beautiful and merited England? Was he a delayed clairvoyant coming from a time which once had been deemed as 'future'? Or was he a lunatic stranger dropped down from the moon with a head filled up with only some milky light? Whatever was that teenager, he was able to feel England as a continuum of growth and its yielding and rewarding pains. Perhaps it was Brother Sohrab's soul within me. It was him who used to see the world that way; he was able to use his own existence as a medium and see the early beginning points in the past. In those early days I had no wish but the improbable wish of having Brother Sohrab and Afsoon with me in England, as they both were from the past, an unblemished continuum of humanity, and the receivers of messages. I am certain that they would have opened their arms and danced to concede and celebrate their presence in a historically beautiful England."

"Gol, we had never heard you speak about England so positively and so beautifully!" said David, ruffling his hair with a tinge of guilt sitting in his eyes, "Do you remember ages ago when I called you 'the most anti-English person ever'! And when you taught me a great listen by a colander and a spoon with holes!"

"Whatever needs to be overtly expressed, has got a missing leg," said Gol, throwing an involuntary look at Cynthia, "It is only a critical mind that is capable of offering you genuine attention and respect."

"Well said, mate," said David, smiling musingly, "Go on, mate, go on."

"After my asylum claim had quickly been processed and accepted," said Gol, throwing another kind smile at David, "I was sent to school, and that was the auspicious beginning of my new life. Up to that point I knew nothing about the whereabouts of my family and Sohrab in Afghanistan, and it took me a while to eventually get in touch with them. My mother and Afsoon had been sent to Kabul to reside in a compound allocated to the Mujahedin's families, and my father and Sohrab had been sent to the Panjshir valley where a heavy battle was going on. I received Afsoon's second letter a month later, in which I found four beautiful pictures—one of my father and Sohrab, which had been taken just hours before they had departed and joined the Mujahedin, and two of Afsoon and my mother, and a fourth one… Could anyone have ever guessed what it was? No. It was an old picture of the donkey that used to patiently carry us to school and back home from Saturday to Thursday! The patient donkey was looking out of the picture with his large and worried eyes fixed on an unknown spot."

"Gol," said Cynthia, putting her hand on his shoulder, "Why have you not shown those letters and pictures to us yet?"

"Right moment, Cynthia," said Gol, touching her hand unwittingly, "I have been waiting for it, and it is about to arise. I will hand them over to you as soon as Sophie is released. Well, after seeing those photos, I became so nostalgic that I wished I could become a bird and fly back to the people I loved so dearly. And if there was any serious desire to do so, it was rendered as impossible in Afsoon's third letter: she and Sohrab had asked me to promise them that I would never even think of going back to Afghanistan. They had also informed me that my father wanted me to join them and fight against the 'infidels' and that I should not allow my still raw emotions to affect my decisions.

"Sohrab had reasoned that the war in Afghanistan was a pointless war for Afghans and it would only need some of their blood only to justify the untenable causes behind it. Of course as a teenager full of bravado and naturally affected by the story of patriotism and the moral obligations to one's country and people, I had some really hard times when dealing with all this. And it was years later that I realised it was love that helped me out; I also realised that love, if approached and understood correctly, can align itself with the mind, and even become a version of it, a more cogent and calmer version of it. If it was not because of my love for Sohrab and Afsoon, I would not have listened to them and definitely gone back to Afghanistan.

After a long while I received the first letter from Sohrab, written in his beautiful handwriting, half of which was about me and the other half about Afsoon, and nothing about himself, and it was then that I realised Afsoon and I were much more than two ordinary human beings to Sohrab—we had become his world, his existence, and he would do whatever he could to protect us. A couple of years passed, and I wrote a letter to my dad and asked him to allow Sohrab and Afsoon marry. Although bitter, but it was something I thought about and experienced at that young age, I mean the dreaded thought of war and death and the fact that Sohrab and Afsoon could have lost their lives at any given moment. I was always imagining and thinking of finding a way to save something of them, something more than their names and their sweet and life-affirming memories. A child, I wanted them to leave behind a child, a continuation of themselves. My dad did not respond to my letter. He had fallen out with me. He had become full of Allah and completely alien to human emotions. The war—guys, I know it is not the right way, but let me finish this story off. The war dragged on. Allah and the good guys and the bad guys stood their grounds firmly and fought right to the end. Sohrab, Afsoon and my mum perished. Sohrab was killed in Panjshir valley and my mum and Afsoon were killed in an air raid. The war ended. A torn apart Afghanistan crumbled down on her broken limbs and kept licking her deep wounds. My dad and Allah survived, and immediately remarried to make more children for the future sacrifices! The war had only two winners: Sohrab and Afsoon. They were the only ones who fought and died for a good cause. They were the lovers."

Chapter 37

"Who is going to cheer Anita up?" asked Gol, stroking his beard and looking at Anita's rather sad face.

"Is a woman's arse part of her or is it an independent thing?" asked Franco, in a deliberately accentuated Italian accent, apparently meant to reveal a sublime piece of Italian humour.

There were a few moments of lingering silence before Cynthia and Anita burst into laughter. Gol followed them suit. Franco's face showed no sign of humour only to look even more humorous. He kept touching his moustache while nodding thoughtfully.

"Would you believe it!" said Cynthia, wiping up her tearful eyes, "That stupid solicitor had actually mentioned this in the covering letter attached to the lawsuit against Gol! He had written that because Gol had fallen in love with Anita's arse, he could have had a strong enough motive to think of murdering Garry!"

"It is so funny," said Franco, his face still rigid, "I didn't know that the men of this country had such a facilitating option available to them! 'Dear lady, unfortunately I can't afford to fall in love with all of what you are. Would you be kind enough to allow me to fall in love with only one of your boobs and one of your legs?' Imagine such a line! It reminds me of those little restaurants in the Middle East where they sell lambs' heads, legs and inner parts: a customer would ask for two legs and a tongue, and another one for a whole head and two legs, and some others, well, they would relish the inner parts without being worried about the legs and the heads and the brains!"

"You did cheer Anita up," said Gol, laughing, "Let's get to the point and make her even happier. I wish Anita and I had crossed paths with each other years ago and I had fallen in love with her, whether with one or two parts of her or with the whole of what she was! But it wasn't destined to happen that way. The only wish now I am curiously eager to fulfil is this inquisitive urge to see inside Anita's head to learn what caused her to fail herself by investing all her emotions on some obviously wrong people and

288

wrong causes for so long. Perhaps Anita can teach us a precious lesson today. You married Garry and soon after you realised that he would not allow you even to cut open a watermelon the way you wished to. But you wasted three decades of your life on a man who would see you as nothing more than a female rat. Why, Anita? To what should we impute this, if imputable to anything normal at all? Was it due to the lack of pride within you or—?"

"Or was it due to too much of it!" interrupted Franco, thoughtfully smiling. "You have a point, Franco. Go on," said Gol.

"Being Greek, invaded and ruled over by the Ottoman Turks, and migrated to England," said Franco, evidently having a point, "There would be an unbearable accumulation of *pride*, an ever-enhancing form of it, making you hallucinating all the time. You would simply mistake a rat for a lion, or vice versa!"

"Should we take it as a joke or as a piece of savvy observation?" asked Gol, crossing his arms on his chest.

"More than that," replied Franco, "Anthropology, biology, psychology, philosophy and history and some other things which are out of my scope of knowledge, they are all incorporated into this. As we all know, these types of subjects should be wrapped in the velvet of humour or they can cause some wrong tingles in some wrong spots of society. So, to safely wrap this up I should say I would have never moved to England had I been a Greek man with a history of being conquered and ruled over by the Ottoman Turks!"

"To avoid mixing mustard with horseradish?" asked Gol, laughing.

"Exactly!" said Franco vivaciously, indulging himself with a wayward and blasting laughter, "Gol, you are an unmatched master of analogies! This is brilliant! Yes, just to avoid such a taste- eradicating mixture."

"Though we have already gone off topic," said Cynthia, laughing, "But what Franco is saying is thoughtfully interesting to me. Franco, are you trying to define the subtle line between pride and arrogance?"

"Cynthia, you have become too foreign!" said Franco, "You wouldn't mind to read between the lines and ask serious questions. Yes, you are spot-on with this. Misconception of self can well be highly demeaning and even destructive, as it creates a sense of grandiosity instead of a clear and tangible picture of the existing reality. Therefore, and based on my own world-view, I believe what kept Anita in a completely wrong relationship

289

for so long was nothing but a hidden and wrongly invigorated sense of grandiosity; otherwise no human soul could have stood that much of humiliation within normal circumstances."

"A sense that keeps reminding one that one is unique and great anyway." said Cynthia, holding her chin.

"Exactly." said Franco.

"Are we allowed to sit here and judge Anita in this manner?" asked Cynthia, with a smile that failed to fully form, perhaps she realised her question was not fully relevant.

"We are," replied Gol, throwing a smile at Anita, "We were pulled into this bizarre game of mockery in which Anita, knowingly and unknowingly, has been playing a role. To work out our own business we have every right to interfere with hers. So let's seriously avoid abusing the language to distort the truth, as wise and viable people would never be afraid of abrasive frictions that can clear and polish their minds. Let's begin at the beginning: where was the beginning point for us? The moment Sophie stepped into Garry's restaurant, and it is none of our business what had gone before that, as that would be the business of the society's conscience. Of course as a woman, Anita knew that Sophie was somewhat confused, and as a result, highly susceptible and vulnerable. She also knew that she would be exploited by her husband, her son, Mervyn, Christopher and Mehmet.

Nobody's business is nobody's business! Perhaps this overridden and deliberately hollowed mantra prevented Anita from taking the right action, not even as much as a few indirect hints. Deliberately wrong approaches to the defining terms that elaborate on human interconnections would definitely yield nothing but degeneracy and decadence. This badly convoluted form of, '*nobody's business is nobody's business*' means, unequivocally, *humanity is nobody's business!*

Oh, yes, nobody's business is nobody's business! Should we be allowed to hold Anita responsible for the loss of three lives and the irreparable damages done to the lives of some others? No, this is not our business! What we would be allowed to do is pamper Anita, shed tears for her broken heart and the pains she has endured, forget all about wrong and right, bury the truth and mind our own business like some decent citizens! The justice has been done immaculately; a hefty punishment has been imposed on the bloodthirsty perpetrator! No, no one has the right to hold Anita accountable for this inhuman game! Those murders wouldn't have taken place had Anita not been so indifferent to what was happening around her. What can I say about what happened to Sophie! Yes, we have tried our best to approach Anita's story in the most possible rational and inclusive manner, and we have all come to this point that Anita was beyond question before and after the death of her husband, and therefore we have decided to see her as one of us. Having said that, I would be immensely grateful to Anita if she would kindly answer a few questions. The purpose behind my questions is clear: we wish to avoid offering you blind and undue empathies."

"I will happily answer your Questions, Gol." said Anita with a flutter in her voice.

"Good!" said Gol, offering her an appreciative smile, "Who was the main manager of your business?"

"I was the manager." replied Anita.

"Who did take on Christopher and Mehmet?" asked Gol, throwing a fleeting look at Cynthia's anxious face.

"I did."

"Good," said Gol, stroking his beard, "You took on these two guys and gave them your full and very generous support. How generous? They would get a pay rise every year! It is exactly what a good manager should do to appreciate quality and commitment and direct them towards bettering the overall functioning of a business. Bearing in mind that you were not as generous to the rest of your staff, could you tell us what did you see in Mehmet and Christopher that could not be found in others, who were left deprived of your generosity?"

"Gol," said Anita, evidently unable even to utter a single word let alone fashion a convincing reply, "I...I..."

"Don't worry, Anita," said Gol, "I am being harsh to you. Am I not? Pustules, Anita, those old pustules within you must be cut open or you will, sooner or later, suffer a severe reversion. There is this Persian saying that goes, 'even a madman knows he is mad.' Anita, you were fully aware of what you were doing. If we accept that your soul and your overall mental state had been undermined by your wrong husband and your wrong son and daughter, then we would have serious problems with digesting the fact that you were so zealously supporting the people of the same nature! Life means all these passing moments, which so many of them go unnoticed. There is a guy who has been working for you people for fifteen years. Did you ever

291

give him a pay rise? Did you ever want to know him? Did you ever want to sit and have a cup of coffee with him? Did you ever think what it would take for a man to be so consistent and loyal all through those years? Did you ever want to know if he had any children? No, because you were busy studying the entire genealogy of Mehmet and Christopher and memorising the size of their shoes, trousers and even their socks and underpants! It is a bitter irony that I have to let you know that that man—who is yet to be given a pay rise after fifteen years!—is a proud father to four decent and educated children. I think I should go back to what Franco said and admit that understanding Anita's story is out of the scope of our knowledge."

"Let's get to the point." said Cynthia, laughing.

"Gol, I have come here to tell you—" said Anita, turning her now hangdog face away from Gol and towards Cynthia.

"Do you not think it is too late, Anita," interrupted Gol, "You have come here to tell me what you should have told me much earlier! It is about what happened between Garry and a Kosovan woman years ago. Isn't it?"

"It is," whispered Anita.

"Keep it for yourself. Let your loyalty remain intact, woman," said Gol, turning his head towards Franco, "Walk Anita home and come back here quickly. We will have two amazing visitors before noon, and I want you to be with us."

An hour later, and after Franco had come back, Cynthia and David set the table in the gallery while trying to guess who the two 'amazing' visitors could be, of course in vain, as they both had failed to notice the tinge of sarcasm Gol had gently added to the word 'amazing'.

"There used to be five of them, of the 'very amazing' men," said Franco, ruffling David's hair, "Two of them were taken. It is a pity. Only Sophie could have told us how 'amazing' are our visitors."

"Franco, you are not going to tell us that—" said Cynthia, now turning towards the door.

"Here we go!" said Franco, laughing loudly, "Look! The amazing Draco and even the more amazing Christopher! It is a great shame that the late great Garry and the even greater late Mehmet are not with them today!"

"Mum, I think we are going to have the most amazing day ever!" said David, looking at Draco's spiky hair that seemed spikier than ever.

"Indeed!" said Cynthia, stretching her hand out to switch on the dimmed lights over the table.

"Gentlemen," said Gol, asking them to take a seat with a gesture of his hand, "Not in a million years, or maybe even more, we could have imagined we would one day be hosting you two gentlemen! Have a seat and let's drink, and then we will see what we can offer each other. David, be quick boy, pour the wine, warm our heads up, as such a unique conversation is categorically in need of a unique form of exaltation."

"I don't think alcohol can cheer Draco up!" said Franco, throwing at him a meaningful crafty look.

"Mate, you are wrong," replied Draco, giving his nose a gentle twist, "My great dad used to say 'if a man is to measure himself against anything, that has to be alcohol'. Yeah, I think he was very much right with this. And honestly, I have always found my true self when under the influence of alcohol."

"Shall I pour you some whisky?" asked Cynthia, reaching for one of the two bottles of Jack Daniel's in the middle of the table.

"That would be awesome, honestly. I would have it with two ice cubes and a wedge of lime, please. The late Mehmet used to have it this way," replied Draco, scratching his right ear.

"Did you ever find out what exactly happened to Mehmet?" asked David, pouring wine for Christopher.

"Yes, man," said Christopher, tuning himself to let out a horsey laugh, "We all know that Mehmet was a great and very decent man. Yeah, man, but there was this fucking Iranian man with his quirky sayings and proverbs. Yeah, he believed, this fucking man, that Mehmet saw the dick but not the pumpkin! And that was why he ended up having it in his throat."

"What the hell is it, this dick and pumpkin thing?" asked David, ruffling his hair and laughing.

"That is one of Rumi's aphorisms!" replied Cynthia, bursting out a hearty laugh, "Christopher, you go on. I will tell David about it later."

"Yeah, man," said Christopher, taking a swig of his glass of wine, "This fucking Iranian man, who used to work for us, believed that Mehmet lost his life to his insatiable greed, but as we all know very well, it was that evil girl, that whatshername who took Mehmet's life with morphine. How much of it? Yeah, man, so much that it had turned his liver into a gooey thing. Horrible, that whatshername was going to get rid of all of us. She had, you might not believe it, prepared six bottles! Yeah man, six of them for all of

293

us. Three of those bottles are with the police. Yeah man, with her fingerprints on them."

"Yeah, honestly, disgusting, whatshername was disgusting," said Draco, carefully taking a dab of his glass of whisky, "The reason for which she took Mehmet's life was that he had stood in her way. She had cunningly planned to marry my dad and own whatever he had. Honestly, yeah, Mehmet, that fine piece of a man, had fallen in love with whatshername, thinking of her as an angel, not knowing what was awaiting him."

"So it wasn't that he saw the cock but failed to see the pumpkin?" asked Cynthia, laughing from the bottom of her heart.

"No, honestly," replied Draco, scratching his neck, "He was badly dejected when whatshername broke his heart, that is why Christopher and I decided to help him by marrying Calypso to him. Yeah, honestly, it was not that he married Calypso to get his hands on her share of what my great dad had left behind. Mehmet was a very religious and highly spiritual man who was far beyond his material needs. Honestly, if you look at it, that is why this country appreciated him so gracefully. Honestly, the good thing about this country is that it never fails to appreciate goodness."

"Look who is here!" said Gol, pointing to the door.

"Tia Maria!" exclaimed Christopher, "Long time. Isn't it, Maria?"

"Happy to see you again," said Maria, walking in, "I am doubly happy to see both of you, you very decent men!"

"Come here, here, sit beside me," asked Christopher, pulling a chair back.

"Let me sit there, opposite you," said Maria, pointing to the chair beside Cynthia's, "I would like to see the faces of both of you."

"Bloody hell, man," said Christopher, "There was this black guy who was going to abuse Maria, yeah, man, bloody hell, I prevented him from doing so. And there was that Romanian gypsy. Remember? She would have been looking after a sick pig and a couple of chickens in a remote village in Romania had I not interfered and taught that pervert a lesson. Yeah, man, the world is full of abusers!"

Franco stared at Christopher's face. David's face fell, his eyes became blank, and his gaze wandered off, hit the walls, bounced off, hit the ceiling and vanished through the open door. Cynthia and Maria looked at each other, as if to make sure that they were sound and sane, and to avoid any unhinging misgivings, they looked at Gol's face that now seemed like a burning book of justice. In some moments of void, they all kept silently staring at the two overly confident faces before them. In some moments of void, they all felt a throbbing pain in their hearts, as if they had just been informed that the entire of their existence had been an ugly misunderstanding! They thought, it was written on their faces, what if they were the ones who had to be ashamed of their abusive existence in the world; what if they were the wrong ones; what if they were the cavemen and left unaware of the drastic changes in moral systems among human beings... The owners of those two confident faces remained unmoved, amusing themselves with alcohol and calmly eyeing around the gallery.

"Wow! What a beautiful painting! What a beautiful girl!" exclaimed Christopher, his eyes glued to a painting on the opposite wall.

"Emily, my daughter," said Cynthia, her voice slightly raised and angry.

"Could you please ask Clement to come upstairs?" Gol asked one of the two waitresses who had brought the food.

"I like Clement," said Draco, a smirk appearing in the corner of his mouth, "Honestly, though not a very good chef, but he is awesome! Years ago, he came to us. My dad put him on minimum wage. He apologised and left."

"Did he apologise because your dad offered him minimum wage?" asked Maria, cocking an eyebrow.

"No, he apologised for failing to see my dad as a great businessman," replied Draco, "Honestly, he said to my dad 'Sir, if I knew you were such a shrewd businessman I would not have bothered you at all'. He knew he wasn't good enough for our place."

"Nonsense! Clement is a MasterChef!" said Maria, bursting into laughter.

"Maria, his dad was right," said Franco, twisting the right side of his moustache, "Only an overly great businessman can put a MasterChef on minimum wage!"

"Guys, let's eat," said Gol, throwing half a smile at Draco.

An hour later, and with the somewhat formal arrival of Usman, some aspects of the unexpected presence of the two 'fine pieces of men' were revealed. Posing as a man of law in action, Usman pulled out from his brown leather shoulder bag some forms and a few pages of blank paper attached to a notepad, put them on the table and with the unmistakable air of impartiality appearing on his face, waited for the two parties to call him in to action.

"Mr Draco Christodoulou is here to sell his restaurant to me," said Gol, turning his face towards Usman, "And I am going to buy it, but I need to be assured that the murder case is really over and Sophie was the murderer. You know what I mean, gentlemen. No wise man would enter a deal when the other side could be exposed to a legal action at any moment."

"Mate, honestly," said Draco, an out-of-control smirk ploughing through his face, "I and Christopher had a meeting with the judge before contacting you, and he assured us, a million percent, that the case had actually been over three days after those murders had taken place. And above all, what type of assurance could be more authentic than whatshername's confession, which had been mentioned and acknowledged by her five times all through her trial? Honestly, mate, we think you should not be so sceptical about such an evidently done and dusted case."

"Well, I think this is a good-enough point, I mean Sophie's confession," said Gol, apparently fully convinced, "Then let's do it. Usman is my solicitor, and he is here to legally arrange the deal for us.

"As we have already haggled over the final price, I have one small request that if you gentlemen accept, then we can seal the deal today, and you will get your cheques. I want you two gentlemen to keep the business going on as usual for, let's say, two months before we manage to take the restaurant over."

"That is absolutely fine, mate," said Draco, scratching his neck, "We have about three months before we initiate the bigger part of our enterprise. Yeah, fine. We can do this for you."

"Good," said Gol, in a tone that evidently made David somewhat worried—calmer than ever.

"Why don't you tell us about your enterprise, you two old mates?" asked Maria, laughing.

"You too could have been part of it," replied Christopher, offering Maria a mulish smile, "You know, people get what they deserve. Bloody hell, you never appreciated our friendship. Yeah, imagine such a massive business. You could have bought yourself an entire island and all its inhabitants! Just the other day Calypso and I were talking about you and your untameable character. 'Restive', Calypso said. 'Maria is a restive mare'. She knows her words, Calypso. She is going to be in the centre of our massive and lucrative business. Yeah, she knows her *portion*; it is what her great late dad believed. Yeah, man, the problem with this society is that most women don't know their *portion*."

"What do you mean, Christopher, what is *portion*?" asked Cynthia with narrowed eyes.

"See," said Christopher, letting out a squeaky laugh and scratching the back of his head, "You women don't know even the meaning of *portion!* It means capacity and the size of wishes and dreams. A woman is a mine of easily-attainable ambitions. Yeah, bloody hell, but they don't know how to materialise them. That is silly of them. Yeah, take, for example, our Calypso, she is one of those little portion of women who know it. She, our Calypso, have been using all the means available to her since a very young age, and bloody hell, she is now so very close to becoming a woman of prosperity and full success in life. This was actually late Garry's idea, this *portion* thing. And he used to experiment it on some young women, one of whom, as we all know, was whatshername, this ungrateful fickle little thing. Late great Garry, and even late Mehmet, used to believe that whatshername was one of those who could have climbed it all the way. Yeah, bloody hell, but she wasn't steady enough."

"Interesting!" said Cynthia, "I am very intrigued with this. Now that Draco is busy with Usman and Gol, I would also love to know a bit more about your future enterprise."

"Bloody hell, man," said Christopher, throwing another look at Emily's face in the painting on the wall, "I appreciate your interest in what we are going to do. Yeah, it was all in great Garry's head. He had seen it long before his unfortunate death. Yeah, the rat, I mean. That Iranian fucking man believed Garry had come from a stinky dungeon in the depth of history, but he was so very wrong—you know these mother-fucker Iranians think they know it all—as our great Garry had come from the core of history, where there is only pure rationality and practicality. You see the rat and then you see the rat, and if you see the rat then it is there, and if it is there, well, it is there because it is there.

"Simple. Bloody hell, you know, pure men would never mistake a rat for a lion, or even a cat. What is the point of seeing a rat and thinking of it as a lion or a cat? I don't know; I really don't understand some bloody people and how they deliberately ignore the core meaning of humanity. Garry, like his son, was a unique intellectual of his time. He saw it, the rat.

297

And we are going to look after it. The other day Draco and I had a meeting with some very understanding council members, and they all agreed that what Garry offered to this society during his fruitful life, had to be acknowledged and celebrated. And they all agreed to grant us a big loan for the rat business."

"Are you really going to breed rats?" asked Maria, her face now a badly overwritten booklet of belief and disbelief.

"We have already begun doing so," replied Christopher, scratching his face with both hands, "Six months ago, we turned one of the restaurants, the one by the waterfront, into a small rat-breeding centre. And guess how many rats people have bought from us so far! Around three hundred thousand! Would you believe this, mate? We have bought five vans, carrying rats all over the country! This marvellous business has already sorted us out: I bought my first house just two months ago, a mansion in the countryside, and two horses, a couple of ponies and a female white donkey. And Calypso—a daughter to an intellectual and a sister to another—has invested all of her money in another amazing and lucrative business. That also had been initially formed in her dad's head. Can you guess what business she has set up?"

"Lizard and snake-breeding, perhaps!" said Maria, laughing.

"It should be related to this rat business," said Cynthia, her face blank, her eyes oozing incredulity.

"Spot on!" said Christopher, letting out a mixed laugh—horse-ish, mulish, rattish, "Spot on, English woman! It is the grand business of dog castrating! A replacement: dogs out, rats in. And we have already registered these two businesses, meaning we will have a monopoly over them. Yeah, man, as ever, and as the history is our great witness, it is only the Greek mind that can guide the stray Westerners by shedding light on them."

"Really!" exclaimed Maria, "If we had any light left for us we would have shed it on ourselves first! Replacing dogs with rats is definitely a step back and not forward, and no sound mind would see it as *shedding light* on some stray people."

"Maria, I have always doubted your blood," said Christopher, scratching the top of his head, "I don't think you have Greek blood in your veins! Even your surname isn't Greek. You could well be a fucking Iranian, or a mongrel thing from the same area. Speaking Greek doesn't make people Greek! Bloody hell, man! I was going to offer you a free share in our business but you made me change my mind right now! Bloody hell, appreciation is like a ladder, and so many women fail to understand this. Fake things like you have discredited the grand Greek culture!"

"Rat-breeders have degraded the grand Greek culture, and not *things* like me," said Maria, laughing loudly, "Where was this rat? Where did you find it, you children of Narcissus? In your own heads! In your own minds!"

"No, mate," said Christopher, evidently badly wounded, "Garry, the most authentic Greek man in our time, did spot it in the head of this society, and then we also saw that he was right. Bloody hell, man, some people don't know the meaning of the word 'prerogative', that is why they open their mouths so carelessly! But we don't care, because this society has chosen us to guide it towards a better and more meaningful future, and we will put our hearts into this. Yeah, man, we are not going to be affected by some rotten things who call themselves 'human' while they are only some living things."

"Christopher, I hope you are mistaken, and all this is based on ignorance," said Cynthia, holding her chin and staring at him, "I mean all of you and this society and this bizarre story of dogs being replaced by rats and some other really alarming implications around all this."

"We are not mistaken; we have absolute faith in what we are doing," replied Christopher, his chickenpox-ridden face now resembling a badly dented old copper pot, "We are the soul of history, and this is what Garry, the great intellectual, believed. How could we be wrong when we are summoned back from the depth of history? And this is what Draco, the conscience of his time, believes. Yeah, man, bloody hell, how could anyone even think of finding fault with us when the entire of this society is behind us? Society has made up its mind, and is set to leave the dogs behind and embrace the rats. What could be, if anything at all, wrong with this? The great Mehmet, who had the blood of an empire in his veins, believed human life is all about pleasure and therefore we must seek it regardless—it could be sought in licking an ice cream, or even shagging a donkey! And that was why Mehmet had set up that donkey farm with that Albanian guy."

"Did you buy your donkey from that Albanian Guy?" asked Maria, her eyes unhinging Christopher.

"Bloody hell, I think we have said enough!" replied Christopher, pushing the chair back, braying hysterically.

"Okay, we are almost done," said Usman, throwing an indifferent look at Christopher , who was staring at him like a horse looking at his shoes, "As you can see, I have already written the cheques, and I will hand them over to you as soon as the rest of the paperwork is done. I would like to congratulate the both sides and wish you all the best."

"I am wondering if Usman could become our solicitor," said Christopher, throwing a look at Draco.

"That would be awesome, honestly," said Draco, almost overwhelmed by a surge of euphoria revolting within him by seeing the four large written cheques, "I am sure that would boost our massive business drastically. Honestly."

"Tell me a bit about your massive business," asked Usman, in a rather business-like tone.

"I have something here with me," said Draco, reaching for his backpack, "Well, these are some samples of our logo and the main signs for our really large business. I think they can impart to you the nature and the enormity of what we are aiming for. Yeah, honestly, I have always believed in the artistic representation of ideas."

"Wow!" exclaimed Usman, holding the first piece of *artistic representation* of Draco's ideas with both hands, "Half man half rat! I think you people have been creating your own mythology! Look at them! Rat heads on human bodies! Marvellous!"

"Mehmet, the exceptionally great Mehmet," replied Draco, overly delighted and proudly boastful, "And my great late dad. And it is going to be our grand emblem, representing us and what we stand for."

"Is this really what you stand for?" asked Usman, now staring at the second picture, "It seems to me they are meant to pander to some crooked and convoluted state of mind."

"Mate, you know your words," replied Draco, scratching his right temple excitedly, "We stand for what society stands for; and we have this from my great dad. He believed great minds pander to whatever contains ample lust and sensuality. Yeah, honestly, my dad used to be an unmatched intellectual. '*Humanity is an empty word*', he would always say, '*And what could you do with a meaningless thing? Use it meaninglessly*'. And, honestly, I think he was so very right."

"Interesting!" said Usman, holding the first picture towards Draco, "So, which one is your dad and which is Mehmet?"

"Evidently, this is my dad," replied Draco, putting his finger on the man-rat in the left of the picture, "And that round plump guy is the great Mehmet, the closest to a full rat, the peculiar mind that knew how to use the meaningless things meaninglessly. I think if any human society is to know their core meaning and what they should stand for, they should look for great minds like Mehmet and my dad."

"How about you, your sister and Christopher? I think you are also great minds," said Usman, in a most serious tone.

"I thank you for the compliment," said Draco, twisting his nose, "But we are not as shrewd as they were. One has to be honest. Yeah, honestly, they were so insightful and infallible with their takes on humans, especially with women. In all, they both knew how to stand for what society was prone to stand for."

"So you mean this society stands for a rat head on a human body?" asked Usman, now gazing at another picture.

"Honestly, mate, this is a very intricate subject," replied Draco, assuming an erudite tone, "My great dad and the great Mehmet used to see the bigger picture in a most comprehensive manner, therefore I do not think we will ever be able to acquire a full understanding of it. What we know for sure is that both of those unrepeatable minds had noticed that this society had gone off the old ways of pleasure-seeking. Honestly, and therefore they decided to offer it a new and more satisfying way. Honestly, my great dad believed in unconstrained passion."

"Unconstrained passion is called *lust*," said Usman without looking at Draco.

"Yeah, honestly," replied Draco, now switching to a language of sophistry, "My great dad and the great Mehmet did not believe in some sections of philosophy, as they rightly believed those sections were meant to manipulate the language and deviate humans from the path of ultimate passion. And if you look at the background, yeah, my dad having the blood and the juice of Greek Mythology and philosophy in his stream-like veins and vessels, and the great Mehmet privileged with having the blood of a very passionate empire in his veins, you would relatively understand them. And they both hated Socrates and Aristotle. Honestly, I have personally never been interested in philosophy. Yeah, great Mehmet believed some philosophers were just some impotent guys, impotent in all aspects of what they were, who were not able to shag even a donkey, and that is exactly why

301

they would highlight *exquisite* human virtues as the tools and the means of obtaining overall satisfaction in life."

"Interesting!" said Usman, now gazing into the depth of Draco's eyes, "I didn't know that Mehmet was such a great mind!"

What a strange and messy battle, this battle against these rat-admirers and donkey-shaggers, these self-proclaimed and society-backed gods of the modern era and the designers of the new sets of virtues! Would Garry and Mehmet's ghosts come to the aid of the defenders of their 'great' imperial and philosophical legacy in the last and final stage of this battle? Would the society stand behind these guys who had so devotedly been standing for what it stood for? And above all, would Sophie offer them another lifeline by another unexpected U-turn, or would she be the one to see them off to a place where they could stand for whatever they wished for the rest of their lives?

Chapter 38

"Have we ever had a more popular prisoner than Sophie!" said a chubby prison officer, standing in the threshold and smiling at Sophie.

"Have I got visitors?" asked Sophie, jumping to her feet.

"Yes."

"Who is it?"

"A very calm and composed and smiling gentleman named Clement."

"There couldn't be any better way to begin a day!" said Sophie, offering the officer one of her unique smiles, "Eileen, let's go! I have always wished to see Clement since I was imprisoned. He is a dear friend of mine—yeah, because Gol is—yes, Gol is a dear friend to him."

Minutes later, and when Magdalena had joined them, they were led towards the visiting area with Sophie fervently recounting snippets of her shared memories with Clement, such as him calling her a 'nimble but aloof Egyptian cat'. And that he would always treat her with care and respect, except for the occasional mumblings about her general passivity towards emotional subtleties; that he would allow her to go into the kitchen while no one else was allowed to; that his overall treatment of her would induce in her a strong sense of belonging, a sense she was unable to understand back then.

"Clement!" shouted Sophie, dashing towards him with her arms open, "Why so late, Clement! Why so late?"

"It isn't late. It is the right time," replied Clement, embracing her, "Remember Gol always doing things at the right time?"

"I do remember. I do remember," said Sophie, now holding Clement's arms, "I am so happy and glad that you have come to visit me! You are a dear friend to me. You have always been. Oh, by the way, these are my friends, Eileen and Magdalena. They are like you and Gol; they both love me dearly; they both believe in me."

"Hello to you, friends," said Clement, offering them a highlighted version of his permanent smile.

"Let's sit down," said Sophie, pulling a chair back for Clement, "I am so happy! Yes, I have never been happier. I am going to take this visit as a good omen, a prelude to freedom and joy."

"You sound very sensible, girlie," said Clement, laughing, "And I am going to take it as a clear and honest sign of craving for goodness."

"Clement, first of all tell me a bit about Gol," asked Sophie, her eyes moistening, "I know that he hasn't aged at all. Just the other day Emily sent me a picture of him and David. I loved it dearly.

"David has turned into a proper man. Yeah, Emily has been sending me all sorts of stuff."

"Gol is very well," said Clement, throwing a smile at Magdalena and Eileen, "He believes your pains and sorrows will soon be over."

"Does he?" asked Sophie, her voice cracked, her heart pounding, "He never gave up hope on me. Did he? Clement, I am so ashamed of myself for what I did to him."

"You shouldn't," said Clement, touching her hand, "And that is exactly what I have come here for.

"Do you remember once I told you that you were only mind and only mind?"

"Yes, Clement, I do remember!" said Sophie, laughing innocently, "That standing in the rain… the dog… the dog owner and the seagull… You brought me a heater… You made me Lamb Balti with freshly baked chapatti… I was only mind and only mind."

"So, you also haven't aged that much!" said Clement, laughing loudly, "Your memory is still in good kilter. Emily has been showing your letters to me, and I have to say that you are now half heart and half mind, and this has turned you into a uniquely charming and beautiful angel—it has even enhanced the beauty outside. I am here today to assure you that you have nothing to be ashamed of, because you have gracefully managed to check in with your real self, and more importantly, to shake yourself off the dust and the soot of the past. And to offer you a decisive guarantee to what you have so far achieved, I should remind you of Gol's unwavering faith in you all through this painful story. Hold your head up and be proud. Gol has offered you what you deserve most. To him, you are still as innocent and loveable as a lamb. He would never blame you."

"It is the nature of goodness. Isn't it?" said Magdalena, pushing back a puff of hair covering Sophie's wet face.

"It is," replied Clement, smiling, "And goodness never rejects or disappoints the ones who knock on its door. Goodness is like a kind and indulgent mother, always praying, always awaiting the return of her travelling children, always worried that some of them might never return to her. Our Sophie knocked on the right door but wasn't patient enough to wait for it to be opened, but luckily that door memorised her touch, her name and her scent."

"Clement," said Sophie, looking him in the eye, "Why has Gol visited me only once since I was imprisoned ages ago?"

"A very good question," replied Clement, "Because he didn't want to reiterate his presence in your mind. That would have made life difficult for you in this cage. But don't worry, he will soon come to visit you."

"Really! Are you being serious Clement?" asked Sophie, half her wet face celebrating and the other half denoting fear and doubt.

"I am being dead serious, Sophie." replied Clement.

"Eileen, I am wondering if I could be bailed out before I am acquitted and released?" asked Sophie, wiping up her tears."

"Of course you could," replied Eileen, "We have more solicitors than we have farmers; and it is because there is nothing impossible in this country."

"I think I can guess why you wish to be bailed out before you are released," said Clement, laughing musingly, "I would have the same wish. Well, let's move on. I would like to have a few serious words with you, my dear Sophie. I called you, 'dear'. Didn't I? Do you remember the day you came to our place and asked me for a job…That hesitation, that uncertainty, that vulnerability…You were guarding something within you, something precious and something so human and worth guarding. I had no doubt, whatsoever, that the moment you would stand before Gol, he would also notice this. He did. Didn't he, Sophie? You fell in love with him and were so eager to deliver the gem within you to him and take a sigh of relief. But there was a problem: you did not know the art of deliverance, as you had never been allowed to acquire it. You did know how to fall in love but you didn't know how to materialise and live it. A mere biological thing, a creature of imitation, a submissive consumer of pre-packaged foods and concepts, a conditioned creature immune to curiosity, a co-dependent, it was our Sophie, the unfortunate carrier of a priceless gem. And you knew— I wish you did not know this piece—that he was the only buyer who could afford the price of that gem. What was the price of it? Heart, a full and loving heart fed by an awakened soul. There is a problem with these types of buyers: they hate haggling over the deal, as they believe it would reduce the price! It is strange. Isn't it, Sophie? Such mad buyers! They wouldn't ask for a discount because they want to pay for it with whatever they have; and therefore a deal open to haggling isn't their cup of tea! You waited for him to open his arms and own you, not knowing that he didn't wish to own you, he wished to unite your soul with his. He could have definitely opened his arms and owned you within the first few days, but what would have been the result? Some carnal pleasure and then some painless pains to deal with, and it wasn't what he could have wished for. Do you know why? Because he had been waiting for you to arrive all through his life."

"Clement," said Sophie, putting her hand on his shoulder, "Do you mean I was really that worthy and priceless?"

"You were and you are," replied Clement, "And that is why he overlooked all those silly things you did. You know what I mean, giving yourself up to the people far beneath you and what followed. And today I am here to remind you of your worth and pricelessness, and make sure that you wouldn't doubt this again. Remember, you are the child of nature, remain as such and listen to its call, and you will soon be fulfilled."

"I think now you understand why Gol asked you not to study science," said Eileen.

"Yes, definitely," said Sophie, "He wanted me to expose myself to the subjects that could remind me of my natural and human form of existence and not to the subjects that could enhance the sense of physicality, mortality and futility; and that is exactly why he has been, via Emily, exposing me to the greatest works in the field of humanities."

"And that is exactly why," said Clement, now beaming at Sophie's excited face, "He offered you those two precious books. Remember?"

"It was Mr Gibran—" said Sophie, pausing, turning her face towards Clement, "Do you mean it was him, Gol?"

"Yes, he had bought those books," replied Clement, watching the reflection of his own face in Sophie's glistening eyes, "And I am sure now you can realise why he did not want you to know this."

"I can, Clement," said Sophie, "And what a silly little thing was I! Perhaps it was an unconscious urge to escape from goodness, I mean misunderstanding Mr Gibran, a man utterly immune to… Oh no, I was so silly. But, Clement, do you know how many times I have read one of those books? Eight times. And books, Clement, I now have found them to be the incredible means that can simply allow one to examine the self and have a better understanding of one's overall existence."

"I am glad to hear this," said Clement, nodding thoughtfully, "And can you now promise me you will never be silly again?"

"I promise you, a promise from my heart and not from my mind," replied Sophie, now looking more innocent than ever.

"Good!" said Clement, "And to appreciate this, I will also make a promise to you."

"What, Clement, what! Tell me," asked Sophie, childishly excited.

"I will speak with Gol about that bailout thing."

"Thank you so much!"

"Sir, may I ask you a question?" asked Eileen, smiling at Clement.

"Yes, of course," replied Clement, highlighting his smile, "Why only one? Ask as many as you wish."

"What have you people seen within Sophie," asked Eileen, putting her arm around Sophie's shoulder, "That has made her so dear to you people?"

"Eileen, you know the answer," replied Clement, throwing a wise look at her face, "I think you wish to hear a different version of it. Well, deposited in her heart, there is an eternal kind of innocence and merit plus a good deal of hidden bravery that could only be felt by a few. She was lucky to cross paths with Gol, who quickly spotted the wealth within her, and helped Mr Gibran and me to notice it too. And I am certain she will soon make all of us proud of herself."

"You are so very right, sir," said Eileen, kissing Sophie on the head, "She is now a ferociously brave woman who knows how to stand up to herself and impose her pricelessness on the world."

"And also a great dancer who knows how to find and unite her moves and charm the world," said Magdalena, offering Sophie a warm smile.

"Very good!" said Clement, looking at Sophie's face, "And now a really nimble Egyptian cat and not aloof at all!"

"Clement, you should watch me dance," said Sophie, "I have become much more than a nimble cat. I have become a rolling flailing ball of fire!"

"You are not going to burn anything. Are you?" asked Clement, indulging himself in another hearty laugh.

"No, I would only be offering warmth and light," replied Sophie, rejoicing in her own realisation and awareness. "And by the way, have you noticed that today I had no problem with understanding your head bobbles and hand gestures?"

"Yes," replied Clement, laughing, "Now you are immune to confusion."

Chapter 39

"Only Satan could have guessed this!" said Usman, laughing while checking his appearance in the full-length mirror, "Safely put in a barrel and attached to the bottom of his boat! What a bloody crafty geezer! And what a bloody craftier Islam! Man, you are potentially the most intelligent and adroit thief ever! And I am potentially so proud of you. That geezer was going to screw a big chunk of money out of Brother Gol. Wasn't he? Okay, brilliant. Put it in my suitcase and carry it to my car. I will be with you in a minute."

Minutes later, the brothers drove off towards Gol's house, where he and others were eagerly waiting for them. With Islam in driving seat, they were both serenely quiet until they reached a small roundabout at which five straight narrow streets had neatly branched out. After a quick exchange of looks with his brother, Islam took the first to the left and drove on until they came to an old primary school with stonewalls.

Although quite the opposite of each other in terms of personality traits, but they had never failed to understand and appreciate each other's inner emotions. It was Usman and the nostalgia and the aftertaste of an unfulfilled but dear past desire, a memory of yearning for innocence and love. They gently pushed the iron gate open and stepped into the small yard. Usman eyed around with a bittersweet smile sitting in his eyes. It was no longer there, the low wooden bench at which Sophie and he used to sit, with Sophie chattering and him listening to her so patiently, as if listening was his only art in the world. The bench had been replaced by a plastic one, and the blueberry bush behind it uprooted. Usman walked over to the plastic bench. Islam followed him. In their minds the blueberry bush still existed, kindly allowing Islam to hide himself behind its full and low branches and watch Sophie frolicking around the yard like a little fawn, with one eye full of admiration and love and the other sadly dismayed.

"What are you doing in here, you guys!" shouted a middle-aged chubby woman, now marching towards them, "You do know that trespassing is a punishable crime. Don't you?"

"Darling, we are here to reminisce an old memory," replied Islam, offering the woman a big smile.

"What?" exclaimed the woman, a very mechanical expression appearing on her pudgy face.

"Do you understand English, darling?" asked Islam, laughing.

"Oh, you naughty boy!" said the woman, now noticing Usman's impressive appearance, "Could one of you two gentlemen tell me what is going on in here?"

"As my brother said," said Usman, smiling, "We are here to reminisce a dear past memory. The gate was open. We didn't barge in."

"Oh, I see," said the woman, now curiously looking at Usman's face, "May I ask you what exactly you are reminiscing?"

"It was Sophie, my brother and me, here in this school. We were schoolmates," replied Usman, gently hoisting his coat over his shoulder.

"I hope you are not talking about a certain Sophie Grandeur," said the woman, unconsciously taking a step back, "'The Morphine Girl' who murdered three innocent human beings!"

"We are talking about a certain Sophie Grandeur," said Islam, laughing, "Apparently you know her very well."

"Goodness gracious!" exclaimed the woman, her green eyes widening, "I got to know her parents years ago, when they had just moved to our town. The would-be Morphine Girl was a little reticent girl. You never know what fate has got in store for you. Gosh! Have you come here to reminisce your memories with an evil murderer! No one would do that!"

"She will be acquitted in two or three weeks. I am her solicitor," said Usman.

"No way!" said the woman, holding her chin in utter disbelief, "So what was all that fuss about in the papers?"

"It was all about fuss!" said Islam, laughing contentedly.

"There was a blueberry bush there," asked Usman, pointing to the far end of the yard, "Do you know what happened to it?"

"Did she use to hide behind it?" asked the woman, now smiling, "A little boy got stuck in its branches and got his balls badly injured, so they decided to uproot the bush."

"No one should uproot a bush because of two little balls!" said Islam, indulging himself in a blasting laugh.

"Do you really mean she didn't commit those murders?" asked the woman, holding her chin again.

"She was exploited. They set her up, the real murderers," replied Usman.

"I see," said the woman, nodding thoughtfully, "I spotted her parents as grandiose as delusional. The poor vulnerable girl!"

"No one should uproot a beautiful blueberry bush because of two little balls!" said Islam again, blasting out another laugh.

As a gaggle of children rushed into the yard, Usman and Islam turned around and left, perhaps to avoid intensifying their nostalgia.

"Life is a bloody ugly beautiful thing. Isn't it, brother?" asked Islam, staring at the red traffic light, "We both loved Sophie. Didn't we, brother? You, the optimistic one, and I, the pessimistic one, we both loved her the way we could. Mine was bitter. Yours was bittersweet, as you wouldn't mind to make your wishful wistful world of fantasies and see Sophie from there, but I was unable to take to such a world. In all, I think it was a love never to be, and if it was not because of you we would have ended up hating her for good."

"It is a very good point, brother," said Usman, taking a gentle sigh, "And now after all these years, we have magnanimously succeeded in turning hatred and disappointment into an elevated form of love and ample respect for her. And today we are happy because she is happy, the girl we once would have ripped out our hearts for and offered them to her is happy, and has turned herself into a most loveable creature, and this is what we should take as our reward."

"Well, my dear friends," said Usman, putting his suitcase on the table and immediately opening it, "Look at this! This camera contained the last piece of evidence we badly needed. You should all thank Islam for his ingenious thievish instinct!"

"And now you have extracted all the footages from other cameras as well—?" asked Gol.

"You are right," interrupted Usman, a triumphant smile brightening up his face, "And they are all here, in my laptop. Well, let me begin from the beginning: as most of you know, ages ago we had a brush with an old geezer at our restaurant. Like all other geezers, our geezer also has got a name, a grand Mr Ian Mitchel, a man of all trades, from chasing the unpaid debts, receiving stolen goods, match fixing of the local football competitions, stealing bicycles, fiddling with the gas and electric metres to blackmailing of petty drug-dealers, and you just name it.

"During that rainy early morning, and when Sophie had just left the flat after noticing the death of Garry and Miss Julie Atkins, Mr Ian Mitchel and his illegitimate son, Mr Kyle Mitchel, arrived at the same flat. As they had not been invited, they knew how to get into the flat, and they did. Both father and son being competent masters of their trade, they immediately noticed that something amiss had taken place before their arrival. What were they after in Garry's flat? A good amount of cocaine, which was supposed to be carried to Scotland the next day, by our own Sophie! Garry had asked Sophie to take some stuff for his eldest sister, who had been sectioned in an asylum in Scotland! Yes, as I was saying, the father and son rushed out of the flat, and like two trained dogs, they kept sniffing until they reached Garry's restaurant. To their amazement, they found the door unlocked. The confident and the competent father and son stepped in and immediately smelled business! Furtively, they walked towards the stairs, and there they heard an anxious argument going on between two of our super stars, Draco and Calypso. They turned around and began a frantic search, and in a matter of minutes, they found what they were searching for: a sack containing a few CCTV cameras, which were supposed to be destroyed by Draco minutes later. A while later, and when Gol had been accused of deceiving and abusing Sophie and all that nonsense, Mr Mitchel and his son approached our Islam and offered him a deal over one of those cameras, the one from the flat, the one which proved who had deceived and abused who. Brother Gol and Islam did a great job with this deal: a big chunk of money was paid but the entire haggling over the deal was secretly filmed and recorded. Mr Mitchel and his son had managed to screw a quarter of a million out of Draco over the same camera when Draco had sold their large house, which of course he refused to give him the camera after he received the money.

"For the next and the most telling piece of evidence we eventually managed to acquire, we should all be grateful to Franco and his impeccable presence of mind: it was him who noticed the absence of what he had noticed its presence long before: a tiny camera over the bar of Garry's restaurant. After having a long and scrutinising discussion with brother Gol, Franco, David and Islam, I suggested that the final precious piece of evidence we badly needed could well be in the heart of that little inquisitive camera. As we found it unwise to stake a big amount towards obtaining the camera, and as we were asked, we left the rest to Islam, and what a cracking job he did! And I am going to display all the footages and give you all the details."

"Shall we go through them after lunch?" asked Emily, throwing an appreciative and admiring smile at him.

"Has the lunch been made by Emily?" asked Usman, looking at David.

"Yes," replied David, ruffling his hair.

"What has she cooked for us?"

"Barberry Pilaf with Chicken."

"Emily," said Usman, turning his face towards her, "Have you ever forgotten, ignored or broken a promise you made? Guys, she promised me some Barberry Pilaf with chicken ages ago. I thought she had forgotten all about it. Emily, you are a committed mother to the world."

"Oh, thank you, Usman," replied Emily, "It is what Gol also believes."

"Okay, the committed mother of the world, be quick. I am starving." said Cynthia, proudly beaming at her daughter.

With David's help, Emily served the food while passionately expressing and philosophising her passion for food and cooking; and how she had applied this passion to her study of philosophy and language at university and her serious interest in other branches of humanities. "Once I imagined a very special and rich meal," said she, "I put a large chopping board on the counter, grabbed a reliable knife and looked at my meticulously chosen and bought needed ingredients: a big chunk of philosophy, a good deal of psychology, a proper cut of history and a good deal of sublime tangy humour, and cooked them in a pot of now and then."

"What spices did you use, Emily?" asked Gol, smiling.

"Old love, imbued in old dreams and beautiful irrationalities and frivolousness," replied Emily, the two burning blue flames appearing in her large eyes, "A touch of melancholia, a handful of sensuality, a mixed dipper of god and sin, a ladle of wild desires and a pinch of common sense, and I garnished it with fresh leaves of freedom."

"What did it taste like?" asked Islam in a low tone, gazing at Emily's face.

"It tasted human," replied Emily, smiling, "Definitely not suitable for automatons, as it can damage their gears and clutches!"

312

"Interesting!" said Islam, still gazing at Emily's face, "If you allow me to interpret 'wild desires' as 'a touch of rascality', then I would say I have been living my life exactly based on this recipe!"

"You are allowed. You wouldn't be that wrong!" said Emily, laughing.

"You are definitely the loveliest and most canny rascal ever; and as useful!" said Gol, indulging himself a light-hearted and infectious laughter.

"Brother Gol!" said Islam, raising both arms and laughing, "This is the ultimate compliment. I absolutely love it. There are only two means available to proper men: ample love and wisdom, or a reasonable amount of rascality, otherwise they would be undone by the world."

"Well said, Islam," said Emily, smiling wisely, "If you were to be a philosopher, you would definitely become a black Nietzsche."

"Who is Nietzsche?" asked Islam, narrowing his eyes.

"He was a werewolf!" replied Emily, laughing.

"What could you expect," said Usman, throwing a wise and admiring look at Emily, "When a cogent philosophy student turns into a chef and invites you over to have lunch with her? Although Islam is not black enough to be seen as black, but I do agree with Emily that he could well be of the same mind. Well, let's leave a comment on Emily's cooking and get on with our main business. Rice fluffy, chicken succulent and lightly spiced, Barberry gently modified to hone the appetite without agitating it. And what can I say about the pistachio, saffron and finely treated zestful dried strips of orange peelings? In all, this meal tasted equally of mind and heart. I wish all the chefs had a bit of knowledge on philosophy!

"Well as I was saying, and now you will be watching in a minute, from Garry's flat cameras we extracted a good deal of very useful information, and it was during scrutinising those footages that I noticed that a piece of the recordings was missing. Going back to Mr Ian Mitchel with a bigger bundle of cash, we managed to obtain the missing bit—thanks to his son who is computer-literate. Now, watch here. See, this is Sophie exiting the flat a while before Garry and Miss Julie Atkins' murder took place. She is going to the restaurant to get some food and drink. And in the next frame you will see her coming back to the flat with two carrier bags under her arms... And there she is, coming in. And now let me skip the scenes we don't need... Here, as you can see, Garry and Miss Julie Atkins are drinking. Fortunately, due to a severe stomach pain she had been suffering from for a couple of days, our Sophie refrains from drinking. See what fate does! Pure blessings within a severe pain. As you can see, the first bottle is almost consumed but the two victims still look fine, and even so euphoric to fancy a bit of flirting with Sophie. As you will see in the next frames, the first bottle did not contain morphine. On the way going back to the flat, Sophie drops one of the bottles, and goes back to take another one. When she enters the restaurant, she finds no one around the bar. She pulls out a bottle from the honeycomb rack without being noticed and goes back to the flat. And now as you can see here, the victims are getting up to go to the bedroom, with Garry reaching for the second bottle… Here, Miss Julie Atkins grabs his glass and follows him. And around an hour later… Let me show you… yes, as you can see, Sophie is walking towards the bedroom… and look here, instinct, intuition or whatever you may call it, tells her that something horrendous has happened. And here she turns the light on… reels back and clasps her chest. According to the coroner, the victims suffered a quick syncope due to a high dose of morphine mixed with alcohol.

"Now, sit firm and watch the most important part. During the afternoon of the same day, Sophie is asked to dust off and clean the shelves and the racks in the bar area, and as you can see here she is taking the bottles off the shelves and the racks and placing them on the counter, obviously leaving her fingerprints on them. Look, this is Draco, entering the bar area while wearing a pair of white gloves, and seconds later you will see… yes, here, he is putting a few of those tiny whisky bottles in the pocket of his large coat.

"And in the next frame you will see Sophie entering the restaurant… there she is… going behind the bar… Sophie Sophie Sophie! She is being a bit naughty here. Isn't she! Look, she gives Draco the finger! And now she turns to her left, grabs two flagons of wine and puts them on the corner of the counter… and now he is asking her to take the flagons off the counter and put them beside the till, the spot that he thinks is out of the reach of cameras, not knowing that Garry and Calypso had craftily had a camera camouflaged onto the ceiling in order to have a close-up and clearer view over the till, from which Draco used to steal! Now Sophie is walking towards the kitchen to order the food… And here, see, Draco is replacing the two flagons with the ones he had already narcotised with morphine. And do not forget that a tiny whisky bottle filled with morphine was found in Sophie's handbag during the early police investigations. That bottle had been hidden in the bottom of her bag by Calypso. Here, watch, with Maria's help I found out that in this scene she is getting the sack... See, she is marching towards the door, and seconds later... wait... yes, here, Sophie is going after her... And now... Calypso grabbing Sophie's bag and going upstairs... And thus, the mysterious afternoon gave way to a feverish evening which in turn gave way to a dark and wet dawn of crime, and landed our Sophie behind bars."

"And who did murder the 'great' Mehmet'?" asked David.

"On his last birthday," replied Usman, "Which was coincident with the night he and Calypso flew to Tenerife; Draco offered him a present, a few different items among which there was a three-fold pack of tiny bottles of whisky, all doped with morphine and all had Sophie's fingerprints on them.

"The main reason behind Mehmet's murder, plus his scorpion-like nature, was his marriage to Calypso. During my study of this case, I realised how greedy and opportunistic Mehmet was. But he was not murdered solely because of his financial intentions in marrying Calypso, he was murdered by the man behind all this, and Draco also had a hand in it. This man has been in a covert and wrong relationship with Calypso."

"Is any one of you going to tell us who this man is?" asked Cynthia, looking at Usman and then at Gol.

"Be patient, Cynthia," said Gol, smiling at her, "Anita will tell you all about him. She and Franco will come over for lunch tomorrow."

Chapter 40

"Around the time when Yugoslavia was still Yugoslavia, not knowing that it would soon cease to remain as such," said Gol, pouring some wine for Anita, "Some bigger guys were calmly making a deal with some smaller guys. The bigger guys were some very proud and scrupulous blokes; and they all hated the word 'rape', as all pious and seemly creatures do. But the smaller guys were unsure, as they were simply capable of loving and hating almost every deed based on their immediate needs and necessities. The good guys sealed the deal, issued permission and handed it to the unsure guys, who draped themselves in their uniforms of amorality and *raped* someone else's land. Cyprus was torn apart. And a while later, Yugoslavia suffered the same fate. What does the Cyprus and Yugoslavia events have to do with us and our story? Well, today Anita is here to tell us. Are you ready, Anita?"

"I am, Gol," replied Anita, a tinge of moral relief appearing in her eyes, "Years ago, Garry confided a secret to me: 'I have a son', he said.

"After the unfortunate death of his eldest brother's family during the Turkish invasion of Cyprus, and receiving the news that one of his brother's children had survived, Garry travelled to Cyprus only to find out that the boy had been taken to Kosovo, then part of Yugoslavia. The boy had been rescued by a Kosovan family fleeing the war in Cyprus. It took Garry a while until he found the family, a couple and their two young children. Obviously, very humane and hospitable, the couple received Garry very warmly and offered him their empathy and condolences for the loss of his brother and his family, and asked him to stay with them for a while and allow them to console the badly traumatised boy. Meanwhile the husband decided to go back to Cyprus in search of his young brother-in-law, entrusting his family to Garry. 'It just happened', he said. 'It wasn't me, it was the woman. She seduced me'. However it happened, it happened. The poor man got stuck in the war and lost his life. Garry stayed there for six months, and then travelled back to England with his twelve-year-old nephew. The moment he was leaving, the woman told him that she was

316

pregnant by him. 'I didn't believe her', he said. 'It could have been someone else. And above all, it wasn't me. It was her who seduced me; that white lush lustful Muslim woman! I was a bereaved anguishing man, well beyond lust and lechery! I asked her to abort it, but she said it was too late!'. The child was born, a boy. And it took his mum eight years to eventually find Garry. Medical test proved him as the father. The case was settled by Garry accepting and taking the boy into his own care and paying the woman a small amount of money. Garry handed the boy to his sweetheart, Miss Julie Atkins, and asked me to keep the secret between ourselves. In all, I don't think Garry was fully responsible in this case. Perhaps it was that lush Muslim woman's lack of morals that tempted him."

Some heavy lingering moments took over. Gol kept staring at the glass of wine before Anita.

David and Franco exchanged two bitter smiles. Cynthia kept fussing with her hair. Usman cocked an eyebrow and gazed at Anita's face.

"Well," said Gol, still looking at the glass of wine before Anita, "Would you mind telling us a bit more about Garry's son?"

"Oh, well," said Anita, slightly embarrassed, "At Garry's request, he moved to this town with Miss Julie Atkins. Brought up by Miss Julie Atkins, I found him a very mysterious yet misleadingly calm and composed creature. Although Garry had told the boy that he had been adopted, I had no doubt that Miss Julie Atkins had revealed the secret to him. As a very frivolous playboy, he had no qualifications and interest in any specific trade. After a while Garry let him into our household, and it was around the same time that I noticed he and Miss Julie Atkins were involved in Garry's investment in drug dealing. And a while later, when my Calypso had just turned fourteen, I realised that she had lost her virginity. My initial guess was that it was him, and I was right. I raised the issue with Garry, and he said, *'If it was not consensual, Calypso would have told us about it! Yeah, it was consensual, and therefore there is nothing wrong with it'*.

It was a short while before Garry's murder that I realised that Calypso had found out that her lover was her half-bother from the beginning of their relationship. And with the late Miss Julie Atkins propagating eagerness and insatiability towards pleasure within them, they decided to get rid of Garry and own his wealth. And we all know that Garry wasn't going to be their only victim: Miss Julie Atkins, who had underestimated the competence of her own students, was a hurdle to be removed at the same time. And then, of course, it would be Sophie and then Draco. Mehmet failed to understand the nature of the relationship between Calypso and her half-brother, and paid for it. Plus this irreversible failure, he had also proven himself as an overly greedy and inquisitive creature.

"Needless to say that Christopher wouldn't even be given a chance to doubt his fate. And who would be the last? Calypso, my poor Calypso."

"Thank you very much, Anita," said Gol, turning towards Usman, "Usman, Cynthia is impatiently waiting for you to reveal the name of our mysterious man, Garry's son."

"Are you, Cynthia?" asked Usman, delightfully looking at her delighted face, "Well, disguised in a cloak offered to him by society, he looks like an incarnation of the young and very innocent Mohammed before being endowed the grand state of prophethood by the Almighty. His real name is Mikhalis, a name Garry chose for him after he was handed to him by his Kosovan mum. But when Garry decided to bring him and Miss Julie Atkins from London to this town, he created a new identity for him: an Italian little boy who had been adopted and brought to England by an English woman. He named the boy Mervyn."

"No way!" exclaimed Cynthia, her eyes bulging, "He looks so innocent!"

"Yes, mate," said Usman, shaking his head, "Like his dad used to, and like his half-brother, Draco, he is also only interested in some specific sets of vocabulary, and his most favourite word has been the word 'consent', the keyword to the very accommodating zone of *consensuality* in the brain of this society! At first glance, one might call this type of people *nothingarian*, but one would be disabused as quickly, given the paradoxical fact that the nothingarians are actually the 'believers', the dishonest and opportunistic creatures who would readily hold their shoulders under the empty and legless beliefs only to hide themselves in their shades and pursue their interests.

"This calm composed and 'God-like' man immediately spotted Sophie as an-easy-to-use prey. Sophie, who had given herself up to indifference and cheapness, failed to notice—or perhaps consciously overlooked it— that this man was not an ordinary abuser; that he would go far beyond abusing her body. With a sealed pass in his pocket—the word 'consent'— he took Sophie with him on his holidays on two occasions, during one of

318

which the idea of getting rid of Garry by using Sophie was inseminated in his mind. He also, like Garry, Mehmet and Christopher, had promised he would have her as the love of his life! Sophie, Sophie, Sophie! How many grooms did you need! Guys, the rest is history."

Franco, who had remained quiet up to that point, cleared his throat to say something, but he decided not to. He looked at Gol's face, and seconds later they both looked at Anita and the half-full glass of red wine she was gently pushing aside.

Chapter 41

"Although I am sure that this case has long been over," said Calypso, gently rubbing her belly, "I think we should have gotten rid of Sophie. Better safe than sorry."

"Are you pregnant with a rat?" asked Mervyn, stroking his brownish beard, a fixed stark schizophrenic stare appearing on his spacious face, "Christopher's. Isn't it? Evil fucking Christopher!"

"Oh, I am so pleased you are so fond of Christopher," said Calypso, her large black eyes, the eyes of a pregnant woman, exhibiting a series of unknown impregnated dark inner desires, "The most suitable choice. Isn't he?"

"You are a brilliant fucking bitch!" said Mervyn, grabbing her wrist and pulling her towards himself, "You know how to stir shit and how to roll it, just like those fucking dung beetles do! Why should we have got rid of Sophie? She is also a brilliant shit roller, capable of making the most impeccable round balls and rolling them like no other. Have you forgotten how brilliantly she would roll Garry's shit and roll it towards me? Do you know what I mean? Of course, you know! You helped her to master the art of shit rolling. But, you, the master and Sophie, the pupil, made a big mistake when you rolled Mehmet's shit towards me. It was much shit, that is why it backlashed and cost him his life. Poor Mehmet, he could have been the superstar within our rat business."

"But I am still worried," said Calypso, her hand creeping between Mervyn's legs, "What if she realises shit rolling isn't a good business and turns against us?"

"Your worries are baseless," replied Mervyn, touching her neck, "She is still in love with Draco, and that is more than enough to create a safe harbour for us. To Sophie, understandably, we are the best form of nourishment. Don't forget, her appetite isn't designed to taste and accept anything else. What has happened to your memory? Have you forgotten that she said to the judge that it was all *consensual* when those CCTV footages showed her being banged by Garry, Christopher, Mehmet, Draco and I?

320

Only a miracle can turn her around. And above all, Gol, this so-called intelligent man, has never mentioned my name as a suspect in this case, and it simply means he will never find the truth."

"Oh, I see," said Calypso, unbuckling her belt, "And are you sure miracles will never happen?"

"The only miracle I know of is the thingy you are about to get out and gobble," said Mervyn slithering his hands round her back and unzipping her skirt, "Fucking is the only miracle, and Sophie loves it. She is fucked up."

"I love it!" said Calypso, her large eyes widening.

"Which one, mine or Sophie's share of miracles?" asked Mervyn, lifting her up and placing her on the table.

"Both of them," replied Calypso, her mouth gaping, "Though not a big one, yours is a sweet miracle."

"Sophie also used to taste it as such," said Mervyn, picking up her skirt and throwing it on the table, "Let's do it before your dear husband turns up."

"You know that he would love it," said Calypso, leaning back on her arms and opening her legs, "He told me he used to walk in on his ex-wife. He said it would arouse him beyond imagination."

"Pervert," said Mervyn, holding her long legs.

"Just like you," whispered Calypso, wrapping her legs around his waist, "Modest-looking, Christ-like but full of glorified shit. There is no pleasure in straight and decent men. I love it with you and Christopher. I used to love it most with Mehmet. You shouldn't have murdered him."

"I made him a martyr!" said Mervyn, squeezing her dark nipples hysterically, "He died for a cause—for two hundred and fifty grams of cheap pussy! Christopher believes he is now in paradise, flirting with some smuggled-in English girls!"

A seagull landed on the kitchen windowsill. Calypso moaned, whined, and wrapped her legs around Mervyn's back and her long arms around his neck. A chair fell over. A pair of grey cats tore round the bulky sofa in the sitting room, stumbled, rolled over, landed on their feet and carried the chase into the kitchen, darting through Mervyn's legs, they both mewed, growled, they both sounded feminine, they both sounded masculine. The seagull, whose gender was also hard-to-tell, tilted its head and stared at Mervyn's face, as if trying to warn him.

"Carry me to the bathroom," whispered Calypso.

"You love riding, and that is why you are the best rider," said Mervyn, putting his hands under her backside and lifting her up.

The seagull kept staring into the kitchen. The two cats were at the end of a long stand-off in the sitting room, now posing to jump at each other. They did, one jumped higher and missed the target.

They landed, one on the carpet and the other on the bulky sofa. They both bounced back on their feet, and after sharing a rather lackadaisical stare, they resumed the chase back into the kitchen, swerved through the chairs legs, hit the opposite wall and came to an abrupt halt, which soon turned into a rather lingering standstill. One had been cornered, the one with the slightly sagging belly. A rasping mew, a feline growl, the cornered one was a female, demanding roughness and, though belligerently, ready to take it.

A clattering noise behind the door, the jingling of a bunch of keys, a key was inserted into the lock and turned, the door was pushed open, and there appeared Christopher, the master of walking in on people and cats and dogs! He held the door for Draco to come in. He was to call his wife's name but his pricked ears drew his attention towards the bathroom. Draco sat in the sofa and immediately crossed his legs and assumed an air of absolute exoneration and entitlement. Christopher walked into the kitchen only to walk in on the cats that were diligently and frantically working it towards a vigorously soaring climax. He put his right hand on the table to bend and have a peep at the cats, but he was immediately distracted by what caught his eyes on the table: two large drops of semen, larger than usual, and Calypso's short black skirt. Seconds later, he noticed a man's underpants and a pair of fabric trousers on one of the chairs.

"What time is it, mate?" asked Christopher, entering the sitting room.

"Quarter to two," replied Draco.

"Wasn't Mervyn supposed to turn up at three, mate?" asked Christopher, walking towards the bathroom door. "He is in there, shagging my fucking wife!"

"He has been shagging your wife since she was fourteen, mate," said Draco, in a very matter-of-fact tone, "Mum told me the other day. And there is something else we didn't know."

"What is it?" asked Christopher, now a gentle twist wriggling through his upper body and down to his lower back and backside.

"He is Garry's son."

"You must be joking! Do you mean he has been shagging his own sister, knowingly?" asked Christopher, his face now resembling that of a fully mythological god—open to manipulation and arbitrary interpretations.

"My dad was well aware of it," said Draco, in a hushed and somewhat husky tone, "He used to believe in *consensuality* as the catalyst in human interconnections and relationships. And you know what a deep and longanimous thinker he was. 'Humans are all but meat' he used to say. And he actually meant that if a chunk of meat touching another chunk of meat could bring pleasure and happiness, then what could be wrong with it."

"What is going on in here!" shouted Christopher, as Calypso stepped out of the bathroom.

"I am sorry," whispered Calypso, holding her head down.

"What are you sorry for?" asked Mervyn, standing behind her, "What is it, mate! I was just washing her. You know, her back, her long legs, below her belly. Pregnant women can't and should not bend down. All fucking men should wash their lovely pregnant women!"

The conviction in Mervyn's voice, the fixed stare and the inexplicable innocence on his face, his squared shoulders and the questioning flame in his eyes outstared and unhinged Christopher, reshuffled his mind only to cause a series of rapid and confounding glitches: no, he had not seen a black skirt and... two marble-looking drops of semen—no, they were only two marbles! No, he had not shagged his wife! He had only washed her back and... he had only seen a cat giving it to his own sister!

Calypso turned around and scurried towards the bedroom. Christopher marched behind her. The door was slammed shut... She moaned. She whined hysterically... "No, he didn't fuck me! He just soaped my back and under my belly! Ouch! No, not that way...!"

"He is shoving it up her arse! She loves it. Doesn't she?" said Mervyn, the entire history of deviant, deranged and dark sexual desires appearing in his eyes on a background of sadism and masochism.

Draco said nothing. He was delighted by good news and narcotised by good stuff, which together, they had pitched him into a phantasmagorical world of eternal prosperity and a well-deserved eventual promotion to the strata of highs and most accomplished creatures. Sitting crossed-legged—a newly acquired habit, an imitation of the late Mehmet—he would indulge

323

himself with a self-assuring sniffle every now and then, inhaling meticulously and exhaling with an air of grandiosity and undisputed deservedness.

Half an hour later, and after Christopher had punished his wife in a godly manner, they sat at a *divine* table, so very akin to that of The Last Supper, with a slightly butt-hurt Magdalena-like Calypso leaning on her husband's arm and divinely enjoying the aftertaste of the pain in her butt!

"Guys, I think we are almost there," said Draco, lifting up his cup of coffee, "I met Gol yesterday. Was it a day yesterday, guys! Will it be repeated ever? Some days will remain only as *some* days! He opened his large safe and showed me loads of cash! He is going to pay the rest of it in cash! Sunday night, guys, he is coming to our restaurant to pay the money and get the keys."

"Are you being serious, mate?" asked Christopher, picking up a piece of pastry from the glass ball in the middle of the table and immediately smelling it, perhaps to make sure it did not smell of semen!

"He is being dead serious," said Mervyn, placing his hand on Calypso's back, "And my *sister* is going to get a slightly bigger share of it."

"Why?" asked Draco, lowering his cup of coffee with the air of a gang leader.

"Because she has been going through a lot of pain—physically and mentally. And don't forget, she has been looking after us so devotedly. If it wasn't because of her, none of you would have the privilege of easily getting access to Sophie's pants, and well, so many other pants."

"Fuck off, man!" said Draco, "No one would say that about their own sisters!"

"And no one would shag their own mothers and even grandmothers!" said Mervyn, his schizophrenic stare disconnecting all the synapses within Draco's brain.

"Mates, I think we are going off track," said Christopher, throwing a very Zeus-like look at Draco, imparting to him that shagging one's mother and grandma would fall into the category of '*a chunk of meat touching another chunk of meat*'! And that if *consensual,* that would completely be fine!

Draco, this fruitful perennial tree of shame, had always hidden himself in the large shadow of society, where he could freely spread his roots around and absorb the very essence of darkness.

324

Draco had mastered, at a very young age, the sociology and the psychology of his surroundings, the duplicities cloaked in civility and mannerism, the veneers of righteousness glued on to an expanse of indifference and denial. Draco was a mine of dark secrets and sublime shame. Draco was a dark mirror, reflecting his own surroundings.

Would Draco and his cronies, believers in *predestination*, these self-proclaimed cankerous *divine* creatures, be allowed to move on and spew slimy dirt on the face of goodness? Or would Sophie write an earthly predestination for them and become their scourge?

Chapter 42

Magdalena had been released, but Eileen had to wait for her latest appeal to be processed and sent to a High Court, an appeal that her solicitor believed would definitely secure her freedom.

Contrary to what she had thought, Sophie had had a peaceful night and many hours of sound sleep, and now was patiently waiting for Gol to arrive. Her bailout, as she had wished, had been arranged.

"Eileen, have a proper look at me and tell me if I look all right," asked Sophie, who had just finished tying her shoelaces.

"You look completely fine," said Eileen, taking the brush off Sophie's hand, "This outfit is simply incredible: Polo black T-shirt, a pair of denims, a grey twilled herringbone blazer and a pair of black Nike sneakers, and all are of the finest quality."

"Gol's choice and taste," said Sophie, turning around to allow Eileen to brush her long hair, "A very solemn and wise mixture of sensuality, spirituality and stability, I would say."

"You are so very right," said Eileen, "Now you know how to deal with the heart-related matters and how to polish them with the use of your mind. And tell me the reason behind this, this long hair reaching down your buttocks? I like it very much."

"Oh, Eileen I am happy you like my hair," said Sophie, her now mature face turning rosy, "When I used to work for him—Oh, those blissful days!—once I decided to cut my long hair, and the next day when I went to work, and when I entered the office, he threw a fleeting look at me, and it was enough for me to notice that he didn't like it. And you know what, Eileen, during the time I spent at Garry's restaurant, I would always keep my hair very short, just like these dykes do in here! Do you know why? Because Gol had liked my long hair, and also my hands, that is why I would use a pair of gloves whenever washing something."

"And now you have a lot more to offer to him: your moonlike face, your talking eyes, your awakened heart and soul and…" said Eileen, patting her backside.

"Eileen, you are being a little bit naughty!" said Sophie, laughing, "Eileen, I just remembered a very funny and very silly thing. So silly of me! When Lucy was trying to persuade me into making all those silly and baseless accusations against Gol, I, with Draco's help, made up a story, which at the time didn't amaze me that much, but now it makes me feel ashamed of myself."

"Tell me what it was," asked Eileen, handing her the brush.

"Eileen, I said a lot of things. All of them silly!" said Sophie, covering her face with both hands, "I said: once, and when Gol had just finished raping me brutally inside his car, he slapped my arse and said if your arse was as great as that of Garry's wife, you would be the sexiest fucking chick in town; and that yours is only one size smaller. What a shameless silly girl I used to be!"

"Stop chiding yourself," said Eileen, a tinge of sensuality appearing in her eyes, "Turn around and let me have a proper look at it."

"At what? My bum?" asked Sophie, involuntarily putting her hands on her hips and turning around.

"It is definitely of the right size now! Simply perfect," said Eileen, laughing light-heartedly, "Although I haven't seen that of Garry's wife, but I can assure you yours is unique."

Sophie remained silent for some long moments with her head held down. Eileen kept watching her calmly. She had something to say, something precious, and something deep and denoting comprehension and appreciation, and Eileen was aware of it. She raised her head, pushed her hair back and said, "I had never before felt my body the way I have been feeling it today and since I woke up. It feels like a conscientious and trustworthy container of what I am, a guardian, if you like, of a truly cultivated flame-like soul that feeds on lyricality and freedom from cheap wants and untoward desires and pleasures. I am now a most expensive woman, and it is what my body have been reminding me of since this morning. And I am going to sell myself to a man who hates haggling over the price. Cynthia told me this. He will pay with whatever he has got at his disposal. I am the owner of a silky body, and who deserves me the most? A man who could make a woman pregnant even by thinking of her. He impregnated me the moment he looked into my eyes, and now I am delivering…"

"Sophie!" shouted a prison officer with a big smile on her face, "You have visitors!"

"Who are they?"

"A dark handsome—"

"Wait! Wait!" interrupted Sophie, putting her hand on her heart, "Are you going to say a dark handsome gentleman and Cynthia?"

"Exactly!" replied the officer, laughing.

Eileen grabbed Sophie's large backpack, and they dashed out of the room and towards the narrow corridor, and minutes later, they entered the prison's large office. It took Sophie a while to see Gol, who was apparently signing some papers with Cynthia sitting beside him. Once again she felt amazed with the way her body was handling her magnanimously. Her heart, now a tuned instrument of its own kind, was not going to play a piece of noisy and cheap jazz but a piece of classic music with all its meaningfulness, inspiring and soothing attributes. She gently walked towards them, approached Gol from behind, wrapped her arms around his neck and pressed her face against his.

Cynthia watched delightfully. Eileen took a sigh of relief and joined them. Gol held both Sophie's small hands in his, the hands that had directed him to the unique world within Sophie. Cynthia got to her feet and opened her arms with all the love and enthusiasm in the world filling her heart. Sophie hurled herself in to her arms, as if she had been waiting for this moment all her life. Cynthia held her firm. They both remained silent. There was a moment to be delivered, a moment of union, a sanctuary and a safe haven to Sophie, and the priceless reward of fulfilment to Cynthia.

Gol and Eileen shared a hug and some savvy words of recognition and appreciation. Eileen did not allow Sophie to shed tears, and neither did herself.

"I don't want you to leave with a heavy heart," said Eileen, holding Sophie's face in her hands, "We are not going to lose each other. We will meet again. Appreciate yourself. So long, my friend."

"I have a present for you, dear Eileen," said Cynthia, unwrapping something which looked like a tableau, "I have sent a copy of it to Magdalena too."

It was a dazzling painting: Eileen, Magdalena and Sophie, with Sophie sitting on Magdalena's lap and looking at her face most innocently.

"This is simply a work of heart," said Eileen, holding the painting with both hands and delightfully looking at it, "I love it. I will treasure it."

Minutes later, a small side door by the heavy prison gate was opened, and they were let out. The clouds were scudding away. The sun was coming out.

"I think she is going to play a little game with you!" said Cynthia, as Gol lifted Sophie's backpack to put it into the car boot.

"Where are you going, Sophie?" asked Gol, laughing.

"There," replied Sophie, pointing to a row of tall trees at the very far end of the large expanse of turf before her, "Remember, Gol? The police station, me telling you that a lion who does not chase is a fake one. And what did you say, Gol? You said even a fake lion is lion enough not to be happy with anything less than a lioness. I am a lioness, and I want a chase."

"What would happen if I failed to catch you?" asked Gol, taking off his jacket and handing it to Cynthia.

"You would go away without me." replied Sophie, taking her blazer coat off and throwing it on the turf.

"Go for it then!" asked Gol.

Sophie turned around, and seconds later, she darted away. Gol dashed behind her. She sped up, running faster and faster, her long slick hair waving behind her, making her look more like a mare than a lioness. Fifty yards… Seventy… A hundred… Midway. Gol was getting closer and closer… She stumbled… going down… No, she kept her balance… The tall trees enlarging… Fifty yards left to go… Gol was catching up with… Closer closer… The mare-looking lioness was brought down. The chase was over… They were lying on the cool turf, panting heavily… Sophie rolled over and placed herself on his chest, pressed her lips on his… The sun had come out…

Cynthia shaded her eyes with her hand and watched them walk back towards her. She felt jealous; a kind of jealousy that immediately enhanced the rich contentment and joy within her heart. She had been insinuated to, by Gol and Sophie, that she was implicated in their story; that her presence, with whatever it entailed, would be unconditionally appreciated. Cynthia, the artist, the woman, the mother, and now the selfless friend, had placed herself above and beyond conditionality, and she was *unconsciously* aware of it. She took a few steps forward, picked up Sophie's blazer and walked towards them

"There is a nipping chill in the air. You might catch a cold," said Cynthia, holding the blazer for Sophie to put on, "And girl, what a brisk gazelle you are!"

"I am not a gazelle. I am a lioness," said Sophie, laughing, "Or perhaps I am... Yes, I am a gazelle and a lioness at the same time. Yes, I am definitely half of each!"

"Okay, gazellioness, let's go," said Gol, lifting her off her feet and hoisting her over his shoulder.

"Gol, I love it! I am gazellioness!" said Sophie, relaxing her body, "Gol, I have always wished to be carried by you!"

"What is the plan, Cynthia?" asked Gol, as soon as they got into the car.

"Well," said Cynthia, "You will take us to a good restaurant, and then we are going to go to Sophie's parents'."

***

She kept looking around as if she was one of the People Of The Cave, the sleepers who remained asleep for so long that their currency was outdated. She was out of prison, out of the cave, and back to society. Sophie and society, now both equally alien to each other, had to reach reconciliation, in one way or another.

She had never before noticed this, the flatness of her hometown, a slugging expanse of inertia, a dreary swathe of land with narrow streets, low-squatted old redbrick houses with small squinting windows, unseemly and unwelcoming doors and black-tiled roofs covered with layers of old and rotting moss. She had never noticed this since she had been born under the low roof of one of the dilapidated houses of this stagnated town. She eyed around with an overwhelmingly incredulous and self-admonishing feeling storming in her head and trickling down to her heart. The dumped garbage, the barricaded doors and passages by the unwanted bulky household items piled up before them, the ever-overflowing rubbish bins... She pulled a face, staggered, winced reprehensively. The seagulls were soaring, the seagulls were landing, and they could be seen all over the town, squawking shrill notes of insatiable greed and hellish appetite. A seagull swooped down on its prey. A fat rat was taken down. A fat rat was gobbled. Outnumbered by the raptors and the rats, the inhabitants of the town were some short-lived and happily unhappy creatures, morbidly rejoicing themselves in watching the ongoing game of carnage between the seagulls and the rats. Attired with three very phallic-like ever-erected smokestacks, and of course its wealth of rats and seagulls, the flat town seemed like a brothel where the state of affairs are out of the question.

"What is it, Sophie?" asked Gol, as they reached a narrow pathway, haphazardly hedged at both sides.

"Oh, me? I am sorry, Gol!" said Sophie, grabbing his hand, "This town---and the way it is---it distracted me. This way, yes, this pathway, it leads to my parents'. Gol, I have always wished to walk hand in hand with you. I have always wanted to be with you."

"And I have always been awaiting your arrival, since centuries ago." said Gol, pressing her hand in his.

"Oh Gol, I Love this!" said Sophie, her green eyes shining, "It gives me this assuring sense of immortality."

"Love and goodness are immortal." said Gol.

"Gol, stop," asked Sophie, pulling her hand off his and opening her arms, "I have always wished to be held and kissed by you!"

"Your innocence and the tinge of naiveté in your tone," said Gol, bending down and wrapping his arms around her, "Have always melted a big chunk of sugar in my heart!"

"Gol, did you fall in love with me when we met first?" rising on her tiptoes and kissing him again.

"I did; I fell in love with the way you fell in love with me," replied Gol, kissing her on the head, "I have always been falling in love with falling in love."

"I can fully comprehend what you mean," said Sophie, her eyes moistening, her face turning into a booklet of yearning for intimacy and oneness, "Gol, don't leave me alone again. I don't want to be lost again."

"You will never be left alone again, because you have found your own self," said Gol, holding her hand and walking on.

Minutes later, they reached Sophie's dad's homestead, where he and his family had spent a big portion of their lives, working on the small farm and raising cattle and occasionally some pigs. The gate to the fenced farm was unlocked, and the farm was empty and eerily quiet. They wheeled their way through the farm and round the small pig enclosure and seconds later, stood behind the door to the house, looking at each other with some already formed questions in their minds.

"I am here, Sophie!" shouted Mr Barry James Grandeur, ushering two black cows in through the gate to the left of the farm.

"What has he got in his hands?" asked Sophie.

"It looks like a rabbit," replied Gol, pushing his hands into the pockets of his jacket.

"You are going to excuse him. Aren't you?" asked Sophie, holding his arm.

"No worries," replied Gol, gently pinching her face.

"You should have shown due patience, my dear daughter," said Mr Barry James Grandeur, now standing a few yards away from them, holding a dead rabbit with both hands so tightly as if it was alive and kicking, "You should have allowed those two gentlemen enough time to free you. You should have allowed us to go about it with great consideration and circumspection. Freedom at what cost? The door is unlocked. Open it. Let me carry this rabbit in."

Sophie pushed the door open. The man and the rabbit entered, one full of life but not kicking and the other dead but kicking! And they both ignored Gol.

"Come in," asked Sophie, holding Gol's hand with a most endearing smile sitting in her eyes.

"Well, you were supposed to come here on your own!" said Mr Barry James Grandeur, entering the large dining room, "You know that I am not very much in favour of some certain type of people."

"May I hold that rabbit for you, sir?" asked Gol, now gazing into Mr Barry James Grandeur's eyes.

"May you hold the rabbit for me!" asked Mr Barry James Grandeur, in a most eccentric tone, "Did you hear what he said, girl? He wants to hold the rabbit for me! Sir, I have always been holding my own rabbit, all through history. How dare you!"

"But I can tell that you have forgotten how to hold a rabbit," said Gol, now noticing the framed black and white pictures lining the painted walls.

"Girl, go and make some coffee," asked Mr Barry James Grandeur, "I need to sit and have a proper chat with this pleb!"

"Dad!" exclaimed Sophie, her face blushing, her eyes widening.

"Go and make some coffee, Sophie," asked Gol, "We need to talk."

Mr Barry James Grandeur, now holding the rabbit under his arm, paced the length of the room several times before he reposed himself in the sofa.

332

Crossing his legs and putting the rabbit on his lap, he stared at the pictures on the wall, eyeing up, down, right and left, very cinematically indeed, and he eventually zoomed on a picture in the centre.

"Do you know that man in the picture, the one in the middle?" asked Mr Barry James Grandeur, throwing an indifferent look at Gol, "No, of course you don't know. What do the plebeians know about the greatness of man? They do not even fret themselves to think, because they have only one thing in their minds: exploitation. Yes, that gentleman in the picture, sitting cross-legged so gracefully, is the great Mustafa Kamal Pasha, the father of the Turks. And this photo had been taken just hours after the triumphant end of the battle of Gallipoli. I bet you know nothing about that battle. He routed the British. Bearing in mind that Mustafa Kamal was born on the soil of Greece, one would not hesitate to propose that his genius and unmatched bravery were the direct result of the fusion of Greek and Turkish blood. What a boon! What a vintage from the vineyard of humanity! What an offer to the world!"

Sophie put a cup of coffee before her dad, and sat beside Gol on the opposite couch. Mr Barry James Grandeur continued, stating that in his *humble* opinion the blood running in the vessels of the grafted Greco-Turkish tree would be the future, and the ones who failed to recognise and use it, well, would be the great losers! And therefore, as he said most ardently and most wistfully, he had always wished a Greco-Turkish husband for his Sophie and all other Sophies in the country; and that he was still holding on to his wish in the hope that Gol would leave her alone so that she could walk the right path. He also expressed his most cherished-for wish that her daughter would either marry Draco or Christopher. Of course, he did not forget to offer a few grand words about the late 'grand' Mehmet by narrating an *amazing* story he had heard from Mehmet's grandfather when he had visited them in Turkey: *Mehmet was an incarnated Mustafa Kamal!* he had said. In another piece of his very *humble* opinions, Mr Barry James Grandeur also proposed that now that the Greeks had gone bankrupt they should all have been invited to move to England and settle here. He also wished that the Europeans would stop being foolishly pessimistic towards the great Turks and allow them to join them. He also wistfully wished that in a near future this country would be joyously and proudly hosting the Greeks and the Turks.

Sophie kept gazing at her father for a while, got up, and with a sweet and somewhat defiant smile sitting in her eyes, she gently placed herself on Gol's lap and pressed her lips on his.

"Dear sir," asked Gol, holding Sophie in his arms, "Do you really believe that Draco and Christopher are the most decent and the most suitable men for your Sophie?"

"Of course, I do!" replied Mr Barry James Grandeur, staring at Gol with bulging eyes, "Only a Greco-Turkish soul could be most suitable for my beloved daughter!"

"Dad, they will be imprisoned in a couple of days," said Sophie, picking at Gol's beard.

"That would be the bungled judgement of this country," said Mr Barry James Grandeur, gently stroking the back of the dead rabbit, "Who could even dare to think of those *fine* gentlemen as criminals!"

"Dad, they were the ones who murdered those three people," said Sophie, "And the ones who deceived and abused me and so many others."

"A shameless setup!" shouted Mr Barry James Grandeur, now pressing the dead rabbit against his chest, "And you silly worthless girl have been brainwashed by these primitive exotic creatures! These diabolic things are connected to the source of evil! Only a possessed and metamorphosed human could think of an angel like Draco as a wrongdoer! Here and now, I disown you, you ungrateful shameless child! You are banished from my household! Go away and live a lecherous life with this primitive man!"

"I would have gone away, anyway," said Sophie, in a low painful tone, "I have come here to take my passport. I would love to see you every now and then, but if this is what you wish, so be it."

It was not what he wished. It was his obligation, his beliefs and all of what he stood for. Mr Barry James Grandeur was a sophist, a victim to himself, a master of ornate folly and impertinence whose thirst for vanity and unjustified grandeur would only be quenched by running away from the sea and drowning himself in the desert!"

"Where is Mum? Where are my sisters?" asked Sophie, handing her passport to Gol.

"They moved to Turkey. They are now married, the three of them," replied Mr Barry James Grandeur, rubbing the dead rabbit's belly, "I gave them permission. I let them go."

Mr Barry James Grandeur, the cattleman, sounded like a castrated old ox, made unfit for copulation and breeding but not disconnected from the source of libido! The memory of when and how he had been castrated had not been registered, due to the application of a gradual and painless procedure!

"Sir, you have banished yourself from the terrain of goodness," said Gol, holding Sophie's hand, "And language, this double-edged blade, will eventually cut your spinal cord."

"Oh, yeah, yeah!" said Mr Barry James Grandeur, a polite euphemistic way of saying 'sod off'!

Out of the house and on to the empty enclosure, Sophie and Gol walked towards the gate close to which there was a small low wooden enclosure with the two Anatolian black cows inside it. To recognise and appreciate his own version of decency and righteousness, Mr Barry James Grandeur had sold all his eighty-five cows and twenty-one oxen except the two Anatolian cows, and had offered all the money to the 'epitomes' of righteousness and chivalry, Draco and Christopher. He had kept the two Anatolian cows only as a sign of his unwavering belief in Mehmet and his *unmatched fairness and morals*!

As they stepped out of the gate, Sophie's eyes caught sight of the family's old dog in the adjacent meadow. The dog immediately sensed a familiar presence, pricked her ears and gently wagged her tail. She took a few heavy steps forward, lowered her head, raised it up and tried to bark but nothing came out of her. Her days were numbered, and she was very well aware of it. She turned around but remained motionless. Sophie and Gol walked over to her. She sat on her hind legs, tilted her head and waited for Sophie to hold her. The dog tried and let out a feeble moan, perhaps a last strong appreciation of loyalty and friendship. Gol touched her head, she sniffed his hand and let out another moan, her eyes moistening. She tottered a few yards away, sat on her hind legs again and stared at a near spot in the meadow. A lone pigeon was pecking the wet soil. The sun was going down. The dog toiled to get to her feet. She tottered towards the pigeon and made it fly away. She turned around and threw a meaningful look at Sophie and Gol, as if asking: 'who will look after this naïve pigeon when I am dead?'.

Sophie buried her face in Gol's chest and cried.

"I think we are going to visit your brother. Aren't we?" asked Gol, holding her hand.

"Yes, and he will really be surprised. I didn't tell him I would be released last time he visited me."

Chapter 43

It was a cold autumn night, heavy and dark, impregnated with a forceful storm. Sophie, wearing a loose hoodie, and Gol were walking through the streets of the now eerily quiet town.

"So, you have always wanted to play baseball!" said Gol, laughing delightfully, "And of all baseball gears you have always wanted to have only the *bat!* And you have always wanted your baseball bat come in a flute case!"

"Gol, you are so good at mimicking me!" said Sophie, hoisting the flute case over her shoulder, "Yes, I have always wanted to play baseball but only once."

"And do you know how to use a baseball bat?" asked Gol, still laughing.

"Gol, Magdalena has turned me into an elastic woman," replied Sophie, holding Gol's hand, "I could be a flailing mass of danger even without a baseball bat."

Minutes later, they reached Garry's restaurant. As it had been agreed, Draco, Christopher, Calypso and Mervyn had already gathered inside the restaurant, and were happily and impatiently waiting for Gol to arrive. Sophie covered her face, peeped in through the glass and seconds later, she knocked on the door and stood behind Gol. They all turned around and looked at Gol, who was waving at them. Calypso opened the door. Gol grabbed Sophie's hand and they stepped in.

"This is a homeless girl. Don't worry," said Gol, "I bumped into her on the way coming here. I am going to take her home with me."

"Oh, good catch!" said Mervyn, laughing loudly, "Why has she covered her face?"

"A bad cold or something," replied Gol.

"She is apparently into music. Isn't she?" asked Christopher, pointing to the flute case in Sophie's hand.

"She seems to be," replied Gol, pulling a chair back, "I asked her but she didn't reply. She seems to be badly depressed. She doesn't want to talk."

"So wise of you, Gol," said Draco, a smirk perfectly formed in the corner of his mouth, "It is easier to use the homeless birds. Isn't it?"

"Oh yes," replied Gol, unhinging Draco by darting a mildly piercing look into his eyes, "And it would cost you nothing. Would it?"

"Only a condom," said Calypso, lustfully looking into Gol's eyes.

"Guys, I think we are going off topic," said Christopher, throwing a very cuckold-ish look at his wife, "Let's finish the deal and move on."

"Mervyn, open the door for David," asked Gol, pointing to the door, "He has got the money with him."

Seconds later, David stepped in, firmly holding a black suitcase on his chest with both hands. He put the suitcase before Gol, wheeled his way to the other side of the table and sat on a chair close to Sophie's. Gol opened the suitcase and pulled out a few papers, put them before Draco and asked him to sign them.

"Read them carefully before you sign them," asked Gol, pushing the chair back, getting to his feet, and seconds later, he walked towards the door, locked it and put the keys in his pocket, and turning around he said, "Better safe than sorry. We have a big chunk of cash here."

"Yes, man," said Mervyn, "I was going to lock it but I forgot."

Calypso, the chameleon, the competent game player, turned towards Gol and darted a look into his eyes, her black eyes revealing dark and strangely lustful horror. She had sensed the danger. She tried to open her mouth and say something but to no avail. Gol's eyes had already riveted her to the chair. "A pregnant woman shouldn't sit on a chair like this," whispered Gol, holding her arms and gently lifting her up, "There, go there and sit on the sofa by the fireplace."

Gol walked back to the table, and after checking the signed papers, he placed his hand on Sophie's shoulder and said, "Well, you 'homeless' girl, did you hear what Calypso said about what it would cost one to get access to your pants? 'Only a condom'! As I am going to take you home with me and definitely have access to your pants, I want to make sure it is not going to cost me anything less than my heart. Is there any way you could prove your worth to me?"

Sophie pushed the chair back, got to her feet, put the flute case on the table, and after gently unzipping it, she threw a look at Gol and nodded. Gol took a few bundles of cash out of the suitcase and put them before Draco. Calypso dared to turn her face towards them but she failed to summon enough courage and utter a word. Draco's eyes brightened up. Gol put a few more bundles before him. Christopher formed his newly mastered smile—donkey-ish, rattish. Sophie lifted the flute case. David ruffled his hair excitedly. Draco stretched his right hand out to touch the brand new banknotes before him, his trademark smirks appearing on his face one after another... It was wielded, aptly and precisely, the baseball bat, and guided by a good deal of well-substantiated indignation, it landed on the intended target... Draco's right hand shattered... The swift impact and the ample pain overwhelmed his nerves and his brain... Mervyn and Christopher desperately tried to get up... They both failed... The baseball bat caught Christopher on the right shoulder... Mervyn's throat clamped in Gol's hand... Sophie jumped on the table... Draco tottered, yelled and down he went... Christopher screamed, squeaked, neighed, brayed, his chickenpox-ridden face now resembling the surface of the moon in a dark night. Gol grabbed Mervyn's shoulders and slang him on the floor... He scrambled to get to his feet... he ran... he stumbled... The baseball bat was raised... It landed... Mervyn twisted, the breath imprisoned in his chest... The bat was raised and landed on the back of his lower legs... Sophie turned, jumped, bounced... A row of wine glasses on a long table shattered... Flying salt and pepper shakers, wood splinters... The chandeliers... crystal rhombic hangings arrowing around... Sophie turned, turning, turning like an ever rolling ball of wrath and indignation... A stack of black boxes fell on the floor... They were full of rats... Terrified, squeaking, chirping, the rats darted around through the chairs legs... A fat round rat running towards Christopher... Sophie batted a large glass vase... A shard of glass hit the fat rat... the rat staggered, rolled, rolling rolling... it came to a halt right under Christopher's nose... The bleeding rat... the bleeding nose... Two tiny streams of blood... they ran... they joined... Sophie took off her hoodie and the scarf covering her face... She turned, turning turning... The two large mirrors on the wall shattered... A large gas flame mimicking lightbulb on the wall... more wine glasses... stacks of plates... Gol and David remained unmoved.

Calypso kept watching with her mouth wide open. Sophie unhurriedly walked towards the bar... Shattering bottles of booze... Her face bespattered by red wine... Breaking shattering pounding... She pounded the till and the printer beside it... a handful of coins, she grabbed... She walked over to Calypso, who was now almost paralysed, bent down and whispered into her ear, "Take these coins and buy yourself some condoms! You are cheaper than a condom!"

She walked over to Christopher, landed another heavy blow on his lower back, waited for him to regain his breath, grabbed his hand and pulled him towards Draco, who was leaning against a chair with his evidently broken hand on his thigh. "Open your eyes," she demanded, in a low steady tone, and when they did, she said, "This was for my smeared dignity and for my parents. You are the quintessence of shame, you two timid empty despicable creatures! You swindled my parents out of whatever they had! You dastards ate a whole barbequed piglet with two bottles of wine and to thank your host, well, you shagged his wife! Why did you shag my mum? Had you not promised her that you would protect her Sophie's dignity? Look at me, you despicable rodents! Raise your heads! Do you still think I need to be protected?"

"That is enough, Sophie," said Gol, laughing.

"Gol, let me have a few words with that Christ-looking son of a rat as well," said Sophie, turning around and walking towards Mervyn, "You innocent-looking psychopath, how many souls have you smeared? You are a prostitute, physically and mentally! Look at that cheaper-than-a-condom bitch! You will soon become an uncle to your own child! What is it? Why are you looking at me like that, you empty little miserable rat? Don't get so butt-hurt! It doesn't suit you! Can you remember what you said about my pussy? 'Your pussy is not fresh' you said! A twenty-two-year-old pussy wasn't fresh enough for you! Son of a rat, move your ass and get ready. The police are coming for you bastards!"

"Did you call them bastards, Sophie?" asked David, laughing, "Bastards are the result of courage, the mums; it would take them a lot of courage to give it to someone else. They are only rats, at their best!"

"Well said, David," said Gol, smiling at him.

Sophie threw the baseball bat away and dashed towards Gol with her arms wide open. She bounced, she flew, and he opened his vigorous arms and caught her in the air. She was sure that she would be caught carefully and eagerly; that it was the first and the most elevating flight of her rather unfortunate life. Wrapping her legs around his back and tightening her arms around his neck, she pressed her face against his and cried, loud and unstrained, her tears sluiced out, her heart began to get unburdened, her consciousness clearing, and above all, she felt a rebirth taking place within

339

her—the child that had been taken away from her was coming back into existence. She moaned feebly, shut her eyes and gradually fell silent. Gol felt her weight in his arms. Franco, Maria and Islam appeared behind the door. Gol turned towards David and said, "Call Usman first, and then sort these guys out quickly and leave before the police arrive."

David pulled the keys out of Gol's pocket and ran towards the door. Franco, Maria and Islam were let in. Gol stepped out. The cool breeze wafted through Sophie's soaked hair. She did not move. She was fast asleep. He walked on, so carefully and so steadily as if he was carrying the planet earth on his shoulders. He was, he thought, carrying his own soul, the prize, and the final fruit of his own existence. At the end of the narrow street, he turned left to walk towards where he had parked his car, but he changed his mind, turned around and walked on. He wished there was an endless road before him. He wished he could keep walking for the rest of his life with the precious load on his shoulders. The autumn wind was gaining momentum. Two passers-by whistled and cheered him on. The wind blew through Sophie's long hair and covered his face by a puff of hair. He inhaled the scent of her hair—a mixture of red rose and freshly baked bread, the scent of life and goodness. He walked on… The wind howling, whistling, whirling…

"Goodness gracious!" exclaimed Cynthia, holding the door.

"She is fine. She is fine," said Gol, before Cynthia could say anything else

"I am fine," whispered Sophie.

"Thank goodness!" said Cynthia, stretching her arms out to hold her, "David just phoned me—Goodness! Her face—"

"It is red wine," interrupted Gol, "Hold her firmly. She is just overwhelmed by joy and indignation."

"Gol, I would have killed you had something happened to my Sophie!" said Cynthia, in a slightly raised tone, "You said you would take her for a walk, but you took her to Garry's restaurant and threw her among those rascals! Did you ever think what would happen to my heart?"

Some solemn moments of silence took over. Sophie, who was sat on the couch, raised her head and gazed at Cynthia's face. She had met Cynthia first at Aziza's restaurant, the down depressed withering woman with a pale face and a very dejected pair of large dimming blue eyes, and an attitude

340

that would have only allowed her to flip the world off!

"Cynthia is a most glamorous woman. Isn't she, Gol?" said Sophie, tilting her head and looking at Gol, her red wine-spattered face resembling that of a lion cub that had been allowed to join in on a feast.

"She is, indeed, a most glamorous woman," replied Gol, bending down and holding Sophie's face in his hands, "And you love her very much. Don't you?"

"I do love her very much," replied Sophie immediately, putting her hands on Gol's.

"I will make the bathtub ready," said Cynthia, evidently being overwhelmed by a surge of emotions, "You need a very good bath."

"Gol, will you wash me?" whispered Sophie, kissing his hand, "I have always wished to be washed by you one day."

"And I have always wished to wash my wife one day," said Gol, holding her arms and lifting her up.

"Is it me, Gol?" she whispered, covered her mouth with both hands.

"It is you, Sophie," replied Gol, holding her arms and looking into her eyes, "Will you marry me, Sophie?"

"Yes! Yes, yes, yes, yes!" replied Sophie, now hitting him on the chest with her palms.

"What is going on, guys?" asked Cynthia, coming out of the bathroom.

"It is me! It is me, Cynthia!" said Sophie, dashing towards her to share her rather unbearable joy with her, "He has always wished to wash his wife one day! He is going to wash me! He is going to wash his wife! Right now, in that bathroom!"

"Who could be happier than me!" said Cynthia, holding her firmly, "I am now fulfilled. I am now consummate pride and gratification."

"But I have a single condition—" whispered Sophie.

"He would accept it, no matter what…," interrupted Cynthia.

"Really?"

"Yes, because you are, both of you, now out of the zone of conditionality."

"I fully understand what you mean."

It was not a moment, their moments had never been discrete, and they both were aware of it. It was not an independent moment of lust—not on its own. It was to be a moment of fully delivered intimacy.

Coming out of his room in a pair of sports shorts, Gol almost bumped

341

into Cynthia, who was walking towards the bathroom with two bathrobes and towels over her hands. They gazed at each other for some long seconds before Gol kissed her on the head. Cynthia's heart sank, bulged, rose; her face blushed, just like it would in her prime days. Cynthia raised her hand and gently placed it on his broad and hairy chest and, involuntarily, turned her face away from him, and seconds later, she said, "You have been sharing your life with me and my children. From now on I want you to focus on yourself and your beautiful wife. I have no expectations and—"

"Cynthia," interrupted Gol, putting his hand over her mouth, "Say no more. There is still a lot we can share. There is still a life we can share."

Cynthia was left speechless. She took a few steps back, covered her mouth with both hands, turned around and disappeared into the kitchen.

"Gol, I thought you would love to watch me get undressed," said Sophie, as soon as Gol entered the bathroom, with her head tilted.

"I'd love to," replied Gol, placing the chair he had carried in by the tub, "Well, let me sit here and watch the most watchable woman in my life."

"Oh, Gol!" said Sophie, reaching for the button of her jeans, "Gol, honestly, am I the most watchable woman for you?"

"And the most loveable," replied Gol, crossing his arms on his chest.

Sophie said nothing. She took off her jeans and her T-shirt rather shyly, and after taking off her bra, she pointed to her underpants, with her face now rosier than ever, and said, "I don't think you want to see this part right now. Do you?"

"I will see that part later," replied Gol, getting to his feet and opening his arms, "To see that part, well, I will have to pay for it with my full heart."

She said no more. No more was needed. She put her face on his bare chest and inhaled his scent, the scent for which she had paid a high price— eight painful years of her life and centuries of her pride, value and dignity. She felt him with all the cells in her body. Her round white breasts, pressed against his body, transmitted to her brain a sort of pleasure so unknown to her: a mixture of sensuality and goodness, a touch of earth and a touch of heaven. He gently lifted her up and carefully lowered her in the tub. He sat back on the chair and watched her ivory body immersed in the warm clear water. He gazed into her green eyes, at her wet hair, at her face and the undeniable eternal charm and innocence on it. To this gnostic man, this seeker of the origin, there was only one medium through which one might be able to catch a glimpse of the source: woman. And he had eventually found his medium, his own woman, his own book of enigmas and captivating hints and clues. He stepped into the tub and soaped her body, gently and patiently. He shampooed her long hair. The tub drained, the shower running, he rinsed her… He wrapped her in a towel… He kissed her eyes… He held the bathrobe for her to put on… He lifted her up and carried her to his room… Cynthia appeared with a hairdryer… He put on a green T-shirt and a pair of black shorts and left the room.

"I love this room!" said Sophie, sitting at the wooden makeup table, "I love this reddish glowing hue of this room, those crimson curtains, this large flowery red carpet, a wealth of mahogany, and of course the large bookshelf and the vases on top of it… But, Cynthia, this makeup table, that large bed… What are they doing in a single man's room?"

"True lovers are strange people. Aren't they?" said Cynthia, plugging in the hairdryer, "They live every moment of their dreams. It all began the day you sent back his jacket to him. Remember? The police station, Aisha and Mr Gibran… An automaton would have taken that as a decisive gesture of rejection, but to him it was the most vocal cry for love and union. It was around the same time that he began sharing his life with you. This room used to be as ascetic as Gol himself."

Sophie said nothing. The hairdryer was turned on. She gazed into her own eyes in the mirror. With an air of amazement and admiration, she noticed her own beauty in a way she had never experienced before. She was a precious woman, she thought, offering herself a smile of appreciation. She was the quintessence of womanhood, she thought, the sensual intellect of the entire existence. The hairdryer was turned off. Her eyes met Cynthia's in the mirror. She turned around, held Cynthia's face in her hands and kissed her cheeks.

"One of those wardrobes is yours, and this is the key to it," said Cynthia, handing her a pair of keys, "Open it, and let's see what is inside it."

Sophie opened the wardrobe, and after having a thoughtful look at all the items in it, she held Cynthia's hand and said, "Cynthia, you are absolutely right, he has been living all the moment of his dream. He has been living with me since we bumped into each other! Look at these clothes! Look at these solemn and meaningfully assorted colours! There is a wisely moderated sense of allurement in them, in all of them. Cynthia, I

343

am sounding like a wise woman. Am I not?"

"You are," replied Cynthia, "What are you going to wear now, wise woman?"

"Cynthia," replied Sophie, reaching for a V neck red blouse, "A lush woman in a red top and a long white skirt, waving, swaying flailing around her full white shanks."

"You do know what you are," said Cynthia with a big smile, "And you do know it differently: you know your worth, and above all, you know what you are going to gain in return."

"He said he would pay for it with his full heart!" said Sophie, taking the bathrobe off, "Cynthia, am I really that worthy?"

"You are. You have proven this to yourself," replied Cynthia, taking the white long skirt off the hanger.

"The simpler the better," said Sophie, putting on the red top, "Eileen advised me to be natural with him and avoid superficiality and flashiness."

"Great advice!" said Cynthia, handing her the skirt.

"What do you think? Do I look seductive enough in this dress?" asked Sophie, posing to show some dance moves.

"Captivating, so sweet!" replied Cynthia, touching her face, "When we get over the remains of this saga, you will dance for us. Won't you?"

"I will, and I will put my full heart into it. I promise," replied Sophie, putting her hand on her heart.

Sophie danced out of the room and into the sitting room, where Gol was patiently waiting for her and Cynthia to join him. Gol pulled a chair back for her to sit, but she sat on his lap, put her head on his chest and remained silent. Cynthia poured the wine with a full smile fixed on her face. Gol handed her a glass of wine. She stared into it, watching the reflection of her own face. She raised her head, smiled at Gol and took a swig of her wine and laughed. She took another large swig and laughed again. Gol grabbed his glass of wine and took a swig of it and laughed. Cynthia took a sip and laughed with them. Sophie took another swig and whispered, *drink all your passion, and be a disgrace*. I am now a disgrace. Am I not, Gol? I am unshackled. I am now a childish little woman."

Gol said nothing. He kissed her on the head, caressed her face and kissed her hands.

"Childish woman, get off his lap and let's eat," said Cynthia, in a most delightful tone.

After having a light dinner and some more wine, Sophie whispered something into Cynthia's ear, kissed her face, turned around, grabbed Gol's hand and they walked towards the bedroom. As they entered the room, Gol crept his arms under hers and held her breasts. She moaned, turned her face and he bent down and kissed her lips passionately. He gently squeezed her breasts; she pressed her hands on his and moaned again. She turned around and opened her arms, he lifted her up, pressed his lips on hers and carried her to the bed. He took off her clothes, stood by the bed and wrapped his long arms around her white milky body. He ran his hands up her back, up on her shoulders, the back of her neck, her long hair, down on her hips, down on her backside... He lifted her up and gently put her on the bed... He took his pants off and...

"Wow! It is—" exclaimed Sophie, her eyes widening. She could not finish describing what she had seen, as he had already reached between her legs... She gasped... She threw her now shaking arms around him, her eyes rolled, breath stuck in her chest... He crept his vigorous arms under her lower back, down and he held her buttocks... He arched his back... He pushed hard... She moaned loudly... His mouth grazing her neck... She clasped her arms around his neck and moaned, yelled, cried, wriggled, her legs shaking, her fingernails now piercing into his back... He squeezed her buttocks... She whined.... She gaped... He arched his back... Her hands reaching for his hips, her legs wrapped around his back, her eyes asking for more... He pressed her mouth on hers, sucking the life out of her... Culminating... culminating... She yelled... Culminated... They remained motionless for a while... She held his face in her hands and cried... He kissed her eyes... He rolled over, stretched his hand out and grabbed some napkins from the drawer of the low desk beside the bed, and cleaned Sophie's... She watched him with ample joy and admiration sitting in her wet eyes... He looked around and found her nickers, and put them on her... He lay beside her, gently lifted and placed her on his chest, pulled the duvet over her body and kept stroking her back and her long hair, just like a pilgrim touching the walls of a sacred shrine for blessings.

"Gol," whispered Sophie, her warm breath caressing his neck, "You have always seen and treated me as if I am a white sacred dove."

"You are."

"How are you going to take care of your white sacred dove?" asked Sophie, kissing his face.

"I am going to take away the freedom of not being free from her."

"I love this. Explain it to me."

"Excessive and unnecessary freedom is the plague of all the tender and precious things," said Gol, kissing her shoulder, "The ones who serve freedom with the use of shovels, are the abusers of goodness. They are the mean traders of cheapness."

"What freedoms are you going to take away from me?" asked Sophie, in a pleasantly conscious and submissive tone.

"The freedom of being cheap," replied Gol, kissing her shoulder again, "The freedom of devoiding yourself of womanhood; the freedom of smearing the silk of your existence; the freedom of spitting your own face; the freedom of not being free."

"Gol, shall we marry in a few days?" asked Sophie, pressing her face against his, "I just can't wait. My heart is bursting."

"Yes," replied Gol, gently rising, "How about on your birthday?"

"Amazing! Amazing!" exclaimed Sophie, now sitting astride on his lap and holding his face in her hands, "Only five days left to go! I want nothing but you! You are my freedom!"

Gol wrapped his arms around her back. She pressed her thin lips on his. After some long minutes of fondling, snuggling and laughing, she whispered something into his ear that made him gaze at an unknown spot for some long moments while firmly holding her in his arms. He held her arms and gently pushed her on the bed… He took off her underpants… He held her legs… They stared at each other… She grabbed his arms and pulled him down… "Gol!" she gasped, "I am taking this as a big 'yes'."

"Take it, girl. It is a big yes," whispered Gol, reaching for her breasts. She opened her mouth to say something… He pressed his mouth on hers…

When he woke up, Sophie was still asleep. He kissed her bare back, pulled the duvet over her, and quietly slipped off the bed. It was an early tranquil morning, but not like any other morning in the entire of his life. It was a morning of victory, a morning of pure joy and fulfilment; it was a morning of home and homecoming. Cynthia, the early bird, had already come downstairs. He heard her speaking with David on the phone in the kitchen.

"Hold on, David, Gol is here," said Cynthia, as Gol appeared on the threshold.

"Hoy, David," said Gol, holding the phone with his left hand and reaching for Cynthia's hair with his right, "Brilliant! That is why I call you

346

a man! Okay, okay. See you then."

"Gol, what is going on in here?" asked Cynthia, her cheeks turning rosy, "You have become so tactile since yesterday."

"Only Sophie knows what is going on in here," replied Gol, now holding a stack of her golden hair in his hand, "I have recently noticed that you have become so touchable; that my sense of touch, very much equally, has also been honing itself."

"I wish I could get up and run away from you, right now," said Cynthia, her face now turning into a tapestry of conflicting emotions: remorse, defeat, victory, shame, pride and compensation, "It is too much. It is too heavy. When hatred is turned into the purest form of love, it gains the weight of the world. Gol, I am only a woman. Look at my shoulders. Could they withstand the weight of the world?"

"Lioness, you are trapped," said Gol, kissing her bare shoulders, "There is no way to escape. And remember, these shoulders are going to withstand only the weight of your trophy. And there is a question here: who owes who and what? You owe me nothing. You purged the heart I fell in love with and brought it back to me. And it is completely unnecessary for you to feel so contrite about the past."

Cynthia burst into tears, wiped her face and shed some more tears, laughed from the bottom of her heart, and turned her wet face towards him, tilted her head and sobbed in a rather childish tone, "What is it that Sophie knows?"

"I love it most when a woman tries to be deliberately silly," said Gol, laughing.

"Gol, am I still young enough?" asked Cynthia, sounding half wise half silly.

"You are a rejuvenating lioness," replied Gol, kissing her face.

"I love this!" said Cynthia, laughing, and now pointing to a cardboard box on the counter, she added, "I have prepared what you asked me for last night."

Gol, now with a very excited face, gently and carefully lifted the box, and as he turned to leave the kitchen, Cynthia asked, "Will you eat breakfast today?"

"Yes, I will, today and all the coming days," replied Gol, "I am now a married man, and therefore I think I will need a bigger belly. Won't I?"

"You should ask Sophie!" said Cynthia, letting out a hearty laughter.

When Gol returned to the bedroom, Sophie was still asleep. He put the box on the bed, and as he opened it, two pairs of blue eyes smiled at him, and seconds later, a little cute head was raised and offered him a most innocent and slightly inquisitive look through a pair of smiling black eyes. He had bought these little divine creatures for his homecoming Sophie four days ago. She rolled over, opened her eyes and turned around as soon as she noticed the absence of Gol beside her.

"Gol!" she said, crawling towards him, "Why are you sitting there?"

"Although I am not intending to spoil you," said he, holding her naked body in his arms and kissing her neck, "I have the first present for you."

"I am so excited!" exclaimed she, sitting cross-legged and shutting her eyes.

"Well, they were fed and cleaned by Cynthia, that is why they are quiet," said Gol, "Open your eyes!"

Three four-week-old puppies were curiously looking at her when she looked into the box. She gazed at them in silence. They gazed back at her with their heads tilted and their ears pricked. She opened her arms, and when they waddled towards her, she burst into tears. She held the three of them in her bosom and kissed them one by one.

"What a blessing way of beginning a new chapter!" she said, "Two white and black female Siberian huskies and a male German Shepherd! Divine, absolutely divine! Two pairs of enchanting blue and a pair of dark and intelligent eyes, they are all here to amplify goodness and laugh with me. And Gol, we will all laugh with you, Cynthia, these puppies and I."

They sat to eat the first breakfast together, Sophie, Cynthia and Gol. The three puppies, placed side by side on the table and to Sophie's right, kept looking at her with their heads placed on their front legs. The German Shepherd let out a low yelp, slightly folded his right ear and crept a few inches closer to Sophie. The huskies followed suit. They gently yelped, and with the German Shepherd as the conductor, they performed a pleasantly clumsy and out of tune show of howling and barking. Sophie stared into the German Shepherd's eyes for some long seconds. Her vision blurred, the puppy's eyes shrank, seemed smaller and smaller, the size of a rat's. She blinked and let out a low gasp, raised her hand and covered her mouth and shook her head. Cynthia and Gol threw a fleeting look at each other, paused a few seconds and resumed eating. The puppy crawled closer and put his head on the back of her hand. She lifted him up and placed him on her lap.

The huskies sat on their hind legs and offered her another round of howling and barking; this time much better.

"The puppies are growing on you so hastily," said Gol, touching her face with the back of his hand.

"They come from heaven," said Sophie, reaching for a slice of toast, "They receive our emotions, purify them and throw them back at us; and such emotions make us immune to numbness, negligence and mental metamorphosis. I am worried about the dogs of this country. I am worried that they might cease to be dogs. Yeah, I love dogs."

Cynthia and Gol offered her two very empathic smiles. The two huskies imparted to her that they too loved to sit on her lap, by some low and rather wheezing growls and some more howls and barks.

David, Usman, Franco and Maria entered the house. Sophie made an affectionate show of friendship and respect with Usman and Maria, and cracked a few jokes with Franco, all about the *pigs* and the red large *apples!* She also made a most passionate show of her puppies.

"Well, David, the man, give us your report," asked Gol, smiling.

"Well," said David, "First of all allow me to thank Franco and Islam who helped me with managing the CCTV cameras covering the entrance to the restaurant. As it had been planned beforehand, the cameras inside the restaurant were taken off the walls hours before you and Sophie entered it. And it all means that we left no piece of decisive evidence behind in relation to what happened in there, and of course to what Sophie did. Amazing job, Sophie! And then it was Usman who revealed an ace: he told them that he had enough evidence to prove the existence of a good deal of class A drugs hidden inside the flat, where Garry and Miss Julie Atkins were murdered. By this, he told them that if it was reported to the police, they would definitely be responsible for that as well.

"And therefore, they agreed to tell the police that what happened inside the restaurant was based on some differences among themselves. And I would like to congratulate Sophie as the eventual and very proud winner of this bizarre story."

"Thank you, David," said Sophie, now pressing the two huskies against her chest, "Maybe Usman can tell us what will happen to their rat business now. I would be severely disappointed if it was handed over to someone else and allowed to exist."

"You have now become full of questions," said Usman, gesturing her to hand him one of the puppies, "As I told you during one of my visits in

349

prison, you should take on a very rational approach towards questioning your society. Yes, their rat business will go on. The council has already assigned two caretakers for the rat breeding factory. Who are they? Who could have been better candidates than Mehmet's brother and Christopher's son! And as I have been told, the piece of land that had been allocated to this grand business by the same grand council could well be handed over to another two superstars: Mr Ian Mitchel and Anita!"

"No! I can't believe this!" exclaimed Cynthia, throwing a questioning look at Franco.

"I can remember once Aisha said that only a miracle could change women like Anita," said Maria, offering Franco a pleasant smile, "I can also remember that Emily, in response to Aisha, said that love was a miracle and Franco's love for her would save her. And unfortunately now we know that she had become too numbed to be able to feel true love."

"And she is about to marry Mr Ian Mitchel," said Usman, "And you, dear Sophie, should take Anita as a perfect sample of the society you are going to question. Love failed to affect and save Anita because she had simply been made immune to it!"

"Do you mean we should sit on our hands and let this rat business go on?" asked Sophie, her face being distorted by the pain of disappointment.

"As soon as you find it possible, let us know, and we will take action," said Usman, kissing the puppy's head, "For the present, look after Gol and your puppies, and let's hope that miracles and love have not lost all of their magic."

Sophie offered Usman a smile and holding his arm, she whispered happily, "Gol and I are going to get married in a few days!"

"Really!"

"Yes, he proposed last night!" replied Sophie, her eyes shining, "And I want you to help us with arranging our wedding. I wish to share these blessing moments with you as my best friend."

"I am overly happy!" said Usman, "And I will be at your disposal from tomorrow morning."

Chapter 44

"Mate, that is why I have never trusted this world," said Draco, staring at his broken hand, "Honestly, humanity is a bad joke. My share of life has been a big and ever-aggravating misfortune, an unfair imposition on me by this cruel world. Honestly, I believe there is no meaning to humanity. Look, mate, look what they have done to me!"

"Mate, don't be so sad," said Christopher, throwing a look at Calypso's blank face, "Now you can imagine what Jesus Christ had to endure. He suffered absolute injustice. He was crucified on the cross he had made with his own hands. He sacrificed himself for the good of his own people. And in the same way, we have also, very knowingly, been making our own crosses. Bloody hell, man. Yeah, we will also be crucified for the good of this society. Yeah, bloody hell, man. History is being repeated. Goodness is to be crucified again!"

"Mate, I don't wish to be sacrificed for the people who have already forgotten me!" said Draco, throwing a supercilious look at Mervyn, who was gazing at the dark blue unrelenting door of the lockup, "Mate, I am amazed at how unlucky we are, honestly, there are only three fucking completely *corrupt* people in this fucking town! And look how the fucking hand of fate has put the three of them in our path! Gol, this fucking policewoman, and that fucking judge! Honestly, mate, I think this society has lost its marbles; otherwise, they would have been banging on the door of this fucking police station demanding our immediate release! Honestly, it has always been because of fucking fickle societies that goodness has been crucified!"

"Yeah, mate, bloody hell," said Christopher; throwing a sneering look at Mervyn, he added, "I think you yourself should have approached this fucking policewoman, this fucking Melanie something, instead of Mervyn."

"Mate, she is not like fucking Elizabeth who begged me to shag her!" said Mervyn, still gazing at the door, "She didn't wish to become *immortal!* This fucking woman isn't being ruled over by her cunt! I did my best. It didn't work."

"Mate, because of you we didn't try it ourselves," said Christopher, "You fucking empty man! You can only bluff! You could only shag your own sister and miserable submissive bitches like Sophie!

"You said you would sort her out by giving her a good bang! Bloody hell, man, bloody hell! Look what she has done to us! Did you hear how respectfully the judge was talking to her at the hearing! Mate, we are going to be badly screwed! These three fucking corrupt people are going to put an end to us! Bloody hell, man, bloody hell! Even Jesus Christ would feel sorry for us!"

"Guys, can you just fuck off and listen to me!" boomed Calypso, creeping closer to her will-be-crucified husband! "Guys, instead of moaning like some old despairing women, for God's sake, be men for a few minutes and listen to me! Based on the moral system of this society, we have done nothing wrong; and it is what matters to us and nothing else. Have you forgotten what Mum and Mr Ian Mitchel said yesterday? The rat business will go on. The Town Council has already issued the licence, allocated the needed piece of land and, more importantly, put up fifty percent of the estimated cost. And this is, if you pussies understand it, our great and very realistic hope. Now, listen carefully: one of us should be let off the hook to go out there and goad the society in to an immediate action and secure the freedom of all of us."

"Oh, I see what you mean!" said Draco, toiling to keep his now sunken eyes open, "Which one of us do you think we should let off the hook?"

"Well," said Calypso, now rubbing her belly, "If the lovely Mehmet had been among us today, it would have definitely had to be him, as he was the only one this society could fully understand and trust. Shame! But he died for a good cause. Anyway, back to our own issue. Should it be Draco? No—"

"Why?" Draco cut in, one of his eyelids refusing to rise!

"Guys, you are not going to interrupt me!" said Calypso, brandishing her index finger at them, "Because Draco is a money-guzzling drug addict whose brain is also now out of service! At times, he could be *excessively* irrelevant. I am sure you haven't forgotten his speech, when Dad had just been murdered, where he listed Nicola Tesla, quantum physics, caesarean, and parallel universes among the dire issues facing the earth and humanity! As that fucking Iranian man used to say 'What does your fart have to do with your temples?'. Draco, you are out."

"It has to be me," said Christopher, picking at the thick gold chain around his neck, "I am the most experienced among us. Bloody hell, man. Yeah, and the most sensible. You know, I have seen it all. And, bloody hell, man, I know this society very well."

"I am younger," said Mervyn, his eyes now a full exhibition of schizophrenia and sadomasochism, "And definitely more handsome than you are. We are talking about some superficial people. Out there, I would be seen as the same innocent lamb; and this is the difference, and therefore I think it has to be me."

"Every fucking piece of evidence is against you!" said Calypso, her eyes widening, "You and Draco met Mr Ian Mitchel five times, at his home, where he recorded all of what was said between you, and sold them to Gol!"

"Hang on a second," said Draco, now both his eyelids refusing to rise, "How have you managed to acquire that much information? Perhaps you have been betraying us!"

"Shut up!" said Calypso, throwing at him a very pitiful look, "This fucking policewoman revealed all the details of our case to me. She believes we should plead guilty to avoid the maximum punishment, which I also think is the right thing to do."

"So, let's suppose we somehow managed to let you off the hook," said Mervyn, touching her face with the back of his hand, "How would you go about finding a way to get us off the hook?"

"I would pull Sophie back into this case," replied Calypso immediately.

"How?" asked Christopher, a very mulish smile forming on his face.

"Mr Ian Mitchel and his son, Kyle, used to shag our Sophie every now and then," said Calypso, nodding thoughtfully, "Mr Mitchel told me."

"Oh, I see! Mr Mitchel told you!" said Christopher, scratching his face, "Okay, fair enough. Go on. Tell us more."

"Bearing in mind that the nature of this crafty man is now known to the police and the court," said Calypso, now holding her belly, "And also taking into account the fact that he is now giving it to my mum, I am sure I would be able to use him and get Sophie and Gol hooked again. Imagine, for example, Mr Mitchel claiming that Sophie approached him with half a million pounds and her pussy and asked him to murder Garry. Sophie's pussy, Gol's money and Anita's arse—don't forget, Gol had fallen in love with my mum's arse—and needless to say, Mr Mitchel's proven insatiable greed and cunningness. 'I declined the offer', he would say. And also bearing in mind how good Mr Mitchel is when it comes to creating and forging evidence, you could simply imagine a good number of other effective scenarios."

"It sounds plausible," said Mervyn, "But you seem to have underestimated Gol, that fucking intelligent man! Have you forgotten that he never mentioned me as a suspect while he knew it was me right from the beginning? How would you tell if he hasn't already devised a plan to get Mr Mitchel hooked as well?"

"Nonsense!" said Christopher, letting out a horsey chuckle, "If he was intelligent, he wouldn't have spent three hundred thousand pounds on Sophie's overused pussy!"

"You said it, mate! Honestly, he is a fucking idiot!" said Draco, his head drooping.

"Guys, you are too daft to understand his intelligence," said Calypso, laughing, "Gol being the wise man and Mr Ian Mitchel the dangerous venomous snake, they both know how to wisely deal with each other. As long as our snake stays in his own terrain, the wise man won't hurt him."

"But how are you going to *use* him if he is supposed to stay in his own terrain?" asked Mervyn, half a wise smile appearing on his face and disappearing as quickly.

"He would devise plans and I would implement them," replied Calypso.

"I see," said Mervyn, a white lamb appearing in his right eye and a black fierce wolf in the other.

"Mates," said Christopher, gesturing Mervyn to raise Draco's head, "I think you two should accept the full responsibility and let Calypso walk away."

"Why only us, mate?" asked Mervyn, darting a half-dead look at Christopher.

"Guys, Stop it! I won't have it!" snapped Calypso, "What would happen if you failed to reach an agreement over this before it is too late? Well, listen to me: we would all be fucked! I am your only fucking hope! Don't fuck me up! Hurry up. Make a decision. We have only twelve hours to salvage a bit of our lives."

"Okay, tell us exactly what you want us to say," said Mervyn, touching her belly.

"I am so sorry, guys," said Calypso, two tiny specs of light appearing in her eyes, "But there is no other option. I am going to claim that you three guys have been abusing me since a very young age—"

"What!" neighed Christopher.

"Let her go on, Christopher!" demanded Mervyn.

"And that you deceived and coerced me into collaborating with you in the crime," said Calypso, two dressed-in-black jokers dancing in her eyes, "And you are going to admit you did, and express some heartfelt remorse for it, which given my pregnancy, would definitely secure my freedom. And you two should show some emotions and bear in your minds that you are the father of the child in my womb."

"How come!" uttered Christopher, his eyes widening, his neck elongating, "How come we both are the father to the child in your womb?"

"Don't be so butt-hurt, my dear husband," replied Calypso, touching his face, "The child will have your name on her or his birth certificate. No one would take much pride in their DNA nowadays. Would they?"

"Bloody hell, mate, how could you do that to me?" asked Christopher, his tone now much lenient.

"It wasn't my fault, mate," replied Mervyn, pinching Calypso's arm, "Your wife isn't an ordinary woman. She is a goddess who lives on ambrosia, a thick creamy form of it. She loves it warm and fresh. What would you expect when you have a cumdumpster for a wife!"

"Mate, I think we are going off track," said Christopher, assuming an air of absolute righteousness on his face, "Bloody hell, man. Yeah, I think we should let my wife off the hook. Yeah, she knows her prerogatives. She knows her way around the games of this bloody world."

"Thank you very much, my sensible husband," said Calypso, throwing a look at Draco whose head was now going down like that of a dying bird; she added, "He is now more unconscious than a cooked chicken! I wish we could find him a pinch of cocaine before being taken to the court."

"Don't worry about him. We will sort him out," said Mervyn.

"Oh, by the way," said Calypso, assuming a supernatural air, "There is something about me you didn't know about, something which will assure you, you made the right decision to let me off the hook. I have a doppelganger!"

"What is a doppelganger?" asked Christopher, scratching the back of his head.

355

"A double, an invisible version of me," replied Calypso, her large eyes brightening up, "It all began a short while prior to Garry's unfortunate death. She appeared to me first when I was out on a date with Mehmet, and warned me about some future disturbing events, among which was Mehmet's fate and my marriage to Christopher and my mum to Mr Ian Mitchel."

"Oh, amazing!" said Christopher, laughing, sounding like an old Spanish donkey.

"Yes, and she also told me that you would all be fine in the end," said Calypso, smiling at her husband affectionately, "That you would all live a graceful long and prosperous life; that Garry, Mehmet and that undertaker were destined to leave the word a bit earlier. And I am certain she will guide me through the remains of this saga."

"Fascinating!" said Christopher, beaming at his wife, "Did she also tell you that Sophie would go back to Gol?"

"No, my doppelganger would only tell me the news about the very decent people," replied Calypso, smiling at Mervyn, "And not about dirty cheap bitches like Sophie!"

"Oh, I see," said Christopher.

The less-conscious-than a cooked chicken gentleman—who had been somewhat sorted out by a strong mug of coffee and some painkillers, and now looking like a crestfallen cockerel—was carried into the grand building of the Crown Court. The three gentlemen and the very gentle woman were ushered and seated at a table in a small consultation room, where their very competent solicitors—three of them—were patiently awaiting them.

After doing the logbook and signing some papers, Officer Melanie Maxwell—one of the only three *corrupt* people in the town—let them know they had half an hour before they would be taken to the courtroom.

With the immediate arrival of a grand Mr Ian Mitchel and his grand wife, Anita, who was once the proud wife of a proud man with the very Greek blood streaming in his very straight veins and vessels, they launched in to an ardent last revision of what they had already agreed upon. Their three solicitors, who were very strict and *dutiful*, expressed their vehement disapproval of their client's decision to plead guilty, as they believed, categorically, that they could turn the case around in their favour! Perhaps they were still manoeuvring around Anita's backside and Gol's love for it!

They also did not hesitate to express their doubts about the success of their plan to let Calypso off the hook.

"It doesn't matter how," said Mr Ian Mitchel, who was now confidently offering them some forms of fast-changing little smiles, thanks to a pair of dentures he had recently had fitted into his mouth, "Just go through it. Do you know what I mean? Just fuck through it and don't be worried about it even a bit. Do you know what I mean? The rat business is pulling off like no other business has ever done! Yeah, mates, do you know what I mean? And with it, we will all be raised higher and higher. Do you know what I mean? What you have offered to this country is even greater than the Magna Carta, and even the entire of the British Empire! This is what my son, Kyle, believes, and he has just begun to write a book about great Garry, and in it, he is going to prove that if Garry had been born and lived before John Locke and Thomas Hobbes, well, this country would have never gone off track!"

"Yes, from now on you should only listen to Mr Mitchel," said Anita, proudly beaming at her husband, "And be assured that society is standing by you because you are now part of a great legacy Garry left behind. Just for you to fully grasp what I mean, I should let you know that during the past ten days since you were arrested, a lot has happened, one of which is the making of statues of your great late dad and the great late Mehmet. The chairman of the Town Council has personally undertaken the supervision of this great job. He has invited eight of the best sculptors in the country and another two from Rome. This great historical project, as the chairman put it, is to start tomorrow. And by the way, I have to apologise to my dear Calypso for failing to understand her. My dear daughter, I do admit that dogs were the past and rats are the future."

"No, not behind the dock," demanded the judge, his tone gentle yet very much resounding, "I would like to have a better view of them. Get them seated here, right before me."

After the security officers seated the three gentlemen and the lone gentlewoman right before the judge, and positioned themselves in their designated spots, the courtroom was draped in a heavy and lingering silence. Moments later, the court clerk read the charges against the defendants, and then the judge, a bearded middle-aged man with a rubicund and very solemn face, kept roving his light blue and very modest eyes round the courtroom until they spotted and met Sophie's. She did not dither. A bright joyful smile sat in the full green of her eyes and she, with her head tilted, offered it to the judge.

"Well," said the judge, after gavelling on the bench three times, "Due to the abundance of some meticulously tested and ratified evidence and also some other factual materials that the court have been provided with by the police; and also as a jury have already had a painstaking study of the case, I do not think we are going to have a long day today. Nonetheless, I am all ears and will attentively listen to the legal representatives of the defendants."

"Your Honour," said one of the solicitors, the one who had highlighted the importance of Anita's arse in this case! "We do believe there are still some dark spots within this case, and we are here today to shed light on them."

"Please, do so," said the judge.

"Your Honour," said the solicitor, clearing his throat, "As we have mentioned it in our covering letter, our clients had no criminal records before these unfortunate incidents where they were subjected to a well-calculated conspiracy devised by an evil mind. Out there, Your Honour, every single member of this society has always deemed our clients as the perfect role models to their youngsters. Just this morning a large number of mostly middle-aged women had gathered before our office to express their anxious support for our clients and urge us to mobilise more women and take a more robust action. It is worth noting that they all believe if our clients are convicted, well, the historical values of this great country will be badly marred. We still believe that the late great Garry, the late great Mehmet and the precious Miss Julie Atkins fell victim to a deranged and sexually deviant man named Gol. Blinded by his hellish lust towards Anita's unique natural elevations—in our case her backside—he turned into a beast and unleashed her demonic wrath towards Garry, that father of fathers, that intellectual of his time. As for the evidence and the factual materials Your Honour mentioned, we are certain that they are all fabricated and there is not even a whit of truth in them. Bearing in mind that this is now the earnest demand of the community, we also demand nothing but immediate justice for our innocent clients who were victimised by the foulest of creatures——"

"Sir," said the judge, raising his right hand, "Leave this part and move on. We will get back to it should need raise."

"Yes, Your Honour," said the solicitor, turning his face towards one of his colleagues, "My colleague will present the next part."

"Your Honour," said the second solicitor, a middle-aged plump dark and rather masculine woman, "To reiterate what my colleague said, I should also maintain the doubtful stand on the authenticity of the evidence and the alibis within this case. However, as the court has apparently deemed our evidence as insufficient and our argument as unsubstantiated, then we will have to accept the course within which the case is now being looked at and help our clients as much as possible. Your Honour, after considering all the facets of this case, we believe one of our clients, Mrs Calypso Christodoulou, could well be acquitted should Your Honour use the right of discretion at your disposal."

"Sure. Convince me, and I will," said the judge, gesturing Calypso to stand up, "Well, Mrs Calypso Christodoulou, tell us your story. Be honest. Help me to help you."

"Thank you very much, Your Honour," said Calypso, holding her head down, "It is a long and bitter story of abuse. It began when I was fourteen."

"Hold your head up and continue," asked the judge, offering her a kind smile.

"Yes, Your Honour," said Calypso, throwing an involuntary look at Mervyn's face, "It all began with the word 'prerogative', as it used to be the basis of my great late dad's philosophy. And I was told that it was my prerogative to do whatever I wished with my body. And then Mikhalis appeared, and he also believed that it was my prerogative, and he abused me, and since then he also kept offering me to his friends. As I was very young, I could not understand that it was not my prerogative to be abused. And when I grew older and around the time I had just begun to think about my true prerogatives, this Mr Christopher Lambrakis appeared and offered me a completely new definition on the word 'prerogative', and began to abuse me. And as we moved on, these two men and my brother, Draco, fooled and coerced me into collaborating with them in this horrible crime. Then Mr Christopher Lambrakis told me if I married him he would protect me. And to make sure I would remain silent and obedient to him, he quickly made me pregnant. Your Honour, I am a woman, and like all women, aspire to goodness; but the deliberate misinterpretation of my great late dad's take on the prerogatives of humans by these indecent men, misled me."

"You can sit down, Mrs Calypso Christodoulou," said the judge, now looking at the three gentlemen sitting before him with their heads held down, "Mr Mikhalis Christodoulou, you have lived a good part of your life under a fake identity. Is it true?"

"Yes, Your Honour," replied Mervyn, now looking as innocent as the lamb that was sacrificed instead of Ishmael!

"And you are Calypso's half-brother?"

"Yes, Your Honour."

"Well, what do you have to say to what Calypso said?"

"Your Honour, I do admit," replied Mervyn, now formally acknowledged as the grand Mr Mikhalis Christodoulou, "I was a young man and therefore unable to fully understand the philosophy of my great late dad. I do admit that it was me who misinterpreted his views and misled and abused my dear sister, Calypso. And I am honestly very much remorseful for my actions and misdeeds."

"You can sit down, Mr Mikhalis Christodoulou," said the judge, slightly perplexed by the innocence splayed on Mikhalis' face, "And you, Mr Christopher Lambrakis, tell us what you have to say."

"Yes, Your Honour," said Christopher, throwing a look at his wife, "I am full of shame and very remorseful. I also admit that our inability in understanding the great late Garry's philosophy misled us and resulted in our abuse of Calypso. Yes, I am very remorseful. Bloody hell, man. Bloody hell."

"You can sit down, Mr Christopher Lambrakis," said the judge, "And you, Mr Draco Christodoulou, was the misunderstanding of your father's *philosophy* conducive to his murder and that of Miss Julie Atkins and Mehmet Kose?"

"Your Honour," said Draco, assuming a look on his face so akin to that of his dad's, "Honestly, as my dad's worldview was based on sacrifice and martyrdom, I think it was his soul that led us to murdering him and his soulmates, Miss Julie Atkins and Mehmet Kose. Honestly, we could have been wrong; I mean we could have misunderstood my dad's soul. Honestly, my dad's philosophy had this element of uncanniness incorporated in it; I mean it was well beyond the realms of nature and obviously hard to understand for the mediocre-minded people."

"Interesting!" said the judge, indulging himself with a solemn laugh, "But as far as I can tell, you and Mr Lambrakis are not *mediocre-minded* people; and thereof you should not have failed to understand the incorporated elements in his philosophy."

"Your Honour," said Draco, now in his own zone, the grandiose zone of impertinence, "Honestly, I think it was because of the community and the rats that we got confused: they had this desirous approach to my dad, which made us believe that my dad was actually a living martyr who had been sent down to earth only to be sacrificed—just like Jesus Christ! Honestly, those people out there made us believe we were actually ordained to undertake this task and create a different theology or philosophy for this society. Honestly, given the intricate nature of the matter we had to deal with, I believe Mr Lambrakis and I could well be exonerated should Your Honour have the case studied by some knowledgeable theologians and mythologists."

"Sit down, Mr Draco Christodoulou," asked the judge, now gavelling on the desk, "We will have a break, and when we are back, I will tell you the verdict."

"Mates," said Christopher, jerking his head towards the solicitors, "You are fucking useless!"

"What is it, Mr Lambrakis!" said the dark plump masculine female solicitor, her eyes widening.

"You shouldn't have put all of our bloody eggs in one basket," replied Christopher, lowering his voice, "Who would invest that much in a fucking woman's arse! You three guys promised us Anita's arse would secure our freedom! See what happened, we are going to rot in prison while that fucking arse will be pampered by a lucky Mr Ian Mitchel!"

"Well," said the judge, throwing a very musing look at Mikhalis' face, "Let us do the better part first. Miss Sophie Grandeur, stand up, please."

"Your Honour," said Sophie, dressed in a black suit, and her hair turned into a single thick long tress, reaching down her chest.

"I have been a bit too casual today, breaching the rules and procedures," said the judge, smiling at Sophie, "Well, here and right now, I gladly let you know that you are acquitted."

Sophie's reaction was priceless: she gazed into the judge's eyes for some long seconds with a different smile blossoming in her eyes. She did not need to jump up, punch the air and celebrate her freedom. She had redeemed herself. She had deservedly earned her freedom.

"Thank you, Your Honour," said Sophie, her eyes moistening, "May I say something?"

"Of course, say whatever you wish," replied the judge.

"Your Honour, I am worried about the dogs of this country," said Sophie, in a clear and slightly raised tone.

A few heads turned towards her. Some faces were on the verge of failing to properly deal with the nature of what was said. The court usher, a wise-looking woman, leaned on the desk and gazed at Sophie. Draco chuckled. Christopher scratched his blotchy face and was about to let out a mulish laugh.

"So am I, my dear," said the judge, nodding thoughtfully, "Sit down, Miss Grandeur. Well, you three gentlemen and you young lady, I acknowledge the fact that some people out there are eagerly demanding your immediate acquittal and release, in particular those middle-aged anxious mothers who think they might fail to properly educate their youngsters without you. Nevertheless, as we are facing some de facto norms and beliefs, I should regretfully let you and those people know that in order for their demand to be fulfilled, they should go to the parliament and put forth an earnest request for those norms and beliefs to be acknowledged and legislated. I am afraid our current laws, norms and beliefs are not *sophisticated* enough to serve the wishful thinking of some people who demand the immediate release of murderers and abusers! What I can, unequivocally, promise you is this: justice will be done. And not to make you completely disappointed, I am going to send you to a place where you will have ample time to think and materialise Mr Garry Christodoulou's intricate philosophy and holiness and offer it to the society that loved him so dearly!"

Half an hour later, the three gentlemen were carried away to be *crucified* for the good of their own people! And the lone gentlewoman, Mrs Calypso Christodoulou, was let off the hook to go back to her people and goad them in to some conscientious actions!

Their hands firmly interlocked, Mr Ian Mitchel and his wife walked, in a gait so precisely coordinated, towards the exit door where Calypso was impatiently waiting for them. The judge blinked, took off his wig and gazed at the chair on which Mikhalis had sat. He blinked again, and a white lamb appeared on the chair, innocently looking at him! He had judged a dark *divine* case, he thought. The anxious middle-aged mothers had gathered outside the court, trying to stop the vehicle which was carrying the three *divine* convicts away.

362

Chapter 45

Gol, holding Sophie's hand in his, was walking through the town streets so triumphantly and so proudly as if he had won the world cup single-handedly and in style, just like Diego Armando Maradona did. Feeling the rejuvenating and ever-existing sensual resonance of life and growth, being transmitted from her hand to his heart, he could feel the nearing steps of the spring right in the middle of a bitterly cold and nipping autumn. She was quiet. He was quiet. They were both listening to the exuberant melody of union and oneness. The words were of no use. While waiting for the green light to appear and allow them to cross the road, they shared a kiss and a smile. Turning into the narrow street, Sophie's eyes caught the sign 'Garry Christodoulou Street'. They stopped, looked at the sign, looked at each other and walked on in silence. Minutes later, they entered the restaurant and were warmly welcomed by Franco and Maria, who were diligently and happily at work. Sophie threw a look at a heap of shattered glass gathered in a corner and smiled.

"Gol, I didn't know you had really bought this restaurant," said Sophie, laughing, "Otherwise I wouldn't have gone too far with my rage."

"It was a need, Sophie," replied Gol, "You needed to give vent to your indignation. And we had decided to change everything in here, anyway."

"Gol, what is your plan for this place?" asked Franco.

"I have just come here to let you and Maria know," replied Gol, gesturing Maria to come closer, "Italiano-Greco, the best of them. You and Maria are going to turn this place into the best—best ever—Italiano-Greco restaurant. Clean it, cleanse it, and leave no sign and no smell of those 'marvellous people'!"

"And as it seems to me," said Sophie, pushing her hair back and forming a big smile on her face, "Franco has finally found his large red delicious apple. Such an apple! I wish I was a horse!"

"Sophie, you are being naughty!" said Maria, kissing Sophie's face noisily, "I have always loved Franco. It took him a while to notice."

"He tried to turn an older apple into cider," said Gol, laughing, "Not knowing that an apple bitten by a rat, would never ferment!"

"You are right, Gol, but my Maria is already a jug of red wine," said Franco delightfully.

Maria hurled herself into Franco's arms. Sophie and Gol wished them lasting love and happiness, and as they were to leave, the door was pushed open and Jack and Jack slipped in quietly.

"Sophie!" they uttered at the same time, gently walking towards her.

"Jack and Jack!" said Sophie, throwing a fleeting appreciative look at Gol.

"We are truly happy to see you again!" said Jack something, embracing Sophie.

"How are you, girl?" said Jack something else, opening his arms, "We both are proud of you."

"Thank you, thank you very much!" said Sophie, now holding their hands, "Do you still believe Mehmet was the most suitable man for me?"

"That Sophie died. Didn't she?" said Jack something, smiling musingly.

"Oh yes, the poor girl died and was immediately cremated!" said Sophie delightfully, now turning her face towards Gol, "Gol, I thank you very much for taking Jack and Jack on!"

"Jack and Jack have no one to thank but themselves," said Gol, now shaking hands with them, "Gentlemen, I welcome you to my life."

***

"Clement!" shouted Sophie, as they entered Gol's restaurant, "I have missed you so much!"

"Glad to see you again!" said Clement, giving her a hug, "Come, come with me. There is someone in the kitchen that is so eager to see you."

Seconds later, Sophie entered the kitchen and faced a face that used to unhinge her during the time she had worked at Garry's restaurant. The two faces stared at each other for some long seconds, and when it became apparent that none was going to be outstared, they both turned into mirrors of pride and smiled at each other.

"Ghena! I have always wished to see you again!" said Sophie, opening her arms and walking towards him.

"It was a long and painful journey. Wasn't it?" said Ghena, kissing her on the head.

"It was," replied Sophie, holding his hands.

"I am proud of you, my friend."

"I am honoured to be your friend. I will always remain your friend."

"I will let you go now. I know how busy you and Gol are these days. We will talk later."

"Yeah, definitely, I would love to talk with you."

"Gol, I've always wished to be carried upstairs by you," said Sophie, opening her arms.

"Oh, the child within you," said Gol, lifting her up, "It was her that guided you out of the dark. Don't allow her to grow up hastily."

"I just love the way you understand and explain me," said Sophie, smiling, "Gol, I am so happy that you have taken Ghena on. He is such a decent human being."

"I am happy to hear this," said Gol, reaching the landing, "He used to admonish you, indirectly. Didn't he?"

"Gol, you've always been studying me since we crossed paths! Haven't you?"

"I have been reading you," replied Gol, lowering her behind the office door, "You left your heart behind when you left me. And inside it, I found a most fascinating novel with a never-ending last chapter."

"Gol, am I really a fascinating novel?" asked Sophie, checking the collar of her red shirt.

"I will let you know when I have finished the last chapter," replied Gol, pushing the door open.

"Wow! What a beautiful office!" exclaimed Sophie, as they entered, "It was not like this those days when I was here. Look at those tableaus and paintings and…"

"It is almost the same as it was back then," said Gol, taking off his coat, "There are only a few additional items, like that portrait done by Cynthia."

Sophie remained silent. She walked round the room, gazing at each item with full attention with a slight tinge of self-deprecation washing over her beautiful face. She stopped before the portrait done by Cynthia, put her hand on her heart, turned her head around and threw a look at Gol. It was a fine portrait of the three of them in one place, with hers in the middle and those of Gol and Cynthia at her right and left. There in Cynthia's eyes she spotted a simultaneously existing hue of fear and hope; and in Gol's she spotted ample faith and tolerance. The date at the left bottom corner told her that it had been done just a few months into her imprisonment. She walked round the room again.

She indulged herself with a self-ratifying smile when she found herself able at understanding the incorporated nuances and the messages within each item on the wall. To the right of one of the large windows there was a large rectangular framed piece of calligraphy which attracted her attention with an-ancient-sounding call. She stood before it. Her green eyes eagerly following the curved, twisted and coiled letters, which initially seemed to her like a big number of newly hatched black snakes badly entangled. But the more she paid attention the clearer they became: they were dancing elastic letters, each bending and twisting to make room for the others, where there seemed to be no room at all. She took a step forward to have an up-close look. She saw, she spotted a full word sitting on the lap of an elongated letter, itself the last part of another word. Those dancing black letters reminded her of Magdalena and her unique approach towards dance.

She walked over to Mr Gibran's desk. She looked at him and her two daughters in a framed picture placed by the wall. She picked up the picture and looked at Aisha and her father's face. 'They are looking back at me,' she thought, smiling. 'I love them. I will apologise to them.'

She walked back to Gol, who was sitting at his desk with his arms crossed on his chest and his eyes closed. She wrapped her arms around his neck and whispered into his ear, "When are you going to unveil my desk? I can't wait to sit there and fall in love with you again and again."

"After the wedding," replied he, holding her hands, "A wise man defined love as a serious mental disease, but he forgot to say that it is the best of all the mental diseases. I am glad that you are going to suffer from this disease for the rest of your life."

"I can understand what you mean," said she, sitting on the chair beside his, "You mean without this disease we would fall into the pit of excessive immunity, and it is exactly there that we would become most vulnerable."

"Well said," said he, now looking at her face musingly, "And this now very cogent-sounding mind of yours is definitely the direct result of inflicting the enlightening pains of such a life-affirming disease on yourself. Sophie, you are well on your way to becoming the essence of your name."

"Am I, Gol?" asked Sophie, tilting her head.

Meanwhile, there was a knock on the door, and seconds later, Mr Gibran came in. Sophie dashed towards him with her arms open. Mr Gibran embraced and held her for some long moments without saying a word, and when she held his face and asked him to forgive her, he planted a kiss on her forehead, and throwing a hello at Gol, he walked to his desk.

"Mr Gibran, you have now forgiven Sophie. Haven't you?" asked Gol with a musing smile.

"I don't know," replied Mr Gibran, gesturing Sophie to go over to him, "Here, Sophie, stand here and look into my eyes and tell us whether I have forgiven you or not."

"Without looking into your eyes, or even at your face," said Sophie, offering him a most endearing smile, "I can tell. Without a shadow of doubt you have forgiven me. *'It is only with the heart that one can see rightly'*. Shall we shake hands and become friends for life, Mr Gibran?"

"I have always been your friend," replied Mr Gibran, shaking her hand, "And from now on we are friends for life, and I will take pride in it."

Sophie smiled at Mr Gibran's face, turned her head and smiled at Gol and laughed a very childish laugh, a laugh coming from a heart imbued in peace and worthiness. She walked over to her desk and stood beside it. She looked at Gol's desk and back at her own, as if trying to measure the distance between them. It was not big, the distance, the difference; it would not have taken eight precious years of her life to travel this short distance had she been allowed to feel whatever was to be felt and understand whatever was to be understood. She paced the distance between her desk and Gol's, and stood beside him, who was calmly watching her.

"The distance from there to here is only around eight feet," said she, putting her hand on her heart, "It took me years to travel this non-existent distance! I was only flesh and mind."

"And what are you now?" asked Gol, stroking his beard.

"What am I now?" said Sophie, and after musing for a while, she bent down and whispered into his ear, "Until last night I had no clue what sex was all about. I felt it with every single cell in my body. I felt it with my heart, my mind, my soul and whatever else that might exist within the sphere of womanhood. Last night sex cleansed my body and my soul, and I discovered myself as a full and dear woman in silky and precious flesh. And above all, I am now dead against *convenient truth*."

"And a very expensive woman," said Gol, holding her hands.

367

"Oh, yeah, I got a big heart for it!" said Sophie, joyfully.

"Look who is here!" said Gol, pointing to the door.

Sophie's show of affection for Emily was something to watch, and Mr Gibran and Gol watched it delightfully. To her, Emily was now much more than a friend; she was her saviour, her herald towards an inner hideaway, where she had succeeded in penetrating into her own psyche and seeing its severed ties with her heart and intuition. Mesmerized by her outside beauty when they had met each other for the first time, and then enchanted by her graceful inner world exposed to her via her letters and her unwavering faith in her, Sophie was deeply grateful and appreciative towards her.

With her head held high, she looked Emily in the eye, as she had done when she had faced Ghena. The compelling beauty, the aura, the manifestation of a polished and elevated soul by an educated heart and the unmatched grace and peace within what Emily was, did not unhinge Sophie, and she quickly noticed this. She was not ashamed of anything, she thought. She belonged in the same zone, the zone within which there was no room for shame, the safe zone of heart.

Emily greeted Mr Gibran, shared a hug with Gol and said, "Gol, congratulations! You have eventually got your Sophie!"

"I have eventually got my Gol!" said Sophie, throwing her arms around and performing a short piece of dance.

"Girls, it is lunchtime," said Gol, taking his coat off the hanger, "Let's go upstairs. Cynthia is waiting for us. And you, Mr Gibran, please join us."

"I will join you when Aisha has arrived. She is coming to see Sophie," said Mr Gibran.

"I can't wait to see Aisha! I love her so much!" said Sophie, her face beaming with joy.

***

Sophie described Cynthia's art gallery as an 'exhibition of heart on a background of philosophy' as they happily sat at the finely set table. After Mr Gibran, Aisha and David joined them, they began with small talks and sipping red wine, but Sophie's animated soul was urging her to immediately deal with the already accumulating serious questions in her mind.

"Emily, could you please tell me more about what you mentioned a few minutes ago?" asked Sophie.

"Oh, yes," said Emily, throwing a smile at Gol, "As I was saying, once, and a while before you got imprisoned, I asked Gol why Sophie was so important to him, and we went on with our talk and reached a point at which I mentioned something that David had said: 'Gol wants Sophie to complete an incomplete image in his mind'. Was David right about this? Definitely. And just put your hands on your hearts and watch: the incomplete image being Cynthia back then, is now sitting side by side by the complement, the dear beautiful Sophie. And you know, you three people might have a great surprise for us! It is the great characters who write worthwhile stories. David and I are so proud to be part of your great story."

"And who is the sweetest fruit of this story?" asked David, offering her sister a most admiring smile.

"It has to be Sophie," replied Emily, stretching her hand out and touching Sophie's face, "This round beautiful face, this fine booklet, had not been meant to be filled with stories of shallowness and unyielding words, and Sophie, by espousing her forgotten inner self, managed to erase the blots of wrongness and rewrite her own hearty and worthy story. And it wouldn't have been possible without the sweet and invigorating mixture of heart and mind."

"Emily, I take this as a great compliment," said Sophie, now looking at Cynthia's face, "But I think the credit should be given to Cynthia, as it was her who actually offered me to Gol by doing a bit of alchemy."

"Well said," said Mr Gibran, nodding thoughtfully, "Can you elaborate this for us, Sophie?"

"Yes," said Sophie, throwing a most affectionate look at Cynthia, "Cynthia was jealous of me.

"And how much heart and personality would it take for one to turn pure envy into pure love and peace and take a step back and watch it flourish and yield the most desirable fruits. And only an alchemist could have done this."

"And do not forget," said Emily, pushing her golden hair back, "It is only pure love that can create an alchemist, and when created, it is only an alchemist that can create love. So interconnected and mutual. Aren't they?"

Sophie and Cynthia fell silent. They calmly gazed at Emily's face, as if looking themselves in a mirror. They both looked at Aisha's face and her large black eyes, and offered her their heartfelt appreciative smiles. In the silver of Mr Gibran's hair and beard they read their own future, the child of their past. And thinking of this child, they turned their faces towards

Clement, who had just stepped in, and pictured his unadulterated permanent smile. And not to forget David and his unuttered well wishes for them and also his selfless efforts all through their painful journey, they both offered him a smile enhanced by the divine and ever-pure feminine affection.

"Sophie," said Clement, smiling, "Do you remember what a mess you made of the crab and the lobster I cooked for you ages ago?"

"Yes, I do remember!" replied Sophie, with her hands raised, "I cut both my hands. They were bleeding like hell! And I was crying like a baby. I made a messy mess of it!"

"And here you are," said Clement, taking the sheet of foil off a silver tray, "A crab and a lobster. I have dismantled them, so you don't have to cut your hands and cry again!"

"I love *human* attention," said Sophie, getting up to give him a hug, "You people have never ceased to amaze me. I am now registered, every piece of me, in the hearts of you dear people; and what a place and what a way of being remembered! This array of emotions within you people, all sequenced, all arriving at the expected time, all arousing the best of feelings within one's heart and mind."

"Wow!" uttered Clement, a big smile sitting in his eyes and a bigger one spreading on his face, "What and who do we have here, Gol? A girl who was unable to differentiate respect and affection from lust and lechery, or simply a lady philosopher? What is she talking about!"

"I am exactly what Gol wanted me to be," said Sophie, indulging herself with a bit of coquettishness by throwing a most inviting wink at Gol, "Priceless, he wanted me to be priceless. He wanted me to be a *woman*; and I am a woman."

"Okay, woman, sit beside your man and enjoy your meal," said Clement, laughing heartily.

"Woman, you are very lush," Gol whispered into Sophie's ear as she sat.

"Man, I love you," Sophie whispered back.

"Take a seat, Clement," asked Gol, pulling out a bottle of red wine and handing it to David.

As Clement sat, Sophie held the back of her hands before him and repeated the question she had asked him seven years ago: "What feeling do my hands induce in your mind?"

Clement laughed at remembering his reply to this question back then, and told her that her hands would elicit nothing in a mind but pure desires for goodness and becoming.

After lunch, Sophie had a savvy conversation with Mr Gibran and Aisha about the necessity of accepting and trying to comprehend the less tangible forms of human existence, with Sophie stating that the ones who ignore, or worse, reject the dichotomy or the trichotomy existence of man, would eventually get stuck in their own-created excruciating vertigo. And on the same note, Aisha, the mythologist, also proposed that man had always used mythology as a means to picture the less tangible forms of his existence; and perhaps, it had been an unconscious try to avoid falling into the trap of his physicality.

"I think I could do with a short nap," said Gol, as they entered the office.

"So could I," said Sophie, looking at the wardrobe by Gol's desk, "Do you still keep your blanket and pillow in there?"

"Yes," replied Gol, walking towards the large leather couch, "Can you go and get them?"

Sophie opened the top part of the wardrobe, took out the pillow and the blanket, and when she turned towards Gol, he said, "Not that one, the other one, in the plastic bag." The blanket in the plastic bag seemed familiar to her. Before taking it out, she looked at it for some seconds, turned her head and threw a look at her desk and smiled.

"Gol, I want to lie beside you but the couch is not wide enough for both of us," said Sophie, handing the pillow to Gol.

"How about my chest, is it wide enough for you to lie on?" asked Gol, placing his head on the pillow, "Now, pull the blanket out and give it to me."

"You have always wanted the best place for me," said Sophie, pulling the blanket out, her eyes moistening, "I wanted to work as a waitress for you, but you offered me an office job. Perhaps you didn't want me to damage my hands. You placed my desk close to that heater on the wall. You bought me a comfortable chair. Hold me, place me on your chest and tell me what it is about this blanket."

"You left your scent in this blanket. Didn't you?" said Gol, throwing the blanket over her body.

"Oh, my God!" uttered Sophie, pressing her face against his, "That

371

night, standing in the rain, coming back into the office… Yes, I wrapped my naked body in the very same blanket!"

"And the next day when I came in, Clement told me the story," said Gol, "And when I found the office door locked, I peeped in through the glass and saw you wrapped in my blanket."

"And you put it in a bag so my scent wouldn't get off it!" said Sophie, emotions ringing in her tone.

"Yes," replied Gol, placing his hands on her back.

"What does my scent mean to you?" asked Sophie, in a lilting lulling tone.

"It means life and goodness."

Sophie laid her face on his chest and allowed the moments of catharsis take her mind and heart over. She had felt these moments since she had stepped out of the prison, she thought. No, she had begun to feel them since Gol had visited her in prison… No, it had happened inside the police station… No, it began since I left him and joined those rat-breeders, she thought.

Two hours later, Sophie was woken up by rhythmic pelting of rain on the window panes. She pressed her face against Gol's and whispered, "Wise man, do you think you would be able to afford some moments of pure childhood?"

"Wise woman, what are you up to?" asked Gol, holding her face in his hands.

"If you get up and come with me, I will tell you," replied Sophie, laughing childishly.

With Sophie walking before him, he followed her, trying to guess what she wanted him to do. As they went down the stairs and reached the bottom landing, Sophie turned towards the back door and pushed it open and stepped out into the lashing rain.

"I have always wished to stand in the rain with you one day," said Sophie, holding her head back and giving her face up to the pelting rain, "It is childish. Isn't it, Gol?"

"It is childishly human," replied Gol, stepping out, "It is an urging call. Isn't it, Lulu?"

"Gol, you called me Lulu! Didn't you? Yes, you did," said Sophie, her now soaked red shirt sticking on to her body, "Yes, your Lulu experienced this inner call just a few days before she left you, here, right in the very same spot. It was some scene: a dog and his indeterminable owner disappeared under a large black umbrella, and a seagull. Inside my head, the dog and the seagull were at a fierce tug-of-war. I let the dog down, and the seagull won. I wasn't recipient enough to hear the call and comprehend all its facets. Come here and hold me, wise man."

Gol approached her from behind and held her in his arms, the rain lashing down on his head and trickling down on her chest. The dusk was gently giving way to the night. The autumn wind was tuning itself, ad-libbing a note here and another there and mixing them with low muffled whistles. He lifted her up and gently placed her on his shoulder, turned around and began walking towards the narrow street.

"Gol, our jackets, our phones, my hand bag——?"

"Do they matter, Sophie?" interrupted Gol.

"No, they don't," replied Sophie, kissing his neck, "Carry me. Just carry me. Take me home. It is the only thing that matters."

Chapter 46

Mr Barry James Grandeur was ambulating towards his farm, with his head held high and his upper lip stiff. When his farm came to view, he stopped, and after blinking several times, he shook his head and let out a half-dead sigh. He blinked again, as if he had just noticed the disused state of his farm. He walked on and blinked again, the farm seemed to be coming back to life, with the opulent bovine creatures roaming around and mooing happily. He changed pace; he marched and whistled a cheering melody in his head, imagining some opulent white girls dancing to his melody in their colourful clothes. 'I will be fine. I have always been fine,' he cogitated, and the word 'fine' began to enlarge in his head until it became his head, grew bigger and bigger and it became all of what he was: he was *fine.*

During the day, and as part of his new job, he had castrated eight calves, all constrained and held firm within tight and secured enclosures, and for the first time in the entire of his life, he had, very cautiously, thought about *castration* in a very *different* way: 'castrated calves will never be the same again; they will no longer enjoy the lush and green grass; they will only be *fine!*'

When he entered his farm, he noticed his wife and daughters had already arrived. They had informed him that they would come over to visit him.

"How have you been doing over there, my dears? I hope you have been happy with your husbands."

"Oh, yeah, we have been doing fine," said Elizabeth, "My husband is a true young gentleman, and what can I say about those of our girls. They are two veteran connoisseurs of appreciation."

"I am very much glad to hear this," said Mr Barry James Grandeur, smiling at his daughters, "I am truly delighted for you two. You could have ruined your lives like Sophie did. She disgraced all of us. Didn't she?"

"What could we do, Barry," said Elizabeth, taking a gentle sigh, "By nature, she is limited, and as a matter of fact, all the lesser beings would struggle with understanding and accepting the truth."

"My dears, I am genuinely elated and prideful that you did understand

374

the truth and accepted it," said Mr Barry James Grandeur, "And to make sure you will never be deviated from the path of truth, I will support you by all means available to me. I will have your back."

"Oh, thank you, Barry!" said Elizabeth, her eyes sparkling, "What would life be worth of without truth. Nothing. It would only be a thankless fagging. Barry, as you know, my husband is a man of grand enterprises, you know, very much driven by courage and endless ambitions. But he doesn't have enough capital to fulfil his dreams. I am wondering if you could sell the farm and——"

"Elizabeth," interrupted Mr Barry James Grandeur, "As you know very well, I only own half of this farm. Have you forgotten that we sold half of it and gave the money to those two fine pieces of men? And there is another thing that you seem to be deliberately ignoring: I am, and have always been a very territorial man. Haven't I? What will happen to me if I lose my territory?"

"I can appreciate this, Barry," said Elizabeth, carefully reading his eyes, "Is there any greater territory than one's country? This country is your territory."

Mr Barry James Grandeur nodded knowingly. Elizabeth was right. He was in his own territory. They both were right. They had always been right. He gazed at his stunningly beautiful daughters and then at their mother. In a fleeting eerie moment, the picture of the last calf he had castrated during the day appeared before his eyes. He felt a sharp pain in his spine, running down to his genitals and back up to his heart and his brain."

"You all right, Barry?" asked Elizabeth, holding his arm.

"Yes, yes, I am fine… I am… Yeah, I am fine," replied Barry, his upper lip getting stiff.

Meanwhile, there was a knock on the door. Mr Barry James Grandeur turned his head towards the door and, through the tinted glass, he spotted the contour of a bearded young man with rather long hair. He got to his feet, threw a second look at the door and with a disdainful huff rushed towards it.

"Oh, David, the metamorphosed David! What the hell are you doing here, you traitor!" shouted Mr Barry James Grandeur.

"Sir, you should let me in," said David, in a gentle tone, containing some consequential denotations.

"You sound like that pleb!" said Mr Barry James Grandeur, "Intolerably assertive and insolent!

375

"Well, come in. Be quick and brief and then get the hell out of here!"

David walked in, threw a hello at Elizabeth and the girls and waited for Mr Barry James Grandeur to sit back in his bulky sofa. He put the suitcase he had with him on the low coffee table, and after pacing the length of the sitting room several times, he threw another look at the girls and stood before Mr Barry James Grandeur and said, "I have come here to inform you that your daughter's wedding will take place tomorrow night."

"Sophie is no longer my daughter!" boomed Mr Barry James Grandeur, his face now a tableau of undisputable righteousness and self-vindication, "She put shame on us! She sold her historical values for a life of lechery and degradation! She sold us for a pleb!"

"Sir," said David, ruffling his hair, "I would have definitely begged to differ had I been tumbled out of an untouched and unfucked vagina. My mum's had been properly pampered before I jumped out of it."

"Get out of my house! Right now!" shouted Mr Barry James Grandeur, apparently another rush of pain in his spine circulating through his genitals and…

"Sir, do not calm the hell down. Stay up there," said David, kneeling beside the coffee table and opening the suitcase, "Look here! This is, more or less, the amount of money those rascals swindled out of you. I would have never allowed this to happen had not the other side been a man named Gol. You do not deserve it. Now you have your money back. Take it and spend it on bloating yourself only to make sure you will eventually bust like a dead cow left in the sun for days."

David left; Mr Barry James Grandeur fell into an abyss of confusion and incredulity, stumbling, rolling, tumbling, falling down. He opened his mouth… nothing came out. He opened his eyes… he saw nothing but the last calf he had castrated… He felt a nerve-shattering pain in his testicles… He opened his mouth… He mooed and mooed and mooed… He came back. He climbed up. He overcame the excruciating pain and delirium. He was *fine!*

"How did he dare to talk to you like that!" said Elizabeth, eagerly looking at the bundles of cash in the suitcase, "How blind and obtuse some people are! Can't they understand how wrong they are? They have ruined the life of our beloved child and yet are so impudent to come here and puke at us! Sophie will see for herself. He is not going to marry her. He is going to fool her around, take her beliefs and soul away from her and, well, turn her into a fucking ruttish jenny! This fucking man can't stand the feminine modesty and chastity! He will definitely metamorphose my poor beautiful Sophie! You all right, Barry?"

"Oh, yes, yes, I am fine," replied Mr Barry James Grandeur, closing the suitcase with his shaking hands and pushing it towards Elizabeth.

"Oh, Barry, thank you very much!" said Elizabeth, interlocking her fingers and placing her hands on her chest, "Only a truly gentleman could afford so much selflessness and generosity."

"You are most welcome, Elizabeth," said Mr Barry James Grandeur, "A man is defined by his authenticity and his manly merits. It is the least I could do for you. Now tell me about your husband and his ambitions. He must be a man of essence, I reckon."

"He is, Barry, he is," said Elizabeth, now sounding most juvenile, "He is twenty six years old and exceptionally handsome. He is from a very dignified descent, you know, from some prominent origins back at the peak of the Ottoman Empire; and very much like his ancestors, he is a man of morals and appreciation. Adding to this, the ever-active volcano of libido within him, what else could an equally merited woman of virtues and fine carnal qualities wish for? Yeah, and he is really hot and passionate, so much so that when he is doing it I feel like a ewe clamped in the jaws of a hyena!

"Yeah, he slobbers all over me! He chews my toes and bites my legs. Yeah, he appreciates all the niches of my body, just like a hyena that wouldn't spare even the bones!"

"What type of business is he into?" asked Mr Barry James Grandeur, evidently delighted by Elizabeth's description of her husband.

"He is——" said Elizabeth, pushing her hair back, "Yeah, he is into the business of buying and selling, yeah, he buys from a few and sells to so many."

While gazing into Elizabeth's green eyes, he was hit by a transient conscious moment. He shook his head so hard, as if trying to shake off some large bats stuck to it. He stiffened his upper lip, threw a smile at Elizabeth and wished her and her husband a very happy and prosperous life. He was fine, he thought. He was a man of truth. He was fine.

Chapter 47

As Sophie had wished, the wedding took place in the vast forest park near the town. As it had been predicted by some, Sophie, Cynthia and Gol had a big surprise for their two hundred invited guests and some casually involved park goers watching them from the margins.

"Sir, wait, please," said Sophie, turning towards the registrar, her face blushed, dithering, fussing with her hair, her heart pounding, "The bride will soon appear! Yeah, she won't be long! I promise."

"What does she mean, sir?" asked the old kind-looking registrar, looking at Gol with a slightly baffled face, "Isn't she the bride?"

"There is another half," said Gol, laughing the laugh of his life, reaching for Sophie's hands, "This gorgeous heavenly bride has got another half. The other half is older, and I have categorised her as classic."

"All right!" said the registrar, stroking his thin soft white beard, "One of you three must be the dearest."

"It is our Sophie," said Gol, kissing her cheek.

There was a pleasant tumult among the guests, the turning of heads towards each other, the huddles and the whispers, the full and lingering smiles, and now the short brisk trips from this table to that. The secret had been leaked, apparently by Emily, who was the only one aware of it. The heads, now coordinated by a call of love and affection, turned towards them, and as Cynthia appeared in the bridal dress, they rose to their feet and gave them a lengthy standing ovation. David, who was standing among the guests, squeezed himself out from among the people and the tables, and dashed towards them.

"Mum!" shouted David, now walking towards her with his arms wide open.

"David," said Cynthia, dashing towards her son.

"No tears, Mum. Not tonight," said David, embracing his mum, "You are fulfilled, Mum.

"Congratulations! You made yourself worthy of love, and it eventually found you. Give me your hand. Let's go. They are impatiently waiting for you."

Minutes later, Emily joined them and, very meticulously and affectionately, checked the overall appearances of the brides and the groom and placed Cynthia on the chair to Gol's right and Sophie to his left, and turning towards the registrar, she said, "Okay, sir, join them together. Let them fly."

"Come here, my dear," asked the registrar, smiling at Emily.

"Yes, sir," said Emily, lowering her head.

"Are you real?" asked the registrar, a kind and admiring smile brightening his face up.

"I am. I am from the earth," replied Emily, smiling.

"Okay, you real girl from the earth," said the registrar, pointing to the brides and the groom, "Can you briefly tell me the story of those three dear people?"

"Well," said Emily, "The older one is my mum. She fell in love with the groom when she was very young. She failed to understand love because she had never been allowed to, and therefore she failed herself. The younger one also walked the same path. And they both eventually heard the same call and redeemed themselves."

"Is it some story, girl!" said the registrar, nodding sagaciously, "Well, let's join them together and let them fly."

"Okay, the dear audience," said the registrar, holding the microphone with both hands, "This is a rare occasion, and we are all privileged to be here today and witness it, as it doesn't happen so often. Give them another round of applause and please be seated."

"James, I am so happy and proud that you are with me today," Sophie whispered into her brother's ear.

"Sophie, I will be with you for the rest of our lives," said James, holding her hand.

"My brother," said Sophie, in a tone as if she had just coined the word 'brother' herself, "Had I ever felt you so dearly as I am feeling you right now? James, you are my brother!"

"Well," said the registrar, clearing his throat, "Let's be conformant to the nature of this wedding. Let's be unusual and casual, and somewhat informal. Let's take a shortcut and ask, Miss Sophie Grandeur, do you solemnly——"

"I do! I do!" shouted Sophie, leaving no room for any possible formalities. "And how about Cynthia——?"

"I do solemnly take Gol as my lawful husband!" shouted Cynthia, her voice youthful and resounding.

The rest of the formalities were breached. They were not needed. Magdalena, wearing a red gown, appeared in the circular empty area among the guests and waited for the music to be played. Usman approached Sophie and whispered something into her ear. She put her hand on her heart and eagerly and curiously looked around. She did not see. She felt, right behind her. "Eileen!" she exclaimed, hurling herself into her arms, "Nothing could have made me happier than this!"

"Usman bailed me out," said Eileen, holding her firmly, "I didn't want to miss the chance of seeing the most beautiful bride ever!"

"Am I, Eileen, am I really beautiful?" asked Sophie, pressing her face against hers.

"Yes, and self-realisation is responsible for that," replied Eileen, now holding her face, "Wisdom doubles even the beauty outside. Now let's join Magdalena."

Magdalena had already mesmerised the guests. Sophie, Cynthia and Eileen joined them. The guests cheered, rose to their feet and clapped for them.

"Who used to call who a 'little bird'?" asked Magdalena, reaching for Sophie's hands and smiling at Cynthia.

"Oh, it was me. I admit it," replied Cynthia, touching Sophie's face affectionately, "She is now definitely a dancing phoenix!"

"What a compliment!" said Magdalena, dancing away with Sophie.

"This is what I call dance," said Aziza, standing beside Gol, "Old boy, congratulations! You truly deserve this gorgeous bride. I wish I was a man so that I could taste the pleasure of holding such a delightful creature in my arms."

"Not a bad wish!" said Gol, laughing, "I will tell you, Aziza. It tastes of heaven and earth. It tastes of the origin."

"And how about Cynthia's?" asked Aziza, evidently delighted by Gol's answer.

"Pure wine. Pure euphoria," replied Gol, watching Sophie dancing towards him.

"Catch her, Gol! Catch your bird!" said Aziza, clapping.

Gol bent down, and wrapping his right arm around Sophie's buttocks, he lifted her up effortlessly, and walked towards Cynthia. At their request, he danced with them. Although not a very good dancer, but his manly qualities and gestures were more than enough appealing to earn him the ardent approval of his brides as well as those of the guests and, of course, Magdalena's. Aziza, who was still watching them from the margins, was evidently grappling with a temptation in her mind. Picking at her scarf while gazing at Gol and his brides, she grabbed the corner of it and gently pulled it off her head. Receiving a timely and well-appreciated gesture of hand from Cynthia, she let her thick long black hair down, asked Allah to look away, and joined them. Though now a woman of age, but her very fit body still was capable of exhibiting a level of appeal and sensuality. As ever, very much aware of what she had at her disposal, she made a show of her busty torso and her shapely backside. Aziza's dance moves together, somehow, implicated a lenient confrontation of an ephemeral lush source of sensuality and *sin* against an eternal source of it! *'If Allah wasn't happy with this, he would have petrified me the moment I decided to do this,'* she thought. *'Allah himself is watching this. Yes, he is also interested in lushness and sensuality, otherwise he wouldn't have bestowed upon women so much beauty and charm. Yes, Allah is, and has to be, a very sensual creator who might even cherish kissing the sweet lips of a most lush and adorable woman like Sophie; and perhaps he has already done this, via Gol's lips! Allah is a lover. Allah is a kisser. Allah is a dancer. Allah will not punish me. Allah has never punished anyone.'*

Chapter 48

"Mum, who chose these names for us?" asked Grace, shading her eyes with her free hand and looking at Sophie's face.

"How many times more are you two going to ask me this question?" asked Sophie, holding their hands and carefully walking them through the craggy path leading to the beach.

"This is the first time," said England, "Isn't it, Grace?"

"Oh, yes, or maybe the second time!" replied Grace, holding her little hand up and showing the number with half a pout.

"I don't know. You might be right," said Sophie, laughing joyfully, "Well, it was your dad, and as I have told you... No, I don't think I have ever told you. Have I? Well, just an hour after you had entered the world, your dad held both of you in his arms and named you, England and Grace."

"Mum, why did you let England enter the world first?" asked Grace, pulling Sophie's hand with a gentle huff and a full pout, "I also wish to have been named England."

"It wasn't me, it was destiny," replied Sophie, bending down and kissing her hand, "Destiny wanted Grace to be welcomed by England."

"I see!" said Grace, smiling at England, "That is why she always waits on me."

"Exactly!" said Sophie, releasing their hands, kneeling down and holding them in her arms, "England is half an hour older than you are, and it means she is the big sister. And what a kind and caring big sister!"

"Mum, did Dad name me England because of his love for England?" asked England, holding Grace's hand.

"How many times have you asked me this question?" asked Sophie, in a most mirthful tone, her heart melting.

"This is the first time. Isn't it, Grace?" said England, shrugging her shoulders and raising her palms.

"Yes, or maybe the second time!" replied Grace, tilting her head.

"Okay. You might be right," said Sophie, laughing, "Your dad named you England because of his love for me."

382

"Mum, you are England," said Grace, stretching her little hand and touching her mum's face.

Tears welled up in Sophie's eyes and she welcomed them. Her six-year-old twins, she thought, had been proudly watching her long before they were born, or perhaps even long before they were inseminated. She let her tears of happiness and appreciation shed. She held the back of her hands up and stared at them. Two large tears dropped on her hands and she immediately felt the warmth of them within her heart. *'From now on, your hands are my prayer rugs,'* she remembered. She laughed. She imagined a miniscule Gol sitting on the back of her hands, dressed in all white and saying his prayers, asking the *source* to grant his Sophie eternal eudaimonia. She laughed. The gentle breeze wafted through her hair and pampered her face. The twins were running towards the water edge. The dogs appeared, hailed Sophie with a few barks and dashed towards the children. Moments later, a scuffle broke out among the dogs: apparently the two huskies believed England and Grace could step into the water unattended, but the German Shepherd, well, being German, was dead against it. Sophie took sides with the German guy with a gesture of hand and the scuffle died down with a few purrs and howls from the huskies.

"Gol, I want to dance for you and Cynthia!" said Sophie, as Cynthia and Gol appeared, taking off her sandals, "You have never watched me dance on the sand. Have you?"

"Another precious moment. isn't it?" said Gol, wiping her wet face with his thumbs and looking into her eyes.

"Yes," replied Sophie, tilting her head.

Gol held her hands and kissed them. She began to dance, move after move, each finding the other effortlessly, each denoting a lingering sense, each representing a corner of her heart, each defining an aspect of her womanhood. She was dancing, she was philosophising her own existence, she was evaluating… She was not an object… She was not an ephemeral or seasonal sweet fruit… She was a divine chunk of sensuality and wisdom, dropped down from the heaven… She was *the meaning*… She was a woman… She was England.

The End.